Praise for
NANCY ROBARDS THOMPSON

"Robards Thompson's sense of emotion is keen."
—*Publishers Weekly*

"Details are brilliant. Readers can look forward to
seeing how Robards Thompson's talent develops."
—*Library Journal*

"Funny, smart and observant,
Thompson writes with charm and flair."
—*Romantic Times BOOKreviews*

"Ms. Thompson's novels are a sure winner
in the eyes of this reviewer."
—*LoveRomance*

"Ms. Thompson has found a way to speak to the heart."
—*Romance Reviews Today*

Dear Reader,

Sometimes it's easier to "fix" someone else's life than it is to deal with our own problems. At least that's how it is for interior designer Rita Brooks, the heroine of *An Angel in Provence*.

Employing her impeccable taste and creative vision, Rita is fabulous at making other people's lives beautiful. That's evident when she nudges her sister Annabelle—the heroine of *What Happens in Paris (Stays in Paris?)*—to go to Paris to pursue her dreams. Too bad Rita can't work a little magic for herself, because her own life is in need of serious remodeling. It's become a little too comfortable, like a threadbare quilt or a favorite chair that fits *just so* after years of faithful use—so much so she's become oblivious to the errant spring poking her in the derriere.

I'm so excited that Harlequin Books has brought you both Rita's and Annabelle's stories in one volume. Though these special ladies need a little push from fate to get out of their comfort zones, both, in their own way, soon realize that no matter where you are in life, it's never too late to begin anew and realize dreams that seemed lost or unattainable.

So brew yourself a café au lait, then settle in and enjoy the ride as you accompany Rita and Annabelle on their life-changing journeys.

Bon voyage!

Nancy Robards Thompson

AN ANGEL
IN PROVENCE

NANCY ROBARDS THOMPSON

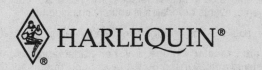

TORONTO • NEW YORK • LONDON
AMSTERDAM • PARIS • SYDNEY • HAMBURG
STOCKHOLM • ATHENS • TOKYO • MILAN • MADRID
PRAGUE • WARSAW • BUDAPEST • AUCKLAND

Recycling programs
for this product may
not exist in your area.

ISBN-13: 978-0-373-23077-8

AN ANGEL IN PROVENCE
Copyright © 2009 by Harlequin Books S.A.

The publisher acknowledges the copyright holder of the individual works as follows:

AN ANGEL IN PROVENCE
Copyright © 2009 by Nancy Robards Thompson

WHAT HAPPENS IN PARIS (STAYS IN PARIS?)
Copyright © 2006 by Nancy Robards Thompson

CONTENTS

AN ANGEL IN PROVENCE

This book is dedicated to
Teresa Brown, Katherine Garbera, Elizabeth Grainger,
Catherine Kean, Kathleen O'Brien, Debbie Pfeiffer,
Caroline Phipps and Mary Louise Wells,
my very own troop of angels who inspire and motivate me.

Acknowledgments

Special thanks to Gail Chasan, Stacy Boyd and
Michelle Grajkowski for being wonderful and
so good at what you do!

A million thanks to Caroline Phipps,
the queen of the midnight edit.
You saved my life.

As always, love and appreciation to Michael and Jennifer,
the loves of my life.

ONE

I KNEW IT was time for a career change when the invisible but perpetual twitch in my right eye progressed to a physical tic that made it appear as if I were winking at the world.

The past few hours spent with my client, Bitsy Van der Berg, had pushed me over the edge. Certain words come to mind at the mere mention of Bitsy Van der Berg: self-absorbed; manipulator; black widow spider, who kills everyone who gets tangled up in her itsy-Bitsy web. Oh, and let's not forget *rich*. The woman was born into one of those families with more money than royalty. She'd popped right out of the womb and straight into the lap of luxury.

What was supposed to be the glorious unveiling of a project that took months of my time—I even designed a prime piece of furniture for this job, had it custom made—and cost me countless nights of sleep had turned into my worst living nightmare. Bitsy swept in from Paris and insisted that the Provençal/Mediterranean interior she signed off on before she left for Paris three months ago was "absolutely wrong."

She claimed the design looked like a peasant's house, particularly hating the armoire I designed.

"No. No. This will never do. Where's my gold-leaf crown molding? Where are my mirrors and chandeliers?"

She'd changed her mind, but she wouldn't admit it. Once she got to Paris and was swept away on her whim du jour, rather than confessing that she'd found something else she liked better—or worse yet, living with the design she'd chosen like the rest of the *peasants* would, she tried to blame me. Pointing the finger was the only possible way out of paying for her fickle notions. Proving, once again, that some of the wealthiest people in the world were also the cheapest bitches, she opted for firing me, saying her lawyer would be in touch.

Well, goody. Maybe I could redecorate his office in oh-so-chic *frivolous lawsuit* motif.

Cursing the evil woman, I parked my white Volvo in the garage, next to my husband Fred's white Saturn. I gathered my briefcase and the bag of Chinese takeout I'd picked up because it was already seven-thirty and cooking and cleaning up yet another mess was the last thing I wanted to do tonight.

Fred had probably been home since five-thirty. He was as punctual and predictable as the quarter-hour chime of the antique grandfather clock in the foyer. That's why I knew before I walked in the door that he'd be hunkered down in his recliner watching TV with his slippers on. The first words out of his mouth would be a listless "Hey…how was your day?" Then, "What's for dinner? I'm starving," as he stared hypnotically at the boob tube.

Normally, it didn't bother me, but tonight before I could stop myself, I snapped, "I don't know, Fred. What did you fix?"

He lowered the television volume and shot me a befuddled look. "Jeez, *someone's* in a foul mood."

I knew I shouldn't take my bad day out on him. I should've checked the ugliness at the door and been happy that my husband was at home, rather than at some corner bar drinking with the boys. Still, I couldn't decide if it was the predictability that irked me or the fact that he'd sit in that damn La-Z-Boy and starve to death before he'd even think of starting dinner.

"Well, yeah, it's been one of those days," I groused.

He sat up, pushed in the footrest and lumbered into the kitchen, watching me as if I might attack.

My eye spasmed again, and I pressed my fingertips to it to quiet the tic.

"What's wrong with your eye? Or are you winking at me?" Fred winked back at me as he walked to the refrigerator and took out an open bottle of Chardonnay and a can of Budweiser.

"Bitsy Van der Berg is what's wrong with my eye. The woman has finally driven me over the edge. Will you remind me why I wanted to design interiors for spoiled women with too much money and nothing to do but cause others grief?"

He handed me a glass of wine, gave me a peck on the lips.

"Because you're damn good at it," Fred offered. "They may have the cash, but you have the taste, my love."

His words soothed me, and I almost felt guilty for being so crabby.

"And because people with deep pockets pay you a lot of money to work your magic." He touched his beer can to my glass.

"Well, she fired me."

Fred's right brow shot up and his jaw dropped, forming his mouth into an "oh."

"What happened?" he asked as we dished out our Chinese meal.

"The woman's crazy." I took my plate and sat down at the table in the great room. "She approved everything before she left for France—the color scheme, the custom-built furniture, the tapestry. She signed off on it, but now she's demanding I send everything back. She says I misled her and misrepresented the design."

As I relived the day in painstaking detail, Fred's gaze drifted to the muted TV visible in the sitting area.

"She's always been a pain in the ass, but she's never gone this far."

Fred didn't say anything. His gaze had been fastened to the television the entire time I was talking. At first I thought he was being a good listener, but now it was obvious he hadn't heard a damn word I'd said.

"Fred?"

"Hmm?"

"Are you listening to me?"

"What? Yeah, Bitsy… I don't know what you're worried about. She signed off on everything, right?"

I nodded.

"Well, there you go. I don't know what's the big deal. You can't stand the woman. Now you don't have to put up with her crap anymore."

Irritation welled inside me, and I suppressed a snort. "It's the principle of the matter, Fred. Don't expect me to be logical about this for at least twenty-four hours."

The phone rang. I got up to answer it, welcoming the diversion.

"Hello?"

"*Bonjour,* Rita, it's Annabelle."

My sister?

"Anna! Hi, my gosh, what time is it in Paris? It's nearly eight o'clock here."

"It's almost two. Jean Luc and I just got back from a party at the art center and I thought I might catch you in."

I glanced at Fred, who'd carried his dinner over to his recliner. The *Jeopardy* theme song rang out as he pointed the remote at the television and restored it to its full volume.

"Anna! Oh, I'm so happy it's you!"

"Hey, Ri," Fred called. Lowering his voice, he muttered, "Since you're up, would you hand me another beer?"

I was too happy to hear my sister's voice to be annoyed at my husband. Although, he could get up and get his own beer if he wanted it that bad.

Waving him off, I took the phone into the bedroom so I wouldn't have to compete with the background noise. "How was the party?"

"It was great. It was the welcome reception for a new round of art center residents."

I sighed. "Tell me everything. Let me live vicariously through you."

It was hard to believe two years had passed since Anna had won a residency at the International Center for the Arts in Paris and ultimately won the one-hundred-thousand-dollar purchase prize for one of her paintings. The residency opportunity had come at a low point in her life. She'd discovered that her husband of eighteen years wasn't the man she thought he was. Or maybe it's more apt to say *she* wasn't *the man* he'd fallen in love with. Discovering the truth about her husband's homosexuality came as a crushing blow. But with a little push from me, she applied for a resident-artist program in Paris, won the spot, moved to France and hadn't looked back.

That aside, what was even harder to believe was two long years had passed since I'd seen my sister. I missed her desperately.

"Rita, when are you coming for a visit?"

"I don't know, honey."

"You and Fred have an anniversary coming up. If my math is right, it's a significant one. Get him to bring you to Paris. You can stay with Jean Luc and me."

It would be twenty years this May. The thought of spending our anniversary in the most romantic city in the world lifted me up and out of the mire I'd been wallowing in all day. Or maybe my change in mood came from hearing my sister's voice. Either way, the anger that had festered inside me earlier fizzled out as we talked.

"You're good," I said. "How can you remember my anniversary? I'm not sure my husband even remembers it."

She laughed. "I won't let him forget. Put him on the phone and I'll refresh his memory."

"*Jeopardy*'s on right now. You wouldn't have much luck. In fact, it would be like talking to a wall."

Anna and I spent the next forty-five minutes catching up on her life in Paris with Jean Luc; the art world; her son, Ben, who'd managed to make several trips over to visit his mother; and how tonight she and Jean Luc had talked to a glassblower from Provence about pooling their resources to buy an old rectory near Avignon. That way, she and Jean Luc could extend their artistic presence into the south of France.

Yes, life was beautiful for my sister. I wanted what she had so badly, envy nearly oozed from my pores.

Especially when Fred shuffled into the bedroom. I glanced at the clock on the dresser. The neon red numbers glowed a decisive nine o'clock. But I could've told you that. It was Fred's bedtime. I also could've told you the routine: he'd shuffle into the bathroom where he'd spend six minutes brushing and flossing his teeth and doing whatever he did in there before he shuffled out in his navy blue striped pajamas. He'd give me a peck on the lips, then stiffly settle himself into bed and sleep contentedly until the alarm sounded at five forty-five, when he would get up and go to work at the Internal Revenue Service, as he had every morning for the past twenty years.

A surge of irritation ripped through me again. Why was I annoyed by my husband's predictable routine? Did I resent him for being happy and content in the life we'd built? I wasn't mad at Anna for being happy in Paris. Even if I did envy her.

Ahhh, Paris. That's where I wanted to be.

"Enough about me," Anna finally said. "Tell me what's happening with you."

I realized with a guilty start that I'd zoned out on Annabelle for a moment, and I struggled to recall what she'd said and think of something positive to say about it. She hadn't called to hear about our evening routine or my bad day or my selfish ex-client. Make no mistake, she would've graciously listened to me recount all the gruesome details, but the truth was, I didn't want to. How tedious. Why inflict that on my sister when even thinking about it bored me?

"Nothing new here—work, work and more work. Then I get up and do it all over the next day."

"Then all the more reason you should get Fred to…" She paused and it sounded as if she put her hand over the receiver because her voice was muffled. Still, I could her laugh and murmur, "Jean Luc, wait… *Mmm*… No…don't…stop… I'll be off the phone in a moment."

The reprimand is more "Don't stop," than "Don't. Stop."

And who could blame her? Even I was straining to hear their exchanges until the sound of Fred gargling his Listerine preempted my eavesdropping.

"I'm sorry, Rita. What were you saying?"

"I *wasn't* saying. You were. Something about how I should get Fred to do something. I hope you were about to suggest I get Fred to do the same thing to me that Jean Luc is doing to you?"

"Oh! No! Oh, I'm so embarrassed—"

"Oh, come on, Annabelle, it's me you're talking to. Don't be embarrassed because you're getting it. You're my heroine. My role model. In fact, you just might have inspired me to shake things up a bit in the Brooks bedroom tonight."

I sighed and Annabelle laughed. It was a sound like light through crystal.

"You go, girl," she said. "But actually, what I started to say was you and Fred really should come to Paris."

The Brooks toilet flushed.

"We're sort of at a standoff on that one. He wants to rent an RV and take a trip to the Grand Canyon this summer."

I wanted Paris. He wanted a Winnebago. If that didn't say it all? An RV was just a La-Z-Boy on wheels. In a split second, the vacation flashed through my mind: I'd get to cook and clean up the messes the entire time, only in a smaller space than usual. Although, I'd draw the line at sanitizing the onboard Port-a-Potty. Fred would get that pleasure. And that was nonnegotiable. But if we went to Paris, we wouldn't even need to have that conversation.

A moment later, my Lazy Boy emerged from the bathroom.

"I'll talk to him about it and let you know," I said. "But I need to run. Fred's going to bed. I have a very short window of opportunity, if you know what I mean."

I glanced over at him, but he wasn't listening to me. He was making his nest.

"*Oooh,* have fun," Annabelle sang. "Love you, bye!"

I hung up and curled up next to him on the bed, my head resting on his shoulder.

"Anna said to tell you hi."

"That's nice… Hi, Annabelle."

With my index finger, I traced the V of skin visible at his throat. His eyes were closed, but he slid his arm under me and pulled me close, nuzzling the top of my head with his cheek.

A surge of *ooohhh-we're-really-going-to-do-this* excitement coursed through me, making my stomach flutter, awakening sleepy, intimate places that hadn't seen action in ages.

I eased my leg over his, so that I was on my side and pressed against him. That way, I had better access to the buttons on his pajama top, which I started working with one hand until I'd undone the top two and could stroke his chest.

He tensed a little and pulled away the slightest bit—so slight I couldn't quite read the signal. Stop? Go?

"Fred?"

"Mmm?"

It sounded more like a sleepy *mmm* than a bring-it-on *mmmmmm*. But I could've been wrong.

"Fred, make love to me."

He was silent for a moment, then he gave me a little squeeze. "Ah, babe, I'm so…tired. I'm sorry. That Chinese gave me a bad case of heartburn and I just—"

I pulled away from him. "Fine." In two quick moves I was sitting rod straight on my side of the bed. "Forget about it."

Tears stung my eyes, and the liquid-velvet sensation I'd felt mere seconds ago dried up like barren desert.

"Aw, Ri, come on." His voice was husky with sleep, like he'd been drugged, but Fred didn't take pills—he wouldn't even go to the doctor. It looked as if it took every ounce of strength he had to force his eyes open.

He reached out for me, his hand landed on my knee. He patted it absently. "We've always got tomorrow, hon," he croaked. "Rain check?"

Low-grade anger flirted with it'll-be-a-cold-day-in-hell-before-I-make-the-first-move-again hurt.

"Yeah. Sure. *Tomorrow.*"

TWO

IT WASN'T HEARTBURN.

The very next day, Fred suffered a massive heart attack and died at his desk.

Just like that. He was here and then he wasn't. As if he were punishing me for only offering my cheek the next morning when he went to kiss me goodbye.

But therein is the rub. He never would've punished me for acting petty.

He wasn't a petty person. *He* didn't hold grudges.

Instead, he'd left me to torture myself knowing that I'd wasted the last kiss we would ever share by offering him my cheek.

My cheek.

Which fate had slapped good and hard.

IT'S BEEN EIGHTEEN months since that awful day, and the crippling devastation I felt when I first learned my husband was dead has settled into a low-grade ache. Despite more than a year of counseling—and several visits from my sister, all the way from Paris—I don't know if I'll ever be able to fully forgive myself for that wasted last kiss.

I'm coping—after listening to my therapist drill into my head that Fred and I had a *good* marriage, even if the physical relationship had waned a bit; that it was natural to feel rejected after I offered myself to him and he turned me down.

It should help, but depending on my mood, it can throw me into a whole new cycle of guilt: Who was I to feel slighted, when he was in the first stages of a heart attack?

"You didn't know," the therapist assures me. "How could you know?"

Overall, therapy has helped.

Along with constant dreams of Fred telling me he loves me and that everything will be okay.

So, after a challenging time of it, I'm slowly emerging from a fog. I've made some changes in my life— I've switched my focus from residential interiors to commercial. The designers within my company handle the residential accounts, since I didn't want to give up that part of the business completely. But after losing Fred, I felt as though I needed to mix it up a bit, needed to do what was best for me and the future of my company—after all, I'm single now, which is scary. Despite Fred's pension and a small insurance policy, I have to be frugal and smart. And emotionally the last thing I need is someone like Bitsy Van der Berg yanking my chain.

That's why it feels good to be out at Drayton College, the expensive private school that's retained my firm to redesign the interior of its music department. Every major firm from

Atlanta to Miami bid on the job. So, landing the project was a major coup. Just the challenge I need to get me up and out. With this project occupying my mind, sometimes I even last a full hour without thinking about Fred.

As long as I keep busy, I'm good.

It's for precisely that reason that I set out to walk the campus this afternoon. Before I get bogged down in sorting paint colors and choosing carpet samples for the offices—trying to figure out whether the Contada Merlot Toile or the Corians Garnet Damask is a better fit for the dean's office and reception area. I want to get a better feel for how my design will fit into the whole of Drayton College.

The campus is an interesting mix of architectural styles. One might call it Spanish Mission meets old Mediterranean. Low-pitched red-tile roofs and projecting eaves, long arcaded corridors with curved gables and white stucco walls. The lush, rolling lawns and ancient oak trees dripping with Spanish moss lend a timeless moneyed air to the college. That and the clusters of trendy, tanned students sipping smoothies and sunning themselves as if they hadn't a care in the world.

Why should they? They're young and gorgeous with their futures stretched out ahead of them.

I've almost walked the entire campus, except for Collier Hall—the dank, dark building that houses the music-rehearsal rooms and a handful of offices. I saved it for last because it's going to take the most work. I suppose I'm avoiding it. However, like any unpleasant task, I can't put it off forever. But it's hot outside—that's October in Florida. While the rest of the world is settling into festive fall weather, Mother Nature forgets to lower the thermostat. Some October days can have highs in the mid-eighties.

Despite the heat, my stomach is complaining that I missed my afternoon snack. So I stop in the bookstore/café for something cold to drink and a treat before I make my way over to inspect the final building.

Another lifestyle change I've made since losing my husband is rekindling my love affair with sweets. For years I didn't touch the stuff. Since I was constantly *helping* Fred lose weight, I never kept junk in the house. But since he's been gone, I must confess I've found comfort in my daily indulgences.

It started with the food that neighbors and colleagues brought over in the days before the funeral. Casseroles, cold-cut platters, whole rotisserie chickens. But it was the cakes and pies that got me. Like old friends who knew precisely what my beleaguered soul needed—only without saccharine words or pitying looks.

It would be a perfect relationship, if not for the extra ten pounds I've packed on.

As I step inside the café, I suck in my stomach, knowing I'll have to curtail these afternoon liaisons soon. But not yet… I breathe in the delightful aroma of freshly brewed coffee and something chocolate baking. Brownies? Cookies? Both?

I hold my breath like a junkie savoring her last toke. Letting the air out slowly, I decide I'll treat myself to both. Why the hell not? The diet can start *tomorrow.*

Most of the people in the café are young. I scan the area until I spy the token *mature student* sitting with a study group. She looks older than I am, I note with some satisfaction, and walk toward the beverage cooler along the far wall.

As I reach for a soda, I spy a guy at a table to my right.

At a glance, he sort of looks like a goat—no, a satyr—with his bald head and big ears, which probably make him look older than he really is. Plus, he has one of those long, matted beards that juts off his chin like a wide, pointing finger. It bothers me the way it sticks out, all red and stiff and phallic-like.

Like a facial-hair erection.

I shudder and my gaze falls to his T-shirt, which says Think Long And Hard…

Oh, God!

An inelegant sound—somewhere between a gasp and a giggle—escapes, which makes him look up. He catches me staring at him. I'm momentarily paralyzed. The way he holds my gaze with his dark, dark eyes is a little unnerving. There's something sexual about the arch of right brow and lazy half smile.

Like an invitation?

No! I could be his mother.

It's that T-shirt, tempting my thoughts to stray into pastures I haven't ventured in a very *long, hard* time.

I'm the first to look away, shifting my focus to my water, concentrating on undoing the flip top as if it's a complicated puzzle. I walk past the bad boy to pay the cashier.

Usually, I like facial hair on men. I do. In fact, I love a close-trimmed goatee, and I even like that little caterpillar of hair some men wear just below the lower lip. I think it's called a soul patch. It's kind of sexy.

Goat Man, however, is *not* sexy.

Sexual, yes. But not sexy.

As I pay for my water and leave the café, I ponder why he bothers me so much. I mean, beyond the obvious year and a half of celibacy and because I'm…*alone* now. I dig a little deeper. Would Goat Man have bothered me when Fred was alive? Better question: Would I have even noticed him and let my mind wander into the seedy, back-alley places his glance led me?

I hold the cool water bottle to my right cheek. Reflexively, my thumb finds the gold band on my left ring finger and slides across the slick surface.

I'm halfway to Collier Hall before I realize I was in such a hurry to get out of there, I forgot to buy my brownies and cookies. *Damn it.*

I contemplate going back, but realize I don't even want them anymore. Just as well, I suppose. I don't need them.

For the first time, I realize I could eat my fill of cookies and it wouldn't satisfy what I'm hungry for.

I blink away the thought.

The sun is leaning toward the western sky. It's getting late in the day, and I have more important things to think about—such as how the maintenance department needs to tackle Collier Hall's mold-infestation problem—before I can begin transforming the place.

In the shade of a magnolia tree near the entrance to Collier Hall, a young couple is making out. They're sitting on the grass, entwined and oblivious to the rest of the world. Like Rodin's statue *The Kiss* comes to life.

Watching them, I nearly run into another couple walking with arms wrapped around each other. The guy's hand is tucked into the waistband of his girlfriend's low-slung jeans. His thumb is rubbing her bronzed bare side where her halter top rises to expose her midriff.

"Excuse me," I murmur, stopping to let them pass.

The whole damn world is paired up.

As I climb the steps of Collier Hall, I force my thoughts back to the interior renovation and the challenge of mold removal to forget feeling alone.

Opening the heavy, wooden door, I glance down at the couple under the tree. It's a sad day when mold removal takes top billing over sex.

I stand there staring at them, a brazen voyeur on the brink of an epiphany.

It's sex.

That's what's wrong with me. Lack of it. No opportunity for it. It's like when you go on a diet that dictates no cookies. All you see, smell and dream of is cookies. Dozens of them. Cookie orgies.

The thing is, I know how to get cookies. I have no clue how to get sex.

I step inside the dimly lit building, and the door slams shut behind me.

I'll have to fix that. The last thing a rehearsal hall needs is a loudly slamming door.

Blinking, my eyes adjust to the low green glow of the sputtering fluorescent light fixture in the center of the long, deserted hall. The overpowering smell of mold is better than a cold shower.

How can they stand this smell of decay? Or the blighted look of the place? The scuffed concrete walls were probably white once. Maybe back in the 1960s. A smattering of cobwebs accent the greenish-gray tinge, no doubt amplified by the fluorescent lights.

Yes, the lights will be at the top of the fix-it list.

After the mold. And the slamming door.

I'm turning to leave, when muted voices drift from one of the rehearsal rooms. Then the sound of someone playing a quick scale on a saxophone, before a woman begins a haunting rendition of "Greensleeves," accompanied by a piano and the sax. It sounds smoky and soulful.

Despite the stench, I stand there and listen.

Funny, I'd always thought of "Greensleeves" as such a silly, old-fashioned song. I never really liked it. Does *anyone* really like that song when it's not disguised as a Christmas carol?

Yet, the trio has slowed the tempo to a hazy, haunting jazzy largo. So different from the traditional tune.

It almost doesn't resemble itself. But it winds its way around my soul.

I brace a hand against the cold, damp concrete wall. The singer croons:

Alas, my love you do me wrong
To cast me off discourteously.
For I have loved you well and long, so long,
Delighting in your company…

The words hit me square in the solar plexus, nearly knocking the breath out of me.

Her voice is so melancholy and the sax is so sad. I close my eyes. The notes drift through the deserted hall, evoking longing, ripping open old wounds.

I'm sorry, Fred. I never meant to—

A gut-wrenching sob bubbles up from a place I thought I'd sealed off tight. Soon its companion tears meander down my cheeks, and I silently weep as if the pain of it all is as fresh and raw now as the day I received the phone call from my husband's boss telling me that Fred was on his way to the hospital.

It's crazy…ridiculous, behaving this way. Eighteen months have gone by. I thought I'd gotten over these sudden cloud-bursts. I'm embarrassed, even if nobody can see me. I try to compose myself, and search my purse for a tissue, which, of course, I don't have because I cleaned out my purse last night.

Then the door to Collier Hall opens and slams shut.

Oh, God.

There's no way out other than the one door. No bath-rooms in sight. No escape.

So, mortified and a little irritated by the intrusion, I turn toward the wall pretending to scratch my eye as I read a poster advertising a student trip to Europe.

"We have room for one more." The masculine Spanish voice makes me jump. "May I interest you?"

I swipe at the remaining tears and clear my throat while preparing a short but polite *No, thank you. I'm just looking.* But before I can answer, he hands me a linen handkerchief embroidered with the initials *JS.*

"I can't bear to see such a beautiful woman so sad."

"Oh, no, I'm fine, really. It's just…" Without turning around, I gesture toward the rehearsal room. "It's the music. It's so beautiful. It brought tears to my eyes."

After one last dab, I turn around and want to fold in on myself when I see the man happens to be every bit as ap-pealing as his European accent.

He eyes me for a moment, drinking me in. "I am Dr. Juan Santiago." He offers his hand. "Professor of music history and appreciation here at the college."

He's tall and handsome. The clean, crisp smell of his aftershave makes me breathe deeper. Fred never wore the stuff. I never realized how nice it is.

"Hello, I'm Rita Brooks."

As we shake hands the music stops.

I venture a guess that he's in his mid-fifties. In fact, probably about Fred's age, although he's nothing like Fred— God rest his soul.

Juan Santiago has a sexy air. *Good God. There's that word again*. But it's true. He's classy, and undeniably sexy. Like Antonio Banderas or Armand Assante.

"Music has that effect sometimes," he says. "Many people attribute this ballad to King Henry VIII, saying he wrote it for his lady Anne Boleyn. In reality, the song is based on an Italian arrangement style that did not reach England until well after Henry passed on."

"Really?" I realize he's still holding on to my hand. I gently pull away. My fingers are hot where he touched them, and I'm suddenly aware that my face must be red and tear-stained. I turn back to the European-trip poster, pretending to look at it as I blot the corners of my eyes. I spy a posting of office hours and a class schedule for Dr. Juan Santiago. This must be his office.

"Are you a student?" he asks. "Because the tour of Europe is a wonderful opportunity and you earn credit, too."

He thinks I'm a student. The thought makes me smile.

I turn back to him. "Oh, no, I don't go to school here. I'm redesigning the music department interior. I'm just having a look around."

He spreads his fingers, palms up, and shrugs.

"More and more…*women* are going back to school later, after children and, well, I just thought…"

He shrugs again.

The trio resumes its practice, and I can hear the singer's voice through the walls.

"It really is a beautiful song, isn't it," Juan says. His back is to me as he unlocks his office door.

"Yes, it is." I'm feeling a little more in control of my emotions now. Though my heart feels hollow and bruised.

His dark gaze is disarmingly direct. He has such nice eyes, I notice now. They shine in the muted light.

"I was just getting ready to brew a pot of coffee," he says. "Won't you join me? I'd love to entice you to join us on the trip."

His smile is warm and inviting, and before I know what I'm doing, I follow him inside the small office.

THREE

MY FRIEND JUDE TURINO is sitting at my kitchen table sipping a margarita and eating salsa and chips. "So this professor was good-looking?"

And how. I nod.

"So go out with him."

"He didn't ask me out."

Jude makes a sound somewhere between a snort and a scoff. "Why does *he* have to do the asking? It's perfectly acceptable for a woman to ask a man out."

The thought nearly paralyzes me. "I was married for more than half my life. I don't remember how to date, much less how to ask out a man. I'm not ready for a new relationship."

"Who said anything about a relationship? You just need to get laid." She delivers her raw proclamation with a hint of sardonic *duh,* as if the remedy is as obvious as advising a starving man to *eat already.*

The protest *I'm married* crawls up the back of my throat, but I take a sip of my drink and swallow it just in time.

"It's too soon," I say instead. The margarita salt reminds me of tears.

"If you're thinking about sex all the time, I'd say it's a good indication that a respectable amount of time has passed. No disrespect to Fred. But if it's not time, why else would you look at a guy's beard and see a penis?"

Since I'd told her about Goat Man and the Professor, she's been prodding me to get out. To…get laid.

Makes me wish I'd kept my mouth shut.

"The imagery a guy's beard conjures isn't exactly valid psychoanalysis. I'd hardly compare it to Rorschach's inkblot test."

I set down my drink and walk back to the ironing board.

"No, but it's a sign of where your head is, sweetie."

I still *feel* married. Yet here I stand in the middle of my kitchen ironing another man's handkerchief while Jude sits at the table I shared with Fred nearly every night for too many years to count, pushing me to have sex with another man.

Sex… Getting to know a stranger's body. All those smells, textures and rhythms. It's so personal. So intimate.

I could read Fred's body like braille. I knew my way around his every dip and turn. I knew what every breath and moan meant before he'd finished them. I knew where my head fit just right in the crook of his shoulder and how his body fit inside mine. Like matching puzzle pieces.

The thought of having sex again seems as daunting as dumping a fifty-thousand-piece jigsaw onto the sheets. Where did I start? How did I find the pieces that fit?

The prospect is too much to comprehend.

"You've gotta get your feet wet sometime." Jude drags a tortilla chip through the bowl of salsa and considers it for a moment. "Might as well jump in, especially if he's as good-looking as you say. Does he have big hands?"

"What?" I know what she's getting at, but I play dumb.

She sticks the entire chip into her mouth and crunches.

"They say the size of a man's hands is a good indication of the hidden package." She points downward as if there's a *hidden package* underneath the table. "You need to check out Juan-Jovi's hands when you return the hankie."

"God, Jude!"

She shrugs, then licks her fingers. "I'm just sayin'."

I retreat into my ironing.

A strange penis.

The thought floors me. And, I must admit, takes my breath away, inspiring a thrill to shudder through my body. It's a wild, naughty thought, musing about penises right here in the kitchen.

I can't say I ever did that when Fred was alive. Sure, the thought might have occasionally occurred to me. In abstract. I mean, come on, it's a body part. Every man has one in the same place, relatively speaking. Just as most have two arms and two legs. It's not like I walked down the street thinking there's a man. He has a penis.

But when you personalize it, start talking about shoe size and hidden packages, it's…different.

In fact, they're all so…*different.*

I haven't seen that many, but even though Fred was my one and only lover, I'd had enough boyfriends to know—okay, three—I've only seen three penises in my life. But that's enough to know that they come in different shapes and sizes.

Short and long. Thin and fat. Left and right listing. Maybe even pointing directly at me like Goat Man's beard.

I spray another layer of heavy starch on the hankie, and breathe in the lemon-scented steam expelled from the hot iron's sputtering sizzle.

It smells domestic. And safe.

A world I'm well acquainted with. A place devoid of penises where I'm completely in my element. I run my hand over the linen square's smooth, stiff surface to be sure I don't inadvertently iron in tiny wrinkles.

"When are you taking back his hankie?" Jude asks.

"I don't know. When I'm out there next. Maybe next week, between meetings. I haven't really thought about it."

"You've gotta have a plan," she protests. "Otherwise it's a missed opportunity."

I have no idea what proper handkerchief etiquette is (do you return it or keep it once it's been offered?), much less how to turn it into an *opportunity*.

So much to relearn. Frankly, it makes me tired thinking about it.

I admit I stopped living after Fred died. I suppose somewhere in my subconscious I believed that if everything remained the way it was before he passed away he'd come back to me.

Rationally, I know it won't *actually* happen. But in the murky twilight of grief, the heart's fantasy isn't always sound.

With my index finger, I trace the *JS* embroidered on the handkerchief. I haven't told Judy that Fred is the only man I've ever been with. I'm not sure I'm ready to start adding to that roster.

I RETURN TO Collier Hall exactly one week after I met Juan Santiago. I carry his clean, crisp linen handkerchief, mindful not to wrinkle the neatly folded reason for my visit.

That's all it is. A friendly call to return an item that belongs to him. No opportunities or hidden agendas.

As I climb the steps, my mouth goes dry and my heart hammers in my chest. I notice that there's no one under the magnolia tree this afternoon. No lovers strolling hand in hand for me to dodge.

I pull open the door to the rehearsal hall and suddenly hope the professor is not in his office. That maybe his being here last week was a fluke. Not his regular hours. I can't remember what was posted on the bulletin board outside his office.

I ease the door shut, not wanting it to slam. I listen, wondering if the "Greensleeves" trio is practicing today. All I hear is the buzz of the fluorescent lights. If not for that and the stench of mold, I might wonder if I'd simply imagined meeting Dr. Santiago last week.

But no, the proof is in my hand. I'd stood in this hall and bawled my eyes out, borrowed a handkerchief from a man I'd only just met and then shared coffee with him in his office.

I hadn't dreamed it up.

As I walk down the dim hall, I see further proof. The door to his office is wide open. He's sitting at his desk. His dark head is bowed over a notebook. He's writing. For a moment I don't know whether to knock or clear my throat. Say something—or turn around and leave.

I'm relieved of that decision when he looks up and smiles warmly at me. "Well, hello."

I like the little turn his accent gives the words. There's a controlled elegance about him in the downturn of his soulful brown eyes, the slight fullness of his lips and the set of his beard-shadowed, chiseled jaw.

"Hi." I'm happy my voice works.

"To what do I owe this pleasure?" He stands, like a true gentleman.

"I've come to return your handkerchief. Don't worry, I washed it."

Ugh, what a dork I am. As if I'd return an unwashed hankie.

I hold it out to him, and he takes it, studying it as he does.

"And pressed it, too, I see." A concerned frown wrinkles his forehead. "You didn't have to go to that trouble. And then come all the way out here to deliver this."

"No trouble. I'm here working on a project for the college. I'm redecorating the interiors of the various buildings that belong to the music department. It wasn't out of my way at all."

He flashes that smile again and it reaches his eyes. "Well, I thank you, and I'm *very* happy to see you."

His words steal my breath. Maybe it's how he said it. Maybe it's simply his accent. But I hear myself blurting, "Would you like to get a cup of coffee with me?"

He frowns. "Right now?"

I nod.

"I'm so sorry, I can't. I have an appointment—" he glances at his watch "—in just a few minutes, as a matter of fact. Perhaps another time."

I feel as if I'm back in high school. Awkward. Rejected. Those feelings never went away, did they?

It's not personal, I remind myself.

"Oh, right… Since I'm redoing the interior of this building, I was just hoping to get your opinion on the colors I'm presenting to the committee tomorrow. But that's okay." I wave away the thought as if it's nothing. "Well, I'm sure you need to prepare for that appointment." I motion toward his desk, as if I know what he's got to do. "So, thank you again for the use of your handkerchief. Maybe I'll see you. Around. While I'm on campus. You know, working."

Ugh, I'm rambling.

"Yes. I hope so."

As I turn to leave he adds, "Tomorrow, perhaps?"

Tomorrow?

I glance at him over my shoulder. I could swear that I see disappointment in his eyes.

"Could we have coffee tomorrow?" he says. "Say, three o'clock?"

My stomach does the most unexpected leap. "Yes, I'll be on campus. It'll be after my meeting with the dean." *Shut up! Why did you say that?* "But, I'll probably be in need of a break after that."

"We could go earlier—say midmorning, after my first class?"

In a split second, I take a chance.

"Three o'clock is fine."

"Great. I'll see you in the café at the student union."

I CHANGED CLOTHES three times this morning before deciding on the baby-blue-and-brown floral skirt and silk button-down. First, I tried a suit with a skirt, but it looked too stuffy. Plus, I hadn't shaved my legs. So, instead, I pulled on my black pants and a twinset. Nope. Too…something…or more like, *not enough*…something.

So, I return to the shower and reacquaint myself with my razor. Don't get me wrong. I haven't neglected personal hygiene since Fred's been gone. I shower daily, but there are certain grooming tasks that have fallen off. Sort of like *natural selection*. Certain habits naturally disappear over time when nature deems them unnecessary.

I've had no sex life, no cuddling, no intimacy. Therefore the need to shave my legs has faded like gills on a creature that no longer takes to the water. Anyway, it's not as bad as it sounds. Actually, the older I've gotten the sparser the hair on my legs seems to grow. Soon enough, I'm shaved, moisturized, in my skirt and heels and out the door.

My meetings last into the afternoon. I present my design boards to the redesign committee. I'm glad to be busy because there's not time to dwell on my coffee... Date? Appointment? What is it exactly? Well, whatever it is, at three o'clock I'm meeting Juan.

I planned to wrap up the design meeting around two-thirty, just enough time to stash my briefcase in the car, touch up my face and walk across campus at a leisurely pace without breaking a sweat. But as fate would have it, I'm tied up until five minutes after three. The only way I manage to break free of the protracted debates over whether the color scheme is too blue or too orange—or maybe they wanted something all together different—*oh, for God's sake. Decide, already! You're musicians. Not visual artists. Don't make this harder than it has to be.*

I'm ashamed of myself for thinking such unprofessional thoughts all in the name of having coffee.

Color is important. I know that as well as anyone.

So, I let them drag it out until I finally excuse myself, saying I'm late for another meeting.

Promising to check in tomorrow, I leave the design boards for the committee to ponder and debate, and hightail it across campus. In heels. Briefcase in hand. Praying that the stifling humidity at the hottest hour of the day will not manifest in the underarms of my light blue silk shirt.

Is this a sign that perhaps it is too soon to start dating? But who said anything about this being a date?

Whatever I'm walking into, I arrive nearly fifteen minutes late, my face glistening with perspiration and no delicate means of checking for pit stains (oh, God, *please* no pit stains…).

For a breathless moment, I don't see Juan among the smattering of people scattered about the various tables.

Did he leave?

A tangle of emotions knot in my stomach. Relief that I won't have to actually go through with it snarls with a thick strand of disappointment. *He left….*

Did he even show?

Then I spy him sitting in a green-and-maroon floral-patterned overstuffed chair in the far corner of the café. His dark, glossy head—remarkably free of gray—is bent over a magazine, while his hand balances a white demitasse on the arm of the chair.

The uncertainty begins again—*he waited; oh my God, what do I do now?*

Don't overthink it.

I turn to the left, toward the coffee bar, grab a napkin and duck behind a rack of magazines to blot my shiny face.

As late as I am, if I wait in line to order my coffee first, he might finish his and leave, thinking I'm a no-show.

Giving my face one last blot, I toss the soggy napkin into the trash can and head toward him.

He doesn't look up as I approach.

"I'm so sorry I'm late. I got tied up in that design meeting."

Now he looks up. And smiles. The contrasting beauty of his dark eyes—which crinkle at the corners—and his straight white teeth—I've always been a sucker for good teeth—make my stomach quiver in a strange way I've never felt before, not even with Fred. Or at least I don't remember quivering like that.

Oh, Fred. I'm so sorry....

Juan stands and gestures to the twin overstuffed chair across from his. "It's no problem."

"I didn't have your number or I would've called you to let you know."

"It is no problem. *Really.* Now, what may I get for you? Cappuccino? Espresso? Mocha?"

The smooth edges of his accent are hypnotizing. I find myself nodding. "Yes, that sounds great."

"A mocha then?"

I'm still nodding and thinking about how nice he looks in his white polo and navy slacks, how he seems remarkably free of the middle-age stomach paunch that seems to claim most men, when he walks away.

I realize, *Wait, no! I don't want a hot drink.*

But he's already on his way to the register to order me a mocha.

I use the time alone to collect myself. Do a few silent yoga breaths.

Breathe in…one…two…three…

Breathe out…one…two…three…four…five…six.

It's a little awkward having someone wait on me, even if he is only fetching my coffee.

I should've ordered a fat-free cappuccino. Actually, I should've ordered water.

I sit there fighting an awkward debate over whether or not I should offer to pay him back.

No. That's tacky.

Or say I'll pay next time.

That's a little presumptuous to assume there will be a next time. I mean, what if I don't like him? What if he slurps or chews with his mouth open or picks his teeth? Or—

Or is completely wonderful?

It all comes full circle back to the handkerchief. A man who carries a monogrammed handkerchief is surely the sort who'd buy a woman a cup of coffee. And probably has impeccable manners.

Just shut up and be gracious.

The problem is, Fred and I never had kids. And in a sense, he became a big kid, letting me wait on him. I did it—I probably encouraged it—because I wanted a child. Desperately.

But because of a childhood illness that rendered him sterile, he couldn't, and wouldn't hear of adoption or artificial insemination.

Impregnate me with another man's sperm? Are you kidding?

So, even though I desperately wanted a child, I went along with it. Because I loved him, and I believed that what we had was enough.

And it was….

"Here you are." Juan is standing in front of me again. "One café mocha. Just for you."

I hold back an awkward apology for his waiting on me

and bite the inside of my cheeks to stifle an offer to get the coffee next time. I opt for a gracious "Thank you."

There. That wasn't so hard, was it?

Sort of.

I sip at the mocha as Juan settles himself. When I lower the cup, I notice he's staring at me with a strange look on his face.

I swipe a finger across my upper lip, in case the whipped cream left a mustache.

Great, a whipped-cream moustache and pit stains.

Such a vision of loveliness.

"May I ask you a question?" he says.

"Sure."

"I hope this doesn't sound indelicate, but are you married?"

He gestures to the gold band on my finger. It's become such a part of me I forget it's there.

"Oh, no. I mean, I was, but now… I'm widowed."

His brown eyes darken with sorrow and he bows his head slightly. "I'm sorry."

"Thank you, but don't be. It's been eighteen months now. It's not easy, but I'm coping."

I don't want to talk about Fred with him. I don't want to downplay the gut-wrenching waves of sadness that sometimes crash down on me and threaten to drown me. I'm sure Dr. Juan Santiago does not want to play grief counselor to a woman he just met. At least he's enough of a gentleman to not ask if I was thinking of Fred last week when he caught me crying.

I change the subject to Juan, and learn that he's taught at the college for three years. In a previous life he traveled the country as a jazz musician. Classical bass is his instrument.

And that he's never been married.

Briefly, it sends up a red flag. Still, I don't ask why, and he doesn't offer an explanation. So we talk about his classes, his personal research. The European tour.

"We have recently opened the tour to the community at large. For some reason, perhaps the economy, we didn't get enough students to meet our minimum numbers. We're hoping that music enthusiasts from the area will join us so we don't have to cancel."

He watches me over his cup as he sips his espresso. "You should consider joining us. It's an incredible value once you consider the entire package."

Package?

Reflexively, I glance at his hands.

Then look away fast. But not before I notice that they're clean. Of medium size. Not overly large. Not inappropriately small. Just the right size, I imagine, to wrap perfectly around...the neck of a classical bass.

I shift in my seat and focus on that despite the one little quirk of lifelong bachelorhood, I'm finding Juan Santiago fascinating. He's smart, funny, philosophical and of medium-sized...hands.

"It must be so stimulating to teach. I've been thinking about taking a class. Something for enrichment."

"The trip." He insists. "Treat yourself."

"Oh, well, I don't know about that. When is it?"

"It's at the end of the semester. The second week in December. For ten days. You'd be back just in time for the holidays."

Hmm...might be nice to go over and then spend Christmas with Annabelle. In Paris. Just a few nights ago, she'd been telling me that

she, Jean Luc and the Provençal glassblower finally purchased the
rectory in Avignon. The one she'd been talking about for the past
year and a half. She was hoping I could come over to give them some
design ideas for the place. Since I was tied up with enough work to
keep me busy through next year, a trip to France was out of the
question anyway.

"It won't work with this job I'm doing for the college,"
I muse aloud. "That's probably when the installation will be
happening. If not the trip, maybe I'll take an evening class.
Maybe when the new term starts."

"That'll be January," Juan says.

I nod.

"That's too long to wait. What I find is that you must act
on these urges as soon as they hit." He cocks his right brow.
"Otherwise you'll keep waiting for *someday*."

Urges? I could read *so* much into his words and it makes
me tingle all over. Instead of speculating, I focus on the fact
that he has a point. I've been saying I've wanted to go back
to school for a long time. "But I can't register until the new
term begins."

"You don't need to." He leans in and his eyes take on a
conspiratorial glint. "I teach music appreciation at seven
o'clock on Tuesday and Thursday evenings. You're welcome
to sit in if you'd like. Of course, you won't get credit for the
class, but you won't have to pay for it, either."

"I don't mind paying."

He waves me off. As if that's beside the point. "The
window for registration is closed. Besides, this way you can
see if you like it, and then maybe you'll sign up for a class officially next term. Why don't you stop by tonight. Room
147, Quinton Hall." He winks at me. He actually *winks*. "If

you need further justification, look at it as a means to get a feel for the students. It just might help with your design project."

FOUR

I WAIT UNTIL the following Tuesday to sit in on the class. Between meeting Juan for coffee last week and finally deciding to go to the music appreciation class, I talked myself out of it at least a dozen times.

"He's lobbed the ball into your court, babe," Jude reminded me several times. "You better take it and run with it. Or better yet, get your butt to class."

I arrive early, half hoping to talk to him before the class starts. Since I was late to our coffee, the other part of me wants to be early to show him lateness is not a habit.

But he's not here yet. A couple of students are already seated. I choose a desk in the back, and settle in, pulling a pen from my bag and placing it on top of the spiral-bound notebook I purchased in the bookstore. Then I pick up the pen again, open the notebook and scratch my name and the date on the top line, resisting the urge to fidget.

As the class begins to fill, I see it's a mixed bag, students of all ages. At least half look to be thirtyish; there's a sprinkling of younger students. Probably the ones who can't wake up for the morning classes—one in particular who catches my eye has the longest fingernails I've ever seen. They stick out a good two inches from the ends of her fingers. They're painted bright purple. I notice them as she lifts a can of sugar-free Rockstar energy drink, which she sips through a straw. Her pinkie is extended, as if she's sipping a proper cup of tea. The dainty gesture is at odds with her matted blond dreadlocks and the purple getup she's wearing. Her outfit sort of resembles a lavender priest's cassock.

But the ensemble is nothing compared to the purple eye shadow, frosted purple lipstick, purple false lashes, which seem to float about her eyes like butterfly wings.

Wow.

I'm transfixed, watching her until she catches me staring.

"You're new," she says.

I nod.

"Cool. I always told my mom she should go back to school. I wish she could see you here."

I guess I might like someone's mom sitting here. I shrug off the feeling of not belonging and search the room for someone my age. She's sitting in the desk to my left. But she's looking down at a book, engrossed in what she's reading.

Juan arrives—at seven on the dot. He walks to the front of the now-full room and says, "We have a lot to cover tonight. Let's get right to work."

He immediately begins to lecture on the canons and fugues of J. S. Bach. Clearly, I've come in midsemester. Good thing this isn't for a grade because I'd be sunk.

"*Canon* is Greek for rule or law. When used in a musical sense, it designates the strictest form of counterpoint in which one voice imitates the rhythm and interval content of another voice."

Counterpoint? Rhythms? Intervals. Oh boy… Yep, I definitely missed some components that would help me get to the *appreciation* part of this lecture.

Speaking of appreciation, I must admit, I'm a little disappointed Juan doesn't notice me right off the bat. In fact, a good twenty minutes of the ninety-minute class goes by before he spies me. A nearly imperceptible flicker registers as his gaze sweeps over me, stutters and moves on. He doesn't skip a beat in his talk.

That's not so unexpected. He's teaching a class, not hosting a party. Plus, I wasn't in class Thursday night. He probably thought I'd blown it off. After class, I take my time stashing my notebook in my purse, finding my keys, waiting for the others to leave.

Out of my peripheral vision, I see Juan walking toward me. My heartbeat kicks against my rib cage.

"Good to see you."

He's standing beside me now.

"Nice lecture," I say brilliantly.

"Thank you. Did it make sense? When I saw you sitting there, I realized this material was a continuation of what we covered last week. So, if you have any questions, don't hesitate to give me a call and I can give you my lecture notes."

That's a generous offer given that I'm not *officially* taking the class. I can't help but wonder if he's that accommodating to all his students….

"Thank you."

He nods. Shifts his notes from one hand to the other,

looking down as he does this. "When you didn't show last week, I feared perhaps I'd frightened you off."

Oooh…

Funny how certain things cause feelings to shift. A word. A gesture. A touch. A look. A combination of any or all of those elements tip the emotions and cause the heart to slide and proclaim, "Yes! This just might work."

The look on Juan's face as he shyly glances up is my tipping point. My stomach spirals and my heart whispers, *You can do this.* Strangely, the accompanying tune is a…tango?

Juan pulls his cell phone from the holster on his belt, glances at it.

"So sorry, I have to take this."

He angles away from me.

Okay, the tango wasn't the sound track to my epiphany. It was his iPhone ringtone.

"Hi, Chris…" His voice betrays nothing, despite how he lowers his tone. "No, I haven't forgotten… Class just ended. I'm talking to a student…"

A student. That would be me.

Hmm…a student. Not a friend. Not a *lady* friend.

"Right…I'll see you in a moment." He disconnects and turns back to me. His posture is all business. His expression betrays nothing. I can't read him.

"Well, duty calls. I have to go."

What? My heart sinks.

As we walk out, I hitch my purse onto my shoulder and hug my notebook close with the other arm. At the door, he angles to walk one way. My car is parked in the other direction.

"So nice to see you tonight, Rita." His polite tone is a

handshake. There's no trace of the man who, before the tango sounded, had *feared he'd frightened me off.* "I'll see you in class on Thursday."

JUDE DEMANDED I call her as soon as I got home. No matter the hour.

"If I don't hear from you," she'd said, "I'll assume you got lucky, and then I'll expect a blow-by-blow. And it better be good."

I put her on speakerphone as I get ready for bed.

"I'm confused," I confess. "I swear there was one point when I thought it was getting…personal."

"Personal?"

Seated at the bathroom vanity, I pull my long brown hair back into a ponytail and then soak a cotton ball with eye-makeup remover.

"Yeah, like he wanted me there because he wanted to see me. But then after the call from this Chris, he all but shook my hand."

I cringe at how clumsy and out of sync I feel.

"Obviously, I misread his intentions. God, it was awkward." The way I stood there expectantly as he rushed out. "I'm not going back."

One last swipe erases the smear of mascara from my lower lid, and I toss the sullied cotton into the trash.

"You have to go back. You don't know his reason for rushing out. Chris could be a guy."

Right. Oh, God, maybe Juan's gay. After what my sister went through with her marriage—discovering her husband of eighteen years preferred men… Well, nothing would surprise me.

"Nah, the class wasn't even that interesting. It's like entering in the middle of a movie—"

"What's his boss's name? Maybe Chris is his boss. If you don't go back, that'll be the end of the line."

Turning on the faucet to a slow trickle—enough so that I can splash my face with water and still hear Jude, I admit, "I think tonight was the end of the line."

I squirt some of my crème cleanser into the palm of my hand and smooth it over my face. It smells clean and familiar. Comforting.

"He invited you to sit in on the class. You have to give him one more chance."

I stare at myself in the mirror and ponder this for a few seconds. "I can't get a read. Beyond his life at Drayton, I really don't know that much about him."

"You've had coffee with the man once. Intimacy comes in time."

"I know it does, but this feels…hard. And honestly, Jude, I don't know if I want to work hard at a relationship right now."

I wet a washcloth and remove the cleanser.

"You give up too easy. Where's your sense of adventure?"

I'm tempted to say it died with Fred, but that sounds pathetic. I may be tired and out of practice, but I'm not pathetic. When I don't answer, Jude says, "I have a plan… Just go with me on this one, okay?"

AT SIX O'CLOCK the next evening Jude calls me from her cell phone.

"I'm at the Publix grocery store on Mills. He's buying a Stouffer's frozen dinner, toilet paper and a quart of milk."

The *he* she's referring to would be Juan Santiago.

I groan. "Oh, my God, Jude, you're crazy. I can't believe you're stalking him."

"Yeah, I know. Why don't you get your ass down here and help me. And please note he's buying *one* frozen dinner. And toilet paper."

"You buy toilet paper. Is that a crime?"

"No, I'm just saying, no wine, no flowers."

I wouldn't go along with Jude's plan to follow Juan Santiago after work. So the next day, she went to his office and looked at the schedule posted outside his door. Got a glimpse of him and was hot on his trail.

Currently, Jude's not working. She's living off the generous settlement from her divorce—but about a year ago she did administrative work for a private investigator. That job only lasted around six months, but ever since she's been bucking to put what she learned to the test.

"Sometimes I don't know if you're fearless or insane," I say. "Then again, I don't know that the two have to be mutually exclusive."

"Where are you?" Jude acts as if she doesn't hear my dig. Or maybe she's ignoring it.

"I'm still out at Drayton. I'm walking to my car—"

Heat rises from the pavement, inviting tiny beads of perspiration to a party on my forehead.

"Wait! He's leaving the store."

"Jude, please tell me you're not shadowing him. If he finds out you're following him and links you back to me, not only will it be embarrassing, it'll look unprofessional. I don't want to do anything to jeopardize my working relationship with the college."

Like sleep with one of the professors.

"Of course I'm not shadowing him. When he got in line I went out and got in my car. This way I'm ready to follow him home."

I cringe. "Or wherever he goes next. Do you want me to let you go?"

I fish in my purse for the remote to unlock my car.

"No, I want you to meet me and keep me company."

I slide behind the wheel. "Oh, right, so he doesn't have to link you to me. That way he can just discover I'm the stalker. God, you know what, Jude? If this doesn't prove you need a job, nothing will. Where are you now?"

"I'm on Mills. Oh, wait! He's turning into the Arbor Ridge town homes. Wow, he lives close to the college."

I put the phone on headset and start the car's ignition.

"Maybe this is where Chris lives?" I snipe.

"How romantic. A frozen dinner, TP and milk. If this *is* Chris's place and Chris is a woman, then thank her for saving you from a lousy date— Wait! He's pulling into a driveway."

"Jude, how closely behind him are you following? He's going to know you're tailing him."

"I'm at the stop sign. I'm going to sit here until he goes inside. Oh—looks like he's unlocking the door with a key. It's got to be his place. Yep, he's inside."

About that time, I pull into my driveway. I'm glad to be home so I can retreat inside and forget what Jude's doing. Erase it from my mind. "Good, you saw him home safely. Now get out of there."

I pull into the garage and kill the engine.

"No way. The fun's just beginning. Get your ass over here and join me."

FIVE

OF COURSE I didn't go.

Despite that, Jude chose to remain on her ridiculous stakeout to make sure Juan didn't get a midnight booty call, she came back with nothing to report. Which is exactly what she was after—*nothing*. Proving to mc hc wasn't otherwise encumbered, and therefore dateworthy.

When she called the next morning to gloat, I made the mistake of pointing out that this one random Wednesday evening wasn't necessarily a valid snapshot of typical. She might get a more realistic picture of what he did in his downtime on a weekend. Big mistake. She jumped at the chance to tail him again.

"You're absolutely right," she said. "He might be one of those weeknight early-to-bed-early-to-rise sorts. Like Fred. I'll tail him this weekend."

"No. Jude, get a job. A *real* job that doesn't involve stalking."

Only then did I realize that I'd fallen right into her trap.

"I'll make a deal with you." she said. "If you'll take the interest he's shown you at face value and go out with him, I'll leave it alone. If not, I'm going to follow him until I have enough evidence that he is, in fact, a good candidate for you to date. Because you know, even if he does date on weekends, it shouldn't be a deal breaker. It's what happens after you get in the relationship that counts."

I know that. I also know that it's hard to go from a twenty-year marriage back into the field.

"Maybe you should get into used-car sales, Jude. You're relentless."

"Do we have a deal?" she pressed.

"A compromise—I'll go back to class."

"And go out with him?"

"If *he* asks."

She huffed a sigh. "I suppose I can live with that."

AT SIX FORTY-FIVE on Thursday evening, I find myself back in Juan's classroom. I sit in the same seat, take out the same notebook, hold the same pen I used last time. I recognize the same faces as they file in and settle down for the lecture.

The Purple Girl arrives, with her false eyelashes and Rockstar energy drink. Once again, she sips through a straw—as if not to muss her frosted-grape lips. She's dressed from neck to foot in purple. This time the getup looks like a violet lamé military uniform with purple combat boots.

Hmm…

I have a tendency to gravitate toward black clothes, for the slimming effect, but it's hard to imagine a wardrobe entirely comprising purple costumes.

I sigh to myself. Oh, the things one could get away with in college. Campus life is a microcosm where idealism and self-expression reign supreme. For four or eight or ten years—if you're on the extended plan—you can try on different roles safe within a romantic cocoon—

"You're new, aren't you?"

I turn to the woman who looks to be about my age sitting at the desk to my left.

"I am."

"Thought so." She has cropped red hair. Her thick, black rectangular glasses give her a bookish air. "I didn't realize they admitted people midsemester."

Oh, boy. Don't want to go there. Just in case she's a Drayton employee who could cause trouble for Juan. She looks like the type who might be a college administrative assistant. I don't know the latitude they afford teachers, but if you got down to brass tacks, by letting me sit in free of charge, he's giving away the school's "product." Though, I suppose one could argue that the credits earned were the actual product rather than the knowledge gained. Either way, I didn't want to cause trouble.

"You're right," I say. "They don't admit people after late registration."

A well-where-did-you-come-from question darkens her face before it works its way out of her mouth. But thank God, before she can ask, Juan arrives and calls the class to order.

This time, first thing, his gaze skim over the class to me, and he smiles. It's just a slight acknowledgment. The others probably didn't notice since they weren't aware of the *situation*. Or at least I hope not. I purposely keep my gaze to the front, not looking over at Curious George to my left. Given her line of questioning a moment ago, if anyone might have noticed, she would've been the one.

Still, Juan is smooth as silk, welcoming everyone and commencing the lecture, a continuation of the Bach canons.

By the time he concludes, I've already made up my mind to ask him for the notes he offered last time. Why not? If nothing else, the knowledge of J. S. Bach will make for good cocktail-party conversation.

As I close my notebook and stand, the woman to my left says, "A bunch of us are going for coffee at the Urban Bean. Would you like to join us? I'm Karen, by the way."

She extends a manicured hand.

"Rita Brooks." I shake her hand, unsure if this extracurricular invitation will lead to a group interrogation. I'm about to beg off when Juan appears at my side.

"Oh, Dr. Santiago, won't you join us for coffee? We're going to the Urban Bean."

Say no.

I know he's going to decline because he tilts his head to the side and smiles graciously. The kind of smile that crinkles the corners of his downward-slanted eyes and makes every fiber in me say, *Ahhhhh.*

"Sounds lovely." He glances at me. "A cup of coffee is exactly what I need right now."

That's when I realize he thinks that Karen's "join *us*" includes me.

"Fantastic." She beams, obviously charmed. "We'll see you there. Rita, why don't you ride with me."

"Oh, no, thank you. I'll take my car. That way you won't have to bring me back."

"It's no problem."

Oh, boy. A persistent one.

Juan looks amused, as if he finds my predicament entertaining.

"Actually, I need to get some notes from Dr. Santiago."

Karen looks at me. Then at Juan. She raises her chin and her brows peak into tiny umbrellas as a knowing look slides over her face.

"*Oooh,* I see." Her pink cheeks flush a deeper hue.

I take it back. She's not just persistent. We have a bona fide busybody in our midst. I knew that from the minute Juan and I left together, Karen would be timing us to see how long it took us to *get the notes. Wink. Wink.*

The three of us walk out of Quinton Hall together. We pause at the door.

"Don't dawdle, kids. We'll be waiting for you at the Bean." As she walks away, she waggles her fingers and smiles as if she's the keeper of a great romantic secret.

Well, the joke was on her.

Still, why was it that everyone—or at least Jude and now Karen—seemed to see something so obvious? A relationship between Juan and me.

As soon as Karen got a safe distance away, I said, "She was asking questions about how I managed to get into the class midsemester."

Juan narrowed his eyes as if he'd not considered the possibility of this snag arising. He thought for a moment, then shrugged as if it should've been obvious.

"What did you say?" he asked.

"Nothing."

"Nothing? Really?"

I smiled. "When she said it wasn't customary, I simply agreed with her and then you entered the room. Right on cue."

"The right place at the right time, for once."

His smile was warm again and he chuckled.

"Well, if she persists, we'll simply have to tell her the truth."

The truth?

"That you're here for...research."

Research. There's that double entendre again. The glint in his eye makes the meaning so ambiguous. I mean, I *am* here for research. Technically...that's the excuse we'd use if someone complained about me starting the class midterm. That makes me think he wants me here. Me, specifically. But then again, perhaps he's just being nice—taking pity on a crying widow. Giving her something to do a couple of nights a week...helping her out with her...*research.*

Nah... His smile suggests something else entirely. And that's the scenario I choose.

We make small talk on the way to Juan's office. I sense that he's good at that—good at putting people at ease.

"How is the redecorating project?"

My first impulse is to say, *"Excruciating,"* but that's so negative. Even if it is true. The committee is more like a hung jury, still unable to agree on a simple color scheme. Honestly, it's like playing referee at a pissing match.

But Juan doesn't need to hear about that. Or, at least, I don't want to talk about it.

"It's fine. Before we know it, we'll be starting the installation."

"Is it still on schedule for the winter break?"

I'm about to nod, just so I can change the subject, but I

realize that the committee's indecision has pushed us back a few weeks. Because his office will be part of the renovation, he'll be bound to notice.

I haven't been able to order the goods or schedule the labor. More than likely, the installation won't happen until January. After the new term begins. Not ideal, but I warned the committee what might happen if they couldn't come to an agreement—

"No, actually. We're running a little behind. You know what happens when you get too many cooks in the kitchen."

A wide smile spreads over his face. "That's fabulous."

I frown. "No it's not. That means certain rooms will be closed for the start of the new term. The rehearsal hall will be off limits for at least a couple of weeks."

As he opens the door to Collier Hall and lets me enter first, he nods enthusiastically. "Don't you see? This means you can join us on the trip to Europe."

He takes care to not let the door slam.

We're outside his office now, and despite the moldy odor, I'm grateful for the distraction while he unlocks the door, steps inside, and turns on the light.

I remain in the hall, suddenly aware I'm out of excuses for not going. I have no family in town with whom to share the holiday. Jude's going skiing in Breckenridge. She did her darnedest to get me to go to Colorado with her for Christmas, but I fended her off until she finally got disgusted and booked the trip without me.

I wonder how she'd take it if I went on a European tour with Juan... Well, not exactly *with* Juan...

That answer was simple enough. Since there was a man involved, she'd pack for me.

"What notes did you need, Rita?"

The way he ever so slightly rolls the *R* in my name makes it sound beautiful. I want to ask him to say it again.

"Anything that will help me understand your Bach canon lecture." I shrug.

He opens a drawer, pulls out a file and thumbs through it. He shakes his head, replaces the file and takes out another. That's when I notice how tidy his office is. Everything is in its place. None of the files are dog-eared. Each is labeled.

Can I hire him to organize my office…and my life?

He removes another file, looks through it, pulls out a page and frowns. Replacing the paper, he aligns all the sheets.

"How about if you give me your e-mail address and I'll send you some information that might help? It will be more efficient than photocopying from the files."

He picks up a small pad of paper and pen from his desk and hands them to me.

E-mail addresses are good. *Very good*.

The new-millennium version of the phone number. Sort of. Actually, texting is the new-millennium phone call, but that involves phone numbers. I think. God, I'll have to get Jude to teach me how to text.

I'm hopeless.

Stop the negative self-talk. Jude's voice scolds me in my head.

Okay, not hopeless, I think as I start to write down my e-mail address…not hopeless. Trainable.

Should I give him my business card?

No. Too formal.

I resume printing in my best block letters, taking extra

care to be neat because the notepaper is fine, cream linen. It's personalized: *From the desk of Dr. Juan Santiago* in script at the top. It's inexplicably both formal and personal. Not business-card formal…. Maybe *classic* is a better word.

I hand the pen and paper back to him.

He glances at what I've written and nods. Approval? "Very good." Tucks the paper into the inside breast pocket of his sport coat.

"Let me grab something and we'll be on our way."

He brushes past me and opens the door of a credenza on the opposite wall of the tiny office. He pulls out a stack of brochures, hands one to me.

It's for the European trip. The counterpart to the poster outside his office that I was pretending to read the day I met him.

My cheeks grow warm.

"Look it over," he said. "Since the design project is delayed, perhaps you will reconsider?"

I study the young, smiling faces on the brochure. Tanned and happy, the group looks as if they're having the time of their lives—a trip abroad. An adventure to give them bragging rights for the rest of their lives.

What is keeping me from going on the tour?

One of my few regrets is that I never went to Europe during my college years. I never did the bohemian-backpacking trek. Fred and I were in love, planning a wedding, a life together, which was so much more important than walking all over Europe. That trip—though maybe not the backpacking version—was for when we retired. Well, it was somewhere on the list after we scrimped and saved and rented the RV and drove to the Grand Canyon.

So why wasn't I jumping at this chance to trade in the fated La-Z-Boy vacation for my very own European trip of a lifetime?

I tiptoe right up to the edge of that question and see that the answer is a longer way down than I'd anticipated. It's at the bottom of a vast list of *why nots* that give me vertigo as I teeter on the ledge, desperately searching for a reason to say yes.

"May I offer you a ride?" His question startles me, pulls me back. "Parking is scarce at the Bean. And it's not safe for a woman to walk the campus alone at night."

There's something in his eyes—or maybe it's his smile. My heart races and the dizziness morphs into a sudden thrill— just as my stomach might drop if I braved a jump off that ledge to claim a reason to go.

He's old-fashioned. Protective, offering me a ride. Looking after me. Then I lose my balance and freefall past all those reasons why not—past work and wedding rings and fear. I tumble softly into the safety net of e-mail addresses and rides and linen handkerchiefs.

The gentle landing makes me catch my breath. Unscathed, I realize I can do this. I hear myself utter, "I would love a ride, thanks."

He gestures toward the door. "Shall we?"

Yes. My gosh. I think we might....

THE URBAN BEAN isn't merely a coffee shop. It's also a wine bar, decadent-dessert den and carnal hot spot all rolled into one.

The moment we walk in the door, I smell the perfume of pheromones mixed in with the scent of strong coffee, warm cinnamon and something alcoholic.

The sound of a funky jazz quartet blends with the electric undercurrent of the place. Everything about the Bean, from the original abstract art on the walls, to the red velvet banquettes to the polished blond-oak floors proclaims: *Hip. Sexy. Now!*

As Juan and I scan the packed room for Karen and the others, his hand is on the small of my back. A barely there pressure that might be an accident. Or he might be touching me…guiding me through the standing-room-only swarm.

Across the room, I notice a blond man who looks about Juan's age waving his arms overhead. He seems to be trying to get our attention, and for a moment I wonder if he's with Karen's party. When Juan sees him, he slants away from me and waves with the hand that had been flirting with my back.

"I believe I see our party over there." He points at a long table in the other direction from where his friend is standing. "If you'll excuse me, I'll join you in a moment."

Oh.

I watch him navigate his way through the crowd. It's obvious he's no stranger to this place. It hits me that while my life has comprised domestic complacency, Juan has been…*here*. Well, not *here* at the Urban Bean, per se, but living a *Hip. Sexy. Now!* life so different from mine. I wonder suddenly if I've misread his intentions—or read more into them than he intended.

I mean, I'm not talking serious relationship…or am I? Do I know anything different?

For some strange reason, as I squeeze through the crowd, I think of roller-skating. When I was a kid, I knew the rhythms, had the grace and balance. I'd get right back up when I fell and start again.

Trying to skate now, after all these years, my feet feel huge and clunky. Everyone is in my way. I can't find the beat to this nouveau jazz. Suddenly I want funky town! Trying this now, I'll probably break every bone in my unpracticed body.

"There she is," Karen shouts over the din and motions to a seat next to her. "Where's Dr. Santiago? Didn't you come together?"

I don't want to answer that question. "He's talking to a friend. He'll be over in a minute."

Karen scans the room. When her greedy gaze latches on to Juan talking to his friend and a couple of young women who look like students, I'm embarrassed by her blatant, hungry assessment. Especially when she turns that gaze on me and demands, "Have you and Dr. Santiago been seeing each other long?"

Three more curious faces stare up at me from the table— Purple Girl, a thirtysomething man and a middle-aged woman I haven't met but recognize from class.

"Hi, I'm Rita Brooks," I say rather than succumbing to Karen's inquisition. "I'm new to class."

"Oh, how rude of me." Karen's voice trumps the noise of the place. "Of course you are. You haven't met everyone, have you? Let me introduce you. Rita, this is Tina Jones, Patty Murphy and Daryl Hodges."

They each murmur a greeting. Then Purple Girl—er— Tina Jones, says, "God, Karen, let her sit down and get a glass of wine before you start grilling her."

With one last glance in Juan's direction, Karen sits down and hands me a wine list. Thank God, Juan returns before my wine arrives. Just as I'd hoped, Karen's nosy questions succumb to teacher-pupil subservience. Though, once Juan had ordered a brandy and a piece of molten-chocolate cake, she did ask, "So where did you come from, Midterm Rita? We're all dying to know."

Midterm Rita? Was that my new name?

I could read the hopeful question in her eyes.

I glanced at Juan, hoping he'd take the lead, but he was busy forking a bite of cake into his mouth, avoiding my gaze.

The floor was all mine. I cleared my throat.

"Actually, I'm not taking the class. Not for credit anyway. I'm doing a redesign of the music department and outlying buildings and…I thought sitting in on a class might help me understand how I could best serve the students."

Four blank faces stared back at me, as if to say, "And…?"

Thank God, Juan cut in. "Have you tried the cake? Paired with the Calvados, it's about as close to heaven as you'll get while still on earth."

The four heads swiveled to look at him. "Here, Rita, taste this." Fork in hand, he leans across the table and feeds me cake. Then he swirls his snifter and hands it to me.

"Wait, smell it first. Savor the apples."

My gaze locks with his and I do as I'm told, inhaling the brandy, sipping, and…*mmm*…closing my eyes to take pleasure in how the rich, warm liquid melds with the deep, dark chocolate.

Oh, God.

It tastes exactly as I imagine Paris might taste, with its hints of pear…and butterscotch…nuts and…chocolate.

Ahhh.

When I open my eyes, everyone is looking at me. Then they flag down the server and order five pieces of molten-chocolate cake and snifters of brandy.

As we eat, Juan passes out the brochures for the European trip.

"Karen, you're going, right?" he asks.

With a fork in her right hand and the brandy in her left, she nods. Her mouth is full, so she doesn't speak.

"I'll be honest," Juan says. "We need just two more people to commit. If not, we must cancel the trip. If we get the two we need, then I can promise you the trip of a lifetime. Come on." He claps his hands like a coach rallying the team. "Let's not let this opportunity pass us by."

Daryl's face shutters. "Sorry, no can do. I just started a new job. With school and a new baby, money's tight. Speaking of—" He looks at his watch. "I'd better get home before my wife comes out looking for me."

He signals the server for his bill.

"So, did you gather us here so you could push the trip?" Tina's looking at the brochure as if it might poison her.

I'm a little tipsy, but cognizant enough to be of like mind with her—which in any other situation might be a scary prospect.

"Oh, no." Juan smiles at her as if he's indulging a bratty child. "Certainly not. I simply don't want you to miss the trip of a lifetime."

The server arrives with bill folders for the table and as we're each digging around for our money, Tina slurs, "Trip of a lifetime? You keep saying that. But it's just a tour. I mean, what's so great about this one in particular that would rank it among *trips of a lifetime?*"

Now Juan looks a little offended. "The trip goes through Barcelona, which is my hometown. Ms. Jones, I've planned to show the students who come along a very special side of

Barcelona. I certainly did not mean to pressure you." His face is pinched. He shrugs as he picks up his glass and drains the last of the Calvados.

Karen scrambles into action. "Tina, you're drunk." She grabs Purple Girl's purse. "I'm driving you home. Come on, let's go."

"I'm not ready to go home." A purply kind of whine.

"Yes, you are. Let's get you out of here." Karen pulls a wad of bills from Tina's purse and settles her bill.

Surprisingly, Tina lets Karen do it. When Karen motions for her, she stumbles to her feet.

"'Night, everyone," Karen says. "Patty, Rita, take it from someone who's never felt as if she was being *sold* by Dr. Santiago, I really hope you'll join the tour. It'll be a great time. And if you don't?" She gives a little *your-loss* quirk of the shoulder. "Come on, Tina, let's go."

"Wait, I'll walk out with you," Patty says.

Then Juan and I are alone in the crowd. He's wearing a funny look, as if he swallowed a marble that's stuck in his windpipe.

Finally he clears his throat. "That was awkward. Not at all as I'd intended. I hope you don't feel as if I'm trying to push this tour on you, Rita."

Uh…the thought had crossed my mind.

I've had just enough wine and brandy that my guard is relaxed. He reads it on my face.

"I'm sorry. This is horrible. Not at all my intention. I mean, I simply wanted to get everyone excited about the tour, but not at the risk of making them uncomfortable." He plants both hands on the table and looks up at the ceiling. *"Ay-γi-γi."*

"But won't there be other trips?" I ask.

He regards me rather sheepishly. "Sort of."

"What does *sort of* mean? Either there will be or there won't."

His gaze, bold and direct, locks with mine. I can see the wheels in his head turning.

"What?" I say. "Just tell me."

"Would you think badly of me if I told you I might have a tiny ulterior motive?"

Thank God he doesn't give me a chance to answer, because what am I supposed to say to that?

"I have a job interview for a summer position at the Valencia School of Music in Barcelona."

Right...?

"It coincides perfectly with the tour." He shrugs, picks up his snifter, stares into the empty bowl, then sets it down. "Honestly, it'll save me a small fortune in airfare and hotel if I can combine it with the trip."

Is that ethical? Even if it is technically, it's a little shady that he'd hound his students to take the trip to fund his next venture.

He looks away and drums his fingers on the table.

But obviously his teaching gig at Drayton wasn't permanent. Don't know why I automatically assumed he'd be here long-term.

When he looks back at me, his expression is an apology. I try to show my sympathetic side.

"Doesn't the school where you're interviewing pay your expenses?"

"Apparently not. Cutbacks, I suppose. This is very embarrassing. I probably shouldn't have mentioned it, but in a small way, I guess I thought by telling you...that you might understand."

He smiles a rueful smile and reaches for the lone bill folder on the table.

"Didn't she bring mine?" I scan the bar for our server.

"I asked her to combine our tabs." He slides a Gold American Express in with the bill. "This is on me."

I'm not sure what to think of this gesture. Obviously, he'd made the arrangements with the server before the evening went south. So, it wasn't as if he was trying to make it up to me. Not that he had anything to make up for.

He wasn't a hustler. Not really. He was just trying to drum up interest for a trip he wanted to take that needed a few more people in order to fly.

"That's very sweet of you," I say, "but it's not necessary. Why don't we have her split it."

He shakes his head and hands the server the bill.

"It's done. *Acabado*."

"Well, thank you."

I pick up one of the brochures. Really, it's more so that I have something to do with my hands as we wait for the server to return. "I hope you find your two people for the trip."

"I was telling the truth when I promised it would be the trip of a lifetime." His posture is more relaxed now. He's leaning back with his hands laced over his tight abs. "I've arranged some extra surprises that aren't on the schedule. Such as a paella dinner at the vineyard home of my cousin. It's just a short day trip. And I will reunite with a quartet I played with when I was in college. There is a concert at an old church in Barcelona. It will be a good time. A chance to experience how the locals live."

The server returns, needing his signature.

His mention of the old church sparks a thought— Just as Juan was combining business and personal pursuits, if, during the Provence part of the trip, I could sneak away and give Annabelle some pointers on her rectory, the trip would be a tax write-off.

I don't know why I hadn't seen it before.

As we navigate our way through the crowd, his hand is on the small of my back again.

This man of the linen hankies and soulful brown eyes means no harm. He is honest, after all. Honest about his intentions. Honestly trying to give those who went the trip of a lifetime.

Out at the car, he opens the door for me. I settle in, click my seat belt into place. By the time he's walked around to the driver's side, I've nearly made up my mind. The only thing I'd need to check on would be whether Annabelle could break away to meet me in Provence during the time frame we're there.

She could even meet Juan.

Oh, but I'm getting ahead of myself.

Still, I wait until we drive back to my car to open the conversation.

"So, if a person was interested in the tour... Would it be possible to follow the Dr. Santiago plan and sneak off for a couple of days to take care of personal business?"

He smiles, but the look is quizzical. "*Pardoné?* I don't understand."

I tell him about Annabelle and the rectory and how if I could do a bit of business while we're over there, I just might be able to swing this trip.

He's elated. After he assures me that he would personally

see to it that my business needs were met, the conversation morphs into how Annabelle came to live in Paris. Then that leads to the branch of his family who are still in Spain.

And before we know it, it's two-thirty in the morning. The car windows are fogged up from hours of conversation, and we've finally run out of things to say.

He walks around and opens my car door and sees me safely to the driver's side of my Acura.

"I will e-mail you the schedule so that you can confer with your sister."

That's when he leans in. I think he's going to give me a proper European kiss on both cheeks, but somehow his lips find mine.

It's just a whisper of a kiss.

Polite, yet not quite chaste.

"This trip is exactly what you need, Rita. And I am so very honored I will be the one to show you the time of your life."

SIX

I CAN'T BELIEVE I'm here. In Europe. Barcelona, to be exact. The first leg of the journey. After I committed, Juan managed to fill the remaining space and here we are.

The group—twenty-five strong—arrived at ten-thirty last night. Some of the younger, more energetic adventurers went out after we'd settled into our hotel rooms. Karen, who is my roommate, and I agreed we'd be doing ourselves a huge favor to forgo the festivities and get a good night's rest. Start fresh in the morning. So we stayed in. I ended up listening to Karen, clad in her Eeyore night shirt, telling me her life story, which basically boiled down to: thrice divorced; thinks men are untrustworthy bastards.

To free myself from her pedantic ranting, I ended up excusing myself, taking my cell phone down to the lobby—for "better reception," *nudge, nudge, wink, wink*—and spending an hour on the phone with my sister, Annabelle, celebrating the novelty of being in the same time zone for the first time in years. Even though my tired body was still on eastern central time, my heart was aching to see my sister. It would still be a week before we saw each other—and that would just be a quick get-together as the tour passed through Paris on the second of four legs of the journey—Spain, France, Austria and Italy. Ten days later, when the group left for home from Rome, I'd hop on the train and meet Annabelle and Jean Luc in Avignon.

We'd spend a couple of nights there, look over their newly purchased rectory. I'd get an idea of what they wanted, make some recommendations. When I offered to draw up some color boards once we got back to Paris—planned to spend the week between Christmas and New Year's with her and Jean Luc before I headed home—she said we'd have to play it by ear because there was some sort of snafu concerning design plans for the rectory. Something about a benefactor—that it was complicated and she'd explain once I got here. But, she said, I shouldn't worry because they still needed my input. "Desperately."

Even though I hadn't seen Juan in three weeks, and I was looking forward to seeing him more than the Eiffel Tower, part of me missed my sister so badly I wanted to hop on the TGV and go to her now.

The romantic in me kicked up a little protest. That time would arrive soon enough. In the meantime, there was Juan....

As I sat in the lobby, in a large wrought-iron chair that resembled a throne with its red velvet cushions, I told Anna about how Juan had flown over ahead of the group to take care of his personal business. That he was meeting us right here in the lobby at eight o'clock the next morning.

"Will I get to meet him when you are in Paris?" Annabelle asked.

My pulse dances a strange little stutter step at the possibility.

In defense, my left thumb instinctively goes for the back of my ring finger, searching for the wedding ring that no longer lives there.

I took it off after Juan kissed me and I committed to the trip.

It just didn't seem right to wear it anymore.

"I don't know, Anna. I guess we'll just have to see."

I've seen Juan three times since that night at the Urban Bean. I missed the following Tuesday-night class because of a meeting with a new client. Then I saw him the following Thursday. That next week the school was closed for Thanksgiving. This year, it was late—November 27. So when we came back that first week in December, I saw him at our regular class meeting.

Then the week after that there was a note on the classroom door that said class was canceled and that the students should see Dr. Santiago's Web site for a study guide for the final exam. Any questions should be e-mailed to him.

I had no reason to take the final since I'd come in midterm. So it was the end of the semester for me. But it was also the beginning of the e-mail portion of my affair with Juan Santiago.

Granted, the majority of cyber correspondence was trip-related and sent en masse to the group, but he always sent me a personal note under separate cover. Something along the lines of:

"Thinking about something you said…"

"Counting the days until Europe…"

"Missing your beautiful smile…"

The next morning, as Karen and I leave our room to join

the others downstairs, I'm giddy as a girl anticipating her prom date. I wonder what it will be like to spend time with him in such a romantic place.

The thought makes me draw in a quick, deep breath, filled with the scent of strong coffee, cinnamon and a hint of orange blossoms. Here, even the hotel smells better than usual. And it's a beautiful place—traditional Spanish style with deep mahogany wood furniture and floors and wrought-iron fixtures.

"What time do you have?" Karen asks as she adjusts her red fanny pack on her little mound of a belly. "I forgot to set my watch."

As I pull my BlackBerry from my purse—I don't wear a watch anymore since I've been carrying the phone—a chorus of laughter rings out as we round the corner.

"I have 7:56."

"Ooh, we'd better hurry." Karen fiddles with her watch. "I'd hate for them to leave without us. That would be just terrible on our first day."

I'm about to reassure her that they wouldn't do that, but there's a knot of college-age kids from our group waiting at the elevator. Three guys and three women. They weren't in the evening class, but I recognize them from the flight over.

"Good morning," I say.

"Hey," they return in unison.

"Did you have fun last night?" Karen asks.

"Uh, *yeah*." A guy with red hair and freckles snickers. "We were just talking about that."

The girls giggle and exchange a look with the guys, who, in turn, play-punch each other in the arm.

Karen shoots me a look I infer to mean *children*. It's almost an eye roll, but the gesture is more implied than actual.

"Never thought I'd see that side of Dr. Santiago," says the tall skinny guy with brown hair.

What? "Dr. Santiago was with you last night?" I try to sound nonchalant and ignore the way Karen's eyebrows shoot up.

"Yeah," says a skinny blonde whose pierced belly button is clearly visible between her high-riding cami and low-slung jeans. "We're going to take him out again tonight and get him drunk. Last night alone was worth hauling my ass all the way across the ocean rather than spending the break at the beach. I thought this tour would be so lame."

"Then why did you come?" Karen sounds cross.

"Yeah, Chris," says a brunette, who until now has been quiet. "Why don't you tell everyone *why* you're here?"

Chris?

Something in the brunette's tone makes my thoughts lurch back to that first night in class. Back to Juan's phone call from an impatient *Chris,* who had him rushing out of the room.

Could this be the woman?

Don't be ridiculous. There must be millions of Chrises—both male and female—in the world. You don't even know if the person who called was a man or a woman.

Chris rolls a sun-streaked strand of hair between her thumb and index finger, bites her full bottom lip as she slants a look at the brunette. "I need the credit. I'm graduating in May and it was either this trip or I'd have to take a fifteen-hour load to make up the humanities class I failed last year."

Karen's mouth flattens into a thin line.

I try to ignore the claw of envy raking at my gut. So I missed the party. Missed seeing Juan.

I push aside this odd feeling. Really, it's not envy, is it? If it is, then it's directed at youth—or lack of it. Jet lag. That's what this out-of-sync feeling is. That's what's causing this frustration burning in the pit of my stomach. It has nothing to do with my being sensible and going to bed rather than partying all night. Yes, jet lag is the reason I barely made it downstairs by eight for a day of sightseeing. It has nothing to do with the fact that I couldn't wear a belly piercing even if I wanted to.

The elevator dings. The doors slide open and we crowd inside like cattle. In the close confines, I smell the afterlife of a night of boozing: sweat, unwashed hair, fruity gum and Chris's too-strong Eternity perfume. I know it's hers because she's standing next to me.

Up close, she looks tired. Fine lines are starting to form underneath her sun-kissed glow. They'd work their way to the surface in a few years if she kept up her sun worshipping.

But that's years away.

This is right now.

Right now she's a young, bronzed, flat-stomached goddess.

And what else matters but *now?*

The elevator dings again and we spill out into the hallway adjacent to the lobby. I go with the flow, travel at their speed, all too aware of life's complicated dance with its ever-changing tempo. I don't always know the steps. Often I fall down. But I've always gotten back up and started again.

That's what matters. The here. The now.

And now, we round the corner and see Juan holding court with the rest of the group—give or take a few.

"Ah, there you are," he says to no one in particular. "Are we all here now?"

"All except for Nina Simons," says a voice in the crowd. "She's hungover. Says she'll join us later."

Poor Nina, whoever she was. She was human. More my speed than some of these hard partyers. I glance around at the group of about twenty-five and notice several look a little green. One guy wears his Ray-Bans inside. I usually don't derive pleasure out of people's pain, but I must admit I get a small degree of satisfaction knowing I'm not the only one who can't handle an all-nighter. If I'd gone out I would've been right where Nina is now.

And I'd much rather be here.

I try to catch Juan's eye, but he's busy writing something on a clipboard. Chris walks by him and I could swear I see her trail a finger along his arm as she passes. But I'm not sure because when he looks up, he says, "*Buenos días,* ladies and gentlemen. I am thrilled to welcome you to my home, Barcelona, where we will kick off our Winter Music Appreciation Tour. I trust you had a good flight and that your rooms are satisfactory. I've already had the pleasure of welcoming some of you. And for those who did not make it to the cantina last night—" he gives a little palms-up shrug that is at once irritating and endearing "—well, judging from last night, there will be many other parties. I'm sure."

Karen leans over. "I like a good glass of wine as much as the next person, but oh, brother, I hope this trip doesn't turn into one big drunken orgy."

Suddenly, I miss Jude, who probably would've dragged

me, kicking and screaming, to last night's party. And what a sweet surprise it would've been to see Juan. Today is the first day of a new beginning. I can sleep on the flight back. I'm just about ready to lean over and whisper to Karen, *What did you expect from a college trip?* when Juan says, "Before we head out and board the bus this morning, it is my great pleasure to introduce you to Christine Mendoza, who will be your tour guide for the duration of the trip."

Christine? Yet another Chris…

An attractive woman steps forward. She's wearing a sleek brown bob and a smart pantsuit that looks as if it might be a Chico's Travlers ensemble—but I have a sneaking suspicion a woman like this wouldn't be caught dead in pants with an elastic waistband. When I glimpse her exquisite red, high-heeled peep-toe pumps, I'm sure of it. There's a murmur of excitement. When she holds up her hand and smiles, a hush falls over the group.

"Welcome, everyone." She has a slight accent I can't identify. "I hope you're as excited as I am to be here today. We have a lot on our itinerary. I suggest we board the bus, and I'll fill you in on the particulars as we travel to Castell de Montjuïc."

Her flawless, ivory complexion and poised command of the group suggest she's probably in her early thirties. Young enough to possess a fading blush of youth, and old enough to know how to use it.

Her lips and nails are shellacked candy-apple red, contrasting with her light skin and the most beautiful deep brown eyes I've ever seen on a woman.

Juan is watching her, transfixed, a sexy half grin tipping up the edges of his mouth. Could this be *the* Chris?

"I'll see everyone on the bus." Confidently, Christine motions toward the front entrance, then struts over to Juan, moving like a model on the catwalk.

As the herd moves toward the buses, she says something to him in Spanish. His expression blooms into a full smile.

They laugh.

A private joke.

I hang back, adjusting my scarf, tucking it into the front of my navy blue double-breasted peacoat. Stalling. Not quite sure if I want to see him or if I want to see how he is with her.

"Come on," Karen demands. "I want a seat up front."

When I agreed to room with her, I didn't intend to become attached at the hip. "Go ahead," I say. "I need to…tie my shoe."

I glance down at my Skechers. The ad in the magazine had promised the shoe would increase my style and comfort. God, what was I thinking? From this vantage, they look so new and white they glow in contrast with the mahogany floors.

Maybe I should've opted for the other style: the less comfortable, but not quite glaring-white sneakers.

At least I don't have a fanny pack.

"I'll save you a seat," Karen says as she moves with the group. "But don't be too long."

I feel dowdy in my slacks and tennies, but the Trip Tips e-mail I received suggested dressing comfortably since we'd be in for long days filled with miles of walking.

Oh, well. This isn't a fashion parade. I'm not trying to impress anyone.

Well, not *everyone*. Maybe just one.

I glance at Juan. He might be standing a little too close to Christine. Then again, it might just be a European thing. But who can blame him? The woman is gorgeous.

Ha! Let's talk at three o'clock this afternoon and see who's comfortable clicking around Barcelona in high heels. Didn't you get the Trip Tips memo?

Although something told me this wasn't Christine's first tour. She was probably well versed in the appropriate footwear for our excursion. Probably one of those women who could traipse all over a city in heels by day and go out dancing in even higher stilettos by night.

That European thing.

I bend over and retie my shoe, wishing I could buy a bottle of that…that…*European thing* and take it home with me. No, scratch that, I'd like to hook myself up to it intravenously and give myself a transfusion.

Naturally, that's when Juan sees me.

"Rita!" He beams. No, he really does. He seems genuinely happy to see me. Even in front of beautiful Christine. "There you are. I was looking for you, but I didn't see you in the crowd."

I straighten so fast I nearly throw my back out. I don't bother to finish retying the stiff, white laces—what, bent over like that, with my butt up in the air? Are you kidding me?

"Christine, may I present my friend Rita Brooks," he says. "She has come all the way from Florida to experience your tour."

Her tour? I thought it was *his* tour. The *Juan Santiago Time of Your Life Tour*. I sense a bait and switch—especially remembering how he said Christine would be our tour guide for the duration of the trip.

But with the way Juan's looking at me, it doesn't really matter. In fact, maybe it would be better if Christine worked, freeing Juan up to play…

"Pleased to meet you." I offer her my hand. She looks less than enthused as she gives it a quick hard squeeze. This is a woman who is not comfortable around other women.

It's a snap judgment, I know, but my first impression is confirmed as she snips off a cool "It's nice to meet you. We should get to the bus."

All of the warmth she exuded when she addressed the group is gone as if she'd flipped a switch.

Christine onstage: warm, smiling, welcoming.

Christine one-on-one: cold, hard, mannequin.

Was it just me? I distinctly saw the smile she gave Juan before he called me over. Not mannequin-like. I decide to put it to the test.

"I heard there was quite a party last night," I say to Juan, but glance at her, hoping her expression will offer a clue whether she was there or not.

Nothing.

"Yes," says Juan. "And you were sorely missed."

He's looking at me the same way he looked at me when we sat in his car after the Urban Bean. Right before he kissed me… My toes curl in my too-white tennies. And darned if I don't feel heat color my cheeks. I pray he doesn't notice.

"Really, we must go if we're going to keep on schedule to be back in time for the opera tonight."

"Ah, *Carmen*," Juan says wistfully.

"Oh, is it *Carmen?* I've seen the opera three times, so that one I know. Finally, something a little more accessible than the canons and fugues of J. S. Bach."

Juan and I laugh.

This time it's our private joke.

Unsmiling, Christine tucks a strand of hair behind her ear, crosses her arms.

Juan smiles at her. "Christine, go ahead and tend to your charges. I will have Rita to the bus in a moment."

The woman's mannequin face doesn't crack. "We leave in five minutes."

"She'll be there in two."

Christine looks skeptical, but turns and walks away.

My heart is beating as if someone is hitting my chest with a hammer. So maybe she wasn't the mysterious Chris. Or if she was, obviously it wasn't romance that made him hurry off. Maybe she needed numbers…facts and figures—

"So you've seen *Carmen* three times?"

I nod.

I want to kiss him again. I want to lean in and savor his lips and see if they taste the way I remember. Like coffee and apples and pears and chocola—

"I have a proposition for you." He's shoved his hands into his front pants pockets and is rocking, ever so slightly, from side to side. A nervous tic?

"A proposition?"

"Since you've seen *Carmen* three times—" he shrugs "—and, well, I've seen it at least three dozen, how would you feel about skipping the opera tonight?"

My heart skips a beat. *Be cool. Calm. And cool.*

"What did you have in mind?" I don't know what to do with my hands. I shrug my purse from my shoulder. It lands in the crook of my arm.

"I promised you a special tour of Barcelona…."

I melt at the way *Barcelona* rolls off his tongue. Like honey or Calvados with its apples and pears.

I bite my bottom lip. Not wanting to seem too eager. Wanting him to speak first. Because in the wrinkled, whacked-out recesses of my mind, I recall Karen being present when he promised that *special tour.* I don't want to jump to conclusions, reading too much or too little into his words.

"Barcelona is a magical city." He smiles. The sultry, smooth-as-apple-brandy way he looks at me makes my head swim with drunken thoughts. I think his Calvados whisper promises, "I know just what you need, Rita Brooks, and I want to give that to you."

But I'm not sure I heard him right over the pulse pounding in my ears. Before I can ask him to clarify, he says he'll text me, bids me a good day and points me in the direction of the bus.

Karen moves her Disney Princesses tote bag, and I fall into the seat next to her. "Where were you? I was so worried they were going to go off and leave you."

We're sitting in the second row from the front, within range of Christine's cold mannequin glare. Even if Karen and I were alone in our hotel room, I wouldn't gossip like a schoolgirl. Later, I'll have to come up with a plausible excuse for skipping out on the opera, but right now I simply say, "I was tying my shoe."

Karen looks at my feet and scrunches up her face. "Well, why is it still untied?"

I LOVE CASTLES.

Really, I do.

In fact, the trip to Castell de Montjuïc was one of the

destinations I had most looked forward to while we were in Barcelona.

That is, until Juan changed my itinerary.

With one sweet promise, he turned me inside out until all I could think about the entire day was exchanging *Carmen* and the rest of the Drayton College group for a private tour of Barcelona heaven with Dr. Juan Santiago.

I was as dreamy and scatty as a teenager with raging hormones, who planned to sneak out of the house to meet her boyfriend in the moonlight.

It was the longest day of my life. And when the bus finally delivered us back to the hotel, with just an hour to get ready for dinner and the opera, I had to feign a headache to get out of the prearranged evening with the others.

"I can't believe you're going to miss it." Karen resembles a shimmery sausage link in her too-tight strapless gown. It's made of that material that looks brown if you look at it from one angle and pink if you look at it from another. "You want me to bring you something back?"

I remove the arm I've thrown over my eyes—for effect— and squint at her. "That's very sweet of you, but I think I will draw a nice hot bath and order in."

Karen blinks at me. Sort of skeptically. Her expression makes me fear she sees right through my story and is about to expose me.

Finally, she gives a quick shake of her head, as if tossing off the thought, hitches her black lace shawl around her shoulders and says, "Well, good night. I hope you feel better. We're doing the town Euro-style tonight. Opera first. Dinner after that. So I don't know what time I'll be back. I'll try not to wake you when I come in."

In my mind, I start to calculate the time I'll need to be back in order to get in before Karen, but stop myself. If I'm out when she gets back, it's none of her business where I went. I simply went…out. For a bite. For a stroll. For a night of mad passionate sex with Juan.

It's none of her business.

As soon as Karen closes the door, I sequester myself in the bathroom. Juan had sent me a text message earlier asking me to meet him in the hotel bar at eight o'clock. Opera curtain time. He wasn't so crass as to point that out, but the unwritten rule was *discretion at all times*. Even though there was nothing wrong with our seeing each other. We were consenting adults. Technically, I wasn't even his student.

Still, I'd feel better not to be the center of gossip and speculation. And, I had to admit that the secrecy added another layer of excitement to the tantalizing promise of an affair.

At exactly eight o'clock, I walk into the dark, smoky hotel bar. Underneath my red dress, I was wearing the underwear I'd purchased at Victoria's Secret and thigh-high stockings. The cherry on top—er, on the bottom—is a pair of black patent, pointy-toe stiletto pumps that force me into a slow, sexy walk across the polished wooden floor.

Juan sits at a high table for two. Champagne is chilling in a bucket beside the table.

His gaze wanders over me as I approach.

When he stands, he takes my hand, lifts it to his lips, then gives me a single red rose. "You look exquisite."

Heat blooms inside me, and I feel desirable for the first time in years.

"Thank you."

He pulls my chair out.

"I thought we would enjoy some champagne," he whispers into my ear. "Then get a bite to eat and then see where the night leads us."

A silent, full-body sigh shudders through me.

This is why I came to Europe. The place where I can give myself permission to live again.

We drink the champagne, make a pretense of eating dinner—then somehow we find ourselves up in Juan's suite.

The moment the door closes, we are a tangle of arms and bodies and discarded clothes. He backs me against the wall and presses himself to me. I can't catch my breath because he's thrust his tongue so deeply inside my mouth that I can't breathe. But then he pulls away, leaving me gasping as he sears a path along my jawline to a secret spot behind my ear that nearly makes me come undone.

A sweltering heat and dampness between my legs has me longing to be naked and underneath him, with his maleness filling me.

I move my hand to touch him, but he catches my wrist and pins it to the wall.

A little rougher than I like, but—

"Right now everything is for you," he says. "Let me pleasure you. I will have my turn later."

He releases my wrist and manages to free me of my bra and panties in what seemed like one continuous motion. Until I am standing naked in only my thigh-highs and heels.

"I want to look at you," he says, suddenly backing away, devouring my vulnerable nakedness with his hooded eyes.

"You are quite exquisite—"

Then I think I hear the door opening.

Oh, my God, did he not lock the door?

The sound of a woman's shriek.

"You cheating bastard! What the hell are you doing?"

It's the Chris of the bare-belly fame from the elevator this morning. She was *the* Chris.

Everything happens in a surreal sort of slow motion. Juan steps away from me, holding up his hands as if his not touching me would absolve him of all guilt.

I am exposed, naked and ashamed. As I scramble for my dress and underclothes—Juan is standing on my bra—I realize Chris isn't the only one there. Others are lurking in the doorway.

"Oh, my God! He's fucking the old broad," shouts a dis-embodied voice. Phantom laughs explode in the hallway. Voyeurs crane their necks to ogle my nakedness as Chris continues to shriek and pummel Juan with her fists.

With my dignity permanently shoved down around my ankles, I hug my dress to the front of my body and scramble in thigh-highs and heels into the shadows of the bathroom. I wish that somehow I could slip between the marble floor tiles or that the room would simply swallow me whole.

SEVEN

I HAD TO get out of Barcelona. I couldn't stay.

Not after that humiliation.

It wasn't simply getting caught in a compromising position. Oh, no, it went much deeper than that.

He went with *her.*

Juan followed Chris out the door begging her forgiveness. He went chasing after that little bare-bellied tanoxeric college student who was young enough to be his daughter. I had no idea Chris was his *girlfriend.* I knew someone named Chris called that first night, but he certainly didn't act like a committed man—kissing me in the parking lot, enticing me to come on the trip. What did it say about a man who thought he could send two women on the same trip and string them along for ten days? What did he plan to do, alternate beds?

Some nerve.

It made me sick to my stomach—that I could be so gullible. That I could have such delusions. As if I'd find another Fred in my lifetime.

Even that thought didn't break through the icy wall that had formed around me after I heard him sniveling, begging her to forgive him. I could hear him through the bathroom door as I wiggled back into my dress and waited for everyone to leave so I could sneak into my room like a prostitute on the lamb.

Nope, humiliation doesn't even begin to cover it.

That's why I was absolutely numb, as I threw my clothing into my suitcase and made a mad dash out of the hotel, praying I wouldn't run into Karen or the lot of cackling jackasses who'd barged in on the *Juan and Rita Floor Show.*

I was in such a hurry to get out of there that it didn't even dawn on me until I was checking in to the Grand Hotel Central near the Barcelona França Train Station, that I'd forgotten all about checking out of the other hotel.

Damn.

I didn't want to just walk away from it—who knew how much expense I might incur if I didn't formally check out. But I wasn't sure how I was supposed to handle it since we were on the tour.

Somehow, through the icy barrier I'd built around myself, I managed to call the hotel, from my newer, less mahoganied, less Spanish, more generic room.

"An emergency prevented me from continuing on the tour and checking out in person," I tell the guest-relations person. "No, I hadn't charged any incidentals to the room. Yes, my roommate will be occupying the room through the duration of the original registration. Yes, I realize I will not receive a refund for the unoccupied nights since the lodging is included in the tour package."

The congenial woman is wishing me well with my *emergency* when Juan's text message comes through.

So sorry. Chris missed me at dinner. Came looking 4 me.
Sorry 2 put U thru that.

I nearly throw my phone against the wall.

Apologizing via text?

Are you kidding me?

How could I ever have thought this man with his smooth
accent and linen hankies a gentleman? Gentlemen did not
pursue other women when they had girlfriends; gentlemen
did not send apologies via text. I don't care if we do live in
the twenty-first century, in the age of technology, only a
coward would apologize that way.

I stared at the message for a moment and then push the
call button.

The bastard-coward wasn't going to get away with it that
easily. Though he'd probably let my call go to voice mail—

"Rita, oh, my God." Damn! He answered. "I am so
sorry, love."

Love?

"I certainly didn't intend for our evening to end up like that."

Love?

"I do humbly beg your pardon."

Love?

"Why didn't you tell me you were involved with someone?" I snap.

There's a pause on the other end of the line that makes
me wonder if he's still there.

"You never asked," he finally says.

I never asked—

"Why would I ask a question like that when you were

leading me on? You kissed me in the parking lot, Juan. Was it all just a ploy to make your numbers for the trip?"

"I don't understand."

He sounds truly confused. Either he's a great actor or he really doesn't get it.

"What's not to understand? You don't sleep with other women when you're involved with someone, Juan. That's Relationships 101. Did you miss that class?"

He clears his throat. "I don't understand what my relationship with Chris has to do with you."

I'm so mad I have to get up and walk around the small room.

"You really don't get it, do you?" I say. "Where's Chris now, Juan? I'm sure she's not any happier with you than I am. And she wasn't standing there stark naked in front of a group of kids young enough to be her…her…*kids.*"

There's another long pause.

"You Americans are all the same, aren't you? Aren't you, Rita?"

"Excuse me?"

"My relationship with you is none of Chris's business. And vice versa. I never promised commitment or fidelity. I offered to give you what *you needed.* Nothing more. Nothing less. Making love is a beautiful exchange between a man and a woman, Rita. Can you not accept it for that? For what I offer you? Nothing more. Nothing less. Give yourself time to experience life. Now that you're finally free, don't settle down with the first man you meet. Won't you quit this foolishness and come back and join the tour?"

His words sting. Like a beautiful, poisonous fish that injects his venom and swims away, leaving his paralyzed victim to die.

No, I won't rejoin the tour. Not after last night's humiliating floor show. How can he be so callous about it? About last night and about the days ahead?

Now that I'm finally free? As if I'd served a prison sentence? My husband—a good, solid, faithful man—a better man than Dr. Juan Santiago would ever be—died. I'm not free. I'm in hell.

"Goodbye, Juan." I hang up the phone.

Nothing more. Nothing less.

SO NOW WHAT?

Annabelle is not expecting me for nine days.

I can't bring myself to call her and tell her I'm a naive idiot. That I ran away from the tour with my tail tucked between my bare butt cheeks.

Oh, God.

The humiliating scene plays over and over in my head. Everywhere I turn I see myself standing there naked and raw.

Blink—I see it in my reflection in the mirror.

Blink—in my image in the window.

Blink—in my mind's eye even when I squeeze my eyes shut tight to block out the horrific picture. But I can't escape it. Or the haunting vision of Fred, looking ashamed of me and betrayed.

After a sleepless night spent mulling over my options, I decide to go to Avignon early. I'll have a look at the rectory (even if it's from the outside). I'll get a feel for the city. Spend some time alone. Make my assessment and, if Annabelle can't get away, I'll talk to her about it over the phone. From my office, a safe distance away from Europe. Because what made me think I could live the same life as my sister?

Getting out of Barcelona is no less complicated than my decision of where to go.

There are no direct trains from Barcelona to Avignon. Although there is an 8:45 from the França Station that arrives at Perpignan, France, at about a quarter to noon. Then on to Montpellier, arriving a little after one o'clock in the afternoon.

I sleepwalk through the hour layover in Montpellier and then I catch a connecting train to Avignon, which dumps me off at my destination an hour later.

And here I stand outside the station. Rolling suitcase in hand. It's cold here. The biting wind whips right through me. I stop to turn up the lapels of my navy peacoat and tighten my scarf around my neck. It reminds me of yesterday, how I stalled in the hotel lobby to get Juan's attention.

A wave on nausea washes over me.

This time I'm tucking in the scarf for real. And the cold is for real, too. Not the chill that had me trembling as I lay in the dark waiting for the first break of dawn so that I could get to the train station and as far away from Barcelona and Juan Santiago as possible.

No, it was even colder in Avignon than it was in Barcelona. As I hail a taxi to drive me into the city center to find a hotel, I wonder if the chill air is a bad omen?

"*Bonjour, madame,*" says the taxi driver.

"*Bonjour, monsieur.*" I search my foggy brain for the words. *"Je voudrais aller…um…à un hôtel."*

"*Oui, quel hôtel?*"

Which hotel?

"Je ne sais pas…um… Parlez-vous Anglais, s'il vous plaît?"

Please speak English.

Normally, I would do my best to communicate in French. After all, I *am* in France. Usually, I would try—and I will, if he doesn't speak English. But right now my head hurts from lack of food and sleep. My lexicon is in my tote bag, which feels as if it weighs tons. Frankly, it's all I can do to heft my baggage into the cab.

"*Oui*—er, yes, I speak English. Which hotel, *madame?*"

"*Je ne sais pas*—I mean, I don't know. Perhaps you could recommend one?"

Two watery blue eyes watch me through the rearview mirror.

"There are several hotels near each other just inside the ramparts. I shall take you there and you can decide for yourself, *bon?*"

"*Oui, très bon. Merci beaucoup.*"

I stare out the window as the cab drives me closer to the walled city. It's after three o'clock now and the light is heading west, and beginning to take on a late-in-the-day golden hue as it washes the ancient city with light and shadow.

I've been to France twice before. But never this far south. Both trips were to Paris. Once with Fred when he indulged me several years ago. The other time was when Annabelle won the artist residency. I brought her over because I was afraid that if I didn't she might not go. Little did I know, she wouldn't leave.

I really want to talk to her, but I just can't bring myself to call her.

Not yet.

Juan's words scat through my brain. *Give yourself time to experience life. Don't settle down with the first man you meet now that you're finally free.*

I wish I could shut out the pesky buzz of his memory.

But the moment I shoo it away, it comes back, buzzing in another part of my brain.

It's not a very long ride. In a matter of minutes, the taxi stops on a narrow cobblestone street lined by stone buildings.

As I pull out my wallet to pay him, I grab the address of Annabelle and Jean Luc's rectory.

"Would you happen to know how far this address is from here?"

He takes the paper and considers it for a moment.

"Not far. Ten minutes by car. A good walk outside the city proper."

I hand him fifteen euros. "*Merci, monsieur.* Keep the change."

"Wait there. Let me help you with that." He gets out and hauls my suitcase from the seat beside me. Then reaches in his pocket and pulls out a card. "If you need a car, you call me, *oui?*"

"*Oui, merci.*"

He waves as he speeds away, leaving me standing on the uneven cobblestones in the shadows of ancient buildings.

EIGHT

I DIDN'T RESEARCH Avignon hotels since I was meeting Annabelle and Jean Luc here. My sister said she had a place for us to stay, so there was no point in it, even though I like researching and planning the trip almost as much as the adventure itself.

So here I stand with my rolling suitcase and carry-on, wearing my too-white Skechers and feeling sorry for myself.

The taxi has dumped me inside Avignon's rampart walls, near three bed-and-breakfasts. A smaller road dead-ends into a busier avenue, forming a *T*. From where I'm standing—at the head of the T with cars rushing by and the occasional person passing on bicycle or foot—I suppose this is actually where the lesser road *begins* rather than ends.

Beginnings.

Endings.

I guess it's a matter of perspective.

All around me the shops and storefronts are decorated for Christmas. There's a festive look to the place. Since I'm definitely not in the mood for festivities, it's not a good time for me to contemplate whether this is the beginning or the end.

It's simply a crossroad.

My stomach grumbles, as if seconding that motion. Well, actually, it's just reminding me that I haven't eaten in nearly twenty-four hours.

The smart plan would be to get the room, stash the luggage and then grab a bite—even though nothing sounds good. But as I stand in the shadows cast by the western listing sun, considering the three inns, I'm suddenly paralyzed by the task of choosing.

Which one?

It's not that hard. Just choose one.

But my legs don't work. I can't force my feet to move, so I can't even get close enough to look in the window of the one closest.

The metallic shimmer of disgust simmers in my veins. I'm cold and I'm tired. I'm mad at myself and Juan and the taxi driver for dropping me here; mad at the bulk and weight of my baggage, at the inns for making me choose, and the chef in the café down the street for cooking something that smells so delectable it's making my stomach grumble like an earthquake—

I put my hand over my rumbling belly. My body is hungry—even if the thought of food repulses me. I'm hanging upside down, caught in the vice of low blood sugar. The only way to right the world again is to get something to eat.

Somehow, I manage to move the mountain that is my body—bags and all—down the street to the café.

As I stare through the window into the empty dining room—what, only six tables for two? Each of them empty. I'm reminded that it's that hazy hour between lunch and dinner.

Is the restaurant open? *Please be open.*

A holly wreath adorns the lace-curtained glass door. As I push it open and haul myself and my baggage inside, a bell tinkles announcing my arrival. The warmth of the place hits me head-on, and a female voice rattles off a string of French I don't understand. I assume it is a greeting. *Please don't let her be saying, "We're not open yet."*

"Bonjour," I call in return. Hopeful.

More disembodied French floats out to me. I have no idea what she's saying.

I stand there, head pounding as I try to gather the basic words I need to communicate.

Should I sit or wait to be seated?

I glance around for a menu, but see none. I don't care. I'll have a plate of whatever's cooking that smells so good.

My stomach rumbles again and my blood sugar slips a notch lower.

Then a petite brunette in a red shirtwaist dress with a wide black patent-leather belt that makes her waist look impossibly tiny appears from behind a three-paneled screen that must section off the small front of the house from the back. She's talking in rapid French, and the words bounce off my ears.

"*Parlez-vous Anglais, s'il vous plaît?*" I ask anxiously.

"*Oui,* yes." She smiles. Her lips are painted the same vivid shade as her dress and her eyes are a startling blue against her dark hair and ivory complexion. She's probably my age, but she has that timeless sort of look. But one thing that strikes me is she looks very Parisian to be running a small Provençal café like this.

She reaches out and touches my arm, and I realize I've been staring at her too long.

"Are you unwell?"

"No, I'm just…famished."

She glances at my baggage, then appraisingly at me, finally the smile returns to her painted lips. "Ah, well, with that I can help you. Have a seat."

She makes a sweeping gesture toward the tables.

"Sit anywhere you like. I am Marie. And you are…?" After I answer, she adds, "Make yourself comfortable, Rita. I will be right back."

As Marie disappears behind the screen, I choose the table by the window so I can look out at the street. I take off my coat because it's so warm in here, and stow my luggage behind me. By the time I'm settled, she returns with a menu, a lacy, white paper place mat, a breadbasket and a glass of water. All of which she places in front of me in a sweeping flurry. That's when I notice her nails, shellacked the same bright red as her ensemble.

"The special today is fricassée de poulet et champignons. I shall give you a moment to look at the menu and then come back to answer any questions. *Bon?*"

Surely she doesn't do the cooking, too? Cook, tend the customers *and* keep a meticulous manicure?

Yeah, she probably does it all. It's that European thing at work again.

She starts to walk away on three-inch black pumps. I cross my feet at the ankles and tuck my sneakers as far out of sight as physically possible.

"Excuse me, Marie. Before you go, I'm wondering, what would you recommend?"

The woman tucks a wisp of hair behind her ear, then clasps her hands in front of her—a ladylike gesture.

"I would suggest the *fricassée de poulet*. It is the special. It is very good."

"Is that what smells so wonderful?"

The woman inclines her head to the side and smiles. "That is what you smell cooking."

"Then that's what I'll have."

She nods and bustles off behind the screen again.

I pluck a small baguette out of the basket. It's warm, and I wonder if she baked it herself. Probably.

I had a warm baguette for breakfast yesterday morning. Was I really in Spain just yesterday? It seems like another lifetime. I ponder it and the situation that sent me packing as I slather butter on the hot bread and watch it melt into the tender white crevices.

Can you not accept it for that? For what I offer you? Nothing more. Nothing less. Give yourself time to experience life. Now that you're finally free, don't settle down with the first man you meet.

Juan's words press down on me.

As much as I hate to admit it, I can see his point. I was ready to give myself away to a man who, as it turns out, is so incredibly wrong for me.

But at the time he seemed right.

So right.

The kind of right that speaks to the part of me that wants to be settled. The part of me that loves going away, but loves coming home even more—and even more than that—loves having someone to come home to.

But that wasn't the real Juan, despite how I tried to make him into that person. Out of nowhere, I think of something I read last week, the results of a study that confirmed that women aren't wired for one-night stands. That when we experience orgasms, our bodies release a "nurturing" hormone that makes us want to cuddle and commit—it makes us want to make a home.

So, Juan or no Juan, even if I tried to convince myself that I was capable of having detached sex, like men do, it would actually go against my natural grain and do more psychological harm than empower me.

Even so, this realization isn't comforting. It leaves me stranded in a no-woman's land.

I take a bite of the bread. *Mmm…delicious.* I'm suddenly overcome by just how ravenous I am. Not simply for food. But for…for…life; for someone or something to fill the void; to bring back the happiness I had with Fred.

I shove the rest of the buttered bread into my mouth. The bite is too big, but I don't care. I immediately start buttering another piece.

Though, I'm not looking for someone to replace Fred. I mean, how could I ever replace him?

He's irreplaceable.

I'll never have my old life back. But I can't live like this. So what am I going to do?

I stop buttering, midmotion; sigh and set down my knife. *I have no idea.*

Maybe Juan was right, if I don't know what I want, I really don't have any business tying myself down—at least not yet. But if not that, then *what?*

I'm only forty-five. Too young to put myself on a shelf.

Too old for casual sex. Or maybe not too old. I've never been cut from that cloth.

I swallow the bite of bread I've been chewing, but rather than devouring the piece I've buttered, I set it down on my bread plate and stare out the window.

The day is cold and gray. Not many people are outside. But soon I see a woman walking by with a cloth grocery bag brimming over with bread and squash and wrapped packages that look like meat. Two young boys bundled in coats and scarves race by on bikes. A horn honks somewhere in the distance, though no cars are visible on the narrow road.

Across the way, an old, stooped woman steps out from the inn—Chez Sabine—on the east side of the street, and sweeps the stone walk in front of her establishment.

Even though this is a small town heavy on tourism, it is home for these people.

Sadness, weighty and dark, looms over me. Even though my house is back in Florida, it's not a home.

That's what I miss.

I want to go *home*. Wherever that might be.

The woman in red reappears, all smiles.

"Have you just arrived in France?"

"Yes, I have."

"I thought so." She steps behind the small mirrored bar along the far wall. "You look travel weary."

That's a good way to put it.

"Where are you staying?"

"I haven't secured a place yet. I'm meeting my sister here, but I've arrived a few days early." I gesture toward the window. "After I eat I was considering one of the three inns around here."

She nods thoughtfully.

"May I recommend Madame LeNoir's establishment, Chez Sabine? She and her husband, Édouard, will make you quite comfortable."

I glance out the window at Chez Sabine, where the old woman had been sweeping. She's no longer outside, but as I gaze across the street, I feel lighter, more settled. That's where I will stay.

I can finally take a deep breath. When I do, the tension floats away as if on the gust of wind that blows a stray piece of newsprint down the street. Maybe Marie and Chez Sabine have a reciprocal agreement, sending customers to each other. If the inn is anything like service here, it will do just fine.

A popping sound draws my attention back to Marie at the bar. She's set out two champagne flutes and a split of champagne.

"I always like to treat myself to a cocktail before the dinner rush," she says as she divides the bubbly between the two flutes. "Won't you join me? It's my treat. A toast to welcome you to Avignon."

"Thank you, Marie. That is very kind."

She hands me the glass. "It is nothing. I am happy to have someone to share this hour. It is always a little lonely between lunch and dinner. *Santé.*" She clinks her glass to mine. "Now, I shall go get your dinner."

I smile as I sip my champagne.

And who said the French were hard to get along with? Who knows, maybe she's a marketing genius. It is the winter off-season. For the price of one welcoming glass of champagne she's hooked a repeat customer. I'll be back.

NINE

PLEASANTLY FULL AND a bit drowsy, I make my way across the street to Chez Sabine. The little reception area smells vaguely of lavender, mothballs and something savory cooking. The desk is unmanned—no sign of the woman who'd been sweeping the walk earlier.

An ancient, small black-and-white television plays softly in the corner. Because of the canned laughter, I'd be willing to guess it's a French sitcom, but I can't understand what they're saying and the picture is rather fuzzy. So, it's hard to know for certain.

The room is clean, but cluttered with knickknacks and kitsch—lace doilies, porcelain figurines and Christmas decorations cover every available inch of surface. Floral-painted plates, framed rough-hewn needlepoint pieces and thickly painted landscapes adorn the rose-printed wallpaper.

The decorating job is so busy, I almost miss the slip of a man hunkered down on the floral-print couch watching television.

Seeing him makes me jump. My hand flutters to my heart.

"Bonjour," I say.

He grunts and barely drags his gaze from the flickering screen to look at me.

"Je voudrais…um…"

I would like… Oh, how do you say a room? Oh!

"Je voudrais une chambre d'hôtel, s'il vous plaît."

He grunts again and mumbles French in a gravelly, low-pitched voice.

I don't understand.

"Pardon? Je ne comprends pas. Parlez-vous Anglais, s'il vous plaît?"

"Non!" He pulls a face that resembles an angry pug, and stares at me a moment before he pushes himself up and shuffles out of the room, muttering under his breath.

Heat burns my face.

Okay. Now what?

I stand there, unsure what to do. Should I wait? Should I leave? Maybe I should've mentioned that Marie from the café sent me.

I would've, but I don't know how to say it in French. A sinking, lead-in-the-belly sensation threatens to drag me down. I'm just turning to go when a light, cheery *"Bonjour!"* stops me.

It's the woman I watched sweeping the walk as I ate my dinner.

"Hello, I am Sabine." Her wrinkled face is an inviting smile. "Please forgive my husband's bad temper. I am pleased to welcome you to Chez Sabine. How may I help you?"

I MUST'VE SLEPT the sleep of the dead, because I lay down on the bed to close my eyes for just a minute, and the next thing I know, bright sunshine is streaming in through the lace curtains on the windows.

I sit up and blink at the light. Sometime during the night, I must have pulled the quilt over me. It looks handmade, a Dolly Madison Star pattern, made out of fabric in shades of reds, pinks and whites. I run my hand over the top of it, admiring the fine stitching.

The room is small and bright. The walls are painted white with a matching chair rail; the floors are blond wood. There's a mirrored dressing table with a delicate stool, a ladder-back chair in the corner and a trunk at the foot of the bed. The decor is much more understated than the reception area—even though there's a small Christmas tree in the corner.

I set my feet on the cold floor and shiver as I walk to the window and push back the curtain. The window in my room overlooks a little stone courtyard at the back of the house. There's a small fountain throwing water toward the sky and a single round, wrought-iron table with a matching chair. It looks inviting—even though it's chilly out there. As evidenced by the cold floor and the air seeping in through the white-painted casement windows—original, judging by the rough-hewn look of them.

It's the last day in Barcelona for Juan and his tour group before they move on to Paris. The thought of him weighs down on me. I try to shrug it off, but it doesn't really work. The memory looms like a disembodied shadow, and I can't tell if it's the thought of him or the cold that makes me shiver.

I rub my hands together as I step away from the window. I need coffee. Not only to warm me up, but to kick-start me. Despite the sound sleep—or maybe because of it—I'm a little groggy. That's the only thing wrong, because as far as I'm concerned, the Juan I knew only existed in a dream I had back in Florida.

A fantasy who only lived in my head.

It is time to get my head together and get to work. Annabelle's design project is waiting.

I check the time on my phone—eight forty-five. Good. Early enough to shower, grab a bite to eat and get myself over to the rectory for a look around.

As I start to shove my phone back into my purse, I hesitate. I should call Annabelle, let her know I'm here.

Nah. I'll do it when I get back from my first look at the rectory. I put the phone away, gather my toiletries and fresh clothing and make my way down the hall to the bathroom.

Soon enough, I'm showered, dressed—and yes, much to my practical dismay, once again wearing my white Skechers. I plan to do a lot of walking today. I don't have a choice.

I head downstairs, following the scent trail of something baking that smells impossibly delicious. *Mmm…I hope it's croissants.* My stomach rumbles.

I take the back steps that lead to the kitchen. Sabine pointed them out last night as she gave me the cursory tour on the way up to my room.

My hostess is standing at the sink washing dishes.

"Good morning," she sings in heavy French-laced English.

"Bonjour, madame," I return. Now that my head is clearer than it was yesterday, at least I can make an effort to speak the language.

"Uh-uh, you must call me Sabine, *s'il vous plaît.* Here, we are not formal."

"Well, good morning, Sabine."

"Did you rest well?"

"I did, thank you."

The large kitchen looks ancient. It's cluttered and clean, like the reception area.

Stone floor. Rough plaster walls washed in ochre. At the far end of the rectangular room a fire burns in the belly of a soot-covered fireplace, which takes up most of the wall— except for the built-in shelving to the left of the hearth. I love the shelves, pieces of unfinished wood that sit on rectangular slats that are affixed to stone recesses in the wall. *Très rustique.* The shelves are covered with dishes, mugs and what looks like antique Provençal crockery.

The room is like a fascinating flea market with treasure stacked upon treasure everywhere the gaze lands.

"I put aside some fresh croissants for you." She answers in English, letting me and my spotty French off the hook. "I didn't know what time you would rise. Have a seat while I put on a fresh pot of coffee."

Oh! I could hug her. "You read my mind. That's exactly what I was hoping for."

She smiles and gestures to a gorgeous farmhouse trestle table in the center of the room. *Ooh,* what one of my clients wouldn't give for a table like that. I sit and put my purse in the cane-bottom chair next to me—one of four on my side of the table. I run my hand over the tabletop's rough wood, admiring the solid, rustic mass of it.

"What brings you to Avignon?" Sabine asks as she measures coffee into a press pot. I notice her knuckles are gnarled. Arthritis maybe? "Are you on vacation?"

Vacation? The tour— No! Stop it.

"I'm here on business."

She pauses to draw some water from the tap. When she's finished, she asks, "What kind of business?"

"I'm an interior designer. My sister and her partner just purchased an old rectory off Rue Delacroix. They asked me to take a look at it and offer some decorating advice."

As Sabine sets the kettle on the gas stove, she cocks her head to the side and her wrinkled brow furrows.

"The Beaulieu Rectory?" She sucks in her cheeks and makes a fish face. "*Non!* That cannot be. I was not aware the property was for sale. It has been in the Beaulieu family for generations. I cannot imagine he would sell it off. In fact, I just spoke with Philippe Beaulieu the other day. He mentioned nothing about it. *Non,* it cannot be."

She shrugs, a gesture that seems to indicate the question has been answered, then slices two grapefruits in half.

"Philippe Beaulieu?" I ask. "The furniture designer?"

"*Oui.*" Her *oui* is so adamant, it sounds like she says *waaaay.* Her chest seems to puff out more with each elongated "aaa."

Wow. Philippe Beaulieu Designs is the gold standard for sleek, modern, custom-made furniture. Over the past century, the company has built an empire, elevating furniture to art, the Beaulieu name evolving into a status symbol. Anybody who was anybody and wanted to prove they had deep pockets furnished their mansions with Beaulieu custom designs.

Not exactly my clientele.

Nor my favorite style of furniture. I found it cold and sterile.

I reach out and trace the wood grain of the tabletop. The

furniture I want to design is just like this. Sturdy. Rugged. Built to weather the test of time.

Still it's pretty fantastical to learn that Sabine knows an icon like Philippe Beaulieu. Sort of like discovering your dry cleaner is on intimate terms with Paul McCartney or Karl Lagerfeld. Go figure.

But it's curious... The company's been around for more than a hundred years. Hmm...Philippe Beaulieu must be pretty old by now.

Maybe Avignon is where furniture designers go when they retire. I hear it has quite an arts community. One of the world's best theater festivals. Or maybe it's his son we were talking about. I pull the address from my purse.

"Perhaps we're not talking about the same rectory. My sister's place is at 89 Rue Delacroix."

I hold up the paper as if it's proof that I'm right.

Stubbornly, Sabine shakes her head and sets down the knife.

"Madame Brooks, Avignon may be big enough for tourists to lose themselves—" she wags her finger at me "—but I assure you it is still *une petite ville.*"

Sounds like she said unpetivee. Um... Oh! Une petite ville. A small town.

"There is only one rectory on Rue Delacroix—" she's still shaking her finger "—and it belongs to Philippe Beaulieu. You, *madame,* have the wrong address."

I hesitate for a moment, staring at the numbers on the paper. Maybe I should call Annabelle and check.

But if I call her, I'll have to explain what I'm doing in Avignon nine days early. My heart tightens as memories of Juan wash over me. I'm getting better at pulling the curtain on the movie screen in my mind, but I still can't quite shake Juan.

I'll have to tell Anna I'm here. Eventually. I certainly can't hide out in this *petite ville* for more than a week. But I don't want to call her now.

Not yet.

Sabine sets a glass of fresh-squeezed juice and a hot croissant in front of me. I refold my paper and stick it in my purse.

Shoving Juan off the outer edge of my mind, I decide 89 Rue Delacroix has to be the right address. I copied and pasted into my travel files directly from the e-mail Anna sent. She said something about the design issues being *complicated*. Maybe Beaulieu is involved.

Yeah, right. Along with McCartney and Lagerfeld. Annabelle would've mentioned that. She knows how much I want to design furniture. Even if Beaulieu isn't my style, it would be such an in.

I sip the grapefruit juice. The tangy citrus makes my mouth want to pucker.

No disrespect to my hostess, but if it is Philippe Beaulieu we're talking about, perhaps he didn't include her in the decision to let go of the property. If it's been in his family for as long as she claims, maybe Monsieur Beaulieu wanted to sidestep being the center of just this type of gossip and speculation. Whatever the case, I'm not going to argue with Sabine. What's the point?

"So you know Philippe Beaulieu well?" I ask.

Okay, so I'm nosy.

"*Ouuui.*" Sounds like she's saying *waaay,* again. She assumes the same puffed-chest stance as before. Possibly even a bit more resolute. "In Avignon, I know *everybody.*"

She thumps her chest with her hand, then locks her jaw in an I-dare-you-to-challenge-me set.

Okay, I see. Sabine fancies herself not just the innkeeper, but also the gatekeeper.

I bite into the warm croissant. *Mmm.* The delicate, buttery layers melt on my tongue. It is quite possibly the best thing I've ever tasted. *Ever.*

I chew slowly, savoring the heavenly flavor.

As I swallow, something inside me tells me I should let go of Beaulieu.

But I don't.

Of course not.

Instead, I lower my voice conspiratorially, "You know, in my line of work, Philippe Beaulieu is something of an icon."

I tear off my next bite, waiting for Sabine to dish. Instead, she pulls a face like she smells something and blows a *pff* between her pursed lips.

"Philippe Beaulieu is a—how do you say—a bum. He is a *bum*."

"Are we talking about the same Philippe Beaulieu? The furniture designer?"

"Ouuuui."

She rolls her eyes as if I've just identified the town drunk—the bum—and mutters to herself in French. I have no idea what she's saying....

But do think I understand a little better. Not that I doubt her— Well... Yes, I do.

Somehow I can't see Sabine and furniture baron Philippe Beaulieu swapping gossip over the white asparagus and squash blossoms at the farmers' market in the square.

We have to be talking about two different people.

As Sabine scurries around tidying up the kitchen, I decide I'll walk the two and a half miles to the Rue Delacroix, have a look around and then I'll call my sister and tell her I'm here.

WHEN SABINE ASKS me about my plans for the day, I tell her I want to take a long walk and acquaint myself with the town before I get to work. She recommends all the obvious places—Notre-Dame des Doms Cathedral, which, she promises, is dwarfed by the Pope's Palace; the Avignon bridge, which is actually called Pont Saint-Bénezet, but was immortalized in the famous nursery rhyme *Le Pont d'Avignon*. She tells me about the opera house, the markets and the various museums.

I nod, doing my best to seem interested, while in my head I'm edging toward the door.

Today, I have other plans. Of course, I won't leave Avignon without visiting all the must-sees, but right now, I'm on a mission. The last thing I want to do is get into a standoff with my hostess over who owns the rectory on Rue Delacroix.

Finally, as I really am edging toward the door, Sabine informs me she and her husband will have a late dinner and they are expecting me to join them.

"Thank you," I say. "It's so nice of you to want to include me, but I'll just grab something while I'm out."

She won't hear of it. In fact, she's so adamant and so offended when I try to decline, I wonder whether I've breached a basic rule in French etiquette—the type such as greeting and saying goodbye to shopkeepers when you enter and leave their establishments. An unintentional faux pas, yet a gaffe nonetheless.

Finally, to make life easier, I agree. I will have plenty of other dinners out—I hope.

It takes nearly forty-five minutes to make the two-and-a-half-mile trek from Chez Sabine to the Rue Delacroix.

At Annabelle's rectory, I'm immediately captivated by the shuttered, seventeenth-century, two-story house. At first glance, it looks like an ideal place to convert into art studios, though I won't know for sure until I get a look inside and see if they'll need to build or tear down walls. As I let myself through the iron gate in the wall that surrounds the back and sides of the property, I'm further encouraged: mature trees and shrubs, spacious, private yard for outdoor projects, a large garden. Lots to work with here. I hope the inside is as promising.

There's a stone walk that leads to a patio made from the same material. Also, there's a set of newish-looking French doors. I look in and get an idea of the condition of the first floor.

The doors lead into a large, empty room with exposed-stone walls and a beamed ceiling.

Just as Annabelle had said, it'll take a lot of work, but it'll be fun. I'll do whatever it takes to renovate it.

I try the door handle. To my great surprise, it's unlocked. I hesitate, thinking of what Sabine had said, that the place belonged to her friend Philippe Beaulieu.

Impossible.

The house is exactly as Annabelle described it.

It's unfurnished. Obviously, no one lives here.

Still, why would they leave the door unlocked? Unless it was the kind of neighborhood where they could. Seeing as how the nearest neighbor was several acres away, it probably *is* that kind of neighborhood.

"Hello?" I call—just in case.

Inside, the old house smells like dampness and decay, but it's surprisingly warm in here considering it's about forty-five degrees outside. The front windows are shuttered, so the only light filters in from the French doors through which I entered.

As I walk to the center of the room, I think I hear a noise, which stops me. A faint sound, like delicate glass shattering. So, I'm not sure if I heard it or simply imagined it. I pause and listen, but no... I don't hear anything else.

Maybe it was a rat or bat or some other pest I don't care to meet face-to-face. The thought makes me shudder. Still, I listen for a couple more seconds. When I don't hear anything, I turn my attention back to the room. It's a generous size, with a hallway leading off of the far end. Stone floors, I notice, as I walk around, kicking at a stray rock over here and a random rusty nail over there. There's dust everywhere.

Even so, the floor is definitely a keeper—quite possibly the original. The beams on the ceiling are definite pluses, too. However, I'll have to take a closer look and see what kind of shape they're in. Depending on what Annabelle and Jean Luc have in mind, whether they want to partition off the room into studios or— Hey, depending on how many studios they want, this area might even serve as gallery space.

I start down the hall, opening closed doors, checking out the small rooms, most of which look as though they've been gutted.

By the time I open the last door at the end of the hall, I certainly don't expect to see a tall man with wild, dark hair standing in the middle of the room. But he's there.

I scream.

As he turns toward me, the long pole he's holding falls. The glass object on the end of the rod shatters as it hits the floor.

It takes only a moment to realize the man has a glassblowing studio set up in the room. In the reflexive process of trying to save his work-in-progress from hitting the floor, he's burned himself.

He yells something in French. Not so much at me, but because he's in pain. My first instinct is to flee, but the pain contorting his face freezes me in my tracks.

TEN

"I'M SO SORRY," I say. "Are you burned badly?"

I start to step toward him, but he looks up as if he's really seeing me for the first time. The fury of hell burns in his dark eyes, as hot as the flames from the furnace he's using to melt his glass.

I quickly realize it's possible that he might not be looking at me that way only because he's burned, but because I'm speaking to him in English.

The only problem is I don't know how to ask if he's all right in French. But I'll try.

"Pardonnez-moi, monsieur." I pull my lexicon from my purse and start looking up how to ask *Are you...* Ugh... what's that verb? *To be. Être.* That would make it *You are*—

"This is private property." He's glowering at me, cradling his burned hand as he bites out words in perfect English. "This is not a place for tourists. Please get out."

He points to the door, emphasizing his command of the

language. The gesture makes him wince, and he turns his attention back to his burn.

Oh, my gosh, he's really hurt.

"I'm so sorry I startled you." I walk toward him. "Let me see how bad—"

"Grrrrrr." He makes a throaty sound, like a growl. It stops me.

"Who are you and what are you doing here?" he roars.

"My name is Rita Brooks, and I'm afraid there's been a mistake. You see, my sister, Annabelle Essex, gave me—"

"Your sister is Annabelle?"

His brow unfurls ever so slightly.

He knows Anna. *Oh, thank God.*

"Annabelle did not tell me you were coming." Still gruff.

"Well, I'm early."

"She is meeting you here today?"

"No, I'm…I'm really early. More than a week." I smile, hoping he has a sense of humor.

But he just scowls down at his hand. "You thought you'd come over and have a nose around?"

A nose around?

"She invited me."

"Next week."

Oh, please.

Then it dawns on me that maybe this surly lummox is the trespasser. After all, he's in Annabelle's rectory. Sometimes the guilty party tries to deflect the blame by assuming an aggressive stance.

Okay, obviously, that's not fair, I know. He's injured, and I'm partially responsible for his burn, which is fueling his bad mood. But now that we've discovered we have someone in common, couldn't he lighten up? After all, I did offer to help him.

"This is my sister's place. I have a right to be here whenever I want. May I ask who you are?"

"Your sister's place?"

He laughs. But it's a humorless sound. If ever there was an example of someone looking down their long, very straight—nearly perfect—nose, this was it.

"Is that what she told you?" His voice drips with a condescension that gives me a sinking feeling.

"And who are you?" I ask.

"I am Philippe Beaulieu. This house has been in my family for generations. It is a bit premature for your sister to claim it as her own."

I CALL ANNABELLE on my walk back to Chez Sabine.

"I'm sorry. I hope I haven't messed up everything for you."

"Don't worry about it," she says. "It's fine. Philippe really is a good guy. He was probably just in pain. How bad was the burn? Wait, why are you in Avignon and not on the tour?"

Despite the earlier chill, it's a good ten degrees warmer now. The sky is a clear, cloudless blue. Really, it's the perfect day for a good long walk. That's what I focus on, rather than the fiery scene I left behind—or Juan, who steals any opportunity to jump onto the stage in my mind.

I ignore her last question. "I don't know how badly he burned himself. He wouldn't let me get close enough to see. I was afraid he'd bite me if I pressed the issue. So I apologized and left. But, Annabelle, *Philippe Beaulieu?* Why didn't you tell me? That's pretty major."

Major, but not at all what I expected. Now Sabine's comments make sense. The guy looks to be in his early to mid-thirties. I do the math in my head. Maybe the great-grandson of the original Philippe Beaulieu? Probably coasting on the family name and fortune. *The petite ville bum.*

I know the type: young, rich, gorgeous. Trust fund baby surfing the high life.

"Don't change the subject, and tell me why you're in Avignon more than a week early? Rita, what happened?"

I stop at a busy intersection: six lanes of cross traffic. In the middle, a car park divides three lanes going one way and the other three going in the opposite direction. The city ramparts lie beyond that, big, beautiful and imposing. Given my track record of late, maybe I should sequester myself in a fortress like this and try to escape future missteps.

Strike one: Juan.

Strike two: the big burn.

"It's a long story. Right now, suffice it to say, it was a college trip for college kids. Big mistake. I'll tell you about it when I see you."

I cross safely to the car-park island and wait for traffic in the other direction to stop before I cross the remaining three lanes.

"But what about Juan?"

"I'll tell you about it later. Philippe Beaulieu. Come on. Spill."

There's a long pause on the other end.

"Anna?"

"Yeah, I'm here. This is also a long, complicated story. I'm just trying to decide where to begin."

"Complicated? Oh, my God. Don't tell me you and Philippe Beaulieu are lovers? I mean, he's gorgeous. Despite his bad temper, I can see why you'd be attracted to him, but what about Jean Luc?"

"Rita. No. I'm not having an affair with Philippe Beaulieu. Though I'm glad you think he's attractive."

I laugh. "I'm just kidding. But gosh, this sounds sort of serious. What's up?"

I make it safely across the final stretch of traffic.

"I guess the reason I didn't mention Philippe in the furniture-empire context you're interested in is because he's estranged from his family. But even so, he's a really great guy."

"Yeah, I guess if you like grizzly bears."

It was a fitting description. The guy was massive, with angry dark eyes and wild, longish hair, dark, curly.

Grizzly bear.

Bum.

Bohemian artist.

All of the above.

"I'm sorry you got a bad first impression," Annabelle says.

"Doesn't get along with the folks, huh?"

"No, unfortunately, he doesn't. Artistic differences. He wanted to go his own direction and the family didn't take it well. He's actually the fourth Philippe Beaulieu, and he was expected to carry on business in the fine Beaulieu tradition."

Phillipe Beaulieu the Fourth? Too much—how about PB IV, for short.

Inside the city ramparts, the air smells of nutmeg, decay and…is that lavender? Couldn't be. It's December, not lavender season.

I draw in another breath, deeper this time. Still, I smell something alluringly floral. Probably wishful thinking on my part.

So, PB IV wanted to go his own way? *Boo-hoo, I don't want to run the family business. Ehhh,* grow up and get over yourself.

"Glassblowing?" I ask. "Luckily for him he has a trust fund."

"Actually, he doesn't. Walked away from that when he walked away from the family business. That's why this rectory deal is so important."

"Why? Is he selling it to you for a cash infusion?"

"Not exactly. He doesn't own the rectory. His grandfather does. But the two have been talking on and off for nearly two years now, trying to come to a meeting of the minds. Negotiating. On one end of the spectrum, Grandpa wants Philippe on board, designing for the family business. On the other end is Philippe, who doesn't care for the product. In the past, Grandpa wouldn't consider anything outside the box. So Philippe walked. Now they're edging toward a meeting in the middle."

Hmm… Two years is a long time to work toward a truce. Then again, the French fought the Hundred Years' War. At least this is in the name of reconciliation.

"Let me see if I have this straight. Grandpa is PB II. Right?"

"Yes, Grandpère is second-generation Philippe Beaulieu."

"I assume PB I is no longer living, right?"

"Yes, he passed on several years ago."

"What about PB III, the father?"

"I don't know. Hasn't come up."

"So PB III stays silently in the background while PB II and PB IV are at odds over design?"

My interest in the Beaulieu family history is purely voy-euristic—an inside scoop to a famous family, I guess. And a good means to keep Anna from asking more questions about Juan.

"Well, Annabelle, at least PB IV and I had one thing in common—traditional Beaulieu designs are not to our taste. And somehow I don't think that would've made a difference after I made him drop his glass and burn his hand."

"Oh, give him a break, will you? I'm sure you wouldn't be the most cordial person under those circumstances. Anyway, they've finally come to a meeting of the minds—and by 'they' I mean Philippe, Grandpa and an executive board. Philippe will get to turn the rectory into an art center, but he must design a line of furniture for it that keeps within the guidelines of Philippe Beaulieu Designs. Those are the two stipulations—Philippe must design the pieces and the art center must be named after the family.

"Grandpère wants something designed by his grandson to be on permanent display in a gallery of the Philippe Beaulieu Art Center. Then Grandpa will deed it over to him, and Jean Luc and I will purchase a half interest. At that time, the board will be dissolved, but the deed will bind us to keep the name and a permanent gallery dedicated to Beaulieu designs."

I turn down Rue des Teinturiers, the famed artisan street. I'd like to buy some dried lavender for my room and maybe some lavender oil, too. I read that a few drops on a tissue helps you sleep. I think it also soothes burns. I'm irritated with myself for replaying Philippe's injury on my mind's movie screen.

"So he caved to Grandpère's ego. PB IV's a sellout after all."

Anna is quiet on the other end of the line and I fear I've pushed it a little too far. He is her friend, after all. And in ways, I suppose I'm as big a sellout as Philippe, since I work a job I no longer love. Only, my excuse is cloaked in the noble guise of cultivating financial stability.

Who's the bigger sellout?

"Can you blame him?" Annabelle's voice is soft and not as accusing as I might have feared. She knows I'm stuck. Not living the life I want to live. Not in the place I dreamed I'd be when I hit the mid-forties. Yet, my gentle, sweet sister doesn't point that out.

"No, can't say I do."

"There's just one thing," she says. "I haven't yet mentioned that I've asked you to help with the interior. If you see him again, you might not want to mention it. Just wait until I get there, okay? I'm sure everything will be fine."

Oh. I'm glad I didn't say anything during our face-off. I'm also a little disappointed that I don't have the job, after all, and I might not get it unless a bunch of people agree with my sister. In any case, I'm still glad I'll be seeing Anna in Auvignon.

"No problem. I'm sure I won't run into him again. I'm sorry for the change of plans, but can you come this week? If you can't make it, I understand. In fact, I saw enough that I can make some recommendations for you to suggest to whomever you hire for the job."

I spy a farmers' market ahead.

"I'll be there, Rita. Jean Luc is finishing up a commission this week. So it'll just be you and me for a couple of days, which is good. It'll give us some time. I'm sorry I was so cryptic about the project. I really want you to get the job, but it's not simply my say. The designer we choose will have to go before the art center's temporary executive board, of which PB II, as you call him, is a member. I guess I should've told you that. I was just afraid you might not come if I did. Besides, you're early."

"Yeah, I guess we've both been a little cryptic."

She laughs.

"Just sit tight. I'll see you tomorrow."

I HEAD DOWN for dinner at seven o'clock on the dot. The kitchen is filled with a mélange of good smells—poultry, garlic, herbs and bread. The bouquet makes my mouth water and I'm suddenly glad I accepted Sabine's invitation to dine with her.

When I reach the kitchen, I'm delighted to discover Marie from the café on the Rue du Remaprt Saint-Lazare sitting at the trestle table in Sabine's kitchen. Once again, she looks Parisian stunning, this time in a knit black turtleneck dress that hugs her curves. She's wearing her red lipstick and matching nails— I wonder if it's her trademark.

The way her dark bob is brushed away from her face, I realize she reminds me of a blue-eyed Juliette Binoche.

"*Bonjour.* So nice to see you again." She kisses me on both cheeks and introduces me to her husband, Bernard.

"You look lovely, Rita," she continues, before I can think of an appropriate thing to say to her. "Your hair is the most beautiful shade of auburn. Isn't she beautiful, Sabine?"

Sabine nods, mutters something in French, then to me, she says, "You see, it is a dinner party. I wanted to surprise you."

She turns to Marie and Bernard and says something in French. They laugh.

Marie must sense my discomfort. "Sabine was telling me how you nearly refused the dinner invitation this morning." *The price of the room only included breakfast.*

I muster my most gracious smile. "Had I known it was a party, I would've said yes from the start."

As Sabine sets out a dish of crudités, Marie shoots me an impish smile and directs her eyes heavenward. Without being rude or hypocritical toward our hostess, the gesture says, *I understand your predicament.*

Bernard pops the cork on a bottle of champagne. I smile to myself as I remember the split that Marie and I shared last night.

Was it only last night? It seems so long ago.

"Where is Édouard?" I ask, remembering how Marie said Sabine *and* Édouard would take care of me at Chez Sabine. So far, Sabine has lived up to her star billing in the business. It seems to be a one-woman show.

But with Sabine's dominant personality, I suspect that's what suits everyone best.

Sabine mumbles something in French and turns back to the boiling pot on the stove.

I learn that Marie is, indeed, from Paris. It's a second marriage for her, Bernard's first. "It was love at first sight," she says, staring adoringly at him. "You might say, he saved me. I thought my life was over. I had my shot and—" She makes a *pfff* sound and a gesture with her hands, as if something has disintegrated into thin air. "Sometimes fate is kind."

He wraps his arms around her from the back, kisses the top of her head. For a fleeting moment, I feel hopeful.

Maybe fate will be kind to me and give me another chance. But fate doesn't smile on all of us equally.

Bernard and Marie make a few suggestions about places off the tourist path that Anna and I should visit once she arrives. I talk about my day, skipping the part about my trek to the Rue Delacroix. It turns out to be one of my better moves. Sabine looks up and exclaims, *"Ah, le voici!"* right about the time I would've been in the middle of my rectory story.

All heads swivel in the direction she's holding out her arms.

My heart nearly stops when I see the bulky frame of Philippe Beaulieu IV filling the door. Clean shaven and dressed in jeans and an ivory fisherman's sweater that emphasizes the width of his shoulders, he looks dark and brooding holding flowers in his left hand.

His right hand, the burned hand, is bandaged.

His eyes flash and his jaw tightens when he sees me.

Oblivious, Sabine walks over and kisses him on each of his cheeks.

"Late as usual," she scolds as she accepts the flowers. She turns to me, and that's when I realize her English is for my benefit. "See, *madame?* Did I not tell you he was a bum? And does this prove to you that I do, indeed, know him?"

She sucks in her cheeks, making that triumphant fish face again as she watches me.

"Philippe, this is my boarder, Madame Brooks. I believe you know Marie and Bernard from Café Cuisine."

Then as she putters back to the stove, she rattles off something in French over her shoulder that I can only imagine is a recounting of our breakfast conversation.

I want to turn to dust and blow away.

But I'm pleasantly surprised when PB IV is cordial and mentions nothing about my appearance at the rectory.

"Philippe, what did you do to your hand?" asks Marie during a lull in the conversation.

His gaze flicks to me. Then away. "Glassblowing accident. Occupational hazard."

I almost want to take back all the bad things I said about him. Maybe Anna was right. Maybe he isn't such a bad guy after all.

There's one point before dinner when everyone was bustling about, pouring wine into glasses and getting food on the dining room table, and Philippe and I find ourselves alone in the kitchen. We pass each other near the doorway. I'm headed out. He's coming in to get the last dish—roasted winter root vegetables. He stops in the doorway, blocking my exit.

I glance up at him, not quite knowing what to say.

"I spoke to your sister," he says, finally breaking the silence. "She's arriving tomorrow?"

I adjust my grip on the breadbasket. "Yes, she is. I called her after—I spoke with her, too. This afternoon."

"Well, then, I'm glad we have this chance to start over before she arrives."

With that, he lets me pass.

I stop in the threshold. "I'm sorry about your hand. I hope it's not injured too badly."

"It is fine. A surface burn. Not to worry."

Okay, so Anna was right. The man is not a rude grizzly bear. She'll be very smug when I admit as much.

At this point Édouard has joined the party. He and

Sabine occupy the chairs at the ends of the table; Sabine instructs Philippe and me to sit across from each other. I'm seated next to Bernard. Marie is seated next to Philippe across from her husband.

I can't quite get a sense of the dinner party's purpose. I'm a paying guest, though dinner is not included in the fee. Would Sabine have gone to so much trouble to simply prove that she does, indeed, know Philippe Beaulieu?

Well, if so…whatever floats her boat. She can gloat all she wants if she feeds me like this: roasted game hen, with wild-mushroom stuffing; wonderfully herbed green beans and the root vegetables Philippe carried to the table.

If I keep eating like this, I'll need to walk every day like I did today to burn it off.

I can handle that, I think as I pull a piece of steaming, fresh bread from the basket.

There's a mixture of French and English spoken at the table, interwoven with periods of reverent silence that are punctuated only by the sound of silverware on china and wine pouring into goblets.

My seat across the table is a good vantage point from which to study Philippe. I'm glad we've had a chance to clear the air. To *start over,* as he put it. I wonder if he knows I know about his history? About his estrangement and imminent re-conciliation with his grandfather—PB II?

Really, it's not so hard to reconcile this rugged bear of a man to the sleek sophistication of Beaulieu Designs. Even if he has gone his own way, done his own thing, he still has a certain *je ne sais quoi.*

If Fred was a La-Z-Boy, then Philippe is a chaise longue. From his family's exclusive line? *Hmm…*

He'd hate me for saying that. Rightfully so. He's not shiny and showy. Yet somehow, he's a little more complicated than the old tried-and-true, well-worn La-Z-Boy.

Philippe looks over and catches me watching him. My face flames and I look away.

Why on earth am I thinking about this? Why would I even include him in the same thought as Fred?

ELEVEN

I MEET ANNABELLE at the Avignon train station the next afternoon. She said she'd meet me at Chez Sabine, but I couldn't wait a minute longer to see my sister.

When she steps onto the platform, she looks impossibly gorgeous with her long, curly auburn hair and infectious smile. She's wearing a moss-green tunic and black leggings. A black leather coat is slung over her arm. Tall, and much more trim than before, she looks as if she should be working the catwalks on Fashion Week.

I can't believe it's been almost two years since I last saw her. *Fred's funeral.* When she hugs me, there's a moment when I almost lose my composure.

"It is *so* good to see you," she says. "I can't believe we let that much time go by between visits. It's awful how time just slips away."

"If you keep talking like that," I say, blinking back tears, "I'm going to start crying."

I step away from her, still holding both of her hands,

admiring how she looks every bit the celebrated Parisian artist she's become over the years. Gosh, what has it been now, nearly five years since she took that leap of faith and moved to Paris?

"No tears," she says. "Only fun. Deal?"

"Deal."

We hug again. That's when I realize just how fit she is. Not skin-and-bones skinny. Her arms are muscled, her legs look long and strong. She was always a little curvy. Now she's curvy in the right places, with a board-flat stomach.

"You look great," I tell her. "I guess the prescription is great sex?"

She arches a brow at me before she puts on her sunglasses. "Actually…yeah. I highly recommend it."

My mind skitters back to the dinner party last night. Philippe standing in the doorway of Sabine's kitchen.

"So, I understand you talked to PB IV yesterday," I say as I grab her bag and roll it toward the stand of taxis.

She links her arm through mine. "I did. And how would you know that?"

I mimic her arched brow. "I had dinner with him last night."

"Did you?"

I nod. "Thanks to Sabine—of Chez Sabine. You'll meet her." I wink because mere words cannot explain. Plus, I'm eager to tell her about the grand reconciliation with PB IV. "So, Sabine decided to put together an impromptu dinner party last night. And she invited Philippe."

Anna and I climb into the taxi. After I give the driver the address, I relay yesterday morning's exchange with Sabine, how she'd been unaware of the plans for the rectory and hadn't believed PB would sell the place. "I can't quite figure it out, but I think the point of the dinner was to prove to me that she knew Philippe. I mean, when she said she knew Philippe Beaulieu, right away I thought she was talking about the grandfather—the furniture baron. I had no idea there was a grandson. It was a surreal day all the way around. But anyway, I'm grateful she went to so much trouble because it gave Philippe and me a chance to clear the air. You're right. He seems to be a good guy."

Anna refrains from saying "I told you so," but insists on calling Philippe and going straight over to the art center as soon as she's met Sabine and stashed her bag in her room.

Today, we take a cab, rather than walking the two and a half miles to the rectory. Philippe is there to meet us. But today he's waiting for us under the cloudless blue sky, out on the patio in front of the French doors. The air is crisp and clean, laced with a slightly grassy note.

Philippe is wearing a black turtleneck and jeans. He looks long and lean. A little thinner than I'm usually attracted to.

"*Bonjour.*" He stands and kisses Anna on both cheeks.

When he puts his hand on my shoulder to kiss me hello, I notice he's not wearing the bandage. I don't know which surprises me more—the kiss or his bare hand.

"*Bonjour,*" I say.

Anna fills him in on Jean Luc's commission—a sculpture someone is giving as a Christmas gift. But he sends his best. Naturally, PB IV sends his in return.

"How's the hand?" I ask.

He shrugs, then smiles. "It is nothing. I think I will live."

I reach in my coat pocket and pull out a small brown vial. "I picked this up for you at the farmers' market in the square."

He looks at it quizzically. "What is this?"

"Lavender oil. It takes the sting out of burns."

I open the bottle and the blue essence of the wild French flower fills the air.

"Hold out your hand," I say.

He does. I'm relieved to see that it's not blistered, only a fat red line running across his palm, perpendicular to his fingers. I sprinkle a few drops on his hand, and as I rub it in I notice his hand is big and a little rough—not unkempt, but masculine.

A man who uses his hands. Big hands.

I stifle a smile. Jude would be proud of me for noticing such details. *Ha!* Jude would be all over this guy.

"There. How does that feel?"

I look up at him and see him watching me with dark, soulful eyes. He has nice eyes...sort of hooded, as if the weight of his long, black lashes is pulling them down.

"It feels good," he says. "Very good."

I look away and release his hand, a jerky motion that splashes some of the oil on my wrist. I replace the cap and then rub away the errant drops that lay like spilled tears on my skin.

"Philippe, I don't know if Rita's had an opportunity to tell you, but she's an interior designer," Anna says. "I've asked her to give us some ideas for the art center. If we're still aiming for an end-of-January opening, we have no time to waste."

I look up, grateful for the change of subject.

"End of January?" I ask. "That's very ambitious. It's only six weeks away, and you'll lose a week during the holidays."

"Exactly," says Anna. "Philippe, how do you feel about Rita offering some advice?"

"Absolument," he says. "I'd love to hear what you have in mind, Rita."

His gaze searches my face, lingers shamelessly on my lips, before finding my eyes again.

For a split second, I'm thrown off kilter by the tingling in the pit of my stomach, but soon enough, I find my balance.

He's a good-looking guy. A Frenchman. *A flirt.* Making a woman feel special as much a part of his DNA as his gorgeous eyes and full bottom lip.

Take PB IV at face value.

Nothing more.

Or to quote a certain professor, "Nothing more. Nothing less." Thank you very much, Dr. Santiago. Lesson learned.

"Since we have no time to waste," Philippe says, "let's go inside and get started."

He opens the door and allows us to enter first. I sense his appreciative gaze on me as I brush past him. I want to feel flattered. But the last thing I need is another slick, good-looking European who thinks he's God's gift to women. To make matters worse, this one couldn't possibly be a day over thirty-five, if that. He probably thinks he can charm the pants off every woman he meets. Probably can. Well, Juan may have fooled me with his savvy sophistication, but there's no way I'll fall again.

It's not as warm inside as it was yesterday. I guess that's because Philippe's glassblowing furnaces aren't firing. As he and Anna give me the official tour of the place, upstairs and down, I discover my assumption is correct. His studio is dark and cold.

They indicate they'd like to transform the main entry area into the Philippe Beaulieu Gallery.

"How many pieces will be on display?" I ask once we've completed the full tour and are standing back in the room with the French doors.

"Ultimately, about ten," he says.

"Will you want to have room to show other pieces? Say, for temporary exhibitions or as space for the art center artists to hang their work?"

"Absolutely. That's how we'd like to utilize the wall space and perhaps have a bit of room for sculpture."

"Have you decided if you'll move your workshop over here, Philippe?" Anna asks.

"*Non*. I will keep it where it is," he says. "I want to keep my work and art separate. I will keep the furniture at my shop and practice glassblowing here."

"Rita, did I mention that Philippe has his own line of furniture apart from Beaulieu Designs?"

Yes. I shake my head, despite everything she told me yesterday.

"You really should show it to her, Philippe. It's exactly the style that Rita's interested in designing herself. She's wanted to do that for ages, but she's so busy with her design company, she just can't seem to find the time."

My cheeks burn at this revelation of my neglected dream.

"She designed a gorgeous armoire for a client a couple of years back. She sent me a photo of it, and I fell in love."

Ugh. The Bitsy Van der Berg debacle. The mammoth piece is in my bedroom since *the spider* refused delivery. We'd come to a financial agreement, but she turned up her nose at the cabinet.

"I've always hoped that someday I could persuade my sister to design something for me." Annabelle elbows me. I have the urge to stomp on her foot to make her shut up.

"You do woodworking?" he asks.

I shake my head. This is precisely the reason I didn't want to talk about it. I can dream the design, but I don't do the hands-on.

"I've only designed one piece, and I sent out the specs to a craftsman."

"But she's always wanted to work with her hands. Do the actual crafting," Annabelle asserts.

It's one thing to want to do something and it's another to do it…and fail. Miserably.

But then I think of Philippe and his glassblowing. His awkward attempt at perfection that ultimately shattered after my surprise entrance.

Perfection. How do I know that's his burden, too? Maybe it's just my hang-up, the reason I've left too many dreams untended, something I'll think about *someday* when I'm not too busy working, or doing any other number of things that keep me from having to try and fail. Again. And again.

I bite my bottom lip until it throbs in time with my pulse.

I don't want to talk about designing dreams. Not right now. Not with the grandson of a furniture baron. The only way around it—other than stomping on my sister's foot, and somehow I don't think that would help—is to change the subject.

"I'm familiar with your family's Philippe Beaulieu Designs," I say to Philippe. "But I didn't realize you had your own furniture line."

PB IV's jaw tightens. I fear for a moment that I've ventured into territory best left unexplored.

"I do," he finally says. "It is Ange de la Provence."

Angel of Provence?

"Ange is his middle name," Annabelle offers.

Philippe shrugs.

"Philippe Ange Beaulieu—" I start to add "The Fourth," but don't. I don't want him to know that I know that much about him. "That's a very nice name."

"It works for the line," he says. "The pieces are rugged. Very much of the Provençal earth and the French countryside."

Interesting. I would've thought the name *Angel* might add a softer feel to an otherwise hard, sturdy product. Then again, with the harder-edged French pronunciation, *Ange* doesn't sound nearly as gentle as the English version, Angel.

As I watch Philippe standing there with his smoldering gaze, big hands and the firm strength of his broad, broad shoulders, there's not a single thing soft or ethereal about him. He's not pretty enough to be angelic. No, he is one hundred percent solid, rugged man-of-the-earth.

"How long are you here?" he asks.

How long? The change of subject throws me. Wow. I don't know. I hadn't really thought about it since my plans had been rearranged.

"You're still staying for Christmas, aren't you?" Annabelle insists.

"But that's more that a week away," I remind her.

I don't want to talk about finances in front of PB IV, but the fee at Chez Sabine's on top of the money I spent on the aborted trip isn't exactly in my budget.

Originally, I was to meet my sister and Jean Luc in Avignon for a couple of days and then go back to Paris for Christmas.

"Philippe, I don't mean to put you on the spot, but would

you be willing to use some of the discretionary funds the board appropriated for securing a designer? To defray some of Rita's expenses? That way she can put together some color boards and draw up a proposal."

This was a little awkward, to say the least. Nothing like putting the guy on the spot. She hadn't even told him I was coming and now she's asking him to fund my lodging—

"I think that's a wonderful idea." There's not a trace of hesitation in his voice. He's looking at me again. That same intense, brooding gaze. "Perhaps during that time, you might like to visit my workshop? Take a look at the Beaulieu pieces I'm producing for the gallery? And see how different my own designs are from what my family produces?"

MY MIND IS full as Anna and I walk back to Chez Sabine— I talk her into walking rather than riding since it is such a beautiful day.

I have to admit, PB IV isn't the spoiled brat I originally pegged him to be. It's interesting that he's studying glassblowing when his road to success is paved in gold via his family's business.

But it's not what he wants to do. So he won't settle. You have to give the guy credit. There's certainly more to PB than meets the eye.

"Sometimes he mistrusts foreigners, but not you, Rita," says Anna. I realize my mind has drifted from what she was saying.

"What?" I'm not sure exactly what she means.

"Really, I don't think it's just because you're my sister. I mean, I've never seen Philippe get dressed up before."

Jeans and a turtleneck.

"That was dressed up?"

She laughs. "For him, yes. Usually, we're talking ripped jeans and T-shirts."

"Are you saying he's a slob?" I tease.

"Not a slob, just…casual."

"*Shh!* You're ruining the fantasy," I say. "I want to believe that type of style is intrinsic to someone so good-looking."

Something victorious flashes in Anna's eyes.

"So you like him then?"

No. Whoa. Wait a minute.

"Of course I like him. In the same way that I like Marie and Bernard from the café and Sabine and even surly Édouard. But not…"

Annabelle is watching me. Scrutinizing me.

"Would you be terribly mad at me if I told you that getting you over here to see the rectory was only part of the reason I wanted you to come to France?"

A sinking feeling drags my stomach down to my toes. I have an inkling where this conversation is heading and I don't like it.

"Rita, I think the two of you would be perfect for each other. I mean, look at him—"

"Yes, I have eyes. I can see." I roll my eyes. "He's a good-looking guy—a kid."

"Not a *kid*. He's thirty-seven."

"Thirty-seven? That's eight years younger than I am. Plus, I'm not looking to get involved. I'm sure a guy like PB IV is looking for some hot twentysomething. Even if I were game, he wouldn't be interested in me."

I'm tempted to tell her exactly what went down with Juan. The words are on the tip of my tongue, that it hurt being toyed with and ultimately passed over for someone half my age. I'm almost ready to spill it, but I can't. And the unspoken words taste like bile as they burn the back of my throat.

No. It's just too humiliating.

"Rita, don't sell yourself short. You're gorgeous."

"Thanks, but you're my sister. You and I have already established our mutual-admiration society."

"Nah, he's into you," she says. "I see it in how he looks at you, in the way he smells of cologne. He even shaved, for God's sake."

"Maybe he did it for God's sake. But not for me."

Anna smiles and holds up a finger. "A week. I give you a week. I'll bet by the time you come up to Paris for Christmas, you'll be singing a different tune."

TWELVE

A DAY AND a half later, I put Annabelle on an early train back to Paris, and I head over to the Rue Delacroix rectory to shoot reference shots so that I can begin formulating my design suggestions.

That's when I run into Philippe.

"Hello," I say as he walks in and smiles at me.

"Good morning. You're up early."

It's eight-thirty.

"I wanted to get here in time to photograph the outside while the light was still soft and pretty," I tell him.

When I'd first gotten here, I had walked around the outside of the house, opening the blue shutters on the ground floor to let some of the natural light into the main space.

"I love the way the light is streaming through the windows." I snap a few photos of the room. I sense his gaze on me and I turn around to see him watching me intently.

I shoot a picture of him standing there, his face in half shadow, half light.

He grins at me. I shoot another.

"So, you're really not moving your furniture studio over here?"

He shakes his head. "It would be too great an ordeal. It has no place here. This is where I will escape. I will work there and come here to get away from work." He sighs. "Except for the furniture that will be in the gallery."

"Is that really so bad?"

"Not if you don't mind being blackmailed."

"Blackmailed? How so?"

He waves off the question as if he wants to change the subject. Not so fast, Monsieur Beaulieu.

"Who's blackmailing you?"

He pierces me with his glance for a moment, as if weighing what he should reveal. "I don't know if you are aware, but I do not hold a position within the family business."

"Really?"

He crosses his arms over the front of him, shuttering himself.

"The pieces I am designing for Beaulieu are by mandate of my grandfather. I do not design that type of furniture, but he wants to put his brand on me. This is his way of doing so. In exchange for the ten pieces of furniture, he gives me the house."

He shifts his weight from one foot to another. Draws in a heavy breath. The sound is amplified by the acoustics of the stone walls.

"If you feel as though you're being blackmailed, why are you doing it? Couldn't you simply purchase the house or even another place for the art center and have it free and clear of any strings?"

"I wish it were that simple. But, you see, my grandfather… He is not well, and we have been on bad terms for so long. Even if I must do something that goes against my principles, I feel it is important that we make amends before it is too late. This is the best way I can see that happening."

I blink at him for a moment.

"Against your principles? I'm sorry, I must not understand. Is he asking you to do something illegal?"

Philippe laughs. A full belly laugh that echoes off the plaster walls throughout the empty house.

"Illegal? *Non*. I suppose we have been at such a standoff over the years, it must seem silly to those not involved."

He looks at me for a moment, rubbing his chin as if considering something.

"I suppose the best way I can illustrate is to show you. Would you care to come to my workshop and see what I'm talking about?"

PHILIPPE'S WORKSHOP OCCUPIES the bottom floor of a converted barn about three miles from the rectory. He lives in the apartment space upstairs.

From the second I step inside his workshop, I'm drawn to the piece in progress on the workbench: a gorgeous Régence-period console table with delicately curved *pied de sabots* legs. I walk over and run my hand along the smooth, unvarnished wood, admiring the graceful, foliated scrollwork of the medallions on the center and sides, and the intricate detail of the motif running down each of the legs.

"Did you carve this yourself?"

"*Oui.*" He manages to carry off pride and humility in the same facial expression. "I will finish it with a marble top."

"It's beautiful."

I sigh inwardly. And just the style I've always dreamed of producing. Though I would never tell him because I wouldn't even know how to begin taking a piece like this from paper to fruition. I could draw it, but I couldn't build it. I'd have to consign the labor—the actual artistry—to a craftsman. That's where you either pay out the wazoo or sacrifice quality for affordability.

"How do you work?" I ask him. "Do you design and build or do you work with designers bringing their clients' ideas to life?"

My heartbeat kicks as a crazy thought skitters through my head. *Philippe could bring my designs to life.* No, it wouldn't exactly be financially practical with him living over here and my clients being in the States. But if a client was willing to pay the price…

"I design and build," he says. "I work with a few designers who do what you do, but it's proved to be tedious interpreting someone else's vision. Most of my work comes from people saying, 'Build me a table or a chair.'"

"And it's lucrative?" The words are out of my mouth before I can stop them. Thank God he doesn't bat an eye.

"Not terribly. A lot of time goes into each piece and sometimes the work takes longer than I imagined. But that is how it goes. Each piece is one of a kind. If I wanted to mass-produce furniture, I would work for my family's business."

His words close the door on the subject, but I slip one last question in, before it slams shut.

"Is that what you meant when you said 'blackmail'? Is this what you wanted to show me?"

"A part of what I wanted you to see." He strides across the room, his long, lean, jean-clad legs covering the distance in a few steps.

He stops in front of a cloth-covered table. "This is what I wanted to show you. *Voilà—*"

He yanks off the cover like a magician unveiling a surprise. A sleek, hard, cold, shiny…*contraption,* which I immediately recognize as in line with Beaulieu designs gleams at me, making its presence known even from the shadows.

"This is my family's way." He gestures to the piece, which seems to be a table taking shape, but at this stage, it's hard to tell.

Then he points to the Régence console on his workbench. "That is my soul."

How can you argue with that? Especially since the only reason he's designing the Beaulieu-branded furniture is so he can meet his grandfather on common ground.

"I don't really care about the house," he says. "It's nice. It will be a good place for artists to work and a monument to the family empire. But I am doing these ten pieces, not to receive the house, but because it is the only ground on which my grandfather and I could meet. The pieces are a onetime venture that Beaulieu is welcome to produce, if they like, and that is the end of my design affiliation with Beaulieu Designs."

"How many of the ten pieces do you have finished?"

"Seven," he said. "So, I have a little over a month to finish the others before we open the gallery. I will be working through Christmas."

My sister estimated that the rectory and the land it sits on carried a price tag of around a million euros. Factored out, that would mean that PB II was paying PB IV around a hundred grand per piece. That's in euros. If you converted it to dollars... Wow!

If furniture design generated that kind of cash, I could afford to make the leap. But the value of the designs goes up with the Beaulieu name—and the inherent, or should I say, inherited—Beaulieu design sensibility. Looking at the contraption he'd just unveiled, it's clear that Philippe gets what his family's company is all about. You'd never know he found the bling-designs so repugnant.

"You see," he says. It's a statement, a shortened version of *I know that you see what I mean.* "With this agreement, I mend my relationship with my grandfather, but it is the end of my modern period."

He smiles. And I'm glad.

It's because he's smiling that I don't ask about PB III, the father whose role has been conspicuously blank in this family saga.

Later. Don't push it.

Philippe's workshop is a convenient setup, and I don't blame him for wanting to keep it here. Especially since he needs a lot of room—probably four of the studios at the place on Rue Delacroix.

"So you see it would be difficult to move everything— and impossible to make this space livable should I abandon it as work space."

I look around, taking in everything. The room is dusty and unkempt by nature of the job—all that sanding and chipping away at wood, but it's also got character. It's a place of organized chaos—like a messy desk with stacks of files. At a moment's notice, the owner of the desk can easily pull exactly what they need from the disorder. But if someone came in and "tidied up," it would be a gesture tantamount to disaster.

All would be lost. The desk owner wouldn't be able to find a thing.

"Lots of work, but not impossible."

I glance around the place for clues to PB IV's life. Who is the man beyond his dark good looks, his stubborn streak and his love of earthy Provençal design?

There's a stack of leather-covered books on a cluttered table. I wonder if they're for show or if he's read them. I edge closer, trying to read the gold, embossed titles on the spine. As I do, I spy a guitar with a worn strap propped in the corner; and pushed off to one side, nearly lost in the muddle is an unframed snapshot tacked by one corner to the wall. I abandon my title quest and walk over to look at it. It's hanging crooked, so I have to tilt my head to the side to get a good look at it. It's a faded snapshot of a family gathered around a table celebrating some sort of festivity. Right away I pick out a young Philippe. I recognize him by the eyes. He's probably in his early teens.

"That's my family." He walks over and stands next to me—so close, his arm brushes mine. He stirs up the scent of wood and leather and—is that lavender again? Just a hint. Lavender isn't typically a masculine scent, but mixed with the wood and smell of him, it works. I breathe in deeply, craving more of the heady scent. But it's not lavender season. Maybe it's the oil I gave him. Or maybe I'm simply imagining it—again?

He unpins the picture from the wall and holds it up, staring at it for a silent minute before he points to a woman in the photo. The lady, who has her arms wrapped around young Philippe, has his eyes.

I know who she is before he says, "That is my mother. She and my uncle died six months after this photo was taken."

I glance up at him in time to catch the flash of sorrow in his eyes. I want to tell him that I know what it's like to lose someone, but I can't find the words.

"This is my grandfather, Philippe Beaulieu II. My uncle, who died, and his wife, Victoria. And that is my father, who shipped me off to boarding school in England after we lost my mother."

In an instant, the sorrow is gone, replaced by a hardening of his face, a tightening of his jaw.

Problems that run deeper than the artistic differences between Philippe and his *grandpère?*

Boarding school… That's why he speaks English so well. Makes sense. I'd wondered if he'd spent any time in the States or the U.K. Boarding school. Hmm…what different worlds we come from.

"Any sisters or brothers?" I ask, hoping to lighten the mood.

"No. I'm an only child, and my uncle…" His throat works and his eyes darken a shade deeper as he considers his words. "He died before he could produce an heir to this *empire.*"

He snorts a very French-sounding *harrumph.* "I have bored you enough with the Beaulieu family history. Would you like to help me work on the console table?"

I blink, but astonishment gives way to a rush of gratitude.

"Yes, I would love to help you."

The next thing I know, three days have passed; we've been working together side by side, him teaching me about the finer points of woodworking; me sharing my design vision for the rectory.

It's very polite the way we respect each other's space. We've asked the well-mannered questions that show interest: he's divorced; they married too young. I'm a widow, who married young and had a good marriage. Nothing too probing: nothing about Juan or how I turned my cheek to Fred the night before he died. Nothing about his father or how his mother died.

It might seem as if it's all on the surface. Yet, I can't deny a certain intangible buzz when we're together, like bubbles in a champagne flute dancing around each other. Especially when he leans in and kisses me.

On my last day in Avignon, I meet him at his workshop, as planned. Tomorrow morning I'm leaving for Paris to spend Christmas week with my sister before going home.

Home. Wow. I haven't thought much about it since I've been gone. I mean, I've checked in daily at the office. Terry, my right-hand man, has it all under control. But beyond that, I haven't thought about what it will be like to return to Florida—to enter that house that is no longer a home; to sleep in the bed I shared with a man that is no longer there; to drive my old routes to and from work that is no longer fulfilling.

It all feels rather empty and depressing. So I don't think about it.

In the time I've been gone, I've become accustomed to my daily walks in Avignon. To that sunny, yellow excitement of *Oh! Philippe, you'll never guess what happened*…knowing he'll smile with those eyes that are so alive as I tell him something Marie said, or report on my latest find at the market, or relay Sabine's latest unintentional dig that could get under my skin if I let it. But I don't, because Philippe is always there with something better.

The winter wind has kicked up, making it seem colder than the mild fifty-five-degree day should feel. They tell me this cold wind is called the mistral. I'm surprised when I discover Philippe has packed a picnic to celebrate my last day in Avignon.

I'm touched. And a little sad.

As we spread a blanket down by the Rhône, near the Avignon Bridge, and eat our picnic of bread, cheese, pâté and fruit, and drink the bottle of champagne from the crystal flutes he's painstakingly rolled in the traditional blue-and-yellow Provençal napkins, I realize this could be the last time I will see this man who has, at the very least, become my friend.

We haven't talked about it, but the question looms: *What's next?*

It's unspoken. It builds, but it gets blown away by the wind before either of us can form the delicate foreign sentence.

It's funny how, when you busy yourself with projects and deadlines, you can block out the little voices that meander through the back of your mind until they take up residence in the frozen crevices of your broken heart.

It's only when you pause—lay down the woodworking tools and design boards and idle chatter—that you can hear those voices over the winter wind. The voice that warns not to let the icy wall that's formed around your heart freeze in the fissures and fractures. Because if that happens, you might make the mistake of believing that your broken heart has been put back together; patched and sealed and frozen so solid that you believe you will never be able to feel again.

That's what happened to me when Fred died; then again in Barcelona. The ice had almost taken over and might have stayed if not for the warmth of Philippe Beaulieu.

But what's next?

I don't know.

Because the wind is kicking up again, and the ice wall is setting.

Philippe leans in and wraps his arms around me, shielding me from the biting cold with his big body. He's warm and smells vaguely of cedar and leather, the top notes of his workshop.

I could get lost here in his arms, I think. I could forget myself. And I do for a while, as he kisses my frozen fingers. One by one. And he leans in and he finds his way to that sensitive spot at the base of my ear, and finally claims my mouth. His lips, hot and sensuous, promise to thaw that ice wall, melting it little by little—an icicle held over a flame.

I want the ice to melt. I will it to melt. But then the wind blows and asks, *What's next?*

And the question—or maybe it's the possible answers—makes me shiver.

"What's wrong?" he asks.

How do I tell him? How do I explain that I have no idea what I'm doing? That I want him, that I want *this,* but I have no idea what *this* is; and the last time I thought I did, it ended so badly.

He gazes down at me with such intensity, his brown eyes squinting against the rush of cold. He looks so open, trying so hard to understand. Yet, for all his patience, how can I expect a man like him to understand a broken woman like me?

He's eight years younger than I am. I've been married and widowed. I feel as though I've already lived a lifetime he hasn't even begun.

"Philippe, I can't—"

He presses a finger to my lips. Kisses my fingertips again, slowly, one by one. And the wind swirls that phantom lavender scent all around us, as if tying us together.

"It's okay," he says. "They say the mistral does bizarre things to people. It can turn them around, makes them do things they'd never dream of doing."

His eyes gleam with mischief. He stands up suddenly, pulling me with him, giving me a quick twirl. In that moment with the wind in his hair, and the sun glinting in his eyes—picking out the amber and umber in the deep brown—more than ever he looks like a boy.

He pulls me back into him and kisses me, soundly, deeply. A searing kiss, the heat of which reaches all the way down into that frozen cavity that houses my broken heart. A searing kiss that makes me feel.

I think, yes, maybe the wind can be seductive that way, inducing wild thoughts and wilder dreams as it blows promises across the river, through the trees and into my ears.

It whispers secrets: this is not Juan. Juan is the sudden spray of winter-leaf confetti that dances away on the breeze; Philippe is the steadfast phantom lavender that lives constant in the Provençal air.

In his arms, I watch the whitecaps roll across the Rhône like waves on the sea. Except, I can see the shore on the other side of this ocean. In fact, I think I can see the future on the horizon, too.

Then the fickle wind changes direction and blows my hair into my eyes. Once more, I'm not sure.

THIRTEEN

IT BEGINS THE moment I leave Avignon.

A nagging restlessness.

A longing that starts as a whisper and grows into a full-fledged shadow voice that calls to me as Anna and I shop on Christmas Eve to find gifts for each other and Jean Luc.

Actually, Anna already has the perfect gift for her love—a painting of the two of them she'd commissioned from an artist friend.

How wonderful to be in love at the holidays, I think as we window-shop in the Marais. Each one a delicate jewel box illuminated with holiday lights and decorations showcasing chocolate in one window, one-of-a-kind clothing in another and out-of-print books in yet another.

Anna and I came here on her first day in Paris when she came over for the art residency. She was the lost one then—and look at her now. Today as we drift from shop to shop, taking in the luscious storefronts, a strange sort of longing pursues me. Thoughts of Philippe spring up in the oddest

places. I see him in the splendid black grillwork, which trans-
forms the unassuming Paris windows into balconies fit for
noblemen; in the heady scent of lavender at the open-air
flower market; in the ghostly reflection cast in the shop
windows of lovers walking hand in hand along the street
behind me.

Fleeting thoughts of him. Shadow glimpses out of the
corner of my eye.

A man with Philippe's same lanky build; a head of hair
the same color as his; a set of broad shoulders that make me
turn my head, only to discover it's not him.

Of course it's not.

I'm here. He's in Avignon.

I know that because he called me yesterday. Just to see how
my trip went. Just to make sure I arrived safely. And then
again this morning, to tell me he missed me, that he's
spending Christmas working on the remaining pieces. For
his grandfather's commission.

As Anna and I wander into an antiques store, I see Philippe's
hand in a nineteenth-century Régence-style armoire. It's an
antique. So he didn't really create it, but the style of it sings
his name. It's carved out of solid oak with a Bacchic mask
centered over an arched cornice. I run my hand along the
paneled doors, admiring the carved shells and delicate, scrol-
ling vines.

He could've made this. He was teaching me how to do
this. Our time together was like one of those dream-job vacations where you test-drive the path of your heart without
ditching the safety net of the career that pays the bills.

And then something shifted. I can't quite put my finger
on when or how. One day we were working together in his

workshop, the next we were on the shore of the Rhône in each other's arms.

I nearly found myself in his bed, but didn't.

I couldn't....

It strikes me that my life really is all about safety nets. That was never so apparent as not making love to Philippe on my last night in Avignon. I wanted to. God, how I wanted to, but my bags were packed and all my excess baggage got in the way: Fred; the fact that Philippe is eight years younger than me; that he'll want children I can't give him; an heir to the Beaulieu throne; and then the sting of what happened with Juan.

And I was going home. Who knows when or if I'll see Philippe again.

Jude will kill me. I can hear her now: *Are you crazy? That would've been the best kind of back-in-the-saddle sex. A young stud to prime the pump. Who cares if you're a little rusty. You never have to see him again.*

And that was exactly why I *couldn't*.

Philippe seemed like an addiction. The more I was with him, the more I wanted to be with him. If I made love with him... Well, I just can't see how it would help.

He's there. And here I stand in Paris, thinking about him, seeing him at every turn.

Well, it's too late to think of should'ves and could'ves now.

A small, masculine-looking gold frame perched on a marble-topped pedestal table next to the armoire catches my eye. I pick it up. The frame is gorgeous with its tiered edges and Grecian urn-like pillars adorning each side.

Hmm...

If I were giving Philippe a Christmas present, this would be it. Perfect for the family photo he's tacked to the wall. It seems only fitting to frame it since he and his grandfather have made amends.

"It's one of a kind," the shopkeeper offers with a smile.

I stare at the frame wistfully.

"It's beautiful," I answer.

I suppose I could get it and leave it for Annabelle to give to him the next time she sees him.

Somehow that doesn't feel right. Especially when I haven't told my sister about the kiss or anything else that might've happened between Philippe and me. I know she wanted to introduce us, but really, there's nothing to tell. We hit it off. But I'm going home and that's that.

I return the frame to its place on the table and stroll around the store looking at all the treasures displayed so beautifully in the tiny space. I find an antique comb for Anna, and a pair of earrings.

When Anna indicates she's ready to go, I say, "I'll be right out. I see something I want to get."

She smiles her sweet smile. "That's fine. Take your time."

As I stand at the wrap stand, waiting as the shopkeeper wraps my sister's gifts, I glance over my shoulder, giving the little gold frame one last regretful glance.

It gleams atop the marble, so perfectly meant to house Philippe's photo.

"Is it too late to add one more item?" I ask.

IT'S NEW YEAR'S EVE.

I've been in Paris with Annabelle and Jean Luc for a week now. Well, nine days to be exact.

We had a nice Christmas, Anna, Jean Luc and I. We stayed in on Christmas Eve night, opened gifts and enjoyed a feast of oyster stew, fresh crusty baguette and ice *aux fraises,* which is an ice made from strawberries and champagne.

Anna loved her comb and earrings, which she wore when we went for Christmas Day brunch at the home of their friends Sandrine and Marc.

It was all very nice, but I was beginning to feel a bit like an interloper. No fault of Anna and Jean Luc's, who couldn't have made me feel more welcome if they'd strewn rose petals in my path.

They were most gracious.

I suppose I was a little homesick, which was strange because I really wasn't in a big hurry to get home. I suppose part of me missed Fred and all our Christmases past. But the feeling was underscored by an odd displacement I couldn't quite put my finger on.

It could've been that this was the first day since I'd left Avignon that I hadn't heard from Philippe.

I was getting used to our daily chats. Looking forward to them, actually. Since both of us were early risers, he'd usually ring me around nine in the morning. Before we started our day, we'd catch up on what we'd done the day before; I'd tell him about ideas for the center that had come to me as Anna and I had been out exploring Paris; we'd talk about his progress with the furniture. He'd even e-mail me photos of his progress.

Sometimes what we'd talk about really wouldn't amount to much, most of all it was simply the joy of hearing his voice, of feeling that connection that started my day off with a smile.

Now here it was, three o'clock, and still no call. But it was New Year's Eve. Surely he had plans. Since he'd worked through Christmas, I hoped he was taking a break on this last day of the year.

Even so, my heart felt a little heavy as I resigned myself to the fact that I probably wouldn't hear from him today. That was okay. I'd call him tomorrow from the airport and wish him a happy new year before I boarded the plane for home.

By five, I was showered and dressed, ready to help with the finishing touches for the small party Anna and Jean Luc were throwing that evening.

She'd invited a small group of friends over—Marc and Sandrine from Christmas Day brunch and a handful of others.

"Have you talked to Philippe today?" Annabelle asks as she dumps a tray of star-shaped ice cubes into an ice bucket.

"There will be single men at the party tonight." She winks at me as she refills the star tray with water.

"Please tell me you're not trying to fix me up again."

Anna slides the tray into the freezer. "Are you saying I didn't do a good job with Philippe?"

No. She did a great job. "Philippe was…just about perfect. It's too bad we didn't meet under different circumstances."

Anna is taking a cheese platter out of the refrigerator. She sets it down and cocks her head to one side. "So you like him?"

I consider the question. Really, I'm buying time because I don't know how to answer her.

By the grace of God, the doorbell rings.

"I'll get that," I offer, winking at her.

"Thanks, that would be a help." There was a note in her voice that said, *Don't think I'm letting you off that easily.* And I know she won't. "The guests aren't arriving for a couple of hours, I wonder who that is."

I walk from the kitchen into the living room. My heels click on the foyer's parquet floor. When I open the large wooden double doors I understand the literal meaning of being weak in the knees. Because Philippe is standing there with a large bouquet of roses and a bottle of wine.

"I'm sorry I didn't call this morning," he says. "But I decided to wish you a happy new year in person instead."

He puts his arms around me and kisses me until we hear Jean Luc clearing his throat behind us. If I wasn't so deliriously happy to see Philippe, I might have been embarrassed. But Philippe acts as if kissing me is natural. I like that.

Come to find out, Anna knew all along that Philippe was planning to surprise me. He's come up for a meeting with PB II about the Philippe Beaulieu Art Center—actually, he'd planned it for New Year's Eve so that we could spend it together.

"So, are you still averse to me fixing you up with a New Year's date?" Anna teases as we're all standing around the large island in the middle of her kitchen.

My face burns. Actually, it starts at the base of my neck and creeps upward.

"I'm glad to hear that." Philippe puts his arm around my shoulder, and I realize it's not that I'm embarrassed by his affection as much as I'm sorry I didn't open up to my sister.

But she smiles at me from across the granite slab. A smile that starts in her heart and brims over in her eyes.

Later, before the guests arrive, when we have a moment

alone, she says, "You know, if I could take that petrifying leap of faith to a better life, so can you, honey. Believe me, it's the only way to fly. He's a great guy."

Before I can find my words, Philippe appears. "May Jean Luc and I intrude for a moment? There's some business we need to discuss before the party starts. I hate to even talk about business issues this evening, but as you know, time is of the essence."

Once we're all gathered around the island, Philippe sets a white linen envelope with the Philippe Beaulieu Designs logo in the upper left-hand corner in front of me.

"As you know, I met with my grandfather today to discuss progress on the art center. He was pleased with what we've done so far and he agreed that if we are to meet our goal of opening the center at the end of January, we need to move swiftly. Because time is of the essence, he has placed the task of hiring a designer in our hands." He nods to Anna and Jean Luc.

"Rita, the three of us have talked and we would like to hire you."

He nudges the envelope toward me. "This is a retainer to get you started. Of course, we can discuss your fee later."

Three hopeful faces stare at me. I realize that I wasn't the sister keeping a secret. Obviously, the three of them had been conspiring since I'd arrived in Paris.

The thought filled me with a warm glow the likes of which I'm not sure I'd ever felt.

"Of course, this means we'll need to keep you in France until the center's opening," Anna says. Oh. Wow. That's right. This wouldn't be an easy job to do long-distance. Without staff to rely on over here, it would be a one-woman task.

That changed things.

I'm quietly calculating the situation: such as how this job has bought me another month in Avignon and given me a valid excuse to stay. I suppose it's feasible for my staff to handle business on that end for another month. Boy, that sounds like a long time, though. But Terry is capable. He's doing a great job overseeing the college installation, which would actually be executed while I was working on this job if I take it.

"You're very quiet," says Philippe. "Perhaps we could sweeten the deal if I threw in the use of my workshop while you are here. Suppose I offered to help you produce, say, ten pieces of the furniture for that line you've been talking about. Then you could use them as prototypes to test-market your work."

"Ten pieces in a month?" I ask. "Considering that I'd have to design and produce them in one month, I'd say *ten* pieces of furniture is an ambitious goal."

"All the more reason you will need a teacher," he says with a wink that makes me blush again.

"This is a little overwhelming," I say. "How about if you give me tonight to think about it. I have a lot to consider— my house in Florida, my business…"

And lots of other things I'm sure will come to me once I've had a chance to distance myself from the heady thought of Philippe's kisses and the feel of his hands on my body.

Later, when the apartment is alive with the New Year's celebration, Philippe pulls me out onto the small balcony. It's cold outside, but it's nice to have a moment alone with him.

"Rita, I hope you will stay." His accent is like warm

honey, and for a moment I'm tempted to lean in and see if I can taste it on his lips. "I know you can't stay forever, but right now all we need is to take it one moment at a time."

I stare down into my champagne flute, at the way the moon is illuminating the golden bubbles that swim in a steady, determined stream up from the bottom so that they can dance on top. And I think maybe.

Maybe this could work.

"Here, I have something for you." From out of nowhere Philippe produces a small gift bag.

I unwrap a perfectly shaped ornament of delicate blue glass. There's a gold ribbon threaded through the glass loop at the top of the sphere.

"It is my first perfect piece, and I wanted you to have it."

"Oh, Philippe, it's beautiful. Thank you."

As I hold up the orb by the gold ribbon, it spins and the full moon shines though it, reminding me of how this fragile bauble is not so dissimilar from life. One careless move and it'll smash on the hard, cold marble patio floor.

But just because it's breakable doesn't necessarily mean it's destined to be broken.

FOURTEEN

SOMETIMES YOU HAVE to close your eyes and leap. You can't think about it too hard, because if you do, you'll spend your entire life standing on the edge of the unfamiliar, too paralyzed to move.

And so I leaped.

Back to Avignon.

Back to Chez Sabine.

Back into the life of a man who is eight years my junior.

I have to admit it feels more like a leap forward rather than a jump backward. It's been three days now. Every day, Philippe and I have worked side by side in his workshop after I finish the set of daily tasks working toward a new design for the rectory. I have a great vision for transforming the place, and Philippe is happy with the progress we're making.

In our downtime, he's been showing me, piece by piece, how to work the various saws and sanders to build the basics.

I've worried that our relationship should be different now

that he is my client. I know how awkward getting *involved* with clients can become. It can end in disaster.

As we're working on one of the pieces for the Beaulieu collection, he reaches out from the stool next to mine and tucks a stray strand of hair behind my ear. I hesitate. But he leans in and kisses me.

I know what comes next.

I want what comes next. But when I put my business head on straight, and exercise sensible judgment, I know this sojourn back to Avignon, back to Philippe, is temporary. We are avoiding the inevitable trip back to real life.

I pull back and put my hand over his, lacing my fingers through his. "Philippe, I don't know…"

He stands up and pulls me into him, my head rests on his belly. "What don't you know, Rita?"

I make no move to free myself. In fact, my arms wrap around him as I sink into his hard-muscled belly. My will-power, so steadfast a moment ago, slips a notch. He smells so good, and I breathe him in, feeling the life juices in me awaken.

He caresses my shoulders, moves his hands down my back then up to my shoulders.

There are so many reasons why we should stop right here. I lean back and look up at him.

"There's a lot that we don't know about each other," I say.

He's quiet for a moment. Sits back on his stool.

"Well, okay then. The only way to get to know each other better is to share. I'll tell you something about me. You tell me something about you."

Something about me?

"You first," I say. "Since it was your idea. Tell me something I don't know—"

I meant to say, "Tell me something I don't know *about you*." But he smiles that smile that melts me from the inside out and I lose my train of thought.

"Something you don't know is your sister said that if I hurt you, she'll take me apart limb from limb."

I laugh because this is the last thing I expect him to say.

"Don't underestimate her. She's telling the truth."

He nods. "I do not doubt it."

We laugh. Then there's silence.

"You and your sister are very close, *non?*"

"Yes. We've always been close. Our parents are no longer living. So, I think that's made us even closer. We are all we've got. Well, figuratively speaking. She does have Jean Luc in her life and I'm glad. But you know what? The object of this was to tell me something I didn't know about you. In fact, if you want to get technical, I could disqualify the tidbit about Anna's promise. She says that to all the guys in my life."

I wink and he laughs. I'm glad, because he gets me. He gets my sense of humor and above many things, that's so important.

"I guess you are right," he concedes. "So, something about me that you don't know…" He gestures toward his family photo that is now housed neatly in the gold frame I purchased for him. "Well, I have already shared that since my grandfather has been aging, I've been learning the importance of family and we've been making progress. You'll meet him at the art center opening. To add to the thread of family conversation, I will tell you that generations of Beaulieus have lived in Avignon for as far back as we can trace. That is why it is important to me that I set my roots here in Avignon.

"When my grandfather and I reopened our line of communication, I purchased an old farmhouse that has been in our family since the eighteenth century."

"It's not the place where you're living now, is it?"

He shakes his head.

"My family home is not in good enough repair for me to live in. It will take much time and money to get it in livable condition. I want to restore it myself."

"That's ambitious, but if anyone can do it, you can. So, I'm confused, were you born in Avignon?"

"No. Paris. But I returned as soon as I was grown. Paris is nice, but I am more at home in Avignon, working with my hands rather than running in the Paris rat race."

"You hardly ever talk about your father," I say.

His face hardens. I've struck a nerve. I sense that I've ventured as far as he'll permit me to go. He lifts one shoulder and lets it fall. He picks up a piece of sandpaper and resumes sanding.

Even so, I push him a little further. "Is he still involved in the business?"

"No. He is not."

His words are sharp, dismissive. We're quiet for a moment, then he says, "My father lost favor in the family when he had an affair with his brother's wife."

I wonder if this is his uncle who is no longer living, but I don't want to ask. Now that he's talking about it, I'm afraid that if I venture off the subject he might follow the new path of conversation.

So I wait and listen.

"When my uncle found out, he wanted to teach my father a lesson about what happens when you take things that don't belong to you."

Philippe stares at his hands for a moment, then back up at me. His eyes look haunted, and his throat works as if he is swallowing an emotion too massive to express.

"My uncle took my mother from us. He killed her and then turned the gun on himself."

I gasp. I don't know what I was expecting him to say, but it certainly wasn't this.

"Oh, Philippe, I'm sorry."

He responds with another one-shoulder shrug. I reach out and put my hand on his arm.

"Maybe that is why I am not so crazy about Paris. That is where it happened. When I finished school, I chose not to return there. Even though it was my father's brother who took my mother from us, I blame my father for driving him to it."

I glance over at the photo in its shiny frame.

"Maybe that's why you have a hard time connecting with Beaulieu Designs. Too many memories?"

He gives his head a quick shake. The gesture is not really a no, but more like he's deflecting the question.

There's so much more I want to ask him— Where is his father now? What about the uncle's wife? Are she and Philippe's father still together?

But those questions will wait for another day.

"Perhaps I've revealed too much about myself?" he finally offers. "I have not discussed that with anyone in years."

He smiles at me, but it doesn't reach his eyes.

"Now, you must tell me two things about you," he says.

Two things. After what he shared with me, I could hardly offer something superficial. I think a moment, weighing my options.

"Okay, two things—I'm still trying to get over Fred…and I'm starting to believe that sex can spoil everything good in a relationship."

He frowns. "It's very sad that you feel that way. Who hurt you, Rita?"

How was I supposed to answer that?

"I haven't even confided in my sister what happened."

His gaze searches my face. "Tell me, Rita."

There's a certain look in his eyes, like he might hurt someone if I asked him to.

"Tell me who hurt you."

His expression makes me realize, maybe I've built this up too much. Sure, Juan hurt me, but—not to the magnitude of how Philippe's uncle hurt him.

"Well, it was just a case of trusting blindly too soon. It really wasn't the other person's fault as much as mine for expecting too much. I guess I'm just not built for the casual…encounter."

"Yes? Continue."

I squirm a little, glance at my watch and see that it's time for me to go back to the bed-and-breakfast so I can check in with my office before they close for the day. But the look on his face convinces me to stay.

He trusted me with his story.

I need to trust him with mine.

"Are you sure you really want to know?"

THE JANUARY WIND, the mistral, has picked up force. I'm tired, cold and wind-weary by the time Chez Sabine is in sight.

I was insane to walk. Philippe tried to talk me into letting him give me a ride, but I wanted to walk.

And I did, with the ghosts of Philippe's mother and uncle on my heels.

Philippe was divorced and came from a family with such tumultuous relations: his father's affair; his uncle so blinded by jealousy that he'd not only kill himself, but he'd take the life of an innocent woman. That he'd take a boy's mother.

It's after four o'clock when I enter the city ramparts. The sullen clouds in the gray afternoon sky look as if they're as fed up with the wind's battering as I am. That they're as sad as a teenage Philippe, who had to endure all alone.

Yet, he could remain so willing to try. So willing to believe in another. He wasn't fazed by my story about Juan, which seemed trite in comparison, though he didn't make me feel that way. He simply said, "The man's an idiot. But I would like the opportunity to thank him someday for leaving me the prize."

The prize.

Ha!

I don't know that anyone has ever considered me *the prize*.

As I approach the cross street off the Rue du Rempart Saint-Lazare that leads to the inn, I see Marie in the window of her café, taking down holiday decorations.

She waves.

Rather than crossing the street toward the inn, I start to pull open the door to the café. A wild gust of wind catches the door and whips it open for me, making the string of bells on the glass sing and dance a frantic jig.

"Oh-la-la!" Marie laughs. She tosses the holly wreath she's removed from the window onto a table and rushes toward me to help me close the door. "*Bonjour,* Rita! *Ça va?*"

I shiver. "Hello, Marie. I'm cold! That wind is biting. How are you?"

"I am quite cozy, *merci*. You will join me for a cup of *café*, *non?* It will warm you."

I rub my hands together. "That sounds just like what I need."

Marie, who looks stunning in an emerald cashmere sweater and tailored black slacks, goes to the bar and prepares the press pot for two cups of coffee. As I settle myself at a table, her husband enters the dining room from the back of the café. He dressed to brave the weather.

"Bonjour! Bonjour!" Bernard waves at me. But his attention is pulled back to Marie. A mile-wide smile overtakes his face at the sight of his wife.

Marie looks no less smitten as she snuggles into his embrace.

"Ah, mon amour." She beams at him, and for a moment they kiss, as if the rest of the world does not exist for a moment.

That's how it should be.

One time over coffee, Marie told me her first marriage wasn't happy, that the two of them were too different, that they wanted different things. The divorce was inevitable. When she met Bernard, who was from Avignon, but in Paris on business, she instantly knew he was her soul mate. That they were meant to be together.

She traded in Paris for Bernard's slower-paced Provençal lifestyle. "It's been five years now, she says each day is better than the next."

L'amour.

As I shamelessly watch them continue their passionate kiss in front of me, I'm struck by the realization that love *does* happen the second time around. It really does—maybe it's only for those who are lucky in love.

Like Sabine and Édouard, who have been married for more than fifty years.

And I was. Fred and I were different, but we loved each other. Deeply. Sometimes he used to disappear inside his head. Whether he was zoned out in front of the television, reading the sports page, or just "thinking," as he'd put it, sometimes he'd drift off to a mental place where I wasn't invited.

I got used to it. In fact, it sort of became a way of life. I came and went as I pleased. As long as I was home to fix dinner, Fred never expected me to report in. I suppose if I were a certain type of woman I could've taken offense— drawn the conclusion that he wasn't interested, didn't care, that we'd come to live separate lives.

I chose to look at it as comfortable silence. The kind that comes only after years of knowing each other so well. But I wouldn't be telling the truth if I said I didn't wish for a little more passion this time around.

My thoughts stray back to Philippe, and the feel of his hands moving on my shoulders. Then back to Marie who is securing Bernard's scarf around his neck before he ventures out into the cold.

Marie is my age—for that matter so is Karen, my roommate on the ill-fated Drayton trip. But never could there be two more different people. How interesting that their relationships reflect their outlook on love.

Wow. Do I want to be a Marie or a Karen?

It's an eye-opening crossroad.

THE NEXT DAY, Philippe takes me to his farmhouse. It's a gorgeous, rambling shambles of a place on acres of rolling land. It's picture-book perfect. Or, at least it will be. Someday. I can see it, as I stand in the gravel driveway squinting my eyes.

Yes, I can see everything that it's meant to be.

I can imagine blue shutters on the white stucco walls, and a shiny, red-clay, barrel-tile roof. And lavender. Lots and lots of lavender. Acres of it perfuming the summer air.

I close my eyes and breathe in deep.

Yes. I can smell it.

When Philippe takes me by the hand and leads me to the dimly lit room that will someday be his master bedroom, I can imagine making love to him on a giant, four-poster bed that he's made himself.

"This place is beautiful," I say. "It has good bones."

"And you have a very good imagination."

He puts his arms around me, dusts my lips with kisses that trail down my throat.

Forget the four-poster bed, I can imagine making love to him right now on the dusty painter's tarp that's spread across the farmhouse floor. I can imagine awakening to a rooster's crow amidst the smell of fresh paint, varnish and wild lavender drifting in from the open windows....

"Oh, you have no idea the things I can imagine," I say, a little breathless.

His sultry smile teases me. Unleashes a need that has me longing to tell him just how I've imagined his kiss...his body...him.

But before the words can find their way past my lips, he leads me to that tarp, and his hands lock on my waist, as if he's taking possession of my body. I want to tell him he can have it, but I don't have to. He already seems to know.

I tuck myself into his chest, bury my face in his shirt, breathe in the scent of him—that delicious smell of cedar, lavender and leather. The scent that is so him that it hits me in a certain place that renders me weak in the knees.

I breathe in deeply and melt with the heat of his body.

He smooths a lock of hair off my forehead, kisses the skin he's just uncovered, then searches my eyes. I answer him with a kiss—*Yes, I want this*—relishing the warmth of him, the scent of his skin that clings to him the same way I want to. I want to be that close to him.

He cradles my face in his palms and kisses me softly, gently, until my fingers find their way into his thick, dark hair, pulling him close, closer until we're kissing with a need so furious it's all-consuming.

The next thing I know, his hands have found mine, and he's laced our fingers together. Our hands tarry a moment, gripping, flexing, hesitating, as if he's silently giving me one last chance to object, to escape, to run away from what's about to happen.

But I want it to happen.

My God, it's going to happen…

A rush of red-hot need spirals through me. He must read it in my face because he lets go of my hands and his arms close around me. In a fevered rush, he claims my mouth, my thoughts, my sanity. My fingers slip into his hair again, and hold him close as my lips part on a sigh and give him full permission to take possession of every inch of me.

I cling to him, relishing the closeness. There's no mistaking his need, his desire, as his hands sweep down the outer edge of my body to claim my bottom.

Then somehow, in a heated whirl of passion, he's tugged

away my sweater, pushed away my jeans and gotten rid of every barrier between us so that we stand naked and wanting. Together.

He holds me so close that I can hear his heart beat. I feel safe for the first time in ages. With every fiber of my being I concentrate on the moment, shoving away the dark curtain of the past that threatens to fall on my desire and silencing the loud voice of the future that's trying to yammer about how young he is, about how ours is a future that doesn't include a life together unless one of us makes drastic changes—

But I want *this*—what we have *right now.*

As his lips find mine again, I shut out everything else. No past… No future.

Only now, only this need that is driving both of us to the brink of insanity.

He kisses my neck, and my fingers sweep over his tight shoulders and muscled arms, before exploring the curve of his derrière, pulling him even closer so that the hardness of him presses into me, urging my legs to part, searching, showing me his need is as strong as mine.

He eases me onto the tarp-covered floor. It's madness how much I want him. Sheer, unmitigated madness.

Above me, he claims my mouth again, capturing my tongue, teasing me until one shock after another vibrates thorough me, until I can't bear it any longer. Pulling away, he smiles down at me. His lips are swollen and red, and I desperately want to taste them again.

A warm, callused palm splays over one of my breasts. His fingers move from one nipple to the other then trail to my belly where they linger and play, tracing small circles that make my stomach muscles tighten and spasm in agonizing pleasure. Then his hand dips farther still, teasing its way down my body, edging toward a silken, hidden place that is begging for his touch.

Thank God, he takes me quickly, those long, strong fingers slide inside me, searching, stroking, coaxing one moan after another from me until my entire body spasms and liquefies like wax at the flame of his touch.

Still, I ache inside, needing more.

So much more.

As if he hears my unspoken plea, he reaches over and grabs his pants, pulls a condom from his pocket and rolls it on. He covers my body with his, and I wrap my legs around his waist, marveling at how perfectly we fit together.

His first thrust steals my breath, drives me deliriously mad. As his own moan escapes his lips, his gaze is locked on mine, and he tucks his hands beneath me helping me match his every smooth, slick glide in and out of my body. His intensity is undeniable and unending.

Each strong, bold, shameless thrust takes greedily, but gives back so much more, until both of us explode together in an ecstasy the likes of which I've never known.

As we lay there, sweaty and spent, Philippe is collapsed protectively on top of me, still buried so deeply inside me I could swear he's touching my heart.

FIFTEEN

TWO DAYS LATER, Annabelle and Jean Luc arrive for a visit. They're eager to see how the rectory is progressing. After a tour, we all come to Philippe's apartment, on the second floor above his studio.

The place is basically a large loft setup, with the kitchen and living room in one big open space with a private bedroom and bathroom.

Jean Luc is in the kitchen, whipping up a feast of steak with cognac-peppercorn sauce, sautéed mushrooms, baked potatoes, grilled white asparagus and, of course, lots of Châteauneuf-du-Pape Burgundy.

Anna, Philippe and I are sitting in the living room chatting and drinking wine.

"Oh, I almost forgot." Anna reaches for her purse. "I brought you something, Rita."

She pulls out a bottle of red nail polish, gets up and hands it to me.

"Thank you," I say, turning the square bottle upside down

to see the name of the color—True-Blue Red. I usually wear more golden red because of the red in my hair, but "It's a very pretty color. It'll look good on my toes."

With that, Philippe pats his lap.

"What?" I ask.

"Put your feet up here."

"Why?"

He smiles. "Just do it."

I give him a look, but I do as he asks, despite the surge of embarrassment. It's just Anna. And Jean Luc, who is busy in the kitchen and not aware of what's going on.

Philippe peels off my socks, takes the polish from me and starts painting my toenails.

I melt a little as I watch him and even more when I look across the room and see my sister staring with open-mouthed envy.

Later that night, back at Chez Sabine's, Anna and I sit in the living room. Jean Luc, Édouard and Sabine have already gone to bed. So Anna and I have the downstairs to ourselves. We're a little tipsy, so I brew us a cup of tea. One of the nice things about staying with Sabine for this month is that she has given me free run of the kitchen. So, on nights when I haven't been at Philippe's, I've been able to brew myself a cup of chamomile tea.

Another good part of our arrangement has been the surprising don't-ask, don't-tell policy. She hasn't asked where I've been sleeping on the nights I haven't been here—though I'm sure it's as transparent as the plate-glass window looking into Marie's café—and I certainly haven't told her.

"Well, Philippe has set a new significant-other standard

painting your toes like that. I'm going to have him give Jean Luc lessons."

I couldn't help feeling a little…what? A little smug? All the times I've envied Anna's sexy new life. Now she was the one in awe. But, *smug* isn't exactly the word. It's more like grateful. It feels good. But, "Significant other?"

The words are out of my mouth before I realize it.

Anna nods. "What would you call him?"

I take a sip of tea. "I'm not sure. It hasn't even been a month. I don't know."

Anna pulls her legs up under her, settling in for the long-overdue sister confessional. "That's long enough to know how you feel about him."

She pauses, probably hoping that I'll continue on the path she's led me. But I don't know how to say it.

That I've fallen in love with Philippe.

There's so much more that I haven't told her. Anna is such a wonderfully gentle woman, she would never prod. That's why she's waited all this time for me to tell her what brought me to Avignon earlier than I'd planned. Now it's time. Being able to talk about it is a good sign—and it's in the back of my mind that Philippe is the one who first helped me to open up.

It's only right that I tell my sister, too.

So I start at the beginning and recap what happened with Juan.

"I have to admit," I say, "I'm a little scared. I don't really know what I'm doing."

Anna smiles her sweet smile. "I'm so sorry that creep misled you. He'd be darn lucky to have a woman in his life as wonderful as you. Obviously, he doesn't deserve you. But don't let him cost you a good guy. I've known Philippe for about as long as I've been in Paris and he's a really good guy, Ri. I can honestly say, I've never seen him like this with anyone. I knew you two would hit it off. The only thing, though, is he'll probably never move away from Avignon. But that just means I'll finally have my sister here in France." Her words jolt me. I knew this. I've known from the beginning that Philippe's roots are firmly set in Provence, but I guess I just hadn't wanted to face up to it. But as my time here draws to a close, the weeks swiftly falling through the hourglass, I know that one day all too soon I'll have to return to the real world. The one that lies far, far across the ocean.

I'm not quite ready to go there just yet.

I HAVE A SECRET. For the past three weeks, in between tearing down walls—both literally in the rectory and figuratively razing the emotional barriers I've built around my heart—and having sex, and plastering, and having sex, and patching, and having sex, and painting... I've been working on a set of design boards for Philippe for the farmhouse.

They're just suggestions, of course. But the more time we spend at the house and the more he tells me about his vision for the place, the better the design came into focus in my mind's eye. So, while I've been pulling together the rectory interior, I've also been preparing these boards for him.

We've arranged to meet here to go over our checklist and make sure we're on schedule for the opening, which will happen at the end of the week. I'm happy because everything seems to be on time. The project has presented its challenging moments, but all in all, considering the short time frame, it's been smooth sailing.

Amazing how being in love will change your outlook.

I prop up the boards in the middle of the floor in the rectory's center gallery. When he walks in, he immediately goes to them.

"What are these?"

Upon closer inspection, he understands. The look that overtakes his face is priceless.

There are photos of the house as it stands now and renderings of how the finished product will look. There are paint chips, tile pieces and fabric samples...

"This is tremendous. I don't know what to say. You've captured the heart of the place."

He pulls me to him and kisses me so soundly that I almost don't hear my phone ringing. It's nine in the morning here. It's 3:00 a.m. in Florida...couldn't be the office...it's probably Anna.

I sink into Philippe's arms and let the phone ring itself to voice mail. We kiss, hands exploring until we hear the door open and turn to greet the team of masons who are there to install the marble floors.

I feel myself flush, but Philippe seems to be unconcerned about being walked in on.

That French thing again.

I sigh and decide to just go with it. To enjoy being carelessly, recklessly, unapologetically...in love.

The thought makes me giddy and it makes me want to pull Philippe into a room somewhere and have my way with him. Good God, it's like someone has opened the floodgates, and sensuality has been flooding my body and brain for weeks.

While the masons haul in boxes of marble tiles, I pull my phone out of my purse.

One missed call. My heart beats a little faster when I realize it's Terry. Why on earth is he calling at three in the morning U.S. time?

I pick up the voice mail:

"Rita, it's me, darling." His voice sounds panicked. "I need to speak to you. Pronto. We have a problem over at Drayton. I've been up all night trying to figure out what happened with the carpet. It's wrong. It's all wrong and the committee is having a hissy. They're asking for you. They want you to come out and fix it. And frankly, I wish you'd get your ass back here and help me. Some of us are trying to work. It's all well and good that you've gone off with your French lover—hell, that's exactly what I need right about now, a French lover. But come on, how can you expect to run your business from the other side of the ocean? It's time to come home."

Oh, Terry.

He was prone to nervous outbursts. In fact, I used to tease him and say that he PMSed worse than I did. Terry's always been the only one at the office who can get away with talking to me like that because he's so darn good at what he does.

Well, Terry, *darling.* There's nothing that can be accomplished at three in the morning. So, I'll let you cool your heels for a little while.

When I put my phone away, Philippe is still studying the boards I made for him.

"These are *magnifique,*" he says. "Why can't all designers be like you?"

I raise a brow at him. "Like me? I don't offer certain services to all my clients, I hope you know."

We laugh.

"I should hope not. But this——" He gestures to the board. "You are always so professional when it comes to your work. You take it seriously. All the time."

He frowns and sets down the board.

"The designer from Paris, the one who has contacted me about some pieces for a client, she called me again this morning with more demands. She has been nothing but trouble since the moment we spoke hello. The woman is impossible."

She's certainly gotten under his skin.

"Have you ever considered hiring a staff interior designer to work for your company? You could arrange it on a commission basis. You might want to consider it, because you're missing out on a huge portion of the market that could be yours. If you had a designer on staff he or she could work with people like this Parisian woman and you wouldn't have to deal with them. Or at least not as often."

He purses his lips and strokes his chin as if he's thinking about something.

"I would like to hire *you*."

He sounds as if he's half joking—a little flirty, but maybe a little serious, too. I can't quite tell. Still, the pseudo offer takes me by surprise.

"If you come to work for me," he says, "I could keep you here in France."

I laugh. "Sorry, buddy, I've worked for myself for far too long to have a boss now. My business is in Florida, and that's where I'm staying. I'm too set in my ways to do anything different."

As the words leave my mouth, it dawns on me with startling clarity that being "set in my ways" was part of what built that hated wall that ran down the center of my marriage to Fred. Was I just as unwilling to change—or let go of my vision of how things should be—as Fred was?

I blink away the thought.

Philippe can't be serious about hiring me, so I play along. "Besides, why would I want to come to work for you?" I joke. "Now that I know all your furniture-making secrets I'll get all the business since I can design both the furniture and the interior."

Philippe laughs. "You don't think I am serious?"

I shake my head.

A strange, indefinable look washes over his gorgeous face. But only for a moment. Then he gets that mischievous glint in his brown eyes that I love so much. He crooks his index finger at me.

"Come and let me prove just how serious I am." Then he kisses me and in that moment, I think it's quite possible that I might agree to nearly anything he asks of me. Well, except for working *for* him.

A FEW HOURS LATER, I'm back in my room at the inn, and I settle in to call Terry back. He's had time to splutter and spew. Plus, the carpet company should be open now, so we can solve the problem.

"Hey, love," he croons. "Shame on you for sending my call to voice mail."

Just as I anticipate, his fit has run its course.

"What were you doing up at that hour anyway, Terry? Are you crazy?"

"Oh, you know me. Deadline insomnia. I never can sleep during an installation."

At the rate he's talking, it sounds like he's gotten a few es-
pressos into his system.

"Did you solve the problem with the carpet? If not, can
you fax me the invoice and the work order?"

"Oh, *hoooney,* that problem's been solved for a good hour.
You underestimate me."

Uh-huh. "Well, you sounded pretty panicked and I just
wanted to check."

"I guess I was just a little jealous of you off with some
gorgeous Frenchman, leaving me here to do all the work. I
suppose you're never going to come home now. You're just
going to shirk all your responsibility and put it on me."

I know he's kidding, but there's a vibe of truth in his voice.
For some reason, it leaves me unsettled.

Especially when he says, "If you're going to stay over
there, you'd better let me buy this business, girl. Don't you
get the wrong idea that I'm going to work myself into an
early grave for you while you're over there rolling around in
the lavender fields with some French god."

"Terry, I'm working on a job over here. Not rolling
around in lavender, as you put it."

Liar.

*Not technically. The lavender doesn't bloom until July. There's been
none to roll in.*

"I'll be home next week," I add.

"Well, Patricia needs to talk to you before then about
some guy from the service club Fred belonged to. He keeps
calling. Something about a memorial scholarship they want
to set up in Fred's name."

Oh. The news sends a zing to my heart.

"When did they call?" I ask, wondering why my administrative assistant hadn't called me with the news herself.

"Sometime this morning or maybe yesterday. How should I know?"

"Well, then have Patricia call me. Why hasn't she called me already?"

"She probably heard about how you screen your calls and wanted to avoid being banished to voice mail purgatory. Listen, doll, I have to run. Toodles."

When I hang up the phone, it's as if the door to reality has swung wide open and dumped out everything I've been hiding. I have left a lot of business unfinished in Florida. Business—personal and professional—that I knew I'd have to deal with sooner or later.

Obviously, the *later* category is full.

IT'S A LONG ROAD from Provence back to the daily grind. So I decide to start training. Small steps toward my reentry—a phone call to Drayton to follow up; a look at the receipts and expenses in the month I've been gone.

But that's enough for now. Next week, I'll have that 24/7. Right now, I want to see as much of Philippe as I can.

I call him to see what he wants to do for dinner. I get his voice mail. It's odd to hear him speaking rapid French, but that's what he does in his message. I can't understand exactly what he says, but it sounds like, "It's Philippe. Leave a message. I'll follow up as soon as I'm able."

So I do.

"Hi, it's Rita. I wanted to see if anything sounded particularly good to you for dinner. I want to cook for you. I'm going to head to the market to see what looks good. Please call me back when you get this."

I find an array of lettuce available. That surprises me because I always think of lettuce and salad as a light, cool summer meal and the cold winter wind is blowing again. But the lettuce looks superb. So do the pumpkins. I decide to make a curly endive and egg salad with pumpkin soup.

My mouth waters thinking about it.

It's a windy walk back from the market, I check my watch. It's after four. Philippe still hasn't called me back. I'll need to bake the pumpkin before I can purée it. So I'll need to get started soon.

I debate what to do. I could always cook the pumpkin in Sabine's oven, but it will be such a hassle to repack everything and take it with me. Plus, it would feel rude not inviting Sabine and Édouard to share the dinner with us.

I really want an evening alone with Philippe.

I walk to the ramparts and hail a cab to take me to Philippe's house because not only are the groceries heavy, but the biting wind is blowing even harder, cutting right through me, pushing against each step I take. Philippe's probably so wrapped up in the final piece of furniture for the gallery he's lost track of time. But when I arrive, the house looks dark. I have a strange feeling that something's not right. I ask the taxi driver to wait, and in a few minutes I'm glad I did. The place is locked up tight. Even his workshop.

I brave the furious wind and walk around the house trying to figure out what to do. I don't have a key. There's never been a need for me to have one since I've always been here with Philippe.

The howling wind warns that something's different, but common sense tells me not to panic.

This may be the first night since I've been back in Avignon that Philippe has gone off on his own. But he's allowed. He doesn't need to check in with me.

We didn't have plans tonight.

I just assumed.

Feeling a little silly, I get back into the waiting cab and ask the driver to take me to the inn.

This is what happens when you assume, I remind myself. You end up feeling like an ass.

THE WIND BLOWS Philippe back to the rectory two days later. By that time, I'm mad. I'm as furious as the biting, howling elements. Of course he doesn't have to check in with me on personal matters—he's free to come and go as he pleases, wherever he wants to go, with whomever he wants. But what galls me is that we're a day away from the art center opening.

You don't just disappear off the face of the earth.

"I'm sorry, Rita," he says. "I know I owe you an explanation."

There's a note to his voice, in his expression. Something distant. Something different. Something has changed.

I try not to think of how Juan left me standing exposed—my lover one minute, a distant man the next. Or at least I thought he was.

All I say is, "We have a lot of work to do. You need to figure out where you want the Beaulieu pieces to go and make arrangements to have them delivered."

My phone rings. It's Anna. I'd called her when Philippe

disappeared. I had questions that needed answers. Questions that couldn't wait.

Part of me hoped he would stay gone until Sunday, when I was on the plane back to the U.S. But no such luck.

"Hi, Anna." I muster my cheeriest voice. "May I call you back? Philippe just walked in."

"Oh, my God. Yes. Yes! Call me back."

I disconnect and start to walk away from him. To unwrap the pedestals that just arrived. They will house his designs. If the last piece that he's been struggling with isn't finished because he's been…away. We'll, that's his problem.

Focus on the work. The day after tomorrow you can leave.

"Rita, we need to talk," he says to my back.

Dread, the weight of a bowling ball, drops in the pit of my stomach.

The we-need-to-talk talk.

I wave him away. "I have too much to do. As I unwrap these, why don't you place them where you want them to go?"

He walks around to face me. "Rita, I'm sorry. You have every right to be mad at me for leaving like that. But my grandfather showed up. He brought my father. I haven't talked to that man in nearly twenty years and he just shows up. Without warning." Philippe is talking with his hands, gesticulating wildly. "My grandfather started talking crazy, changing the rules, saying that a reconciliation between my father and me is now part of the price of the rectory. I had to leave so I could process everything."

I'm trying not to make this personal. Even though it is. But it's not about me. It hurts that he had to leave for forty-eight hours, to leave me, in order to process things. I'm sure

it was a lot to face: a man who'd abandoned him after causing his mother's death. His father was responsible—albeit
indirectly—and then he sent his son away.

"I'm sorry," I say.

He nods, but the look on his face tells me the appearance
of his father wasn't the only thing that sent Philippe running
away on the wind.

SIXTEEN

THE MISTRAL HAS finally exhausted itself. Now, it's so quiet outside, it's eerie. Not a breath of wind. The calm before the storm. I keep telling myself, if I can just make it through this day, I can do anything. It's opening day of the Philippe Beaulieu Art Center opening. Actually, the party isn't until tonight, but there's still plenty of work to be done.

It's a little awkward with Philippe, but I'm a professional. In less than twenty-four hours, I will be on the plane home. Maybe then I'll be able to process everything that's happened.

Yesterday, Philippe finally admitted that the reality of our situation hit him when he offered me the job and I so steadfastly insisted that my business was in Florida.

"Rita, I love you but I don't see how this can work. The reality is we can't fly back and forth once a week to see each other."

He's right. So, I'm doing the best that I can to enjoy this sojourn with my Angel in Provence for what it is. Nothing more. Nothing less.

Maybe once I'm far enough away to see things clearly, I'll be able to convince myself that this was an opportunity for growth. A chance to get back in touch with myself—the real me.

But right now, it hurts.

Annabelle and Jean Luc are here helping with the last-minute details. Jean Luc and Philippe are in the main gallery adjusting the lighting.

Anna and I are in a studio upstairs cleaning and shining everything—getting rid of the last of the construction dust.

"I'm sorry you're sad," she says. "I'm sorry both of you are sad. You're perfect for each other. I just wish there were some way that you two could meet in the middle."

"If we met in the middle that would be in the Atlantic Ocean. It's not going to work, Anna."

I shrug. "I mean, he's a great guy, I lov—"

I snap my mouth shut before the rest of the confession can pop out.

"You love him," Anna says. "I know you do. He loves you, too. I can't understand why neither of you will budge."

"If it were only that simple," I say. I toss my soiled disposable dusting cloth, grab a roll of paper towels and some glass cleaner and get ready to tackle the windows.

Anna is standing in the middle of the room with her hands on her hips. She has her serious face on. "If you'll remember, Jean Luc and I faced a similar situation when my residency was up. But we worked it out."

The comparison makes my heart ache. I know my sister is trying to help, but I wish we could change the subject.

"I'm happy for you and Jean Luc, but Philippe and I are not you two. Philippe and I aren't even a couple. We never were."

That's the reason I want to drop it. We've had a great time for the better part of a month. Only a month.

In the dance of intimacy, that time frame is usually one of the first hurdles. It's when the luster of the new relationship starts to dull, you start seeing the real person.

Lots of people decide to move on at that point. For whatever reason, Philippe and I did not make it over that first hurdle. Even though the luster hadn't dulled in my eyes, reality did cast its ugly shadow, proving that the situation wouldn't work.

"Not a couple? Are you kidding me? Then what were you?"

I don't know what's going on in Philippe's head and I think I'd rather go home clinging to the you-live-there-I-live-here-it'll-never-work, but-if-only-we-lived-closer excuse than learn it just wasn't fun for him anymore. That it was time to move on. That my luster lost its shine.

I shrug because I can't talk any longer. This stupid lump in my throat is holding back my words and damming up my tears.

I will not cry. I cried myself to sleep last night and that's enough.

"I think you're both stubborn and afraid," Anna says as she steps up beside me and works on the window next to the one I'm shining. "Rita, I love the change I've seen in you since you've been here—since you've been with Philippe. It's a softer, freer, more relaxed you. Can't you see that Philippe is obviously in love with you? Are you just going to leave that behind? My gosh, for the first time since I can remember, you've seemed truly happy—all the way down to your red, painted toenails."

Okay, that's a low blow.

The memory of him painting my toenails nearly makes me come unhinged. But the part about me leaving him behind, as if it's solely my fault, makes me mad.

"You don't see him up here begging me to stay, do you?"

"You're missing the point—"

"No, the point is, he's eight years younger than I am. He'll want kids, which I can't give him. Not at forty-five. Besides, I can't commit to anything new because I don't even know what I'm doing right now. I have a house and business back in Florida. I've sorely neglected both. Anna, I haven't even sorted through Fred's things. My husband died and I haven't even had closure there. I can't drift along in this Provençal-lavender haze any longer than I already have."

Anna shakes her head slowly. Looks at me like I'm a hopeless case.

"It's only January, Rita. The lavender hasn't even bloomed yet."

THE NEXT MORNING, much to my surprise, Philippe meets Anna, Jean Luc and me at the train station. When I first see him, a heady burst of possibility courses through me, like a lightning strike. That fast. And then it is gone.

With good reason.

He makes stiff, polite noises about my taking care of myself, that he'll miss me. Then he stays on the platform, looking a little lost, as he watches our train pull out of the station.

The only reason I keep my face turned toward the window to see him is that I don't want Anna and Jean Luc to see the tears streaming out from under my sunglasses.

I'VE BEEN BACK in Florida—for how long now? Days? Weeks?

Who knows?

All I know is that one colorless day blends into the next like an endless loop of nothingness.

Okay, I'll admit it. I'm absolutely miserable living with the imagined ghost of Fred and the shadow of what might have been with Philippe.

The first thing I did when I got home was to go through Fred's clothes. I donated them to Goodwill, keeping two of his shirts that I'd loved the most.

Funny, I've "cleaned house." But it still doesn't feel like home. There's a strange filmy haze looming over my life that no amount of housecleaning can fix. Even when I go to the office, I don't find what I need.

I chalk it up to prolonged jet lag.

Ha. Let's see how long I can get away with that excuse.

Today, I have to mentally whip myself into shape because I'm meeting Terry out at Drayton College to do a walk-though of the music department redesign. It's not the formal walk-through. Terry did that himself a few days ago.

It's a courtesy. I go as the company owner who is interested in making sure her clients are completely satisfied.

Terry and the staff did well, holding down the fort while I was gone, and that is never so evident as when I hear the glowing remarks from the committee.

"We are just thrilled," says a woman from the committee who was particularly difficult to work with in the early stages. "That Terry is an absolute genius. I never thought this place could look so good. Especially the rehearsal hall."

Terry is here for the meeting, which is good PR since he

was the one in the trenches while I was gone. He can't stay for the walk-through because of a meeting, but he's intimately acquainted with the results since he's lived out here 24/7.

Ugh. How depressing.

But sometimes that's what it takes, I remind myself. It's good business and obviously it made the client very happy.

Come on, Rita. Get with the program.

I'm happy when I learn that for various reasons, the committee members can't join me on my walk-through. One has a meeting. Another has a conference call. Yet another is the only one in the office and can't step away.

"It's fine," I reassure them. "I know my way around. I just want to see how pretty everything looks."

This sets off another round of *Oh-so-pretty-we-can't-believe-it's-the-same-place* twittering.

When I'm finally able to extract myself, I discover they're right. The buildings that were once overrun with mold and buzzing, green-tinged fluorescent lights are completely transformed. They look stately and moneyed, like a college where affluent parents would be happy to send their kids.

Eventually, as I go through the redesigned buildings, I find myself in the rehearsal hall. I didn't consciously save it for last, it just sort of came up that way.

The first thing I notice is that the door no longer slams. It glides to a silent closing not disturbing the diligent young musicians who might be practicing.

The second thing I notice is Dr. Juan Santiago is gone. There's a new professor in his office—or so says the name and class schedule on the bulletin board.

Figures.

I laugh out loud. I can't help it.

Was I really such an idiot to not see through him? But a little voice inside me comes to my defense, "You trusted. What's so wrong with that? Don't stop trusting. Don't let him rob you of that."

As I stand in the same spot I stood that first day when I cried over "Greensleeves," I listen. Today the hall is quiet. No forlorn sax, no discordant piano, no slow, mournful tune playing in the background to move me to tears.

So, why do I feel so melancholy?

It's a strange feeling. Sort of like being homesick. But how can I be homesick when I'm at home?

IT TAKES ME a while to admit that I'm homesick for Avignon. That magical place. And for the people I met there: Marie, Sabine, surly old Édouard. And especially Philippe. I miss his smile, his laugh, his dark eyes and big hands and the way it felt to lie in his arms.

In the month I was there, it felt more like home than… home. Transforming the rectory, putting together the design boards for Philippe's beautiful house, working side by side with him in his studio. It gave me a true a sense of purpose, a sense of true joy and inner peace—*real* joy and peace, the likes of which I haven't felt since…well, since I've been back in Florida.

Now that I've had a chance to let everything process, it's okay to admit it was in Avignon where I finally found myself and discovered that I could, indeed, love again. No one will ever replace Fred, but isn't falling in love again a testament to how much I loved him?

Somehow, I know that Fred would want me to pursue this new chapter of my life. Or at least he wouldn't want me to resign myself to being the La-Z-Girl since it was never my true nature. At this stage, I'm feeling a little more drawn to the chaise longue rather the La-Z-Girl lifestyle.

So, then, what the hell am I doing here? I didn't even get to see the lavender bloom.

IT HAPPENS WHEN I'm coming home at lunchtime to meet with the Realtor. I'm selling the house and the first step toward that is to interview Realtors to see who will be the best fit.

Naturally, when I turn down the street and see the white Toyota in the driveway, I'm expecting a woman named Martha from Coldwell Banker to step out of the car.

I nearly drive through the garage door when I look over and see Philippe, getting out of the car. In the time it takes me to unbuckle my seat belt and step out of the car, he's already standing there waiting for me.

"Hi," he says, without waiting for me to speak. "My life is something of a mess and I understand I can find a good designer here to help me spruce it up a bit."

For a moment, I can't think of a word to say.

Then he says, "I would've called, but—"

I don't know what moves me to do such a thing—well, yes, I do, I'm in love with the guy—but right there in the middle of the driveway at high noon, I throw my arms around him and kiss him soundly.

And he kisses me back.

Then he starts talking in rapid-fire English laced with that French accent that makes me swoon. He tells me he's in love with me and starts talking about the future. He wants me to move into the farmhouse with him, but if I want we can split our time between Florida and Avignon.

"As long as you'll share my life," he says.

My head is spinning. I'm afraid to blink for fear he might be a mirage caused by the tears streaming from my eyes. But these are happy tears.

So, of course, I squeeze my eyes shut and when I open them again, he's still there.

He's still there.

"Will you, Rita? Will you marry me?"

PHILIPPE AND I are married in July in the middle of a lavender field across the way from the farmhouse.

It's a small wedding, but all the people who matter to us are there: Anna is my matron of honor, Jean Luc makes a very handsome best man; Jude and Terry, who bought me out of the business, came over from the States; there's Sabine and Édouard; Marie and Bernard; and Philippe Beaulieu II and III.

The relationship between Philippe and his father is still a work in progress, but they're making strides. Just as we are doing with the farmhouse that we've begun to renovate. His father gave us a very generous check as a wedding present, meant to expedite our restoration of the old Beaulieu home.

PB II has even agreed to test-market a line of more traditional furniture that Philippe will design. His grandest gesture yet, to reach out to his grandson.

Philippe graciously met him halfway by agreeing, though he is adamant about remaining an independent contractor. I support him in that decision, especially since we have merged our businesses. We decided to keep the name Angel of Provence because it works on so many levels.

IT'S HARD TO believe we're approaching our first anniversary. As I stand here at the window of the master bedroom—the very room where Philippe and I made love for the first time—I'm gazing out at lavender fields in full bloom. Very much the same way that my belly is blooming with our son.

Carrying a baby at forty-six isn't an easy journey, but the doctor has monitored my progress and all tests indicate that we will welcome a healthy baby boy into our family next month.

Philippe Beaulieu V. I rub my belly and whisper to our child that he will be born into quite a legacy. But that's fine. No reason to be frightened.

After all, the journey of a lifetime begins with a single leap of faith. If our baby boy ever forgets, his parents will provide a living testament.

WHAT HAPPENS IN PARIS
(STAYS IN PARIS?)

This book is dedicated to Michael and that kiss we shared on the quay of the River Seine. Here's to many more. *Je t'aime.*

And to Jennifer, who patiently understands that the only way books get written is when Mommy spends long stretches of uninterrupted time at the computer. Jen, you are my sunshine. *Je t'aime.*

Acknowledgments

Thanks to my editor, Gail Chasan, Tara Gavin and all the wonderful people at Harlequin who make it possible for me to do what I love.

Thanks to my agent, Michelle Grajkowski, for everything!

Thanks to my critique partners, Teresa Brown, Elizabeth Grainger and Catherine Kean, who make the hard parts of writing fun. Special thanks to Elizabeth for double-checking my French.

I couldn't have written this book without valuable insight from attorney Adam Reiss. Thanks for the lowdown on laws pertaining to lewd and lascivious behavior and bailing oneself out of jail, and filling me in on other—umm—interesting aspects of getting arrested; and special thanks to my good friend Carol Reiss, who did not bat an eye when I told her I needed to discuss lewdness and lasciviousness with her husband. It's all in a day's work, right?

"*Grandmère*, marriage is sacred," says the girl.

The old lady quivers. "*Love* is sacred," she replies. "Often, marriage and love have no connection. You get married to found a family and you found a family to constitute society. Society cannot do without marriage. If society is a chain, then every family is a link in that chain. When one gets married, one is bound to respect a social code…but one may love twenty times because nature has made us that way inclined. You see, marriage is a law, and love is an instinct that moves us to the right or to the left."

—*Conseils d'une Grandmère*, Guy de Maupassant
(1850–1893)

ONE

MY FIRST CLUE should have been the infestation of gold-embossed, cream-linen envelopes from various law firms. Thirty-three of them I counted in our mailbox on that otherwise ordinary Friday evening. Each one addressed to my husband, Blake Essex.

My second hint should have been the way Blake swept them out of sight, nonchalantly shrugging them off when I asked about them.

"Who knows?" he said. "If I had the money they spend on postage for the worthless junk mail I get, I'd be a wealthy man."

That was enough for me. I mean, he was right. We did get an excessive amount of junk mail. Just never from attorneys. Still, it was Friday night and all I wanted was a gin and tonic—not a fight. I'd had enough stress at work that week. The wonderful world of marketing can take its toll.

I shoved all thoughts of the unopened lawyer letters to the back shelf in my mind—the place where I stored nagging doubts and discrepancies that didn't quite add up but couldn't be explained—and mixed us a drink.

We went on with our Friday-night ritual as we had for the past eighteen years, politely working together to get dinner, cleaning up afterward, watching a DVD, performing our bedtime routine, giving each other a peck on the lips, and falling asleep, back to back, on our separate sides of the big, king-size bed.

Standard MO for an old married couple.

That's what I used to tell myself.

But now that I think about it, the letters weren't my first clue. By the time they arrived, it was as if the universe was at its wits end and had resorted to slapping me up the side of the head and shouting, *Open your eyes, you blind idiot. Can't you see the truth?*

Even so, I didn't put two and two together until the next day when my sister, Rita, and I were on our way to Saint Petersburg to catch Le Cycle des Nymphéas—Monet's water lilies—exhibit at the Museum of Fine Arts.

Rita was driving and I was reading the newspaper, skimming each page diligently to make sure the competition didn't somehow get a leg up on the retirement company I do marketing and advertising for, scoring free press in the paper. I'd finished with the main section and moved on to the local and state when I spied mug shots of two men that gave me pause.

One man looked like Blake.

I did a double take and realized the name under the photo was *Essex*. The other was of a basketball coach at one of the high schools.

Every little inkling lurking in the murky shadows of my

subconscious jumped to attention and my worst fears were confirmed—right there for all of central Florida to read in twelve-point type.

My husband had been arrested for lewd and lascivious behavior after being caught in a *sex act* with—*another man?*

The high-school basketball coach.

Thursday, they were caught in a secluded park in Seminole County. According to the paper, it's a place frequented by people—especially men—who are looking to exchange sexual favors. The coach had been arrested there before, but the school had no knowledge of his run-in with the law.

That's why the story was in the newspaper.

For everyone to read—

"Oh my God! Oh my God!" I was shrieking. I couldn't stop myself. "Rita, pull over. I'm going to be sick."

She swerved a little bit. "What's the matter?" She glanced at me, then back at the road as if she didn't know what to do.

"Just pull over. Hurry!"

She veered off onto the interstate's shoulder, and I tossed the paper in her lap as I stumbled from the car in the nick of time before upchucking my bagel.

The next thing I knew, Rita's hand was on my back and she was handing me a bottle of water.

"Here, rinse your mouth."

I took it without looking at her and did just that.

"Did you read it?" I asked.

"Enough to get the gist."

I turned to face her. Hot tears of anger and humiliation and disbelief brimmed and spilled. "Oh my God! What am

I going to do? What am I going to say to him? To everyone who knows us? How could he let me find out like this?" I realized I was screaming because the words scalded my throat and I started choking.

Rita took my quaking arm and led me in the direction of the car. But I shook out of her grasp and stumbled back a few steps.

"How could he do this? I hate him! How could he do this?"

I landed hard on my rump in the sparse grass, in the midst of the sharp-edged rocks and sand, sobbing with my head in my hands. In the periphery of my mind I heard my sister urging me to get in the car, then I heard the crunch of tires pulling off the side of the road.

I looked up and saw a cop. Rita confirmed that, yes, I was okay. I'd just suffered a shock after receiving some bad news and needed some fresh air.

All I could think was, *Oh God, if the cop runs my name, he'll know I'm married to Blake. Then it dawned on me that this was how it would be for the rest of my life. Look, there's Annabelle Essex. She was married to Blake Essex, that guy caught having sex with another man.*

I put my head on my knees until I felt a shadow block out the sun. I looked up and the cop loomed over me.

"You okay, lady? You need me to call an ambulance or something?"

I wiped a sand-gritty hand over my face and shook my head. "I—I'm fine."

"Then get back in your car and move on. It's not safe to loiter on the side of the highway like this."

For a split second I contemplated that perhaps getting flattened by a large truck was preferable to getting in Rita's car and driving back to my ruined life. But then good sense rallied and I realized I'd rather be alive to torture Blake.

He'd have hell to pay for this.

I intended to collect in full.

HAVING YOUR DIRTY laundry aired in the newspaper feels like standing in the middle of a busy street stark naked. No, it's more like standing in the middle of a busy intersection and not realizing the world is looking at you standing there stark naked until it's too late and—oops, the joke's on you.

Oh, look—I'm naked.

I'm standing here like a fool.

With that newspaper article, the whole of me was reduced to what was printed on page B–1 of the *Sentinel*'s Local and State section. Gee, all that and *my* name wasn't even mentioned.

It didn't have to be. Blake's mug shot and name spoke for both of us.

I'd been oblivious to the gawks Saturday morning as I walked down the driveway to my sister's car to begin our drive to Saint Pete; blissfully unaware that the reason Joe Phillips next door stopped mowing his lawn and stared at me wasn't because he thought I looked hot in my new pink sweater that showed just a hint of décolletage. He didn't speak; didn't wave. He just stood and gaped at me across the stretch of Saint Augustine grass with a bewildered look on his face.

Ha! And I thought he was ogling my cleavage.

Later, when I realized the truth— Well, you can understand why coming to terms with Blake's betrayal would be even harder knowing I had to face people who'd read all about it in the newspaper.

Even before I knew, others were devouring the juicy details with perverse excitement because they actually *knew* the guy who got caught with his pants down in the park.

Oh, and his poor wife. Didn't she know her husband was gay? But they have a kid. Maybe it was one of "those kinds" of marriages...? What do they call it? A marriage of convenience?

How was I going to explain this to our son, Ben? He'd be wrecked.

Wait a minute. I didn't have to explain anything. I was not the guilty party, despite the guilt-by-association factor.

Or stupidity by association.

I had to stop blaming myself, thinking this wouldn't have happened if I'd been a better wife; a little thinner; more in touch with his needs....

More of a woman.

Or at least enough of a woman to keep my man from turning gay.

Rita and I drove to Saint Pete, but we never made it to the Monet exhibit. Good thing because I didn't want to forever associate Monet's water-lily paintings with Blake's coming out of the closet.

Instead of going to the museum, we walked on the beach. We must have walked for miles, me in my low-cut pink sweater that didn't seem so sexy anymore, and my sister with her sandals in her hand and her white pants rolled to the knee.

She let me talk.

"Ri, you weren't surprised when you heard about Blake, were you?"

She shrugged, pushed a wisp of short blond hair out of her eyes.

"Rita? Are you saying you knew all along?"

She opened her mouth to speak, but closed it on a sigh, and shrugged again. "Come on, Anna. He was just a little too…" She dragged out the word as if stalling for time.

Finally with a look of resignation she said, "He was a little too in touch with his feminine side. I mean, either that or you'd snagged every woman's dream man."

Snagged him? Was that what I did?

Blake and I never had a sweep-you-off-your-feet courtship. We met our senior year of college and dated for about two months before I got pregnant.

No snagging intended. I was as surprised as he was. I was prepared to raise the child on my own. He was the one who insisted he wanted to be a *family*.

Rita snapped her fingers. "Oh, I read something the other day where someone said something about a man who was 'just gay enough.'" Rita made air quotes with her fingers. "That's how I always thought of Blake."

I must have made a face because she grimaced. "Sorry. I probably shouldn't have said that."

Afterward, we mostly walked in silence.

BLAKE WASN'T HOME when I walked into the dark house Saturday night. He slinked in rather sheepishly Sunday, late morning.

I sat in the living room trying—unsuccessfully—to distract myself with a biography on the artist Georgia O'Keeffe when he walked in.

He flinched when he saw me and shoved his hands into his pockets. Dark circles under his eyes hinted he hadn't slept well.

"I'm sorry," he murmured, looking stiff and pale and a little bewildered standing there in his pressed khakis, crisp kelly green polo and navy blue espadrilles that once seemed so Palm Beach, but now just looked...

I wondered where he stayed last night and how his clothing could look so fresh given the circumstances, but I refused to ask.

His gaze darted around the living room, looking everywhere but at me. He seemed so frazzled, like if I made a loud noise or erratic gesture he'd jump out of his skin.

It took a few beats to find my voice. "Why didn't you tell me, Blake? How could you let me find out like this?"

At least he had the decency to hang his head. "What was I supposed to say?"

"Something." I set the book on the end table and pulled my knees to my chest. "For God's sake, anything would have been better than letting me read it in the newspaper."

He didn't reply, just raked his hand through his hair—he always messed with his hair when he was anxious—and stared at his espadrilles. I worried the fabric of my pink velour sweatpants.

"I didn't know it was going to be in the paper," he murmured so softly I could barely hear him.

I traced a zigzag in my pants' velvetlike texture and decided he was probably telling the truth.

The paper said his *partner in crime* was a high-school coach who'd been arrested twice for public indecency. The story admonished the county for its lax screening of teachers more than it focused on exposing the men who meet at Live Oak Park to exchange sexual favors.

Of course. Blake's name and mug shot made the paper

because he made the fateful choice of having sex with the wrong man.

"Was this the first time, Blake, or have there been others?"

He took a deep breath and closed his eyes. "Do you really want me to answer that?"

"Never mind, you just did." Tears welled in the corners of my eyes.

"Would it make a difference if I said it was just a one-time mistake?"

I gritted my teeth before I answered.

"Do *you* want it to make a difference?"

I didn't hate myself for asking the question as much as I loathed the tiny spark of hope his words ignited. *Was* it just a onetime mistake? I held my breath, waiting for his answer.

All that followed was silence like cold water dousing an ember of hope.

Hope? Good God.

A bomb had detonated in our marriage leaving nothing but rubble; everything we'd built together blown to bits by his wanton act of selfishness. It nauseated me to think about it. More than that, it made me angry.

"We have to call Ben," I said. "Right now."

His gaze snapped to mine, a look of utter terror on his face.

I put my bare feet on the floor and pushed forward on the chair. "Blake, the story was in the paper, and it affects our son as much as you and me. People who know him have probably read it, and some wiseass is bound to call or e-mail him sooner or later and say, *Hey, I heard about your dad*. It's better he hears it from us first."

Blake closed his eyes and pinched the bridge of his nose. "It's Sunday morning. We won't catch him in."

I threw up my hands.

"Call his cell phone. He always carries it."

Blake shrugged, deflated. "Okay. Fine. Let's get it over with."

I turned off the reading lamp, which left the living room with its drawn curtains sad and dark. I tried to ignore the tightening knot in my stomach as I followed him into the kitchen.

"His cell phone is number one on speed dial."

Blake's shoulders rose and fell on a noisy shallow breath. He kept his back to me as he picked up the phone and dialed. Every muscle in my body tensed, making me second-guess myself. Were we doing this the right way? Panic screamed and threatened to put me in a headlock. Perhaps we shouldn't break the bad news over the phone.

Ben was in school at the University of Montana. It wasn't as if we could drop by and tell him in person. He'd come home for spring break just two weeks ago and wouldn't be home again until summer. What other choice did we have but to tell him over the phone?

"Hello, Ben? It's Dad. Did I wake you?... Oh, yes, I'm fine... She's fine, too. And you?"

He listened for a minute. I edged closer to see if I could hear what Ben was saying. I couldn't, but I noticed Blake's free hand shook as he raked it through his hair.

My God, he was really a wreck over this. I hadn't realized it until then.

I turned away and straightened my Eiffel Tower refrigerator magnet. Why was I feeling sorry for him? This was *his* fault. Facing the refrigerator, I folded my arms as if I could block out the emotions that were weakening me.

Then the stupidest thought barreled through my mind. What if, faced with dismantling his family, Blake realized the enormity of his mistake?

I mean he screwed up—*and how*—but should we have talked about it a little more before we told Ben?

I'd pushed Blake to make the call, and even though I truly had Ben's best interest at heart, part of me wanted to see Blake squirm to punish him.

He was squirming.

My God, the man was shaking.

Admitting a mistake of this magnitude to your son must be second only to confessing to God. Well, maybe it was tied for second because he seemed pretty wrecked that I knew—

"I'm glad to hear you're doing so well, son—" Blake's voice broke on the last word.

Oh…he was only human. If it was just a mistake, should he have to pay for it with his family?

Encroaching sympathy warred with the thought that Blake should have considered the cost before he dropped his pants.

I remembered a time when I was young. I tried to steal a blouse from Casual Corner, but the store manager caught me before I could leave the shop. She scared me to death, telling me that she could call the police and have me arrested. She went on and on about how this one stupid mistake could ruin my life.

In the end, she didn't call the police or my parents. Instead, she made me promise never to steal again.

She let me go. She gave me a second chance rather than ruining my life.

I learned from that mistake, and I'd like to think I grew into a better person because of her understanding.

Maybe Blake had learned his lesson. Maybe we just needed to talk about it, get counseling. It wouldn't be easy, of course, but perhaps if we could surmount this, it was a chance for our relationship to grow.

I reached out to touch him, to take the phone from him so I could tell Ben we'd call him back later. But before my hand fell on Blake's shoulder, he said, "Ben, I'm calling with bad news. Your mother and I are divorcing because I'm gay."

AFTER BLAKE LEFT, the late-morning sun streamed in through the kitchen window. It made my head hurt.

I slipped into the darkness of the living room, and lay down on the cool leather couch, flinging my free arm over my eyes.

Divorce.

He'd already made up his mind.

Ben took the news hard. I'd never heard such language from him. Called his father a bastard. Said he hated him and never wanted to see him again.

First, I was glad because I wanted Blake to hurt as badly as I hurt. Then I felt guilty because Ben was hurting. My baby. It was hard enough for me to learn the truth, but imagine finding out the person you'd looked up to your entire life had lied to you.

I'd never been homophobic and had raised my son to be tolerant of all people…. This was the ultimate test. The logical side of me knew it was ridiculous to hate an entire subpopulation based on the actions of one man. Oh…but this was so personal. It hurt too bad to form any conclusions.

While I sat at the café table in the kitchen, trying to talk Ben down from the ledge, Blake disappeared upstairs.

He came back down after I'd hung up, and all he said was, "Will you water the orchids, please?"

He had about twenty-five plants in a small greenhouse in the backyard. I knew they were valuable, but I couldn't believe he was thinking about them in the wake of what had just happened.

Selfish bastard.

"No. I won't." I loved flowers, but he fussed over those stupid plants like an old maid. I didn't care if they died.

"Fine. I'll come by and get them this week. When would be a good time?"

"Should I get an AIDS test?"

He squinted at my non sequitur. "Would it make you feel better?"

Anger sliced through me. "You are such a jackass. I don't want an AIDS test to make myself feel better. You had sex with a stranger—with a *man*. And my life could be in danger because of it."

AIDS was only one in a jumble of questions logjammed in my mind, tangled up with the likes of how many sexual partners he'd had over the past eighteen years? Did he practice safe sex? Or did he think too little of me to do so? Even though we only had sex maybe once a year over the span of our marriage it only took one time—kind of like getting pregnant.

Only AIDS killed.

Turning onto my side on the couch in the dark living room, I drew my knees up in a fetal position and listened to the sounds of the house that used to be our home—the tick of the grandfather clock, the phantom creaks and pops as the house settled; the refrigerator and air-conditioning that cycled on and off; and the full magnitude of how alone I was pressed down on me and unleashed the tears.

They came in torrents, in great heaving sobs that choked and nearly drowned me.

All the while, one single thought burned in my mind: How long would Blake have lived a double life had he not been involuntarily outted?

TWO

THE NEXT DAY, I did what any self-respecting woman caught in the middle of an undeserved scandal would do—I called in sick to my marketing job at Heartfield Retirement Communities, then cut all the blooms off Blake's orchids.

Good harvest. About twenty stems with at least three flowers each. I gathered them into a bundle, tied them with a ribbon and made an exotic bouquet.

Flowers for me.

Originally, I intended to sit in the middle of the greenhouse and pluck off all the petals: He loves me... He loves me not, because he's gay and loves men... He loves men... He loves men not because he promised to love, honor and cherish me for all the days of my life....

That was just too maudlin.

The blooms were so beautiful, I arranged them in a crystal vase so I could enjoy them as I gorged on slightly stale *beignet*—that's French for doughnut.

I never realized orchids were such exquisite little works of art. They were always Blake's babies. I fingered a lush maroon petal that draped down past another cream petal shaped like a pouch the size of a chicken egg.

In the greenhouse, he'd labeled this one Showy Lady's Slipper Orchid. The name conjured images of cross-dressing, but I blinked the thought away and ate another doughnut.

I lifted the curious little pouch-petal with my finger. I'd never looked at an orchid up close like this, certainly not a stem cut free from the potted plants Blake sequestered in the greenhouse for optimum growing conditions (rather than optimum enjoyment).

I plucked Lady's Slipper from the vase, held it up and slowly twirled the stem in my fingers, getting a three-hundred-and-sixty-degree look at the flower.

Blake was going to be so pissed when he found his naked plants. He'd studied orchids like he was going for a master's degree, and coddled them, coaxing the temperamental things to blossom. All to end up in a vase on the kitchen table.

Oops. My bad.

Since we were getting a divorce it only seemed fair we shared them fifty-fifty. Florida was a community-property state. After eighteen years of contributing my fair share to our egalitarian marriage, I wanted my half.

He'd get the plant. I'd get the flower.

Fifty-fifty.

I'D DOWNED SEVEN of the twelve doughnuts by ten-thirty and was so disgusted with myself I decided I had to get out of the house before I died an unnatural death.

Death by *beignet*. Or murder by irate, flower-worshipping, estranged husband.

The thought made me shudder, or perhaps the thought of venturing out into the world?

I pushed the doughnut box out of my reach. It wasn't as if the paparazzi were camped on my doorstep. The sensible side of me knew the story of Blake's arrest had faded from the minds of most people in central Florida.

Old news.

But in my world of neighbors, colleagues and husband-and-wife acquaintances the story lived on. Suddenly *my world* seemed like the whole world; as if *everyone* knew.

I couldn't go to work.

I couldn't even walk out onto my driveway.

Good thing the car was in the garage.

After a few moments' contemplation, I decided to seek refuge with an old friend. A dear friend I'd neglected for a long, long time—my painting studio at the Orlando Center for the Arts.

I would go there and paint…orchids.

Because if I didn't get out of the house, I was afraid I might lock the doors and never find the strength to venture outside again.

I waited until I was sure most of the neighbors were gone before I grabbed the vase and drove to the studio.

Far better than staying home and eating until I couldn't fit through the door, or making myself crazy thinking about how I'd rearrange the furniture to make it appear as if nothing were missing once Blake took his fifty percent.

The only way to keep myself from dwelling on the ne'er-do-well was to focus on me. I'd neglected my interests—such as painting, and fresh flowers, and eating entire boxes of doughnuts—far too long.

I read in the Georgia O'Keeffe bio that she used to leave her husband, Alfred Stieglitz, for months on end to go paint in a place she called "Faraway."

It was only New Mexico, actually. I'm sure "Faraway" sounded much more romantic than "Alfred, honey, you're getting on my last nerve. I'm leaving now so I can refill my well. You'll have to get your own dinner, and pick up your own dry cleaning."

I know, I know, they probably didn't have dry cleaning back in those days and if they did, I'm sure a woman who had the gumption to go "Faraway" probably wouldn't have picked it up anyway.

My point being she took time to nurture herself, to foster her creative spirit. And Stieglitz was waiting for her when she decided to come home.

Paris would've been my "Faraway." Once upon a dream, I wanted to study art there, but life's obligations preempted those dreams. The big problem was that it was always so *far away*, and as a wife and mother, I had too much responsibility. Blake hated the French and had no desire to go to Paris. Not even for me.

AFTER STOPS AT Sam Flax for new art supplies (it had been so long since I'd purchased anything there, there was no chance anyone would recognize me) and Panera Bread for nourishment (frequent purchases there, but they didn't know I was married to Blake), I pulled into a parking space at the Orlando Center for the Arts. I sat in the car for a few minutes with the engine running and the air-conditioning blowing cold air on my face.

OCA sat at the crest of a hill sloping down to a beautiful lake. The compound was actually a series of old buildings united by lush gardens and courtyards. Fantasy architecture, I'd heard it called once, with Mayan/Aztec motifs gracing the aged concrete walls and bejeweled stepping-stones and fountains scattered liberally throughout the grounds. Red clay tile roofs graced buildings with worn cream stucco walls dating back to the early 1900s.

A magical place that always made me feel artsy and organic. As if anything were possible.

I picked up the maroon lady's slipper again and turned it around and around, trying to decide the angle I'd paint, but my heart felt so heavy I didn't know if I'd be able to drag myself out of the car so I could get to my paints.

Okay, Anna, you're starting over, who are you going to be now?

Good question.

I'd been daughter, sister, wife, mother. More successful at some roles than others.

What next?

In the rearview mirror I spied a smirking Mayan tribal mask etched into the garden wall behind my car.

"What are you looking at?" I murmured.

I could almost hear it answer, *He's gay. Is that what you want for yourself? Are you really willing to settle for a man who doesn't love you?*

My first thought was, *Yes, I just want my life back.* The scorned woman in me sounded a hearty, *Absolutely not.*

Feeling shaky, angry and vulnerable all at once, I stuck the orchid behind my ear, killed the engine and hauled myself and the vase of flowers out of the cool sanctuary of the car into the oppressive heat.

It was only March, for God's sake. It was never this hot in March.

In Florida, the relentless, lingering dog days of August were bad enough, but it was brutal punishment when the heat came early.

The weatherman said better days were on the way.

Yeah, promises, promises.

Until then, all the more reason to hole up in my studio with my big fat bag of comfort from Panera Bread—broccoli cheese soup, Caesar salad and a raspberry Danish—God knows I wasn't hungry, but I would be later. This way I wouldn't have to go out and get dinner.

I could stay there…indefinitely.

Or until I got hungry again.

Since I was still so full I'd probably never eat again. I was banking on a long stay.

I nudged the car door shut with my rump and adjusted my grip on the Panera sack, careful not to smash the Danish. The paper bag crinkled in my hands, and I had a brief second of panic when I realized pastry had been the sexiest thing going on in my life for a long time.

As quickly as the panic flashed, it dissipated. It was okay to turn to comfort food—

Comfort food and oil paints. The combination made an unlikely elixir, but what the hell?

The baked asphalt radiated heat like the basalt rocks they used in hot-stone massages. A brown lizard dashed across the pavement, heading for the grass, and I nearly tripped over myself to keep from stepping on it—or letting it scurry over my foot.

Logically, I knew they were harmless, but I had a lizard

phobia. When I was a kid, one ran up my pant leg once at a picnic, and I did an embarrassing striptease trying to get it off me. I was traumatized. Ever since, they've made the hair on the back of my neck stand up, and I always end up nearly hurting myself trying to steer clear of them.

Classic case of once bitten, twice shy.

When I was in college, I studied phobias in a psychology class and learned they're usually traced back to an event that caused the fear, and when you're faced with similar circumstances, the fear and panic return.

My professor likened phobias to monsters we manufactured in our minds. Since there are no limits to our imagination, the only way we can dismantle the monsters is by facing them, by reaching out and touching them.

Beads of sweat broke free and pooled in my cleavage, teased by the hint of a breeze blowing in from the lake on the other side of the grounds.

There was no way in hell I was going to reach out and touch a lizard. In fact, the hot weather and the creepy-crawlies made me wonder why I lived here when there were so many other places I could go to avoid them—and Blake.

Ben was at college in Montana. I was free to go, if I wanted to. Just as the orchids cut free from the plant traveled to my studio where I could paint them.

The thought floored me. Did being free equal being unwanted? Cut free to wither and die just like the orchids?

I swiped at the moisture welling in my eyes—"Damn humidity"—and stepped into the grassy courtyard that hosted my studio. I tried to unlock the door, but the key stuck in the lock. I had to set down the bag and flowers so I could jiggle the knob.

It was mad at me for staying away for so long.

Fair-weather friend returning only after exhausting all other options.

After a little coaxing, the door opened with a squeak and I stepped into the shoebox of a room.

The shutters were drawn over the wall of windows and despite the darkness, the space was hot and dank. When I flipped on the light, it bounced off the white stucco walls.

A wooden easel stood bare in the corner below a cluster of cobwebs; a stack of forgotten blank canvases lined the wall; an empty coffee can for brush cleaner and a paint-splattered palette lay on the table, right where I'd left them the last time I was here—a good three months ago.

The first thing I needed to do was get some natural light into the room. I sidestepped a dead palmetto bug and screamed when I inadvertently dislodged a lizard carcass as I threw open the shutters. I couldn't even kick it into the corner.

The windows looked out into an adjacent courtyard. A large live oak shaded a blue mosaic fountain surrounded by an overgrowth of purple foxgloves, red, white and pink impatiens, hibiscus and azaleas.

It took me back to the day Blake brought me here the first time, when he leased the studio for me. Art was where we connected. When all else failed in our relationship— when we went months without touching—I'd return to his support of the creative me.

It was hard not to slip into doubt. Since he was not who he pretended to be, did that mean everything else he upheld was a lie, too?

How he said I was talented; that he loved me and wanted a family.

I mean, what was love? It wasn't quantifiable. You couldn't measure it by any means other than faith and feeling.

When we met he was a good man with a promising future as an architect. He treated me well, if not passionately.

There's more to life than passion. Passion was the flame that burned so furiously it burnt out and left you wanting.

I always believed a good marriage was born of the slow, steady rhythm of a man and woman, developed after passion flared and faltered.

Now I don't know what to believe.

We got married and four months later Ben was born.

I loved Blake. I wouldn't have married him if I thought he hadn't loved me.

I stood at my studio window staring at the courtyard, waiting for the pretty view to permeate me and work its magic the way it did that first day, but all I felt was empty. And hot.

Good God, it was sweltering in here.

I reached over and turned on the air-conditioning unit that stuck out of the top of the last set of windows like a boxy appendage. It chugged to life, shaking and rattling as if it would burn itself out before it cooled down the place.

Hmmph. Passion.

It took three trips from my car to the studio to schlepp in all of the supplies I'd picked up at Sam Flax—new paints and brushes, a large bottle of gesso and twenty more stretched canvases of varying sizes—I'd forgotten about the extras in the studio.

Finally, I shut the door on the outside world, determined to rediscover the joy of my studio and the painting process.

I started painting again after our son, Ben, began junior high school. I set up an easel on the screened-in back porch, but I couldn't leave my paintings out there since it was too damp. I used to talk about how great it would be to have a real space of my own; a spot where I could leave all my supplies and canvases—a real artist's studio.

The spot at OCA was a reward for sticking it out in a marketing job I detested. Since Blake had broken away from Hartman and Eagle, the architectural firm he'd been with for fifteen years, to start his own business, we relied on my company-funded benefits.

The studio was a compromise. Blake got to be his own boss. I got four walls to call my own. But I didn't have time for it, really. Working full-time, cooking and cleaning, raising a child and washing Blake's dirty underwear didn't leave much time or energy for creativity.

I'd bet over the five years I'd leased the studio, the cumulative amount of time I spent there barely averaged a once-a-month visit; that was more often than we had sex. Every once in a while Blake would get on my case about not using it and threaten to cancel the lease, which would force me to drag myself in there to create. So, coming here today, I decided that until I discovered my own style, I would paint flowers of all shapes and sizes, in the tradition of Georgia O'Keeffe; fragile Lady's Slipper orchids; big fat roses; vibrant sunflowers.

I set a large canvas on the easel and positioned the maroon orchid on a paper towel.

This would be therapeutic. I could mix the paint to any shade I desired; place it anywhere on the canvas I wanted. I could wash it on in thin, translucent wisps or glob it on in thick, heavy layers.

I set out the new tubes of oil paint I'd purchased, and one by one squeezed a dab of each on my old crusty palette.

If I wanted to paint roses blue, I could. If I wanted to render sunflowers purple—no problem. I might even paint this pretty orchid black to match my mood.

It was my choice.

Paint complied. It would stay true to whatever image I created. It wouldn't start out as one thing and transform itself into something totally foreign.

Unless I wanted it to.

I picked up the paintbrush, regarded the blank canvas and made a split-second decision not to paint the orchid. Nope. On my canvas, I would honor the traditional. I touched my brush to the glob of alizarin crimson.

Roses are red.

Violets are blue.

My husband is gay.

Shit.

Who knew?

The brush fell from my hand, *pinged* and clattered on the rough concrete floor. I pressed my shaking fingers to my temples.

Who knew?

Everyone in the world but me?

The small room started spinning, and I edged backward until my butt hit the wall. My knees gave way and I slid down until I half crouched, half sat.

I had no idea what came over me, but suddenly I knew exactly what to do to that canvas.

BY THE TIME Rita knocked on my studio door at seven o'clock that evening, I'd painted three canvases. Two florals and what you might call a *Picasso-inspired* portrait of Blake, though I've never been much of a Picasso fan. Rita likes him, but I've always thought of him as a creepy misogynist.

Appropriate inspiration for Blake's portrait.

I painted him with two heads (one male, one female), Medusa-like orchid blooms for hair and a spear driven through his chest. I'd used washes of blues and blacks with a spattering of bloodred applied with a palette knife for emphasis.

"This one's a little scary." My sister held up the canvas of Blake. "If he turns up dead, you'd better destroy this or they'll have all the evidence they need to hang you for the crime."

I shrugged, not in a jovial mood.

"What's Fred doing tonight?" I wiped excess paint off my brush with a paper towel, then walked to the sink to wash the residual from the bristles.

Rita and Fred had such a good marriage, after twenty-five years they were even starting to look like each other. Sometimes—especially after the hell I'd just been through—I wondered if my sister hadn't snagged the last decent man alive.

"He's at the all-night driving range, getting his golf fix. Where did those come from?" She pointed at the vase of orchid blossoms.

"From Blake's greenhouse."

Her blue eyes flew open wide. "Oh. My. God. If you leave right now, you might be able to outrun him. Let me rephrase what I said earlier. *He's* going to be the one hung for murder because he's going to kill you when he sees what you've done."

I smoothed the bristles back into shape and put the

brushes in a jar to dry. "I know. I feel kind of bad about it. I didn't realize how pretty they were. Do you think he'll notice if I superglue them back on?"

Rita burst out laughing. "He's going to flip."

She walked over and picked up a painting of a huge sunflower I'd leaned against the wall. "This is nice. Sort of Van Gogh–esque." She set it down and stepped back to view it, tilting her head from one side to the other.

"I wasn't really going for *nice* when I painted it."

My sister ignored me. "May I take it with me to show a client who lives in Bay Hill? The colors are perfect for her family room."

Rita was an interior designer and some of the houses she decorated cost more than I hoped to make in a lifetime.

"You know," she said, "we really should make some slides of your work. I could probably sell them for you. I don't know why I didn't think of this sooner. Are you coming here after work tomorrow?"

"I'm not working tomorrow." I picked up one of the brushes I'd just cleaned, dipped it in paint and drew a thick sienna line about a third of the way down the canvas.

"You're not?"

I shook my head. "I'm taking two weeks' vacation. I called human resources this afternoon and squared away my leave. They didn't even ask if I'd cleared it with my boss, Jackie."

I stole a glance at my sister, who'd crossed her thin arms over her tiny middle. She nodded.

"It's probably a good idea for you to take some time off. If you have the time, you should use it. What are you going to do? Do you want to go away somewhere?"

I shook my head and wiped my hands on a rag. "Nope. I'm going to paint."

Rita's eyes widened. "That's great. That's exactly what you should do."

What she didn't say was, *It will be good for you to pour all your anguish into something creative.*

"Plus, it will give us plenty of time to photograph your work. So, can I take the sunflower with me, Van Gogh?"

"Sure."

I watched my sister walk over and carefully pick up the painting and study it again.

Was it this kind of anguish that caused Van Gogh to cut off his ear?

What would Blake do if I sent him my bloodied ear all wrapped up nice and neat in a pretty little package? I could put an orchid on top of the box.

Nah. He wasn't worth it.

"Is the paint still wet?" Rita asked.

"Nope. That's the beauty of acrylics."

I tried not to get my hopes up, but I thought if I sold a few paintings, it would help offset the cost of the studio. I wouldn't be able to afford it when Blake and I divorced. Because I was sure once he saw how I'd sheared the blooms from his beloved orchids, he'd go for the jugular, saying I had to pay the rent on my studio because he couldn't afford it, knowing damn good and well I couldn't, either.

"I'll tell you what," Rita said. "Why don't you spend the rest of the week painting, and I'll come over Saturday to shoot the fruits of your labor."

"Saturday? Don't you have plans with Fred?"

"Fred knows I'm on standby right now."

I rolled my eyes. Sweet of her, but I didn't want to become her charity case. "I'm fine, Rita. Really. In fact, I'm sure I can go to Target and purchase a roll of slide film and shoot them myself. Does Target sell slide film?"

"No, Target does not sell slide film. That shows what you know. Fred already has his heart set on golfing this weekend. So you're stuck with me."

TUESDAY BLAKE CAME over for dinner. I hadn't seen him since we'd called Ben on Sunday, and I was a little nervous about the orchids massacre. But we needed to talk—to discuss money, who'd get what. All the things soon-to-be-divorced people talked about.

Nothing like a divorce to jump start the conversation. In fact, we had so much to talk about, I figured I could tell him I'd watered the plants and then distract him with conversation to keep him out of the greenhouse. It would work for now, and I'd make a point to be out of the house when he came to pick up the plants.

I wanted to meet in a restaurant. A nice, neutral, public place where things wouldn't get too intense (translate: far away from the orchids).

He insisted we meet at the house. Since he'd moved out, he wanted to look at everything and start making lists.

Lists?

Okay. Right. Lists.

That wasn't nearly as unsettling as when he said he hoped this was the first step to us becoming friends since we'd be forever connected by our son.

It just smacked of an HBO movie: *My Best Friend Is My Gay Ex-Husband.*

The absurdity really hit me as we sat in the dining room at our usual opposite ends of the long mahogany table. The dinnertime arrangement seemed natural when Ben was at home filling the empty space in the middle. We'd grown so accustomed to our places, when Ben left for college six months earlier, it never occurred to us to change.

To move closer.

Blake was his usual nontalkative self, but it was bizarre sitting there as we had countless times over the years, eating my homemade potato-leek soup, the ominous strains of Wagner filling the silence.

He looked so indifferent sitting there as if he belonged at my table. Sitting there in a clumsy, conversation-free stand-off, I thought, *This is the man I married, the father of my child,* but I might as well have been staring at a stranger. Had he suffered at least a modicum of embarrassment or regret over the scandal? Had he lost clients? Was the thrill worth public humiliation and losing his family?

I was so nonplussed by his nonchalance that I meant to take a bite of soup, but instead the words "How long have you known you're gay?" rolled from my mouth like a piece of errant chewing gum.

"Annabelle." His tone was reprimanding, a blend of shock and annoyance, but he looked at me for the first time that evening, his soupspoon poised in midair.

The look on his face made me crazy.

"What? Does the word *gay* offend you? Do you prefer *homosexual* or another more veiled term? Tell me, Blake, because I'd like to know *something* before the rest of metro Orlando finds out."

His eyes flashed and he glared at me for the span of one

deep sigh, before lowering his spoon. "I suppose I've known for quite some time."

The unflinching touché of words knocked the breath out of me. Reality slammed down between us like a thick sheet of ice. All I could do was stare at him through the surreal haze until he averted his gaze and resumed eating.

Hello? How could he eat at a time like this?

"If you've *known for quite some time,* why didn't you clue me in?"

He didn't answer me, but continued spooning soup into his expressionless face. I pushed away my bowl, and the creamy contents splashed over the rim. "All along I wrote it off that you were simply a man who was in touch with his feminine side. But you know, now that I think about it, it might as well have been written in big, bold script across the bedroom wall. How could I have not known?"

He shrugged and hunched over his bowl a little more, tuning me out. I had questions, and he was going to answer them. So I raised my voice.

"Living with you all these years, what did that make me, Blake? An idiot? Your beard? A fag hag?" Somewhere through the icy miasma of my anger I saw him set down his spoon.

He cleared his throat. "I thought we could discuss this like rational adults, but apparently we can't." He dabbed the corners of his mouth with his napkin. "I'll have my attorney contact yours. But in the meantime, I thought you should know so you can start making plans. We're going to have to sell the house or you'll have to buy me out."

"Talk to my attorney." *Don't have one yet.* "I don't want to move and I shouldn't have to buy you out, either. My standard of living should not change because your lifestyle did."

His chair didn't make a sound as he pushed away from the table and stood. He hesitated for a moment. I saw his throat work in a swallow as his long, manicured fingers worried a button on his shirt. I fully expected him to say something. Instead, he turned and walked out.

A dull ache spread through me as I watched the tall, slim man I'd tried so desperately to make love me disappear into the other room.

A few minutes later or maybe it was a few hours later—who knows how long I sat there contemplating the ruins of our life—I heard the back door slam open.

"What the hell happened to my orchids?"

THREE

SATURDAY, AS I painted the finishing touches on a still life of foxgloves, Rita appeared in the doorway of my studio clutching her camera.

It was still hot outside—so much for the weatherman's promise. The heady scent of gardenia wafted in, and I thought I heard the lake breeze whispering that relief from the stifling heat was just around the corner.

Be patient.

I was wrong. It wasn't the breeze or anything remotely so romantic. It was merely the air-conditioning cycling on, its cold blast merging with the muggy outside air.

Rita stepped inside and closed the door before the humidity flooded in and took over. "Ready to shoot?"

She set her Canon on the counter and stood there with a funny look on her face.

"What?" I said, laying down my brush and wiping cadmium yellow off my hands with a rag. "I recognize that look. You're up to something."

She nodded. Smiled.

"Before we get started—" She pulled a split of champagne and two paper cups from her shoulder bag. "I have a surprise for you."

She set them on the counter, then handed me a plain white envelope.

"What's this?"

She grinned, nearly dancing. "Open it."

I did. Suddenly, I was staring at a check for seven hundred and fifty dollars—written to me?

"What's this for?"

"Your sunflower painting."

I squinted at her, confused.

"The sunflower painting," she repeated. "My client loved it. She bought it— Is seven-fifty enough? I guess I should have asked how much you wanted for it. But that seemed like a fair price. If it's not, I'll—"

"No, it's fine. It's fabulous. I can't believe you sold my painting."

With a look of pride on her face, she popped the cork and poured two glasses of bubbly.

She sold my painting.

She *sold* my painting. As I stared at the dollar amount, I couldn't fathom someone actually paying money for something I'd created.

Holding the check made me light-headed. This was enough for two months' studio rent with a little to spare for supplies.

Rita handed me a cup and raised hers. "A toast. To there being more where this came from."

Nice idea, but I was a realist. I painted for fun. I painted for me. But for seven hundred and fifty dollars I could be commissioned.

Holding her cup, Rita walked to the middle of the room and turned in a slow circle, surveying my new work that lined the wall; in some places they were stacked four and six canvases deep, starting to overrun the small space.

She whistled. "You've been busy since the last time I was here, huh?"

I nodded. Thirty-three new pieces since her last visit.

"It's amazing how much I can get done when I don't sleep."

I set down my cup and shoved an empty plastic soup bowl—lunch from Panera again—into a sack and put it in the garbage as my sister walked over and flipped through a stack of paintings.

I watched her as she studied my work, and wondered what she was thinking. It suddenly seemed a little amateurish producing thirty-three paintings in the span of five days. Some artists agonized over a single painting for twice as long and here I was mass-producing them.

She paused to take in a brilliant pink camellia blossom, flipped past it and pulled out the close-up of the maroon orchid.

"Has Blake picked up his babies yet?"

I rolled my eyes. "He came by Thursday while I was here and whisked them away. The greenhouse is empty."

She nodded absently and gestured to the canvas. "I really like this. Reminds me of Georgia O'Keeffe."

My breath hitched. In O'Keeffe's biography she said, "Most people in the city rush around so, they have no time to look at a flower. I want them to see it whether they want to or not."

I read that she painted fragments of things because they made a statement better than the entire object. She created an equivalent for what she felt about something...never copying it form for form. I borrowed the same philosophy in the dark, almost morbid lines of the orchid close-up. No harm in borrowing a style until I found my own.

"Thanks, Ri, that's quite a compliment." I pulled out a stool and sat down.

"I'm serious, Anna. These are really good." She put the canvas back where she found it and picked up her purse again. "I have something else for you."

I poured a little more bubbly into my cup. "The champagne and check were plenty."

She nudged my hand with a slim packet of papers. "It's an application. Here, take it."

I did so, hesitantly, and set down the paper cup. "A job application? I have a job, Rita, and despite how I hate it, I'm not up for another major life change."

"It's not that kind of application. It's for an artist residency in Paris. Is this not perfect?"

"I'm sure it's perfect for someone, but I can't go."

She put her hands on her hips, and tapped the papers with her index finger's deep-red acrylic nail. "Anna, this is *Paris.*"

She held it out again, and I took it.

Artist-In-Residence Fellowship—Call For
Applications.

The City of Paris, France, and the French Ministry of Foreign Affairs seek applications from foreign artists of any discipline who wish to participate in an artist-in-residence program. The winners will receive a monthly allowance

and a three-month stay in a workshop/studio at the Delacroix International Exchange Centre, a former convent in
the heart of Paris. At the end of the residency, one of the
finalists will win a one-hundred-thousand-dollar purchase
award given by the French government. The winner's artwork will become part of the permanent collection of the
Museum of American Exchange in Paris, France.

By the time I reached the bottom of the first page, I knew
there was no reason to keep reading. I shook my head and
tried to give the papers back to her. She wouldn't take them.

"If you went to Paris, I could sell your paintings for you."

"You just sold one without me going."

"I know, but that was a lucky fit."

My heart sank. "A lucky fit. Gee, thanks."

"Come on, you know you're good, but it's the whole
French-mystique thing. My clients would just eat it up. The
artist just got back from Paris."

"Oh, validation. That sucks. My going to Paris isn't going
to change the way I paint. You know what Gertrude Stein
said about a rose is a rose is a rose…"

"Right, but everyone finds Parisian roses a hell of a lot
more appealing than the varieties we grow here. Come on,
Anna, what's stopping you?"

Oh, let's see…my job. The fact that I was forty-one and
broke and if I gave up that job, at my age I may not find another. And don't get me started on the huge ocean between
the States and Europe and the foreign language I didn't speak
beyond *bonjour* and *au revoir*. Even if I attempted to utter those
words, I was sure some surly Frenchman would toss me off
the side of the Eiffel Tower for butchering his language.

"I can't."

"Give me one good reason that doesn't have to do with your being afraid of something you've always wanted."

I closed my eyes and tried to put into words the litany of good reasons I'd just ticked off in my head, but all that came out was "If I go I'll lose my studio space." Ridiculous—even I had to admit it. The absurdity hung in the air between us like a bad smell. Rita regarded me with a confused grin, as if she was waiting for the punch line of my bad joke.

"You'll forgo Paris to keep your rented studio?" She looked around, and I could see her considering her words before she spoke.

"*Paris*, Anna. *And* you could sell your work to the French government for tons of money. What's not to love?"

When I didn't answer, she sighed. "They're choosing twelve artists. You have to apply. Cross the bridge about going once they offer you the residency."

I set the application on the table, feeling faintly sick.

"Just think about it," she said. "You don't have to decide now."

WORKING AT HEARTFIELD Retirement Communities was like living in a scene from George Orwell's *1984*. My boss, Jackie King—or the Jackal, as I called her—was always on red alert, watching and waiting for someone to screw up so she could sound the alarm and shine a great big spotlight. No wonder the day before I returned to my job as assistant director of marketing, I had a giant panic attack over what I'd face in the wake of Blake's arrest.

Exactly sixteen days had passed since the story appeared in the paper. I knew I couldn't hibernate indefinitely. The longer I put off plunging back into the real world, the harder it would be.

Cold hard reality dictated that since I was getting a divorce, I needed this job. Selling a painting had only lulled me into a false sense of security. Even if my attorney negotiated a decent settlement, I'd still need an income to support myself. Unfortunately, that meant that keeping my job had taken on new importance.

Talk about adding insult to injury.

Jackie King would almost smile if she knew how she had me under her thumb.

The Jackal rarely smiled.

Three of us made up the Heartfield Retirement Communities' marketing and advertising department: Jackie, the director of marketing, a real piece of work who had no life beyond her job; her administrative-ass, Lolly Rhone, who fancied she ran the organization; and me, the marketing misfit.

The Dynamic Duo. And me.

I'd been blackballed from their *club de deux* for a holy trinity of sins: my refusal to give my life to Heartfield Retirement Communities; my refusal to kiss Jackie's ass; and my blatant refusal to play their game.

I had nothing in common with Jackie, and she hated anyone who was different from her. She was a shop-at-WalMart-all-you-can-eat buffet-white-cake-bland kind of normal. Anyone too different, she mocked mercilessly (behind their backs, of course) for the term of her employment.

She cleansed her soul by going to church on Sundays and spending her vacations on mission trips to third-world countries where she built houses and shelters while her daughter stayed home with a sitter. Then she'd come back to work and treat anyone in her way like shit. But that was okay. She did church work.

She and Lolly were like two rotten peas in a pod. They traveled together, ate lunch together, socialized after hours. Jackie even baby-sat Lolly's kids. Yes, the boss baby-sat the administrative-ass's kids. In return, Lolly had her face so firmly buried in Jackie's behind she couldn't see their "close-ness" bordered on incest.

We had our weekly department meetings—Jackie insisted the three of us have department meetings: one hour of hell consisting of a five-minute delegation of assignments for the week and fifty-five minutes of listening to Jackie's harangue about how her boss, Ezekiel Bergdorf, had screwed up the previous week and how she could have done so much better. She wanted his job as vice president of operations so badly she nearly foamed at the mouth. I was willing to bet that over time she would systematically destroy him to get what she wanted.

Therein lay the irony. Jackie's weekly rants left her wide open for me to cause her serious professional harm; it was as if she was playing career chicken, daring me to take her tirades to the brass. She knew I wouldn't do it.

I didn't rat on others (I'm sure in the catch-22 of her small mind she considered that a weakness) and I had no designs on her job.

Sad to admit, but I wasn't ambitious when it came to Heartfield Retirement Communities. I did my job and did it well, but come five o'clock, I was gone. Contrast that with Jackie-the-martyr whose life revolved around the company. She was divorced, had a nanny for her daughter and spent more time on the road than at home. She couldn't fathom why *everyone* didn't sell their soul to the company.

My marketing job started out as a temporary gig that stretched to twelve long years. In the beginning it was a part-time position that provided enough flexibility that I could work while Ben was in school—he was in second grade when I started—and leave the job behind when I went home. It allowed me to keep my foot in the workplace, but still take care of our son—

Who was I kidding? I used to feed myself that line of crap when I started feeling bad about not being able to be the room-mother for Ben's class or chaperon his field trips because Blake was adamant that I bring in my fair share of the livelihood. Heaven forbid that he be the sole supporter of his family.

Looking back, all I really wanted was to paint and be a mother to my baby (not necessarily in that order). My heart was never in marketing an overpriced retirement community. I suppose I should have left a long time ago rather than stay so long my boss regarded me as an inoperable tumor she was forced to live with because Heartfield never fired anyone—short of them murdering their boss.

No wonder Jackie had it in for me. She had no patience for a woman who preferred her child to climbing the corporate ladder.

Looking back, I should have done a lot of things differently. Now, all I could do was try not to look down as I crossed this rickety bridge over the canyon-of-major-life-changes. It was enough to make me contemplate curling up in a fetal position for the rest of my life. Instead, I walked in wearing my hair back in a tight chignon, the same as I had every weekday for the past twelve years. The place smelled of burnt coffee, carpet shampoo and office supplies, the same as it had every day for the past twelve years. I greeted our receptionist, Vicki, and started my approach to the break room to stash my salad in the fridge, the same as I had every day for the past twelve years.

"Oh! Annabelle."

I stopped and glanced back into an uncomfortable pause that lasted a few beats too long. But I reminded myself to hold my head up and look her straight in the eye.

"Yes?" I said.

"Um…welcome back."

"Thank you, Vicki."

Then by the grace of God her phone rang, and I beat a hasty retreat down the long hallway that contained a row of offices on the left and a liberal sprinkling of cubicles on the right. I made it unscathed, stashed my lunch and made myself a cup of tea (no break-room coffee, thank you, because it looked like dirty water and tasted worse).

Clutching my cup, I started to my desk, looking each person in the eye, greeting them. My personal life was *my* business, and I dared anyone to ask. But as I wound my way through the maze of cubicles, my coworkers honored my privacy.

Perhaps returning to work wasn't so bad. It reminded me of a little kid going to the doctor for a shot. The more she dwelled on it, the more it scared her, until she'd built it up to be something so monumentally frightening that even the thought nearly paralyzed her.

I'd turned going back to work into the mother of all shots. This wasn't going to be so bad after all.

Then I ran headlong into the Dynamic Duo.

There they were. Jackie was standing outside Lolly's cubicle, which, like it or not, I had to pass on the way to my office.

Jackie darted a quick glance at me, but kept on with her canned let's-pretend-we're-talking-about-something-so-important-we-haven't-noticed-Annabelle conversation. Good, maybe she'd let me pass without a passive-aggressive dig or contemptuous look. I was almost relieved, because I'd rehearsed this encounter in my mind, prepared several pointed comebacks I preferred not to use.

For instance, if one of them asked "How was your vacation?" I'd smile and say "Lovely, thanks." Or if I felt strong enough to volley, I could say "Why would you ask me that?" Then stare them down until they crawled into their respective holes, and then as I walked away say "I am not in the mood for your *crap.*"

Good God, this was just like junior high school. Of course, since I was prepared, Jackie took another tactic. As I walked past she said, "Lolly, hold my calls. Annabelle, good morning. Please come into my office."

Oh, shit. "Sure. Let me put away my briefcase and I'll be right there."

I was *not* prepared to deal with her one-on-one.

"Right. Take your time."

Take my time? She almost sounded... What was that vaguely familiar tone in her voice? Was she being...nice? Jackie King was a lot of things, but *nice* wasn't in her repertoire. She was too mean to be nice.

Oh God, maybe she *was* going to fire me.

Surely she wasn't *that* mean? She liked to pretend she had

a conscience, and firing me now, when I really needed this lousy job, would be unconscionable.

She told me to take my time, so I did.

I shut my office door, placed my purse and briefcase on a shelf in the small closet. I closed the bifold door carefully so it wouldn't jump the track, adjusted the clip taming my long auburn curls, smoothed the back of my black skirt before I sat down at my desk and picked a piece of lint off my stocking before I started my computer.

The Windows logo had emblazoned the screen, and I had just lifted my mug to take a sip of tea when I spied Blake's face smirking at me from the five-by-seven gilded frame perched on the left corner of my desk. A vision of the mug shot that ran in the paper flashed in my mind. My heart ached as the hole in it tore open a little bit wider.

I pressed my hand to my chest for a few seconds before smacking the photo facedown and sweeping it—like a dead bug—off my desktop into a drawer.

Tears stung my eyes. I dabbed them away and gave myself a pep talk: I was not going to cry. He was not worth it. I closed my eyes for a good minute, until the burning subsided, then I took a deep breath, donned my emotional armor and prepared to march into battle.

"ANNABELLE, COME IN. Close the door. Sit."

Jackie's lips curved down, even when she smiled. She looked at me, radiating a forced creepy-warmth that made me think of the funeral director who helped me make arrangements for my mother's burial last year. An I-can-be-as-empathetic-as-you-want-while-you're-giving-me-your-money kind of look, but it wasn't money Jackie wanted.

Oh, no, no, no. It was details. I sensed it the minute I walked into her office.

She folded her hands on her desk, cocked her head to one side and looked at me. "I just wanted to make sure you were okay."

Liar. She didn't give a damn about me. She wanted the inside scoop—big fat play-by-play juicy details of Blake's arrest—and she was willing to make nice to get me to spill my guts.

"I'm fine."

"I wanted you to know I'm here for you."

Right. How about a pay raise and a transfer to another department? She'd never been there for me one day in the entire time I'd worked with her. And she'd be there for me now for as long as it took to get the goods and have a titillating oh-my-God-can-you-believe-that lunch with Lolly, because Jackie King was that kind of person.

It took me years to understand what this woman was made of—because there was a time in the beginning when I allowed myself to be taken in by her—and I'd rather ask Blake to move back and bring his lovers home than confide in the Jackal.

"Is there anything else?" My words were icy, yet I managed to curve my lips upward; not into a smile of gratitude, but one that closed this too-personal vein of conversation.

Her funeral-director smile faded to a nearly expressionless mask of comprehension. She unfolded her hands and crossed her arms.

"There is something else," she said as I started to stand. "I don't like the direction you're taking with the new marketing campaign."

She opened the file on top of her desk and pulled out my

preliminary design for the new brochure—the design I hadn't shown to anyone yet. Where did she—

"Home is where the heart is...Heartfield Retirement Communities...?" She scrunched up her nose. "That's a little clichéd, don't you think? Come up with something else by this afternoon. We're way behind."

I glared at her in disbelief, trying to think of something to put her in her place, but as usual, my mind went blank with rage.

"Where did you get that?"

She wouldn't look me in the eye. "I peeked at your files while you were gone. After all, some of us had to work these past two weeks."

Some of us had to work? What the— Ohh, that martyr bitch. I was not out on a pleasure cruise and she knew it. She was just mad because I wouldn't talk to her about it. Even worse, she'd snooped through my office and taken one of my files.

"I need that back." I held out my hand and made a mental note to lock my desk from now on.

She closed the file and handed it to me, then started straightening the stacks of paper on her desk to avoid looking at me.

Coward.

Before I turned to leave, I stood there for a moment, towering over her, waiting to see how long it would take her to look at me. But she spun her chair around so that her back was to me and started typing on the computer perched on the credenza behind her desk.

She was a coward.

It dawned on me that the hardest parts of this crisis— telling Ben and going back to work—were over.

"You can leave now," she said without turning around.

Yes. Yes, I could. Perhaps it was time.

I SMELLED THE scent of gardenias before I saw the movement in my peripheral vision. My gaze snapped from my easel to the doorway and there stood Rita in the threshold of my studio. I nearly jumped out of my skin.

Yanking off my MP3 earphones, I said, "For God's sake, you scared me to death."

She smiled and waved a stack of transparency sleeves at me. "Sorry about that. I knocked, but you didn't answer. Your car's out front so I figured you were here—wait till you see what I have." She sang the words as she shut the door and dangled a plastic sheet between two fingers. "I think you'll forgive me when you see these."

"The slides of my work?"

She nodded. "They look fabulous."

I set down my brush, tossed the MP3 player on the table and met her halfway. She pulled a small slide viewer from her bag and popped in the first image. "Here, take a look."

The boxy magnifier lay cool and light in my palm. As I pressed the button and the light engaged, the oddest sensation enveloped me that my future sat in my hand.

It was crazy—merely wishful thinking that I could make a living doing what I love, especially now that life was so messed up with Blake and I was ensconced in the new marketing campaign at work. All the ideas I came up with after Jackie vetoed "Home is where the heart is…" seemed trite and hackneyed.

I breathed in the heady scent of oil paint—I was experimenting with a new medium. It comingled with the gardenia essence that had marked my sister's entrance. I peered into the light box and saw the lavender foxgloves I'd painted last week. The delicate purple blossoms dangled from the stems like glorious pieces of amethyst standing out bold against the rich emerald background.

My breath hitched. I loved foxgloves and these looked good, if I did say so myself. There was a whole planter full of them across the courtyard from my studio. The slide reminded me of how soothing it was to lose myself in the painting process.

If nothing else, at least I had my art. Something to call my own, something constant in this world of madness.

Rita handed me another slide, and then another until we established a silent rhythm of viewing and changing. My discard pile grew. Her handoff pile waned. We sank into the comfortable silence that sisters weren't compelled to fill.

When I'd viewed the last slide, Rita said, "They look good, huh?"

"Yeah, they do. Thanks for photographing them, Ri."

She nodded, chewing her bottom lip as if she had something else to say.

"What?" I asked, putting the slides back into their sleeves.

"Don't kill me, okay?"

"Why would I do that? You're not going to tell me you've slept with Blake, too, are you?"

She scrunched up her nose. "Ew. No."

"Oh, I forgot, you're not his type. You don't have a penis." My sister didn't laugh.

I held up the transparency of the foxgloves to the light and looked at it again, and when I looked over at her she shot me a weird sort-of smirk.

"You know it would be really good for you to get away

from here. Go somewhere fresh where the word *penis* doesn't automatically evoke nightmares."

"What are you talking about?"

I nudged the last slide into place, skimmed the sleeve to the center of the table and turned my attention to Rita.

"You know I shot two sets of slides, right?"

"No, I didn't know that. Is it a problem?"

"Only if you hate me for sending them to Paris…with the artist-in-residency application."

I crossed my arms in front of me. "You did what?"

"I sent your work—"

"I heard you the first time. I just— Rita, I can't go to Paris. I told you that. That's why I didn't send them myself."

She pulled out a stool and perched on the edge of it. "I know you did. Your mind is kind of on automatic pilot."

I threw up my hands. "Well, I'm kind of preoccupied trying to figure out how I'll take care of myself after I'm divorced. As of right now, that plan does not include moving to Paris for three months."

She looked disappointed and lowered her voice the way our mother used to when she tried to win us over to her way of thinking. "Why can't you see that would be the very best way for you to *take care of yourself?* A change of scenery, a change of career."

I hated this logical side of my sister. I walked over to my easel and picked up my brush. "Okay. Okay. Fine. I'm not going to fight with you over this. Thank you for thinking enough of my work…for thinking enough of me—"

The words burned the back of my throat, and made my eyes water. I swallowed hard.

"Thank you for doing that for me. But you know, you have to stop—"

I shook my head and stabbed my brush in the gob of cadmium yellow on my palette so hard the bristles flared.

"What were you going to say?"

Out of the corner of my eye I saw Rita stand.

"That I have to stop interfering with your cocoon-building? Well, I'm not going to, Anna."

I swiped a slash of yellow across the canvas. "This is not worth fighting over. Tell me where I can find a telephone number and I'll call and withdraw."

"Withdraw?" She laughed and stood behind me, but I didn't turn around. "If you feel the need to withdraw, then you think you might win a spot."

I shrugged, and dipped my brush into the black paint. "I don't. I don't know what I think. Just stop."

"Why would you not go for this?"

A funnel of fear rose and whirled around my stomach, but I ignored it, focusing instead on how I should've been mad at my sister for putting me in this position; for going against my wishes and entering my work in that contest. And I would've been mad at her if I hadn't been so numb. But despite the numbness, deep inside in the very center of my soul, down in the tiny little speck of heart that hadn't frozen solid, I knew she was right. Only, there was a wide cavern between what I should do and what I was capable of doing just then.

"Well, Ri, I'll add *painting in Paris* to my to-do list right behind finding a decent divorce attorney and securing another place to live because Blake is barking about putting the house on the market."

She clucked her tongue and sighed. Loudly. As if she'd just learned I'd pierced my nipples and planned to shave my hair into a Mohawk.

"Look, it's easy to judge when your ass isn't on the line," I said over my shoulder.

"Yeah, I guess so. And I guess it's easy to use Blake as an excuse for not living your life. As big a bastard as he is, he's not the one keeping you from Paris. You're doing this to yourself."

I whirled to face her. "That is so unfair."

"I know it is. The entire scenario that's brought you to this juncture sucks. But Anna, what would really be unfair is if you used this crap as an excuse to curl up into a little ball and fade away."

I turned back to my canvas before the first tears broke free and meandered down my cheek. I wiped them away with my sleeve.

"You blame Blake for taking away your life. Don't give him your soul."

I heard Rita's sandals clicking on the concrete floor, walking away from me. I wanted to shout at her, *If I'd wanted to go to Paris I would have sent in the damn application myself.* Well, okay, I wanted to go to Paris. Someday. Just not right now.

Arrgh. Too much. Too much. Too much was coming at me too fast.

"I have a challenge for you." My sister's voice was softer. I glanced over to see her hitching her purse up on her shoulder.

"Don't withdraw. Just let the application ride. Toss it up to fate and see what happens. Okay?"

FOUR

AFTER SIX WEEKS of having the bed to myself, I decided I liked sleeping alone. I woke up at six-thirty that particular morning smack-dab in the middle of the king-size bed. No one poked me in the back and told me to keep to my own side of the bed. No one elbowed me for inadvertently kicking him when I stretched out.

It was kind of nice, this newfound personal space. If I wanted to I could take my half out of the middle. It was a good thing, sleeping alone. I lay there and waited for reality to jolt my sleep-befuddled mind and expose the big dark hole that had taken up residence where my heart used to live.

I waited, but the familiar pain didn't stir.

A good sign.

Never mind that waking up was the easy part. Going to bed alone was still a challenge. After eighteen years of sleeping with the same person, I'd found comfort and reassurance in being able to reach out and touch Blake whenever I wanted—even though we rarely touched.

There was something in just knowing he was there, something comforting in the occasional brush of his foot against mine, no matter how unintentional; something in the rhythmic ebb and flow of his breathing; even something in his snoring, although until I discovered earplugs it used to drive me nuts.

I guess my newfound personal space—room to stretch—was one fringe benefit of living alone.

I spread my arms and legs to the four corners of the bed, just because I could, and moved them back and forth like a child making a snow angel. I reveled in the softness of the sheets under my body, and then lay spread-eagle for a moment, and listened to the quiet until the shrill ring of the telephone interrupted my calm.

"Annabelle, I didn't wake you, did I?"

Blake. My heart skipped a beat. "No, I'm up."

"Good. I wanted to catch you before you went to work."

His brisk tone hinted that I might not like what he had to say. But I waited, holding firmly to the old adage she who speaks first loses.

"Annabelle, are you there?"

"Yes."

"Listen, I've secured a Realtor, Jared Helmsley, to list the house for us."

"Excuse me?"

I sat up and swung my feet over the side of the bed.

Not quite a fighting stance, but at least I wasn't taking it lying down.

"I'd like to bring him by this afternoon to see the place so we can get it on the market as soon as possible."

"No."

"No?"

"No, Blake. I told you at least ten times already, I'm not ready to list the house." I'd just found an attorney to represent me and we hadn't gotten that far yet. "I'm not doing anything until I talk to my lawyer. So just cool your jets."

He heaved a sigh in my ear. A huffy, sissy sigh that irked me to the core. *Oh, be a man.*

He cleared his throat. "Annabelle, we're going to have to do something soon because my partner and I are starting our own business and we need the capital. I want my half."

Whoa! Wait a minute. Rewind. The implication propelled me to my feet.

"Your partner? Since when do you have a partner? You always worked better alone. That was the principal reason you broke off from the firm and started your own business."

He cleared his throat again. God, it sounded like a chain saw sputtering and dying in my ear, and it was getting on my nerves. I got to my feet and started downstairs to keep myself from snipping at him about the ugly noise. On the way down, I caught a glimpse of myself in the mirror on the stairs. Holding the phone with one hand, I tried to tame my wild curls, which sprang out in every direction and made me look like the Raisin Bran sun.

"Not that kind of partner. Jared Helmsley is my…um… my partner."

I braced myself on the kitchen counter. It took a few seconds before it sank in. "Oh my God, this Realtor is your boyfriend? Well, you certainly work fast. Tell me where you two met. No, wait—let me guess. Live Oak Park, right? Aww, I love hearing about blossoming romance."

Not.

"Don't be crass, Annabelle."

Don't be a pansy, Blake.

"I'm retiring from architecture, and Jared and I are starting an antiques business."

Antiques. How typical. My husband was a gay cliché.

So much for the small pleasures of sheet angels and taking my half out of the middle of the bed. I needed a good strong cup of joe after waking up to this. I picked up my French-press coffeepot, measured water from the refrigerator and poured it into the kettle to boil.

"Don't you think it's a risky move to cash it all in and set up shop with a guy you just met?"

"I've known Jared a while."

"Like six weeks a while? Or longer a while?"

"Longer."

"How much longer, Blake?" I dumped some French-roast beans into the grinder. I pressed the start button and the machine hummed and chomped; the rich, aromatic promise of a good cup of coffee lulled me into hoping the day would get better.

He planned it this way, didn't he? He had to have some sort of Annabelle Happiness Radar that sounded an alarm when my misery dropped to a bearable level. Because just when I started to feel okay he'd fling another doozy. I turned around and picked up the glass pot, getting it ready for the fresh coffee.

"Jared and I have been together for three years."

I caught the answer just as the grinder stopped. The press pot slipped from my hands and shattered on the slate floor.

"What?"

He'd been in a relationship for three years?

"Did something break?" Blake's voice sounded miles away. But as far as I was concerned, if he were in China it wouldn't have been far enough.

Oh my God! Where was I when all this was going on? How could I have missed this? How could I have been so pathetically ignorant?

My free hand flew to my mouth, as much to stop the bile that was making its way up my esophagus as to contain my shock. My heart beat as if it were trying to break free from my chest.

As I moved around the glass shards, trying not to step on them with bare feet, I wished my heart would just break free and fall into the glass so that I could give it a decent burial. Like the coffeepot, it, too, was shattered beyond repair.

"Annabelle? Are you there?"

When he got arrested, not only was he cheating on me, he was cheating on the one with whom he was cheating on me. Obviously Jared was a little more forgiving than I was.

I wanted to scream at Blake for being so callous, for making a mockery out of our marriage, for making me feel so utterly, disgustingly unlovable. For making me feel as if this were somehow my fault.

"Yeah, I'm here. But you know what? I have to get ready for work. No Realtors, Blake. Just—just go away."

I NEVER GOT my coffee.

I didn't have time to tame my hair into my old reliable chignon and stop at Starbucks and get to work in time for the big unveiling of our new marketing campaign to the Heartfield brass. It was the trial presentation before we took our "new image" to the board of directors. I couldn't don my game face with wild hair.

So with or without coffee, life marched on.

For that matter, with or without Blake, with or without boyfriends and antiques businesses and whatever else Blake planned to spring on me around the next bend, I had to put it all aside and go to work.

Could life get any worse?

Oh, yes, it could.

Jackie had choreographed a boardroom extravaganza that rivaled Ringling Brothers. I'd spent the past two days assembling goodie bags with T-shirts, hats, key chains, pens and Post-it notes bearing the new slogan "Cutting-edge living for today's savvy senior" for Jackie to give to the Heartfield muckety-mucks after they finished telling her how brilliant she was for reinventing their image. She thought up the "cutting-edge" bit all by herself in a fit of martyrdom because "it reflects the new technology-minded older adult."

Because it provided the perfect opportunity for her to spend the better part of a week muttering about how she "had to do everything…" and how "the ineptitude in the office was killing her…" *Blah. Blah. Blah.*

I was surprised she trusted me to assist Lolly in handing out goodie bags and playing my role in the show: As she gave the preamble to the unveiling, Lolly and I were to put on sunglasses and walk up and stand on either side of the screen on to which Jackie would project her PowerPoint presentation. When she gave the cue, we were to whip off our jackets to reveal T-shirts with the new logo at the precise moment she flashed the new slogan on the big screen.

It was the cheesiest, most demeaning assignment she'd

ever given me, but I guess Jackie got paid the big bucks to discern the gold in what we minions mistook for trash.

When I sat down at my desk, I hadn't even had a chance to turn on my computer, much less change into the T-shirt hanging in the closet or transport the goodie bags to the conference room before my phone rang. The extension on the LCD screen showed the conference-room extension.

"For God's sake, I'm coming. Chill out," I muttered to the phone before lifting the receiver.

"Hello?"

"Change of plans," Lolly hissed. "Bergdorf wants to meet with us before we unveil the new marketing campaign. Jackie and I are in the conference room. Forget the bags. Forget the shirt. Major change of tactic."

She slammed down the phone.

Did that mean I should meet *them* in the conference room or was this a Jackie and Lolly production?

I should be so lucky.

I decided not to leave it up to chance and checked to see if Jackie had a new assignment for me that Lolly forgot to deliver.

If worse came to worst and I wasn't invited, I could always seize the opportunity to make myself a cup of English Breakfast.

Perhaps Jackie had come to her senses overnight and realized what an ass she'd make of herself and us by having us flash the brass?

Better not get my hopes up until I found out what was going on. We still had a good hour before the scheduled meeting with the rest of them. Best not to celebrate prematurely.

When I walked into the conference room, Jackie was hunched over her laptop. She didn't even turn around when I opened the door. She just kept typing like a maniac.

Lolly was setting out Danish and doughnuts. The coffee was brewing. God, it smelled wonderful, even for office coffee.

Despite the hold on the goodie bags and T-shirts, everything seemed to be forging ahead according to the original plan. Then I caught sight of Lolly's harried expression. She bustled around setting out cups and napkins wearing a grim look. Then Jackie turned around. She looked as if she'd been up all night.

"Could someone tell me what's going on?" I said.

Jackie and Lolly exchanged a glance, and Bergdorf walked in looking none too pleased.

Something was up.

I took a seat and folded my hands in my lap, eager to see what kind of mess Jackie had gotten herself into and better yet, how she was going to dig herself out.

"This better be good," he said. "Because based on what you showed me last night, the other campaign was a disaster. Maybe we should just reschedule the meeting and rethink this—"

"No!" Jackie's eyes flashed, but in an instant she composed herself. "Mr. Bergdorf, I was up all night putting this new angle together. I think you'll like it. The marketing department came up with the cutting-edge campaign…"

What? The marketing department did *not!*

"…and while I knew it was a complete departure from what we've done in the past. Well, let's just say, I now understand your concerns, and I think I've come up with a new campaign that will knock your socks off. Sit down and let me show you."

He glanced at his watch. "You have exactly two minutes."

"I only need one minute of your time." The usual superior self-assurance returned to Jackie's demeanor. But I thought I saw tiny beads of sweat glistening on her upper lip. As she turned toward her computer, she swiped her hand across her mouth and signaled Lolly to dim the lights.

Bergdorf pulled out a chair and sat down at the table, and Jackie started a spiel about how in recent years there'd been a return to family values. "Even though family values is a trendy buzzword—"

Bergdorf cut her off. "Can't you understand, our market share does not relate to trendy buzzwords?" He started to stand.

"Mr. Bergdorf, just hear me out, please. Actually, I think my new campaign will say it better than I can."

She pushed a button and the slogan "Home is where the heart is…Heartfield Retirement Communities" appeared on the screen.

"I HATE HER."

I said the words aloud as I steered the car onto Orange Avenue, but saying them only made me more furious.

She stole my slogan.

She stood right there and took credit for my— What did she call it? My *clichéd* slogan.

Of course Bergdorf loved it and fell all over himself congratulating her on the "brilliant comeback."

Jackie stood there soaking it up, a couple of crooked, yellow teeth flashing through her upside-down smile.

Shark.

Jackal.

Bitch.

She wouldn't even look at me.

No wonder she didn't mention my absence from the big unveiling, which I suppose went off without a hitch.

No way I was going to sit there and watch her take credit for something she'd loathed four weeks ago. So I went in my office and stayed there with the door shut all day. The only time I ventured out was to get my lunch.

She knew what she did because not once did she bother me. Not once did she try to explain.

"Annabelle, I was so frantic to prove to him I'm not a total loser that I inadvertently stole your idea. Come on, let's go tell Bergdorf that you're the author of the Home is where the heart is *slogan."*

I should have gone to the big meeting. I should have stood up and screamed "This is my idea and that conniving bitch is taking all the credit." Then I would have handed out all the goodie bags I'd wasted my time putting together so the CEO and the CFO and all the other acronyms in the room could see how much of the stockholders' money their talented little Jackal had wasted on all that useless collateral.

No, on second thought, I wouldn't have handed out the goodie bags. I would have dumped each one in the middle of the boardroom table and thrown all the notepads and pens and key chains up in the air like a bunch of trash confetti.

I would have stood in the middle of the table and pointed to the mess and said, "Hers. This is hers."

Then pointed to the big screen and said, "Mine.

"Hers. Mine."

Okay, so I wouldn't have really done it. But God, it would have felt good.

I was so sick of being crapped on.

I did my best, did what I was supposed to do, and for

what? So my husband could leave me for another man and my boss could take cheap shots at me and then take credit for the very idea she'd belittled.

I was done.

I was over it.

If I could divorce my husband, I could—

I couldn't leave my job.

Not in a huff.

Once again, the reality hit me like a wall of water. I depended on this job I hated so much. Even if I left I needed the reference. I mean, after twelve years, I couldn't just walk away with nothing.

The only thing I could do was start searching for a new job. But where?

I was forty-one years old. Not exactly at the top of my profession. Who was going to hire me for the money I needed?

I needed...

I needed coffee, the whole day was so overwhelming. I drove to Starbucks and pulled into the drive-thru line. It was a long line. At five-fifteen you'd think everyone in the world would have had their fill of coffee for the day.

Okay, move aside, people. This is my first cup of the day and if I don't get it soon, I'm liable to take someone's head off.

The line moved at a snail's pace but finally, it was my turn to order.

"What'll you have?"

I'd planned on ordering my usual nonfat, grande cappuccino. But it was after five. I decided it would be prudent to order decaf unless I wanted to be up all night on a caffeine buzz walking the floor, brooding over what had happened.

But something sweet sounded tempting, too.

A Valencia mocha?

A white-chocolate mocha? Ooooh, that sounded good.

But what about something cool since it was so warm outside? Yum—a mint-chocolate frappuccino. Mmm, it sounded like a dessert. But then again the—

"I haven't got all day, lady. Are you going to order or not?" The man's voice crackled through the drive-thru speaker. I blinked and waited for a laugh, a "No, seriously, take your time, I'm here to serve you when you're ready," qualifier— anything to prove the guy working the coffee line wasn't as rude as he sounded.

Stern silence followed his upbraiding.

He didn't have all day? What? Did he have better things to do? Was I keeping him from an important engagement? From a baristas' summit on world peace?

I could see it—coffee brewers of the world unite to further world peace.

Well, he could start practicing right away by changing his attitude. I didn't want to sit in this line shelling out four dollars and fifty cents for a cup of coffee any more, it seemed, than he wanted to take my order.

If I wanted coffee, I had no choice.

I deserved something to soothe my soul.

"Hello? I'm ready to order. Are you there?"

"Obviously. I have nothing better to do than wait for you."

Was this a joke? Hot irritation roiled through my veins. I wondered if I should warn him that I had a history of using coffeepots as weapons when pushed.

Instead, I took a deep breath, ordered a venti, nonfat, decaffeinated Valencia mocha and inched my car up to the drive-thru window.

Snippy Starbucks Man, who turned out to be a fairly decent-looking middle-aged guy despite the deep frown lines etched onto his forehead, greeted me with a frown and told me how much I owed. He thrust my large Valencia mocha at me, then stuck his hand out for the money.

What is your problem?

I wondered if somehow I'd been transported to a world where all men hated women.

"Come on, come on, come on, already. Just pay me and move along." He spat the words, simultaneously snapping his fingers.

I think someone is a little caffeine cranky. He obviously had his coffee today.

I knew how to fix his wagon. I grabbed a handful of pennies from the car ashtray, matched his glare and proceeded to count the copper coins into his hand.

…ten…eleven…twelve…

He started muttering under his breath. The only words I caught were *lazy bitch* and *drive-thru*.

I stopped counting and looked up at his lined face. "Excuse me? Did you say something?"

His brows shot up. "I said it astounds me how lazy people are. They can't even brew themselves a cup of coffee much less drag their fat asses out of their cars to get it."

I opened my mouth to say something, but I was so appalled I couldn't form the appropriate words to do so. Finally, I resorted to the tried-and-true, "That was a very mean thing to say. Because we drag our fat asses here, you have a job. Why are you so angry?"

He rolled his eyes and something inside of me snapped.

"I'd like to talk to your manager."

He let loose a bitter laugh. "So would I, lady, but she's off today."

He turned over his hand and the twelve pennies fell to the pavement. Then he waved me through.

"I quit. So don't waste your time getting in a tizzy and writing a letter. Just take your coffee and go."

He stepped back. The drive-thru window slid closed like a final curtain, and I realized, with a heavy heart, I understood how a person could go through so much crap he became so bitter he lashed out at strangers.

The one thing Snippy Starbucks Man had over me was the courage to leave a place that made him miserable rather than sticking around waiting for people to throw hot coffee in his face.

No matter how much Blake put me through or how many times Jackie double-crossed me, I would not let them make me as bitter as Snippy Starbucks Man. Unless I intended to do something about it.

I took my twelve-cent venti, skinny, decaffeinated Valencia mocha and drove home, thinking that maybe later I'd go to the mall and get another press pot. Perhaps I'd get an espresso machine, too. My reward for not standing in the middle of the boardroom table throwing Jackie's useless collateral in the air like confetti.

THE PHONE WAS ringing when I walked in the door.

I speculated it would be Rita and started formulating excuses for not seeing her tonight without hurting her feelings. She had been so good to me, but I just needed a little alone time.

All I wanted to do was savor my coffee while I read the

newspaper that I didn't get to read this morning. I wanted to focus on stories about people all over the world who were worse off than I was and then sit back and count my blessings that even though life seemed pretty bleak, at least Ben was well, my car ran, I didn't have cancer and on and on until my list of how much worse life could be was so much longer than my current shit-list that my problems seemed to amount to nothing.

I contemplated letting the answering machine pick up, but decided that since I'd have to call my sister back it was better to beg off now.

"Hello?"

"*Allô?* May I speak to Annabelle Essex, please?"

The heavily accented voice on the other end of the line was most definitely not Rita—unless she'd suddenly become a Frenchman.

"This is she."

"Ahh, *oui,* this is Jacques Jauvert phoning from the Delacroix International Exchange Centre in Paris, France."

My heart skipped a beat.

"Congratulations, madame, I am calling to offer you a three-month artist residency at the Delacroix Centre."

AFTER I HUNG UP, I stood in the kitchen shaking. I vaguely remembered heavily accented mention of a plane ticket and paperwork to arrive within the week. He asked if I had a passport. Yes. Once I had a pipe dream that if I got mine, perhaps it would move Blake to get his and we would visit Paris together.

Key word: *pipe dream.* Blake had no use for the French and no intention of ever going to Paris.

I didn't tell Jacques Jauvert that story. I completely forgot to tell him I couldn't accept the residency.

Sure, it was nice to have my talent recognized.

Even better to have been given the nod by someone who knew something about art.

A French someone, no less.

All because of Rita. I didn't know whether to hug her or never speak to her again for getting me into this mess. I had to admit, it was a pretty flattering mess in which to find myself.

I picked up the phone and dialed her number, but hung up on the second ring. She'd be all over this. She'd come over and start packing for me.

I stood in the middle of the kitchen holding the cordless phone in my hand. The setting sun painted the canvas of sky framed by the window over the sink in hues of red, blue and gold. Inside, the room grew darker and shadows crept over the walls.

This was it. This was my ticket out of town. So why couldn't I—

The phone rang and my scream could have cracked the window. I almost dropped the receiver, but instead I managed to push the talk button and press the phone to my ear.

Maybe Jacques Jauvert was calling back. If so, I'd tell him thanks, but—

"Hello?"

"Anna?" Oh, no. It was Rita. "Did you just call?"

Damn. Caller ID.

"I did."

"Oh, we must have gotten disconnected."

"Something like that."

"What's up?"

I swallowed and tried to think of a last-ditch diversion. Finally I decided to tell her the news.

"You'll never believe what just happened."

"What? Are you okay?"

"I'm not sure. I just got a call from Paris."

"Paris? Who— Oh my God, Paris! The residency? Did you get it? Tell me you got it?"

"They offered it to me."

"Oh, wow! Oh, fabulous. When do we leave? I'm going with you. For a week, anyway. We'll go over early and do all the touristy stuff. My assistant, Tatia, knows this guy who rents his apartment by the week. I'll see if it's available."

She paused as if waiting for me to start singing the "Hallelujah Chorus."

"Rita, I don't see how I can go."

"I'll go with you and show you. I'll even come over and help you pack."

My palm clutching the receiver grew damp at the thought. Like I could just drop everything to jet off to Paris. If only it were that simple. Just pack a bag, jump on a plane and go.

"What about Ben?" I asked.

"What about him?"

"What will he do with his mother half a world away? He still comes home on school breaks and he's been calling home once a week to make sure I was doing okay since Blake moved out. We'd spend a fortune in overseas calls."

"He can come visit you once school's out. What college kid doesn't want to go to Europe?"

She was making too much sense.

"But what about the house? I've kind of been holding out on Blake, fighting him about putting it on the market."

"So throw him a bone. It won't kill you to let him have his way. It'll be more money for you to spend on calling Ben while you're in *Par-ree.*"

Oh, for God's sake.

She was right. If I sold the house, I could pay off what little credit-card debt I had and bank the rest of the money. The mortgage and all the bills associated with it were the mainstay of my money worries. My car was paid for. Other than my studio, the house and half of Ben's tuition, I really didn't have any expenses.

Rita wasn't making this very easy by overcoming all my objections. What kind of sister was she? The worst part was she was making me feel like I *could* do this. Like all the planets were lining up to send me across the ocean.

"You should have been a salesperson," I said. "You're selling me on the idea, making it way too doable."

She laughed. "This is so doable you *have to* do it."

The sun dropped down below the horizon, leaving me standing in the dark.

"And what about my job?" I said. "What am I supposed to do in three months when the Parisian love affair ends and the government sends me packing back to the United States? What then, Rita? No job, dwindling savings, slightly better grasp of the French language—at least I hope I come away with that. Which reminds me, I don't even speak the language."

A bitter taste filled my mouth, but it wasn't caused by the language barrier. It was the memory of Jackie, the idea-stealing bitch, smiling her self-satisfied Jackal grin. "I won't even waste my breath on that one," Rita said. "You can move in with Fred and me when you get back."

"Oh, I'm sure he'd love that. There's a limit to in-law tolerance."

"I'm serious, Anna. If you give up Paris to keep that job you've hated for eleven-and-a-half of the twelve years you've held it, you deserve to be miserable."

Oh my God. She was right. "I deserved that."

"Perhaps, but you don't deserve to be miserable. That's what I've been trying to make you see. This is all I can do, Anna. You have to decide you want to be happy."

Ouch. I deserved that, too. Even though she didn't say it, there was something in her voice that said she'd propped me up as long as she could. It was time I started taking steps on my own.

Panic whirred inside my head, screaming things such as, *What if you fail? Locking yourself away in your studio is so safe; you don't have to put yourself to the test, put your "talent" on the line. What if you get to Paris and prove you're a great big failure? What if you go all that way and they don't want you anymore, just like Blake didn't?*

Snippy Starbucks Man's irritated visage superimposed itself over my mental picture of the Jackal baring her teeth. He frowned. *They lay Paris in your lap and you have to think about it? Oh, just kill me now.* He disappeared behind the sliding drive-thru window.

"Ri, I'm going to call Ben and talk to him about it. Let me call you back."

"You'd better."

BEN HAD TWO simple sentences for me:

"Are you crazy, Mom? Go for it."

Go for it.

I was finally going *Faraway*.

I was going to Paris.

THE NEXT THREE weeks were a whirlwind of packing, listing the house, putting the majority of my worldly possessions in storage, giving Rita temporary custody of the furniture our mother had given me, deciding what to take, what to trash, what to store and what to give away.

What does one pack for three months in Paris?

Starting over was like a psych evaluation if you really think about it: When it comes to "baggage" which do you choose:

A) Nothing. I'll start fresh when I get there.

B) Pack a single suitcase.

C) Take all your excess baggage with you.

I'd have to think long and hard about that one.

Blake's elation over my agreeing to list the house was short-lived due to my motivation.

"Annabelle, you can't just jet off to Paris."

"Yes, I can, and that's exactly what I'm going to do."

"Our divorce isn't final. Your taking off for three months will cause major problems with the proceedings."

"Well, that's not my problem. I guess you'll just have to wait, won't you? Your change of lifestyle has caused our family *major problems.* So I guess it's my turn, isn't it?

"I leave three weeks from today and I'm on a tight schedule to get everything done. When can you come over and take the furniture you want?"

"I thought you wanted to wait and go through the attorney?"

"As far as I'm concerned, you can have anything that didn't belong to my mother."

RITA CALLED ME before I left for work to tell me her friend's fashionable, sixth arrondissement, Saint-Germain-des-Prés apartment was available. The way everything was falling into place made it so much more satisfying to give Jackie notice.

When I walked in, her door was closed, so I told Lolly I needed to talk to Jackie right away.

"She's got meetings most of the day."

"I need one minute."

Lolly smirked. "I'll let her know."

I didn't trust her. I left my office door open so I could hear when Jackie came up for air.

It didn't take long. After about ten minutes of waiting, her door opened and her loud voice rang out over the office telling Bergdorf how she planned to implement the new marketing plan.

It still made my insides boil, but I was beginning to care a little less that she claimed credit.

She could have it.

I had Paris.

I walked up to her and Bergdorf in the hall and stood looking at them until the Jackal frowned at me. "Do you need something, Annabelle?"

"Yes, I need to meet with you this morning."

"Sorry, no can do. I'm booked all day. How about first thing tomorrow?"

"No, how about now? I quit."

FIVE

THREE WEEKS LATER, our plane landed in Paris at seven-thirty in the morning. By the time we wound our way through the Plexiglas tubes of Charles de Gaulle airport, went through customs and claimed our bags, it was close to nine o'clock.

François, the driver Rita hired, stood in the airport atrium holding a sign that said, Essex and Roberts.

I was exhausted and overwhelmed but grateful Rita had the foresight to arrange for a car to pick us up. Nothing like traveling with a woman of the world to smooth out some of the bumps for a first-timer.

The first time she and Fred went to Paris they made the mistake of schlepping their luggage from the airport to the train to the metro, finally walking another seven blocks before they reached their hotel.

Never again, she insisted.

I could see why. It may have been nine in the morning here, but as I settled into the black leather seat of the sedan, my inner clock screamed, *Turn off the damn sun!* My body was still on eastern standard time, where the six-hour time difference translated to the middle of the night. I hadn't slept in more than twenty-four hours.

On the flight over, I dozed in a fitful half slumber. One time I dreamt I was chasing Blake, who kept running from me, just out of my reach, occasionally glancing back with a horrified expression on his face. I awoke shaking. The next time I drifted off, I dreamt I was lost in Paris, which had become a giant maze. I wandered in vain, searching, but not finding whatever—or whoever—it was I looked for.

I didn't bother to tell Rita about the dreams because they were so painfully self-explanatory. Besides, she seemed to be resting pretty well, snuggled up in her afghan with her eye mask firmly in place like a Do Not Disturb sign.

At one point her mouth gaped wide open and a line of drool trickled down her chin. I dabbed it away with a tissue.

My only solace was at least I didn't have my typical dream in which I realized I'd forgotten my passport as I tried to board the plane. Even if the new dreams were disagreeable, perhaps they evidenced I was breaking old patterns.

Safely on the ground, I was enthralled with my first glimpses of France, despite my grogginess. It wasn't quite what I'd expected. I guess I thought I'd step from the plane straight into the heart of Paris.

Au contraire.

Charles de Gaulle was about thirty kilometers outside of the city, a good forty-five-minute commute during the morning rush hour, down a highway that shot through an industrial area, gradually giving way to the suburbs, until

Paris appeared, confident and proud, like an elegant lady. The buildings seemed to emerge from the River Seine like Botticelli's *Birth of Venus* rising out of the sea.

I waited for the scene to take my breath away, but lack of rest coupled with the excitement and adrenaline coursing through my veins blended to create a hyperalert awareness of everything around me.

The light seemed brighter, the shadows deeper and more symphonic. The trees and grass looked a vivid, almost velvet green. I couldn't take it all in fast enough to satisfy my senses.

I was the worst kind of tourist, pointing and oohing and aahing over buildings and bridges, shops and flower stands. Everywhere I looked something new and exciting caught my eye. I saw François, who claimed not to speak a lick of English, stealing glances at me in the rearview mirror.

I didn't care.

"Look, Rita." I gasped and grabbed her arm, pointing to a great white domed building glowing high atop a hill. Set against the clear blue sky, it looked like a culinary confection or perhaps a sleeping giant overlooking the city. "What is that?"

"Sacré-Coeur basilica. It's up there in Montmartre, where all the artists and the windmills are."

We traveled a little farther and the City of Light whizzed by in a blur of tall, tin-roofed buildings, fountains and sculptures.

"Le Musée du Louvre." François gestured to a massive sand-colored building. It looked like faded gold in the morning light. I turned around in my seat to see it as we pulled onto a bridge and crossed from the right bank to the left.

"Le Pont Neuf," François said.

"He's telling us the name of this bridge is the Pont Neuf. It's the oldest bridge in the city," Rita said.

Finally, the driver stopped in front of a crêpe stand set into a storefront. It was part of a long row of businesses in this ancient-looking building that ran the length of the city block, in the fashionable Saint-Germain-des-Prés district.

Crêpes, the Parisian fast food.

He killed the engine. *"Voilà."*

My sister said something to him in broken French I could not understand. Then she turned to me. "This is it. The apartment's on the fourth floor."

I got out and looked up, counting up five sets of windows. The French count the ground floor as zero, and what we would consider the second floor they call the first floor.

So much to take in. So much to learn if I was going to live here for three months. The thought made my stomach dip. I glanced at the signs and advertisements, most of which only had a word or two I could actually read.

So much for four years of studying the language in college and the conversational French class I took in the weeks preceding the trip.

That was what it felt like to be illiterate.

A tall young woman knocked into me as she passed on the sidewalk. She turned and scowled.

"Pardonnez-moi," she said.

"I'm sorry."

She tossed her head and muttered, *"Américaine."*

Welcome to Paris.

I don't know why her disdain bothered me, but it did. All

that was bright, shiny, new and hopeful about this strange place seemed remote.

In an instant my anticipation was gone, and so was the car and François. He pulled away, leaving Rita and me in the midst of the busy sidewalk with our bags at our feet and our vulnerability on our sleeves.

My vulnerability, I should say. My sister fit in like part of the ancient rue de l'Ancienne Comédie woodwork. Cars whizzed by and most everyone else moved with purpose, on their way to important places, I presumed, judging by the rush.

The overwhelming sensation of being alone in a crowd—alone in a foreign country—engulfed me, and I had a moment where I wanted to hit the rewind button and retrace my steps—back to the car, wind back the highway with the forty-five-minute journey to the airport, over the ocean back home again. Only, where I came from, there was no home.

Rita glanced at the piece of paper then back at the building.

It was actually a series of several buildings built one into the next so they formed a continuous row that stretched all the way down to the Boulevard Saint Germain owning the street; the four-, five- and six-story structures had magnificent windows in neat rows across the face. Some were adorned with shutters, others sported window boxes with red geraniums vivid against the white background; still others boasted stately grillwork that lent the humble casements the air of aristocratic balconies.

My God, this place was magnificent. And ancient. When Rita told me we were staying here I researched it and found out that most of the buildings on this famous street were built in the seventeenth century.

I tried to replace the cloaking wistfulness with a reverent awe for the history standing right in front of me, right under my feet. To think of all the wars and upheaval this place had lived through. In comparison, my problems were grains of sand on an antediluvian beach of change.

The thought humbled me.

I took a deep breath and turned a slow circle, trying to take it all in. Across the street I spied a Nicolas wine shop with a red awning that touted *Le spécialiste du vin, depuis 1822;* a twenty-four-hour bread and croissants shop called Boulangerie de l'Ancienne Comédie; a hotel; a café with tables lining the sidewalk. Right next door was a…pizza shop? Okay, Parisian pizza. I suppose the French like pizza, too.

A sign hanging two doors down from where we stood gave me pause: Le Procope.

A chill ran through me.

Voilà—the world's first coffeehouse, where it was rumored Voltaire drank forty cups a day and Napoleon left his hat as security as he went scrounging for money to pay his bill. In addition to them, a virtual who's who of historical, literary, artistic and political figures, the likes of Balzac, Robespierre, Victor Hugo and even Benjamin Franklin, purportedly hung out there in their respective times over the past four hundred years.

It was too romantic, all that history.

I took another deep breath and let it all sink in.

I was in *Paris.*

Oh my God. I was *really* in Paris.

I waited for the rapture I'd always known I'd feel once I

got here to unfurl inside me. But nothing happened. Just traces of the lingering wistfulness I'd felt since I'd disembarked.

Must be jet lag.

"I'm guessing this is the way in?" Rita, still worrying the folder with her notes, gestured to an unobtrusive brown door with a gold number six above it. The entrance faded into the shadows, overwhelmed by the red-canopied crêpe stand that stood next door. Funny, I noticed the wine shop and the pizzeria, but number six rue de l'Ancienne Comédie slipped by until Rita pointed it out. Perhaps my oblivion to subtle detail had caused me to miss the telltale signs of Blake's secret life. Once my eyes were opened, they were there, right in front of my face, just like this plain brown door.

My stomach clenched; my heart weighed heavy and full, like all the pain would spill out of me onto the street.

"Must be it."

Well, I would just have to be more observant while I was in Paris. Here, I would learn to *really see* the details around me instead of wandering absently from place to place looking but not really seeing.

As we grabbed our bags and approached the building, I tried to see past the obvious to the sound of the morning traffic; to the way the face of the building lay in shadow as the sun crouched in the eastern sky. I inhaled the interesting mélange of aromas: savory crêpes, rich coffee, cigarette smoke and—car exhaust.

Not very romantic.

But it was real.

I guess one didn't step outside and think, *Lovely smell of traffic fumes this morning.* Okay, maybe that was taking detail a little too far. But how about the small group of guys who looked to be in their mid to late twenties loitering around the *crêperie?* Five of them, I counted, all talking at once, two sitting, three standing, the Frenchness of them claiming tangible space.

They seemed to be the only people in all of Paris, other than Rita and me, who were standing still. They weren't eating, didn't appear to be working. While they didn't look like a gang of hoodlums—this was Saint-Germain-des-Prés after all, it wasn't a ghetto—I wondered why they'd gathered there at this hour.

Perhaps I was distracted by the melodious combination of deep, accented man-voices; perhaps I was tired from the trip and intoxicated by all the different sights, sounds, smells and emotions, but I stared a little too long, until I saw one of the men staring back at me.

I looked away and tucked a flyaway, auburn curl that had escaped my chignon behind my ear as Rita tried for the third time to enter the correct door code.

The young guy who'd caught me gawking unfolded himself from a chair, did a smooth side step past his buddies, punched in the code for her and held open the door.

Oh, good, the entire neighborhood knew the code. That was comforting.

"Merci beaucoup, monsieur," Rita sang, managing to sound confident and even a tad flirty as she hoisted her bag into the dimly lit vestibule.

The young man was tall and rail thin with short, light brown hair. He nodded and swept his hand, inviting me to enter. As his friends murmured in French and laughed in the background, the guy's gaze didn't waver from mine.

I felt so painfully American, it couldn't have been more apparent if I had a big sign above my head with neon arrows pointing down at me. I managed to stammer, *"Merci."*

He smiled again. *"Avec plaisir."*

The words rolled off his tongue and a shiver skittered through my body. I'd always been a sucker for a man with an accent. Especially a French accent.

He quirked a brow, and I realized he probably wasn't much older than Ben. Perhaps six or eight years. I blinked to free myself from his lingering gaze and joined Rita who stood by a broom-closet-size lift.

The entrance hall smelled musty and old, the ancient odor merging with the men's cigarettes and the *crêperie's* kitchen smells.

"There's no way we'll both fit in here with all our luggage," she said. "We'll have to go up one at a time—or one of us could use the stairs."

She pushed the elevator call button. "The owner is supposed to be waiting for us in the apartment. Why don't I go up first and talk to him."

Fine with me. Her grasp of the language was far better than mine. The lift bell announced its arrival.

"Do you want to leave your suitcase here with me?"

Rita stepped through the doors and wheeled her obscenely small bag in next to her. "No, mine will fit." She motioned to my three suitcases. "But you might have to haul the green monster and family up five flights of steps. I don't know how you're going to fit it all in here."

The elevator door barely cleared her nose as it slid shut. I took off my trench coat and protectively regarded the "green monster," as Rita so fondly deemed my oversize floral suitcase.

"You could pack a family of four and their belongings in that thing," Rita had said yesterday as she watched her husband, Fred, nearly give himself a hernia hoisting my bag into the trunk before we took off for the airport.

"Since I'm staying so long I have a valid excuse for overpacking. Be quiet and let me enjoy the moment."

"Touché," she'd replied.

With that justification smugly in mind, I gathered my luggage, scooting my other bags closer to the green monster and arranging them in ascending order of height. Since Rita had only packed one bag, I took the opportunity to bring a total of three: my two permitted bags and a third, which Rita checked for me.

Why not? Only an idiot wouldn't take maximum advantage of the baggage rule. But now that I was here, I did wonder how in heck I'd get the excess baggage upstairs.

"*Madame,* you are arriving in Paris this morning?"

The deep voice startled me. I turned and saw the guy who'd opened the door for us lingering in the threshold. Seeing him there made me stand a little straighter and finger the pearls hanging down on my cream cashmere sweater. "*Oui.*" I don't know why I answered him in French because it only invited dialogue in his language—a language I didn't speak well enough to carry on a conversation.

"*Vous restez ici combien de temps?*" he said.

I gave him my best blank stare and he answered, "*Vous comprenez?*"

I understood his question well enough to know he'd asked if I understood what he said. It took a moment, but I recalled the appropriate answer.

"*Non, je ne comprends pas. Je suis Américaine.*"

"You speak a little French?" It was hard to explain the expression on his face—not a smile, but not quite a frown—as his gaze raked over my body.

"Just enough to get into trouble."

His gaze snapped back to mine and he arched a brow. I didn't mean to say the words aloud, and I bit my bottom lip to keep anything else from inadvertently slipping out.

A smirk teased up the left side of his mouth. "You like trouble, no?"

I suppose a more vulnerable woman might have been uncomfortable finding herself alone with him in the dim, dank entryway. But his words weren't threatening. *Au contraire.* How could they be, floating out there on such a flirtatious note?

The faint echo of the lift bell reverberated, announcing Rita's arrival five floors up. I glanced at the staircase and tightened my grip on the green monster.

"My name is Étienne. Are you married?" He stood much too close to me and offered his hand. Still gripping the handle of my suitcase, I put my right hand in his.

"*Je m'appelle* Annabelle." Reflexively, my thumb rubbed the bare space where my wedding ring used to be. Was I married? Good question. Technically, yes. Emotionally—

"No. I'm not married."

"*Bienvenu,* Annabelle." He pulled my hand to his lips, glancing up at me as he brushed an air kiss over my knuckles. He was cute. Long black lashes fringing caramel-colored eyes. But, my God, he was a baby. How would I feel if some middle-aged soon-to-be-divorcée was picking up Ben?

"You are very beautiful," he said.

Oh, my…and quite charming for a boy half my age. Okay, perhaps not *quite* half my age, but close enough.

I suppose a more vulnerable woman might have been tempted to believe he actually *was* flirting with her. And technically, I guess he was—he was French after all.

According to everything I'd read, flirtation was France's second national language. But I was old enough and wise enough to step back and assess the situation: opportunistic, flirty French boy hangs out at the entrance of building containing short-term rentals. He spies two middle-aged—obviously American—women arriving alone in a foreign country...

It smacked of *Shirley Valentine*. You know, that movie in which Shirley, a slightly long-in-the-tooth housewife, gets fed up with her mundane life and takes herself on vacation to Greece? A handsome local sweeps in and seduces her. Poor unsuspecting Shirley realizes too late that her oh-so-romantic Casanova is actually a well-rehearsed cad who uses the same tired lines on the steady stream of middle-aged malcontents who flock to the island looking for love in all the wrong places.

Well, Flirty French Boy, I am not Shirley Valentine.

FLIRTY FRENCH BOY offered to haul the green monster up the spiral staircase after my unsuccessful attempt to cram everything and myself into the lift. With his offer, visions of Shirley V. evaporated and paranoia set in: horror visions of Flirty French Boy tucking me safely inside the coffin-size lift and disappearing into the streets with my worldly possessions.

"Thank you for offering, but I can manage."

I lifted the smallest bag onto the green monster. I could lug one in each hand. If I went slowly, it would work.

Looking up the stairs to the first landing made me wish I'd told Rita I'd send my bags up after her. She could have taken them off the elevator.

Oh, well. Schlepping was better than standing there doing nothing.

As I mounted the third step and pulled the bags up behind me, the small one slid off the larger one.

Étienne caught the handle and jerked it upright in one motion. "Let me help you. I will not run away with your cases, if that is what worries you."

Well…don't be so pushy.

My cheeks warmed—from frustration or embarrassment? Perhaps both. I read once that some rapists ingratiate themselves to victims before striking. They offered help or some other random act of kindness and made the victim feel like an ingrate for refusing.

He was already ahead of me and halfway up to the first landing with two of my bags when I said, "You know, my sister is right upstairs. She'll be out to help me in just a minute. You really don't have to do this."

As we bumped and scraped the luggage up the steps, I lagged behind him at a safe distance, berating myself for bringing all this crap.

By the time I reached the third landing, I heard Rita's voice in muffled conversation.

"Fifth floor?" Étienne called over his shoulder from the fourth floor.

"That's right." I huffed out the words between steps. This was the secret to how Frenchwomen stayed so thin—through these sneaky mini workouts. By making the elevators impossibly small, they automatically weeded out all the overweight, out-of-shape people. You had no choice; you either got into serious shape or you died trying.

"Are you staying in Monsieur Bernard's place?"

"I believe so… Do you know him?"

"*Oui.* I did not realize he was going away this month."

I hoped Monsieur Bernard was going away because I didn't care to share the accommodations with a stranger. Before I could shrug off the question, Étienne disappeared down the fifth-floor hall. As I pulled my suitcase up the last steps, I heard Rita's voice.

"Oh, I knew I should have called you myself to check rather than relying on Tatia. *Merci, monsieur.* I appreciate your being so gracious."

What?

Rita stood in the hallway, across from a frazzled-looking bald man who appeared to be in his late thirties. Étienne stood to her right, leaning on the suitcase and conversing with the man in French.

She turned to me as I approached, an anxious look on her face. "Anna, there's a bit of a mix-up with our reservation, but everything is okay. This is Benoît Bernard, our landlord. *Monsieur,* this is my sister, Anna Essex."

"*Bonjour, madame.*" He frowned, wringing his hands, and spoke again to Étienne.

"What is going on?" I asked Rita.

"He thought we were coming next month."

"You're kidding."

"I wish I were." Rita swiped her hand over her eyes. "He does not speak English, and I've been trying to communicate with him in what little French I know. It's been a nightmare."

"He says if you give him three hours," said Étienne, "he will vacate the apartment and go to his home in Provence."

"Yes, I believe we had established that— Who is this?" Rita looked at Flirty French Boy as if seeing him for the first time.

"This is Étienne. He…he helped me carry my bags up."

"That's very nice of you, um—Étienne. *Merci*. I'm Rita, Anna's sister."

They shook hands and I noticed that Flirty French Boy did not kiss Rita's hand. For some absurd reason, I found that satisfying. And then I felt ashamed of myself for being so ridiculous when there were more pressing issues at hand— such as whether Rita and I had a place to stay for the next ten days.

"You speak English very well," Rita said.

Flirty French Boy gave a smug nod, his mouth puckered in self-satisfaction. So very French.

"Would you mind translating what I say into French for Monsieur Bernard?" Rita asked.

"It would be my pleasure."

"Please ask *monsieur* if he would mind letting us leave our bags here for the time being, while we get out of his hair?"

My stomach lurched and my eyes darted to the green monster. Flirty French Boy had finally relinquished his grasp on it and it sat propped against the wall adjacent to Monsieur Bernard's door. The smaller bag leaned against it, as if exhausted from the long journey across the sea and the bump-and-scrape adventure five flights up.

Étienne scrunched up his face. "What do you mean, *out of his hair*? I do not know what you mean."

Rita laughed.

"Rita." I grabbed her arm and shook my head.

"Oh, you're right, I should watch my slang. I mean we want to leave the bags here while we allow him to—"

"Rita, no! Come over here for a minute." I jerked my head in the direction opposite of Étienne. "I need to talk to you."

Rita frowned at me. "Excuse me."

I tugged her down three steps, a good enough distance to talk privately if we whispered.

"What are you doing?" I asked.

"I should have called before we left, but I took it for granted my assistant, Tatia, had arranged everything. There must have been some kind of communication breakdown, because he was expecting us this time next month. But isn't it great of him to vacate the place for us?"

I looked up to see Flirty French Boy staring down at us, and I turned my back on him, stepping in closer to Rita.

"Yes, it's very nice, but we can't just go off and leave our stuff here. We don't know these people. What if Monsieur Bernard takes off for his home in Provence with our things?"

"Don't be ridiculous. What are we supposed to do with our baggage for three hours if we don't leave it here?"

"Take it with us, I suppose."

The thought of hauling the bags down then back up again was not appealing, but it was better than turning over everything I owned—well, everything I needed for the next three months—to a man who was not expecting us, but kindly, miraculously offered to vacate on the spur of the moment. And he was helped along by this boy thief.

Gypsies. That's what these two men were. They were gypsies working together to fleece unsuspecting tourists out of everything but the shirts off their backs.

I hitched my purse up higher on my shoulder. If we went along with their flimsy plan we were setting ourselves up to be robbed blind.

In that case, we were even *more* naive than Shirley Valentine.

"I am worn out," Rita said. "You do what you want, but I'm not schlepping bags all over Paris."

She turned and went back upstairs. I followed her, arriving in front of Monsieur Bernard's door in time to see Étienne wheeling the green monster and family inside.

SIX

I DIDN'T WANT to spend my first day in Paris obsessing over luggage. Really, I didn't. I wanted to get out and walk in the sun. I wanted to celebrate coming this far.

I wanted to see the Eiffel Tower.

I wanted to see Paris.

So I shelved my doubts, compartmentalizing them in that tiny place in the back of my mind. I forced myself to have faith when Rita insisted Benoît Bernard and Flirty French Boy—she didn't say that, she called him Étienne—would *not* take off with our suitcases.

"Tatia knows Bernard. He's a friend of her family's. They go way back. If the place is all boarded up and our stuff is gone, Tatia will know where to find him. Okay?"

"This would be the same Tatia who reserved the apartment for *next month?*"

Rita gave me a look before she walked out of the apartment building's dark vestibule. I followed her out into the sunlight bathing the rue de l'Ancienne Comédie. That expression didn't grace her face very often, but I knew it meant she wasn't in the mood to argue.

I took a deep breath and let simmer the prickly sensation needling me to bicker.

She was right. I was being an anxious idiot for worrying. But when you're so tired you can't see straight, sometimes the obvious looks a little off-kilter.

She wanted to go to the Musée Picasso. She said it was the only thing she wanted to do; if we could just get it out of the way first she'd do whatever I wanted.

We walked in silence, the turbulent morning sending us into our respective shells. When we got to the museum, housed in the former mansion of the Lord of Fontenay, we went our separate ways, viewing the collection solo, at our own pace.

That was okay. In fact, it was better that way. It would give us time to decompress, time to breathe.

If nothing else, the large house was magnificent. The entryway boasted an elaborate staircase adorned with sculptures. Picasso's work was arranged chronologically, starting with the self-portrait he painted in 1901 and ending with *Seated Old Man*, one of his last paintings, done in 1971. It was interesting to see the evolution of Picasso unfold right before my eyes, even if I didn't care for his work.

If I didn't know better, it felt as if I was actually beginning to understand where the guy was coming from with his Minotaurs and dead matadors and portraits of broken people quartered and drawn into geometric shapes.

It *must* have been the exhaustion speaking. I'd *never* identified with Picasso before, except for that brief moment of insanity when I painted the hideous blue portrait of Blake.

O'Keeffe was more my style. Because my style was all about curves, flowers and blooming possibility. Yes, possibility, despite everything.

Imagine that.

Obviously, the flowers worked since they won me a ticket to Paris.

Picasso was all about cubes, flat, hard angles and grotesque distortion. His body of work contained exceptions to this rule, of course, but monstrous, misshapen, hard lines were what I thought of when he came to mind.

As I stared at the *Portrait of Jaime Sabartés* that he painted in 1939, the way he angled the glasses to the right and had the subject's nose pointing off the left side of his face, it looked as if someone had been so mad at poor Jaime they'd slapped him. Perhaps Picasso caught him the split second the blow displaced his features. Just as in my mind's eye, the angry rage that gripped me over Blake's duplicity conjured the image of the blue two-headed beast.

From the little I knew about Picasso, he was so disagreeable, he probably would have disdained anyone who *identified* with his art, or worse yet tried to attach meaning to it. But wandering the galleries in the old seventeenth-century mansion, I floated in a dreamlike state and felt a kinship I never knew existed. Especially when I happened upon a plaque that translated:

Painting isn't an aesthetic operation; it's a form of magic designed as a mediator between this strange, hostile world and us, a way of seizing the power by giving form to our terrors as well as our desires.

When I came to that realization, I knew I had found my way.

—Pablo Picasso, 1946

A message.

Right.

But it was a nice thought, a nice quote, a serendipitous hook on which to hang my confidence as I ventured forth to make art in this city in which so many great artists had come before me.

I wandered into the last gallery, one I almost skipped because, according to the guidebook, it housed the work of a nineteenth-century female artist I'd never heard of, not to mention, it was getting close to the time Rita and I had agreed to meet. But I popped in for a quick look around before heading back downstairs.

The collection of pastel portraits captured me at first glance. They were both bold and understated at the same time, like Toulouse-Lautrec, only more human. The portraits captured people in out-of-the-ordinary ways—exaggerated shadows and colors. The work was extremely feminine, yet amazingly, for a nineteenth-century female artist, it spoke volumes about her independence, unheard of for a woman of that era. I studied the faces for a long time, trying to figure out how the artist, Camille Deveau, had accomplished such a feat.

Interesting that her work was housed in the same museum as Picasso. It was such a contrast to his.

I was so caught up in the anomaly of her work compared to Picasso's, or perhaps the slight similarity to my own, I stayed much longer than I should have. As I turned to leave,

I noticed an old black-and-white photograph hanging on the wall near the door. I must have missed it when I entered.

The photo was of Deveau and her family. Something about the expression on her face gave me an odd sense of déjà vu, an almost out-of-body sensation, and I had to blink to ward off the unsettling feeling.

It was past noon when I finally met up with Rita.

"I thought I was in the wrong place," she said. "I was about to come looking for you."

"I'm sorry. I was swept away by the exhibit upstairs. Did you see it? Her name is Camille Deveau. Interesting, I've never heard of her. Have you?"

Rita shook her head. "I got swept into the gift shop. I just love museum shops."

She smiled and I was glad she wasn't irritated with me for keeping her waiting.

"Her work is lovely. Portraits. They have a haunting quality."

"Sorry I missed it," she said. "How about some lunch?"

"Sure, let's just start walking and see what we can find."

Outside of the museum, the air was cool and the sun shone bright in the cloudless sky. A perfect day for walking. Much better than the unrelenting Florida heat.

"I wish I could have stayed longer," I said. "There was a whole wall of Deveau's paintings I didn't get to see."

"You should have said something before we left. We could have gone back."

I shrugged. "That was fine for today. Perhaps we can go back another day."

"Sure we can," said Rita. "I'd like to see her work."

As we walked, Rita flipped through her guidebook, reading me interesting facts about the Marais quarter, which translated to swamp. "Once the neighborhood of royalty and noblemen, the place descended into an architectural wasteland after the French Revolution. In the 1960s the government recognized its historical significance and began restoring it."

We strolled the narrow, winding streets past chic galleries and boutiques, *boulangeries* and cafés, the stylish and fashionable shops incongruent with the splendid seventeenth-century mansions that once housed French nobility and their mistresses. When we got to an intersection I realized I was looking at everything but not really seeing. My mind kept floating back to the photograph of Camille Deveau. The same unsettled feeling of displacement engulfed me again.

I reminded myself to breathe and tried to let the charm of the old blending with the new weave a spell that would take my breath away, just as I'd always dreamed it would. The scents of lavender and perfume soothed me. They lingered in the air, mingling with the sweet smell of the flower shops and savory aroma of baking bread, fried onions and garlic.

So much to take in—the sounds, smells, sights, all that history. I looked down at the ancient cobblestone street beneath my feet and wondered if perhaps Napoleon or Marie Antoinette had walked this path, or if Camille Desmoulins had trodden this passage on his way to the Palais-Royal before shouting, "To the Bastille!"

It was like faking an orgasm.

I kept waiting for it to take my breath away. I kept thinking I should be *so* happy. I kept telling myself, I am in *Paris*. It was supposed to be love at first sight with this city. *What's wrong with you?*

A haunting sort of melancholy, a longing for something familiar gripped me. I glanced over at Rita and felt ashamed when I realized the sadness stemmed from missing Blake. She was not the person I was supposed to be strolling these streets with. In my dream of *Paris love at first sight,* Blake was supposed to be at my side. A second honeymoon where we walked hand in hand along the quays and he kissed me on the banks of the River Seine.

He was not going to spoil Paris for me because he did not deserve my sadness.

Rita did not deserve my ungratefulness.

So right there in the middle of the Marais, I'd made up my mind. I would snap out of it.

All right, so I did the best I could. Complete transformations took time.

"You know what I *really* want to do?" A new sparkle danced in Rita's eyes, which made me feel better. "For our first meal in Paris, I want to find a little café where we can sit outside and dine on *jambon et fromage* sandwiches on those thin, crispy baguettes. Mmm…I can taste it now."

"Ham and cheese?" I smiled at her, feeling a little more like myself again. "You really want to be a tourist today."

"Oui, madame."

"All right, I'm with you, but I have a special request. As long as we're being tourists, let's go all out and go to the top of the Eiffel Tower. The Delacroix Centre is over there. I can check it out, see where I'm going to live, and we can eat ham-and-cheese baguettes and act like first-class tourists atop *la Tour Eiffel.*"

After looking at the map, we decided the walk, which would take us from the right bank to the left, was too far to attempt. So we decided to take the metro. We walked down to the rue Saint Antoine, bought a ticket at Bastille and picked up line number eight toward Balard. The train wasn't very crowded and we sat on the first seats inside the door. As the metro pulled away, a man started playing an accordion and a woman began singing "La Vie en Rose."

The performance was so hokey, it was priceless. First-class catering to the tourists. Wasn't that song quintessential Paris?

But as I glanced around the car, most of the riders didn't seem to notice—a young woman sat with her eyes closed listening to her MP3 player, a businessman worried his mustache as he studied the contents of a file, an older woman read a book.

Rita and I were probably the only tourists in the car. I put a euro in the singer's cup, which brought renewed energy to the middle of the song she was now singing for me.

"Don't pay them," Rita whispered. "Metro buskers are like stray cats. If you pay attention to them, they'll never leave."

I glanced at the woman. She smiled and redoubled her efforts, thrusting the cup at me again.

I lowered my gaze to Rita's tour book.

"May I see that?"

I took the guidebook and opened it to the colorful metro map. It reminded me of a picture of a child's game of pick-up sticks, with some of the pieces bent into strange trajectories.

Rita figured out our route from the Marais to the seventh arrondissement. She'd mastered the metro on her last trip to Paris. I hadn't even been on an American subway. If I was going to have any sort of life in Paris, I knew I'd better learn to read the metro map *tout de suite*.

"How did you know this is the right train?"

"We're here. We want to go here." She gave me a quick metro lesson and had me track the stops until we reached the École Militaire stop.

"I have a feeling you're going to use this metro station a lot," said Rita. "Get familiar with it."

On the platform, the air smelled faintly of urine, body odor and cigarette smoke. There was a man sitting on the ground near the exit steps strumming a guitar.

We made our way up and out into daylight, winding through the streets, passing dozens of red-canopied cafés and people rushing here and there, until we stood in front of the wrought-iron gates that led into the Delacroix Centre. Beyond the stately black grillwork, lush trees and flowers framed a winding stone path. It had the aura of a secret garden. I had a sudden rush of anticipation. Or was it foreboding? I couldn't tell the difference. All I knew was this was real.

In nine days Rita would leave me here and I would be on my own. The thought made me light-headed.

"Shall we go in?" Rita said.

As I thought about reaching out to open the gate, contemplated taking my first step into the courtyard, a couple approached the gate from the inside and I stepped back to let them pass.

A stunning couple, he was tall and broad-shouldered with longish, dark, unruly hair and a shadow of unshaven beard. His black shirt, jeans and work boots were spattered with a substance that looked like plaster.

A member of the exchange program?

She was a tiny blonde with long thick, stick-straight blunt-cut hair that hung down to her waist. The kind of hair I used to dream of. Something in her swollen lips and tiny nose, or maybe it was her eyes—something about her reminded me of Brigitte Bardot.

The couple stopped outside the gate and she spat words at him so venomously it seemed she could have poisoned him with her tongue. All in French, of course, so I had no clue what she said.

He made a *pffff* sound and walked on a few yards, leaving her where she stood. She yelled something after him. He stopped, turned around and answered her, gesturing with both hands. He seemed more exasperated than angry as he raked both hands through his hair, made a little growl, staring at the heavens for a few beats before turning and walking off.

She hurried after him, her impossibly high heels clicking on the sidewalk. I couldn't fathom how she could run in heels and a pencil skirt.

"What was that?" Rita said.

I shrugged, watching the blonde catch up to him before they disappeared around a corner.

What a gorgeous couple they made. He was so big and so...so French. If he was French, he probably wasn't part of the exchange... Well then, what was he doing at the center besides fighting with his wife or girlfriend, or whoever she was?

Even when Blake and I fought, there was never that much fervor in our battles. I couldn't help but wonder if they made up as passionately as they fought.

The voyeur in me wished I knew what they were saying, but I didn't, which was a reminder that living in Paris would be a challenge.

I could learn.

I'd have to learn.

I stepped back from the gate. "I don't think I want to go in. Not right now. I just wanted to see it. Get familiar with the area. Let's get some lunch, climb to the top of the Eiffel Tower and then go back and see if your Benoît Bernard is ready for us."

"Are you sure?"

I nodded.

"Okay, we'll come back again another day. But, hey, watching them fight reminds me…" Rita rummaged in her purse, and pulled out a small bag. "I got you something at the Picasso museum."

Inside was a small refrigerator magnet that said, *Painting is not done to decorate apartments. It is an instrument of war.* —*Picasso*

THE VIEW FROM the Eiffel Tower's top observation deck was the only aphrodisiac one needed to get in the mood for Paris. From one side the view stretched across the green lawn of the Champ de Mars to the palatial École Militaire. On the other side, the Seine lay like a moat in front of the Trocadéro. It was all there. Paris in panorama. One need only make the effort to look, and if a person couldn't get in the mood up there, well, I suppose she had no business being in Paris.

I was in much better humor as we headed back to the apartment. Benoît Bernard was waiting for us. His bags were packed; ours lay untouched, right where Flirty French Boy deposited them. We paid Bernard ten days' rent and he gave us the keys.

Voilà. The worst was behind us.

I should have felt silly for making such a fuss, but I was too exhausted. Rita and I retired to our separate bedrooms and napped for the rest of the afternoon.

I awoke to the sound of someone knocking on the door and Rita's subsequent, "I'll get it."

Still groggy from deep sleep, I lay on the bed staring out the window at the golden glow the setting sun cast on the white building across the way. The morning's events seemed like a strange dream, and I was happy to awaken from it. I stretched and felt the delicious pull of the move all the way down to my toes. Coming out of the stretch, I noticed the pamphlet I'd picked up at the Picasso museum lying on the nightstand and I picked it up to look at it.

"*Bonsoir, madame.*" The familiar voice carried down the hall into my room, penetrating the closed door.

Flirty French Boy. What did he want? I paged through the pamphlet until I came to a small paragraph about Camille Deveau.

"Good evening, *monsieur.*" Rita sounded way too cheery. How long had she been awake? "Étienne, right?"

I stopped reading. What was with this *monsieur* business? He was a *boy,* not a *monsieur.* I'd have to school Rita on the difference.

Come to think of it, I wasn't exactly thrilled about being called *madame* every time someone addressed me. It felt like a dressed-up version of *ma'am.* Being called ma'am made me feel old. I suppose the alternative *mademoiselle* would have been a little creepy, because *mademoiselle* was for a girl. Or for someone Flirty French Boy's age.

"I told Monsieur Bernard I would check to assure you were comfortable."

My gaze skimmed the paragraph telling about how Deveau was a proper nineteenth-century lady who came from a wealthy family, but defied convention to paint.

"Thank you," said Rita. "Would you like to come in?"

Oh, Rita, no. Don't encourage him. I put the brochure aside and snuggled deeper into the comforter.

"Annabelle is asleep," she said. "We're a little jet-lagged."

"*Merci, non.* I will not intrude. I just wanted to inquire that you have everything you desire and bring you these crêpes for your enjoyment. They're from my restaurant downstairs."

Did he say *his* restaurant? His as in *he worked there,* or his as in *he owned the place?*

"Thank you," Rita said. "I was just going to wake Anna so we could discuss dinner plans."

"I would offer to escort you to dinner, but I must work tonight. The evening hours are always busiest."

"Have you worked there long?"

"It is a family business started by my great-grandfather. You must try it sometime, but on your first evening you should have a special meal. I recommend Le Bosquet."

He gave Rita the restaurant address and said, "For authentic French food, it will not disappoint. Perhaps tomorrow evening you will allow me to show you authentic Paris? It would be my honor."

Say no! It was awfully nice of him to offer, but—

I sat up and contemplated going out there and telling him thanks, but no thanks. But I caught a glimpse of myself in the mirror and saw that my hair was a little too unruly and I was in my underwear. And the thought of going out there and telling him no was more terrifying than just letting him show us *authentic Paris.*

It wasn't as if he was trying to pick us up.

"I shall pick you up at nine o'clock tomorrow evening, *oui?*"

So he was picking us up, in a different sense of the word. I laughed out loud because the play on words was so ridiculous.

Looking at myself in the mirror I thought, *Get over yourself. You should be so lucky as to have a young French guy try to pick you up.*

I dressed to the sound of Étienne bidding Rita *adieu.* When I was sure the coast was clear, I ventured out of my room and found Rita in the kitchen inspecting the crêpes.

"You just missed your boyfriend."

She scavenged through the kitchen drawers until she found a knife and fork.

"My boyfriend? Sounded to me like he made a date with you."

She cut into what looked like a ham-and-cheese crêpe and took a bite. "You were eavesdropping?"

"You were right there in the hall. I couldn't help but hear."

"Then why didn't you come out and say hi?"

"Because you were doing just fine by yourself."

"Mmm, this is good." She took another bite. "He's very cute, you know."

"He could be my son."

"Really? No, he must be at least twenty-five. You would've been—"

"I'd be furious if Ben came home with someone closer to my age than his. The standard goes both ways."

"If Étienne's twenty-five, you would have been sixteen when he was born."

Ignoring her, I took a glass from the cupboard and drew some tap water.

She gestured at me with the fork. "I think you need to find yourself a lover while you're here, and if he's sixteen years younger, all the better. There's a bigger age difference between Demi and Ashton."

"I am not Demi Moore."

"He likes you." She leaned on the counter and took another bite of crêpe. "Look, he even brought you a gift of love from his family's restaurant. In some cultures that would be a marriage proposal."

"Oh, great, just what I need, a marriage proposal when I'm not even divorced yet. And if he brought the crêpes to *me*, why are *you* eating them?"

"Here…" Rita held out the foil with the remnants of the feast. Semicongealed white cheese oozed out of a delicate pancake. "Have the rest. It's delicious."

I took it from her, tasted the remains.

"Good, huh?"

"Mmm." I forked another bite.

Rita unwrapped the other foil, stuck her finger in and tasted the dark sauce. "Oh my God… Chocolate…and orange. This has to be Grand Marnier. *I* would sleep with Étienne for Grand Marnier crêpes."

"You're too easy. And what will you tell Fred?"

"Fred who?"

ÉTIENNE CALLED PROMPTLY at nine the next evening just as he'd promised. In-line skates dangled from his shoulder.

"What's this?" Rita asked, eyeing the skates as she showed him into the living room.

He smiled at me and waved. He looked like a little boy. "I thought you might want to see the real Paris by night."

"That sounds nice," I said. "But I'd like to live to tell about it."

Étienne laughed. "You do not skate? Everybody in Paris skates."

I shook my head. I'd never tried in-line skating. "No, the woman I saw coming out of the Chanel boutique yesterday was definitely not wearing in-line skates. Not *everyone* skates. Sorry, French Boy, I'll pass."

I looked at Rita for backup, but she just gave a noncommittal shrug and busied herself.

Étienne scrunched his face into a mask of consternation. "I beg your pardon? French Boy?"

Oops. I didn't mean to hurt his feelings.

"Sorry. *Étienne.* Look, it's very sweet of you to offer to show us around, but I know my limits. This body is not primed for skating."

He looked me up and down, his gaze lingering unapologetically in *certain* places before returning to my eyes. "American Woman, I think your body is fine. "

Did he just call me— "Did you call me American Woman?" I laughed and so did he. I liked this kid. He was fun.

So we settled on watching the skaters who gathered at the base of the Montparnasse Tower, then we decided to explore the area and get a bite to eat.

It was a little awkward letting him lead us around Paris, but we did. It was also a little disconcerting when each time I'd glance at him I caught him staring at me—he had this piercing, unwavering gaze that kind of gave me the heebie-jeebies.

At one point while we rode a particularly crowded metro, sharing the same metal pole, he reached out and fingered a piece of hair that had broken free from my chignon. I pretended not to notice.

I was wedged into a cramped space just inside the door and had nowhere to move. A smelly man clung to the pole directly in front me, a row of occupied seats blocked me from moving to my right and Étienne stood to my left. Rita was on the other side of him looking all around, taking it all in. I tried to catch her eye, but she was too busy people watching.

So as I stood there hanging on to the pole thinking of that song by the Police, "Don't Stand So Close To Me," I brushed the errant piece of hair back as if his hand weren't even there then leaned in and said, "Look at Rita."

Étienne glanced over his shoulder, then smiled back at me. "She is *obiblious* to us watching her."

"She's what?" I thought he was mixing French and English and I wanted to learn as much of the language as I could.

"She is *obiblious*."

"*Obiblious?* What does that mean?"

He looked baffled. "*Obiblious.* It is an English word, no? It means to be unaware."

"*Oblivious.*" I couldn't help it. I laughed and hoped that my French blunders would be half as adorable as his English mistakes. *Obiblious.* Ha! Cute.

The brakes squealed as the train slowed down to enter a

station. The force pushed him into me. He steadied himself with a caressing hand on my shoulder.

A sweet gesture, but a little too familiar for my comfort zone. When the doors opened and a woman vacated the seat in front of me, I took it, relieved to regain some of my personal space.

As I sat there, glancing up at Étienne occasionally, I wondered what was wrong with me. Why didn't I want to lean into him and flirt back? Why didn't I want to call his bluff and see if the vibes he emitted were what I thought they were. He really was a cute guy.

Not that cute was the be-all and end-all.

Even if he had a *Shirley Valentine* hobby of picking up middle-aged women tourists, why not go for the thrill of a no-strings-attached foreign fling? A cute guy. Hot sex. It might be good for me.

The train rumbled on. Was it the age difference that bothered me?

I'd never been hung up on age.

I didn't mind being forty-one.

I didn't even flinch at turning forty.

What *did* bother me was how fast time had slipped away.

Yesterday, I was at the starting line, then all of a sudden the gun went off and life came at me so fast and furiously I didn't even have time for my head to spin.

I blinked and missed it. I'd slept away my youth and awakened to find myself in this foreign land called middle age.

I'd given Blake the best years of my life.

Now that I was free, this is when life really began.

Glancing up at Flirty French Boy, I decided I'd have to ponder my options.

We took the metro stop that allowed us to walk past Luxembourg Gardens and the Montparnasse train station before we arrived at the Montparnasse Tower. Étienne laced on his skates while Rita and I sat at a café table. He was like a kid restricted by grown-ups.

"Étienne, if you want to skate, please don't let us hold you up," Rita said. "We will be fine here."

He swirled to a stop and planted himself in a chair. "Absolutely not. You are my dates and I shall ensure you have a good time."

Rita and I exchanged a quick glance. *His mama raised him right.*

We ordered cappuccino all the way around. After the server left, I asked, "Do you have a girlfriend?"

He shook his head, watching the skaters gather en masse at the bottom of the Montparnasse Tower.

"Why not?"

He shrugged.

"A good-looking kid like you should not be out with two middle-aged ladies on a Friday night."

Rita kicked me under the table. A reprimand. *This guy's into you. Don't blow it.*

By ten o'clock the street was flooded with thousands of people of all ages on in-line skates. It seemed as if everyone in Paris *did* skate. I watched in amazement as people older than I was rolled by. It was as if someone had opened the floodgates and let in all these people. Étienne sat next to me, rolling his skate-clad feet back and forth as if he was revving his engine.

It really did look like fun.

"Is it hard to skate?"

He shook his head. "I could give you a lesson." He was on his feet, trying to pull me to mine.

"One slight problem. I don't have skates."

"There is a skate shop right over there." He pointed somewhere over my shoulder. "We can rent you a pair."

I looked at Rita to see if she had any interest whatsoever in skating.

"I will if you will," I said.

Rita shook her head and waved me off. "Go on, though. Really. I'll be fine right here."

I tugged out of Étienne's grasp. "No. Not unless you do."

"Will you please get out there?" She smiled and pulled her cell phone from her purse. "I need to call Fred and then I'll enjoy the show sitting right here. Go on."

Étienne was already down on the street, motioning for me to join him. I knew it was insane. I'd probably fall and break my butt. With one last glance at Rita, I joined him and we walked down the block, dodging the skaters, to a skate shop where a friend of Étienne's fitted me with skates and head-to-toe gear.

Skating was easier than I thought. I fell on my rear end a couple of times, but I managed to pick up the basics quickly. It was similar to ice skating, which I'd done when I was a child, and it came back fast.

Soon Étienne and I were out in the thick of things, and I was feeling pretty proud of myself. Together, we rolled over miles of road, pacing up and down the streets of Paris until I was so exhausted I had to sit down.

"Come on, let's rest a minute." I landed hard on a wooden bench outside a tobacco shop. Étienne spun in a half circle in front of me to stop himself.

"You're a show-off, French Boy."

"I like how you call me that."

"What? Show-off or French Boy?"

He grinned. "French Boy. But shouldn't you say French Man?"

I considered it for a minute and shook my head. "French Boy. It suits you."

We sat quietly for a moment, watching the skaters stream by. "I started to ask you earlier. Why isn't a nice guy like you out with a girl his own age on a Friday night?"

He raised one shoulder to his ear. "I go where I want. I suppose I prefer the company of mature women to those my own age. You have more to say. Opinions."

Mature women. Ouch. At least he appreciates quality.

"Besides," he said, "I have a *crush for* American women."

A crush for... "Oh, you mean you prefer American women to French?"

He nodded.

"Usually we say I have a crush *on*. It usually relates to one particular person."

He watched my lips as I talked, occasionally lifting his gaze to my eyes. "Someday I would hope to *marriage* an American woman and move to the United States and open my own restaurant."

I forced myself not to correct him this time. His English was far better than my French. I'd be mortified if someone corrected my every other word of French. "You don't need to get married to do that."

"It makes it much easier if I am *marriaged, non?*"

Okay, I got it. *Shirley Valentine* wasn't his movie. It was *Green Card*. He was a young Gérard Depardieu in training.

"No, it doesn't make it easier. At least not in the long run." I looked at his soft baby face and shook my head. "French

Boy, find a nice French girl your own age and get married for the *right* reasons."

My mind skittered to the night I told Blake I was pregnant and how he came to me the next day with the decision that we should marry. I wondered if he really didn't know he was gay when he proposed or if I'd just served a convenient purpose?

Étienne leaned and whispered in my ear, "I have a crush for *you*."

"I have a crush *on* you," I said.

He smiled and his eyes lit up, "Then you will *marriage* me? *Non?*"

SEVEN

EVEN AFTER I turned down his green-card marriage proposal, Étienne still hung around, bringing us crêpes from his
restaurant and showing us off-the-beaten-track Paris. The
time flew by.

Rita's last day arrived too fast. She had a three o'clock
flight, and I would begin my residency at the Delacroix International Exchange Centre.

No more vacation.

No more sight-seeing.

Time to get to work, prove my worth.

Étienne took our bags ahead to the center so Rita and I
could walk leisurely on our last day together in Paris.

"I'd like to get some lavender and olive oil to take back
with me," said Rita.

"Let's go to the rue de Buci. There's an Olivier & Co.
over there and lots of florists."

We walked past the corner café, which was crowded with
revelers sitting under its red awning, sipping coffee and eat-

ing baguettes. We turned the corner and the market-street rue de Buci burst forth with color, scent and people. Stalls spilled onto the street from shops that lined the tiny road.

We passed a cheese vendor, a chocolatier, and I inhaled the mouthwatering scent of cocoa. It gave way to the fresh sea smell of crabs, oysters and lobsters that crowded an icy bed at the fish stall, then to the tantalizing scent of espresso from an elegant *salon-de-thé,* and finally to the subtle aroma of fresh fruit from the corner produce stall.

And then there were the flowers.

The most beautiful flowers in Paris were on the rue de Buci, and while Rita ducked into the Mediterranean gourmet shop to buy her souvenirs, I strolled over to a magnificent flower stand.

Heaped in huge buckets, the blooms' sweet, exotic scent lured me into the shop. Reds and violets, blues, pinks and oranges, each blossom looked as if it were carefully crafted by hand, every delicate petal cut and shaped into the perfect bloom.

Three clerks helped customers. One arranged a bouquet of fresh spring flowers for a tall, slim, fashionable woman; another wrapped a spidery green plant for an elderly woman; and the third presented the unique creations the shop offered to a handsome man in an expensive-looking suit, probably Armani. She spoke too fast for me to catch a hint of what she was saying, but she pointed to each selection, which had hand-written tags bearing the names of the arrangements:

Le Bouquet Gourmand, which appeared to be Cézanne roses, freesias and other ruffly blooms in every shade of pink available, arranged in a basket large enough to carry to market once the blooms faded.

The man's upper lip curled and he shook his head.

Next, she pointed to *Soleils de Nos Jardins,* sunflowers, plain and simple, arranged into a cheery bouquet.

He eyed the offering and shrugged, a bored, borderline-disgusted look on his face, before finally shaking his head.

No to the market basket; no to the casual sunflowers; for whom would such a man purchase flowers at this hour of the morning…?

Next she offered *Le Bouquet Parfumé,* a cameo of red and yellow roses, carnations and freesias.

He shrugged again, but this time the gesture held more possibility. Ah, roses and freesias. Romantic. Must be a lover.

Finally she presented *La Multitude de Roses*—a bouquet of three dozen multicolored roses, surrounded by wispy foliage. A classic bouquet, full of charm and beauty, I imagined the woman saying.

The man pursed his lips and nodded, and the woman gathered perfect long-stemmed roses from large green tubs. Each of the rose tubs had cards bearing women's names. Carol, Blanche, Gabrielle, Isabelle, Sophie, Sabine…

"*Bonjour, madame.*"

I turned to see a man at the counter peering at me from behind a dozen red-tipped yellow roses he was arranging in a crystal vase.

"*Bonjour.*"

He must have caught my accent because he immediately switched to English. "May I help you?"

"*Oui, s'il vous plaît.* I am looking for dried lavender."

He held up a finger. "Ah, *lavande, oui.*"

He disappeared behind a curtain. That's when I spied the

bucket of roses named Annabelle right next to a bucket of white roses labeled Camille.

A double thrill, startling and pleasing, to find a rose named after me sitting right next to one named Camille, because it reminded me of Camille Deveau.

More than that, it was comfort, as if I'd found a friend.

The man in the Armani suit brushed past me carrying the large bouquet of roses by the stems, blooms down. Even though it seemed a grave disrespect to the delicate blossoms, the way he moved seemed like it must have been the correct way to carry the flowers.

To a lover, no doubt. Or perhaps an apology to his wife for staying overnight *with* the lover? No, they were for the lover, I decided, lifting one of the Annabelle roses to my nose.

It was a spectacular creamy soft pink with dark pink tips and splashes of hot pink on the outside petals. Just the rose I'd hope a lover would have chosen for me.

"Voilà, madame." The florist returned with a generous bag of dried lavender, which I supposed was what Rita wanted to take back with her. I doubted she could get fresh flowers through customs.

With a pang of regret, I replaced the Annabelle stem in the tub and walked over to the counter.

"You would like some roses?" asked the shopkeeper.

"Yes, I would, but—"

I would love some roses and a lover to bring them to me. Étienne's face flashed in my mind. Thinking of him in the context of lover made me cringe a little.

So unfair to him. Some woman would be very lucky to have his attentions. He was just not for me. I was not ready for…for *anyone*.

The shopkeeper walked over to the cooler of roses and plucked out a stem of Annabelle. "You like?"

A wild thought rushed through me. Why wait for a lover to bring me flowers? Why not purchase them as a sort of *housewarming* present for myself? To welcome me to my new studio. A chill wound its way through my veins. Who better to take care of me than me?

"*Oui*. Annabelle is my name."

The shopkeeper smiled.

If I needed justification...I would paint them. The Annabelle rose, my first project.

I asked for a dozen Annabelles and one Camille (for the symbolism), and the shopkeeper threw in six additional Annabelles.

"Gratis." His gaze lingered for a moment and he arched his right brow. Heat spread through my cheeks and I dropped my gaze to his ringless left hand.

I was beginning to see a common trait among Frenchmen. For lack of a better word, I'd have to call it "the look." It was this sultry way they looked at you that made you feel beautiful and appreciated. Why was it that when the majority of American men looked at women it felt as if they were undressing you?

Just one of the many cultural differences.

"*Merci, monsieur. Au revoir.*"

"*Au revoir, madame.* Do permit me the pleasure of serving you again."

I carried my bouquet by the stems, blooms down, and met Rita, who was still browsing, at Olivier & Co. After she finished, we continued our journey toward the Delacroix Centre. Turning onto a quiet wisp of a winding cobblestone street about the width of a sidewalk, I gave her the package of dried lavender.

"Thank you." She stopped and hugged me.

A sweep of seventeenth-century buildings stretched above us as if waking from a sound night's sleep.

It reminded me of how I lay awake most of the night, contemplating that today I'd be on my own in this big city.

"I don't know what I'm going to do without you," I said. My eyes welled with a mixture of emotions—gratitude for my sister, fear for what lay ahead.

"Can't you just stay?"

My voice broke on the last word. Rita pulled back, holding me at arm's length. "You are going to be just fine."

Tears brimmed in her eyes, too, and for a minute I feared we were both going to lose our composure.

"There's always Étienne. The poor boy is smitten."

I rolled my wet eyes and we laughed together, right there, two sisters—two friends—standing in the gray shadows of the ancient buildings that were silhouetted by the early morning sun.

As we walked in silence, counting down the numbers to the Delacroix Centre, I buried my face in the roses and inhaled the sweet scent.

I didn't have to stay if I didn't want to.

I could get on a plane and go home.

My mouth went dry, and I desperately wanted another cup of coffee, perhaps with a couple of shots of brandy in it. But Rita didn't have time to stop. She wanted to get to the airport three hours before her flight, which meant she had to be there by noon. The drive took an hour, and by the time we found my studio, looked around the grounds a bit and gathered her luggage, it was nearly a quarter until eleven.

I thought about trying to convince her she didn't need to go quite that early, that we should stop and have one last café crème. But she was ready to go.

I couldn't blame her.

Since I'd learned of Blake's secret, she'd been there for me around the clock, even going so far as to fly to Paris to deliver me to the next chapter of my life.

She'd done more than one woman should be expected to do within the bounds of sisterhood.

I realized at that moment that when life felt as if it was crashing down on me, all I had to do was focus on how blessed I was to have the gift of her in my life.

I wanted to tell her this. I wanted to somehow express how grateful I was for everything she'd done, but I couldn't articulate the words without losing my composure. So, after I hugged my sister one last time, I handed her one perfectly formed, long-stemmed pink Annabelle rose.

She reached in her bag and handed me a beautifully wrapped box.

"This is for your stay in Paris."

Her cab pulled away, and I wandered the center's gardens for a while before I made my way back to my studio to unpack and settle in before the evening's welcome reception.

The studios were small Mediterranean-style bungalows with white stucco walls and clay tile roofs. From what I gathered during my stroll, they were scattered randomly throughout the twenty-acre grounds, grouped in pairs or quads.

My studio sat a good distance away from the entrance, next to a larger bungalow situated across a brick walkway.

Mine had a bedroom and private bath, a small kitchenette and a large, open space that served as both living room and studio space.

What I particularly loved was the French doors on the back wall that opened onto a patio surrounded by a privacy wall.

Pretty darn nice, I had to admit.

They'd left a fruit basket, a wedge of Brie and a nice bottle of Côtes du Rhône on the middle of the small wooden café table situated outside the kitchenette. There was also a welcome letter from Jacques Jauvert, the center director who'd called me with the good news that I'd won the residency.

I was eager to meet Monsieur Jauvert, whom I'd already decided I liked, based solely on his choice of wine, cheese and *me.*

Since it was a little early in the day for the Côtes du Rhône, I set the bottle on the kitchen counter next to the present Rita gave me, and my roses, which I'd arranged in a pitcher I found in one of the cupboards.

I eyed the box. What in the world had Rita done now? She'd already given me an Hermès scarf. I couldn't imagine how she'd top that.

Carefully, I unstuck the tape and folded back the floral wrapping paper to reveal—

Condoms?

Oh my God.

Ten boxes of ten condoms.

What in the hell was I going to do with one hundred rubbers?

Rita had enclosed a note:

Have sex. That's what you're supposed to do with one hundred rubbers.

I laughed out loud—my sister knew me too well—and contemplated opening the bottle of wine. But instead, I chose a pear from the basket and sat at the table to read the rest of Jauvert's letter.

Along with an outline of basic rules and regulations—work ethic, quiet hours, respecting others' privacy, procedure for receiving visitors, the end-of-residency exhibit and the purchase prize, among other things—was a list of the other artists participating in the program.

Interesting bunch, the twelve of us: in addition to me, there were two other women—a mixed-media artist, Lesya Sokolov from Romania, and Mei Ling, a photographer from Beijing; and a total of nine men—two African men—a potter and sculptor; a guy from Argentina who did watercolors; and then there was the delegation of European men—four painters, one pastel artist and a metal sculptor.

I finished the pear and the biographies, and searched for the thermostat because it was a little stuffy, but I realized the bungalow wasn't equipped with an air conditioner.

Okay. Well, at least Paris wasn't as hot and humid as Florida.

I threw back the shutters and opened the French doors and casement windows, hoping to create a cross-breeze.

That's when I saw them—or at least a fleeting glimpse of them—the man and the blonde I'd seen fighting outside the entrance when Rita and I came here our first day. He unlocked the studio situated across the cobblestone walkway from mine and they walked in.

That was *his* studio? Across from mine?

For some odd reason my stomach spiraled. I pressed my hand to my belly.

Oh lord.

He left his front door open, as if he couldn't be bothered to close it, and I hurried to open the other window in my studio, hoping to catch a peek inside his quarters.

No such luck. His door was ajar at an angle that obstructed my view and he didn't open the windows. The gentle peal of wind chimes drew my eye up to the weathered eave above his door.

I stood rooted to the spot, staring at his studio as if I could will him to open the place for my viewing pleasure or will myself X-ray vision to see inside. Finally, I grew tired of staring at the water-stained white stucco facade, at the garden hose coiled under the window, at the blue bucket spackled with plaster and the faded red towel that looked as if it had been lying there so long it had been bleached by the sun.

So much for the "rule" that asked artists to keep their space tidy "for the visual comfort of others."

He appeared again and dumped a cupful of food into a small dish sitting on the ground outside his door.

The rules said no pets.

Yes, he definitely had the air of a guy to whom the rules didn't apply. And for some reason that made me smile.

Judging from the lived-in look of his studio and the fat gray-and-brown tiger-striped cat that sauntered up and ate the freshly deposited food, the guy wasn't here on a three-month residency. His place had the kind of well-worn look that took a while to achieve.

I didn't remember if the brochure in my acceptance packet mentioned long-term residents. I'd assumed the words *international,* and *exchange* in Delacroix International Exchange Centre were literal.

I was beginning to suspect most Parisian rules were put in place simply to be broken.

I started unpacking the green monster, contemplating what I'd wear to the welcome reception that evening, when strains of music started across the way. The mournful voice of a woman singing what sounded like the saddest song ever written floated through my open windows. She sang in a language I couldn't place. Not French. No, it wasn't Spanish, though the flowery acoustic guitar sounded Latin. Perhaps it was an Italian ballad? But that didn't sound quite right, either.

As I hung up my clothing, the music evoked the uninvited wistful longing I'd fended off since I'd arrived in Paris. I shook off the haunting sensation that fluctuated somewhere between melancholy homesick and wistful displacement.

For some strange reason it called to mind an old poem by Robinson Jeffers that advised not to worry about hating yourself, but to love instead your eyes that can see and your mind for hearing music.

The first song faded into a second and he cranked up the volume.

So much for rule number two on the list asking us to respect the peace and "creative quiet" of the other artists.

At least he wasn't into AC/DC or some obnoxious rap band I couldn't even begin to name.

Tonight at the reception it would give me something to talk to my handsome neighbor about. I could tell him I liked his taste in music and ask him about the language.

Yes, it would serve as a nice icebreaker.

ONE OF THE self-help books I picked up after Blake left introduced me to the power of personal affirmations.

The theory was if you told yourself something—repeated it over and over—eventually it would come to be by virtue of your belief.

When I started getting a little nervous about the welcome reception, I went into the bathroom, stared into the mirror and did my daily half dozen.

"I, Annabelle Essex, am okay."

I looked at myself in the mirror, waiting until I stopped inwardly cringing before I moved on to the next one. It took a while with this one.

In a perfect world, I wouldn't need affirmations. I would simply exude confidence like the perfume emanating from the women at the mall cosmetics counters.

Someday I would believe this bunk. In the meantime, I could dream.

"Just because Blake's life was a lie does not mean by virtue of association, mine was, too."

That one was a little more palatable.

"I loved him. I upheld my vows. I refuse to assume the blame for his screwup.

"I'm smart, talented and I suppose men might find me reasonably attractive—if they like small, thin, soon-to-be-divorced middle-aged women with wild, curly hair."

I reached up and pulled out the elastic that held my hair in place and shook it free. My curls sprang to life and I immediately quashed the urge to gather up the strands and tame them into submission. Maybe if I learned to love my curls. I bent at the waist, flipped my hair forward then back. The shoulder-length mass grew twofold in volume. I smoothed it down. *Let's not get carried away.*

I refocused and said my last affirmation.

"I have the rest of my life ahead of me.

"My future is a blank canvas that I can embellish however I choose. I will paint myself a new life."

The burning question was, how long did I have to repeat the damn affirmations before they took root?

I PAIRED A black handkerchief-hemline skirt with a simple black tank, tamed my hair into a neat twist, and started out about five minutes after eight toward the Delacroix Gallery, which was located about midway between my studio and the entrance to the center.

The lights blazed inside the studio across the way and thanks to the light, I caught a glimpse inside. There was a table just inside the door with pieces of marble each about the size of a concrete block.

He must be a sculptor. As I started to walk away, I heard what sounded like the start of an argument. The blonde said something in a sharp, shrill tone; he answered in an equally short, escalating tone of voice.

Oh, great. I hoped I wasn't in for three months of bickering.

When I opened the heavy wooden door and walked into the gallery, the first thing I saw was two very young, very chic, Parisian-looking women—one blond, one brunette—talking to a short, dour-looking middle-aged man whose face seemed incapable of smiling. All three heads swiveled in my direction just as it registered that I was the first to arrive.

"Bonsoir," said the man.

"Bonsoir," I said in return.

The Parisian Barbies murmured *bonsoir* in unison, and stood perfectly coiffed and made up, holding their wineglasses by the stem, dainty pinkies extended. They regarded me as if they expected me to start performing tricks like a trained monkey.

"I am Jacques Jauvert and you are——?"

"Oh, I'm Annabelle Essex."

I extended my hand. Jacques Jauvert regarded it with expressionless eyes before giving it a limp shake.

"You are the first of the artists to arrive. You are so prompt. Would you care for a glass of wine?" Before I could answer, he snapped his fingers and said something in French to Blond Barbie, who fetched me a glass of white.

"Merci."

She gave a curt nod.

I gathered punctuality was not a virtue around here. Another quirky difference between French and Americans? I should have waited fifteen more minutes—or perhaps a half hour—before leaving my bungalow. I hated functions like this, and being the first to arrive was excruciating. There was no turning back now.

"Make yourself at home, look around—the artist in the exhibit is a Brazilian. We shall start after everyone arrives."

Carrying my wineglass by the delicate stem à la Parisian Barbie, I wandered around the open space looking at the paintings, skirting twelve cloth-covered easels. I hoped they were examples of everyone's work. I'd love to see examples of the talent that landed everyone here.

I wandered around for about twenty minutes looking at the Brazilian landscapes before the others began arriving.

Was there some unwritten rule stating if the function started at eight o'clock it was really code for eight-thirty?

I'd keep that in mind for future functions, so I wouldn't show up looking like the punctual American dork. I noticed the two women wandering around looking as lost as I felt and decided to be the one who reached out.

I tried to introduce myself to Mei Ling, the photographer from Beijing, who didn't look a day over twelve, but she didn't speak English and didn't seem eager to communicate. I couldn't blame her, because I didn't speak Chinese and didn't want to resort to a game of charades.

That made me hesitant to approach the others directly. Instead, I opted for standing back, trying to make eye contact with them.

I realized with a thudding dread that I was easily the oldest person in the bunch, with the exception of one of the European painters who made me look masculine.

Five of the men chatted as if they'd already gotten acquainted. All in all it was a rather icy mixer, with the majority focusing their attention on the art exhibition. Probably pretending to look occupied while secretly sizing up the others just as I was. I don't know why I thought we'd instantly become one big happy multicultural family. There was a one-hundred-thousand-dollar cash prize at stake. Money did funny things to people.

I looked for my neighbor, but he wasn't among the fashionably late. Oh well, this was a working residency—not a social trip abroad.

I was glad when Jacques Jauvert began his opening spiel, which he repeated in English. The Parisian Barbie who'd brought me the wine served as a Chinese interpreter for Mei

Ling, who was the only one in the bunch who did not speak French or English.

Oh, I got it. *Interpreter Barbie.* You could probably buy her in Toys "R" Us right next to Veterinarian and Hawaiian Hula Barbies.

"I hope each of you had the opportunity to read the biographies I supplied. I realize some of you arrived this evening. I would like to make introductions so that you start putting names with faces."

He scanned the room and his unflinching gaze fell on me. "I shall start with our punctual American, Annabelle Essex, since she was the first to arrive tonight."

I smiled, feeling vaguely embarrassed by his backhanded compliment.

"Madame Essex is a painter," he said. "Out of all of the exchange residents, I expect to see the most growth from her when each of you presents your end-of-residency show."

Excuse me? My mouth went dry. If the first was a backhanded compliment, this felt like a full-on slap. With every eye in the room trained on me, I didn't like being singled out as the one with the most growth potential.

Come on. I knew I had room to improve, but need he share it with the entire group of artists?

I tilted my chin up a little higher.

"In all the years I've headed the program," Jauvert continued, "I've never granted a fellowship based solely on one work of art. Until now."

With this slam, I lost all feeling in my extremities.

Well, except for my face, on which I felt the start of a slow, deep burn. Judging by the look on his face, I had the sinking feeling things were rushing from bad to worse.

"In the entire body of work Madame Essex submitted, only one slide caught my eye—a large portrait in which I could see subtle influences of Picasso. But a fresh take, mind you, and vastly different from the *pretty,* decorative little florals that comprised the majority of her work."

In my peripheral vision, the walls melted like a Salvador Dali painting and the magnitude of how alone I was in this foreign city snapped into sharp focus.

Then, just when I thought the evening couldn't get any worse, the brunette Parisian Barbie whipped the cloth off a huge blowup of my blue painting of Blake.

Why didn't someone just kill me now?

EIGHT

I DIDN'T COME to Paris to prime canvases for three months. But I couldn't paint anything else. Not after Jacques Jauvert dragged my self-esteem—and my flowers—through artistic mud.

"...*pretty*, decorative little florals..."

I hated the way his upper lip curled when he said it. I'd never heard the word *pretty* sound so *ugly*.

How could he like that hideous blue painting of Blake? It wasn't even a painting; it was a—a rant; the visual equivalent of a betrayed lover's diary entry. I'd never been good with words. That's why I painted.

Now I couldn't even paint and with no TV, no stereo, no Internet or telephone—except for my cell phone, which I had to use judiciously because overseas calls cost a fortune—I was about to go stir-crazy.

Even if I could talk to Ben or Rita longer than our once-a-week "I miss you!" conversations, I couldn't bring myself to cry on their shoulders over Jauvert's disparaging remarks.

It was embarrassing.

I felt like the butt of some French joke; let's bring over the stupid American and hold her up to pubic ridicule.

Let's prove to the Parisian art community she has absolutely no talent.

Rationally, I knew that was ridiculous. They wouldn't invest the money in me for the sake of a good laugh. I knew that and for a short while, it imbued me with enough will to attempt a "blue" portrait of Jauvert.

I mean, if he liked the one of Blake so much I'd create one just for him: the sour little director sucking on lemons, with his hand tucked inside his jacket, Napoleon-style.

After several false starts, each of which I ended up priming over, I dropped my brush on the table.

I didn't want to paint. I wanted to be anywhere but here, stuck inside this studio. It was sucking all the life out of me.

This had been the bulk of my existence for three weeks, except for my daily trips to the market for nourishment and fresh flowers. Read: chocolate, bread, cheese, fresh fruit and vegetables, wine and coffee for the new French press I'd purchased as a going-away present for myself before I left.

One of the pleasures of being on my own was this new freedom to eat how I wanted when I wanted. My daily trips to the Parisian markets were just about as close to heaven on earth as I'd ever find.

But back at the studio, it was hell.

That's when I realized I had to take a real field trip or risk going crazy. I grabbed my jacket and decided to get the hell out of the studio before I went insane.

As I set out, I noticed that the sculptor's studio was shut

up tight. At least one person in this place hadn't witnessed my humiliation that first night.

Subtle influences of Picasso, my ass.

I decided to go back to the Picasso museum. Just as I had declared a kinship with him on that first jet-lagged day, today I intended to divorce myself from his influence now that I was acclimated.

I wasn't a cubist painter. I didn't intend to copy his style, it just sort of erupted onto the canvas in a fit of cathartic expression. I was beginning to regret ever painting the portrait.

I accepted this residency intending to paint flowers, and if Jauvert and his board of critics expected more cubist distortions... Well, I just didn't have it in me.

At the museum, I stared at the key Picasso works that had moved me on that first day. But when they failed to spark any sort of feeling, I decided to go upstairs and visit Camille Deveau. I mounted the staircase and made my way up to her gallery, but her work was gone, replaced by an exhibit of contrasty black-and-white photographs.

I looked around as if they'd simply moved Deveau's work and I'd discover them behind me, but all I saw was photographs of the American West à la Ansel Adams and a docent slumping on a little stool next to the door.

"*Excusez-moi, monsieur,*" I said. "*Parlez-vous anglais?*"

"Yes."

"The exhibit that was here before, Camille Deveau? Where did it go, *s'il vous plaît?*"

He scratched his bald head. "It ended three days ago. Next, it travels to Italy."

Disappointed and mad at myself for putting off a second visit, I wandered around the old mansion a little more until

I finally found myself in the museum shop. Like Rita, I'm a sucker for museum gift shops. I can't get enough of all the little trinkets and art books and postcards. No matter how inaccessible the artist's work, the gift shop always managed to bring it to a human level.

I had just turned to leave, when a small book on the counter near the register caught my eye: a beautiful little biography of Camille Deveau.

I bought the book and took it to the Jardin des Tuileries, to a garden café situated under a thick canopy of trees just down from the Louvre.

The place crawled with tourists, people of all nationalities—lovers sipping wine in the afternoon; parties dressed in shorts and sneakers with cameras dangling from their necks, relaxing under the red umbrella tables after a morning of sight-seeing; others huddled together in close groups, posing for photos to preserve the memory of their time in Paris.

I chose a seat near the open building and sat down alone. Not a local, but not a tourist. Merely a stranger not particularly welcome in this strange land.

ONE OF THE things I love about Paris is that when you sit down at a café, there's no rush. You can sit there all day savoring your espresso or pastis. I did just that and sat at my little table under the canopy of trees reading Camille Deveau's biography from start to finish.

It wasn't until I closed the book and blinked at the thinning café crowd that I realized I couldn't remember the last time I sat uninterrupted and read a book from cover to cover.

Her biography read like a tragic novel: a woman ahead of

her time. Painter of beautiful flowers. A great talent gone unrecognized and unappreciated.

Now, this was a soul sister I could relate to. Filled with the sad beauty of her story, I wanted to put what I'd read into context, give her an actual sense of place. I took the metro to the Latour-Maubourg Varenne stop, one exit before my usual, because supposedly, this was the area where Camille Deveau lived with her family—right off the rue de Varenne.

The Deveaus and other wealthy residents who formerly lived in the Marais (ironically, the area where the Musée Picasso now stood) moved to this area and built the aristocratic town houses in the Invalides district.

I walked along the boulevard des Invalides, across the street from the imposing Hôtel National des Invalides—in France a *hôtel* was not a hotel in the American sense, but rather a large home. This place was built in the seventeenth century to house wounded and homeless veterans. It was the cornerstone of the posh neighborhood all those years ago. Following a map in the book, I ventured off the boulevard and walked down the tiny rue de Varenne.

To my right was the Musée Rodin—though it wasn't actually the Musée Rodin in the nineteenth century, as Rodin was still a struggling artist, but the mansion was there. To my left were the town houses the book talked about. The road was so narrow it seemed I could stretch out my arms and touch the ivy-covered wall fronting the museum and the old houses. But I stayed to my right so that I could get a better feel for the houses. I wanted to try to guess which one was hers because the book didn't say.

It was just a game. I knew it was. But what was the harm?

If I squinted my eyes and blocked out the traffic noise coming from the busy street behind me, it was as if I'd traveled back in time.

I followed the stone wall until it gave way to a wrought-iron fence and I could see inside the grounds to a fabulous rose garden, home to hundreds of roses. My first thought was, *Oh, I want to paint them,* because I could tell from looking those weren't Gertrude Stein's ordinary roses, those were Parisian roses set against the elegant mansion in the background that stood as proud and stately in Camille Deveau's time as it did today. I turned around and saw the casement windows on the town house behind me.

The oddest sensation skittered through my veins, raising gooseflesh on my arms and the hair on the back of my neck.

This was it. This had to be where she lived. I paused and stared at the garden, the road, the old houses, overcome by the strange sensation I'd been here before. This was the first time I'd set foot on this street, yet there was something oddly familiar in the smell of the air, the narrowness of the old street, the courtyards and doorways.

I rubbed my arms and squeezed my eyes shut against the perplexing sensation pulsing inside me, but it didn't go away.

Blake and I once got into a debate over reincarnation. I loved the romantic notion that we'd all lived many lives— that death wasn't the end—and in those lives we gravitated to the souls who'd had an impact on us in the past.

"How else would you explain déjà vu?" I'd said.

"Maybe it's familiarity passed down through the genes, generation after generation," he said. "A person's ancestors are Irish, so he's drawn to all that's Irish because it's in his blood."

Killjoy.

Just like Jauvert and his curled upper lip denigrating my "...*pretty,* decorative little florals..."

I gave the roses one last wistful look and turned back toward the boulevard des Invalides. The setting sun glinted off the Dôme Church that housed Napoleon's tomb and a cool breeze whispered through the trees lining the street. Cars whizzed by on the boulevard, setting me firmly in the twenty-first century.

I GOT BACK to the center just before dark, still feeling displaced but a little less alone thanks to my new insight into Camille Deveau's life.

Tomorrow, I'd go to the library—the *bibliothèque* (only the French could make a library sound like a nightclub)—and see what else I could discover about Camille. If I wasn't going to paint, I might as well do something productive.

I walked in the dark through the garden and up the winding path that led to my bungalow. As I approached, I saw lights on in the sculptor's studio. The same plaintive music I'd heard the first day I arrived—the last time I'd seen him at the studio—drifted through the open door and windows.

So did the soft sound of a woman laughing as I paused in the shadow of my dark bungalow and looked inside the open door of his studio. I had a better view tonight, thanks to the lights on inside his place.

I caught a glimpse of him through the window. He wasn't wearing a shirt and a red bandanna covered his head. His chiseled features looked even more pronounced in the low light. Then he was gone.

Ominously sexy—were the words that sprang to mind.

He looked about my age.

He appeared in the window again, lighting a cigarette, and I turned around to act as if I was unlocking my door just in case he saw me.

But the woman laughed again and the musical lilt of her voice enticed me to turn around.

He wasn't at the window anymore, but I could smell his cigarette mingling with the faint scent of jasmine. He answered her in a sexy, low voice.

What were they talking about? None of my business, but I was still curious. They weren't being loud, but loud enough that I *could* hear them.

I don't know why I did it, but I walked closer to the window. Not right up to it, but to the edge of the shadows, just close enough to see the blonde standing stark naked in the middle of the floor—well, not stark naked—she wore a G-string and a pair of high heels. Naked enough.

The music hit a shrill, mournful note that made me back away fast—before I could see if he was naked, too, or register many details about his studio beyond the large marble sculptures.

Heat warmed my cheeks. That's what I got for peeping in windows.

As I unlocked my door—this time for real—and stepped inside, the blonde woman's lyrical voice took an edge and before I could shut the door behind me, she was shouting at him.

He shouted back.

How vulnerable one must feel to fight when she's stripped naked—literally and emotionally.

I opened my windows—because the place was stuffy after

I'd been out all day—and left my lights off. The couple fought for several minutes, so loud I was sure their voices must have carried over the entire compound, but no one came to quiet them down.

Then as abruptly as the shouting started, it stopped. I waited for one of them to storm out, but neither did.

The only sound was the woman on the CD singing her melancholy song. I shut the windows and latched the shutters, not wanting to hear how they made up.

Surely two people who fought so passionately made up just as passionately.

I didn't want to know.

Instead, I picked up my brush and put paint to canvas. Inspired for the first time since I'd arrived.

NINE

IF AMERICAN WOMEN were truthful with themselves, they'd confess their envy of Frenchwomen, to whom style seems intrinsic and fat is something unfortunate that happens to other people.

They never have to loosen the waistbands of their tiny designer samples after polishing off a five-course meal, which includes, of course, large amounts of butter and cream, a cheese plate and something yummy such as *crème brûlée* or *baba au rhum*.

Their pouts translate to sultry and seductive to the male species.

They know how to wear scarves.

When I laid it all out, it seemed pretty clear that Frenchwomen had made a deal with the devil.

Oh well, my life had gone to hell.

I might as well join them.

Right. If only.

After staying up all night painting a scene I'd titled *The Bed,* depicting the passionate reconciliation of fighting lovers, I got stuck when it came to painting the woman's face.

The big white bed, heaped with sheets and pillows—no problem. The *ominously sexy,* brooding man—no problem.

The woman? Big problem.

Since Jacques Jauvert implied that my flowers were an insult to Georgia O'Keeffe, I decided to borrow Camille Deveau's bold portrait style. I'd come to a standstill when I forced myself to drop O'Keeffe's methods. There was nothing wrong with borrowing someone else's approach until I found my own way. It was better than priming canvases.

My new line of attack was working. Except for the woman's face, which I'd started and painted over at least a dozen times.

I was tired.

At about nine o'clock in the morning I decided to take a break. I considered getting some sleep, but I was too keyed up to rest.

Instead, I flipped through *French Vogue.* I'd taken to pretending it was a study guide to help improve my French. I'd learned a lot, actually. I could translate the Prada and Dolce & Gabbana ads.

So Prada and Dolce & Gabbana in French read the same as they do in English. I was starting with simple one-word ads and working my way up.

The Lierac Solaire self-tanner ad was what caught my eye—the one with the bronze topless woman, lounging as if she hadn't a care in the world. Before coming here, I never considered myself prudish, but I had to admit, I wasn't quite as uninhibited as the average Frenchwoman who thought nothing of parading topless—with the doors and windows open so that any nosy person who peeped in would get an eyeful.

Like Sexy Man's girlfriend across the way, who walked around his studio in her uniform of G-string and high heels. She moved as if she was so confident in her own skin she didn't care if the whole world was watching.

More power to you, honey.

If I had a body like hers, I'd walk around naked, too.

Just because I could.

I just wasn't quite that…liberated.

So what did that make me?

A prude?

I didn't want to be a prude.

I tossed the magazine aside and got up off the couch, closed the shutters and walked to the bathroom mirror.

I slipped out of my jeans, and closed my eyes, trying to imagine myself sunbathing topless on the Riviera.

So glamorous. Such a deep, dark tan. No tan lines.

I opened my eyes and spied myself standing there in my shirt and underwear and the ridiculousness of it made me laugh out loud.

Why? What was so funny? Because I wasn't comfortable with the thought of sunbathing topless?

Maybe I *was* a prude.

No.

If I got to the point where I was comfortable with my body, I could do it.

I undid the bottom two buttons on my shirt and lifted it, just barely, so I could examine my stomach.

My not-quite-flat-midriff hadn't seen the light of day since…. Since… Well, let's just say it had been a very long time. As I feared, I was frightfully pale. More than pale, actually. I edged the shirt up a little more. The white-fright factor conjured the word *fish-belly.*

How long *had* it been since I'd even had a tan? When I was a teenager, I used to spend most weekends at the beach and I looked great. But Blake hated the beach and had an obsessive fear of skin cancer. Plus, working nine-to-five and raising a son preempted the simple pleasure of sun-worshiping.

I pushed my shirt up under my breasts and did a quick turn and spied something even more horrifying than my pallid tummy: cellulite. On the back of my legs.

Holy shit.

Where did that come from?

I blinked at my legs, trying to imagine how I could shower daily and not notice the unsightly mess. Can we really go years without looking at ourselves? And how about that butt that didn't sit quite as high as it used to?

My focus snapped back to my legs.

I ran my hand over the mottled surface.

They were old legs. Tired legs. Unloved legs.

Dropping my shirttail, I walked out into the hall and grabbed my jeans. But before I could dress, I spied the naked Lierac Solaire woman scowling at me from the *Vogue* ad as if she wanted to jump out of the magazine and slap me for being a disgrace to womankind.

"*You* don't have cellulite. Or a saggy ass. And you're not forty-one years old. I'll bet a man never left you for another man."

I kicked the magazine closed and stood glaring at it in the dim light.

"Don't let him make this your fault." I said the words aloud and a feeling washed over me until a voice deep down inside bubbled up to the surface.

"It's not my fault."

I went to the closet and retrieved the one and only pair of high-heeled sandals I brought with me—the ones I almost didn't bring because they were flirty and this was supposed to be a serious painting trip, but I ended up packing them because I had to bring something halfway fashionable. I mean, come on, it is Paris.

I slipped my feet into them. The leather soles felt cool. I took a step and glanced down and liked the way my ankles looked. I'd always had nice ankles. Thin ankles. And that was good, because not even a plastic surgeon could fix bad ankles.

Liposuction could fix cellulite, but pity the darling with fat ankles.

I walked in my high-heeled sandals and shirt back over to the mirror. I couldn't look at myself, but slowly, one, by one, I unbuttoned the shirt the rest of the way and shrugged it off, then I stepped out of my plain flesh-colored briefs and stood there until I could steal shy quick glances at myself.

Tears burned my eyes and I wrapped my arms around my middle.

"I, Annabelle Essex, am going to be okay," I said to the broken, vulnerable naked woman in the mirror. The words rang hollow, but a few seconds later, I noticed the woman in the mirror stood up straighter, with her shoulders back.

Maybe someday I'd have liposuction.

Maybe I wouldn't.

Maybe I needed to learn to love myself just the way I was.

Maybe I could use a little color.

I grabbed a towel, draped my big shirt around my bare shoulders and crept out onto the patio as if I were breaking and entering a quiet house in the middle of the night.

The morning sun shone bright, bathing the patio in gentle light. I hugged the towel to me as I surveyed the stucco walls, assessing the privacy factor. Satisfied that no one except the birds could see in, I spread my towel on the ground, slipped out of my shirt and sandals and lay down to soak up the sun—naked.

Naked as the woman in the Lierac Solaire self-tanner.

Nope. More naked. She was only topless.

More naked than the sculptor's girlfriend.

I lay there like that for the first time in my life deliciously soaking up the sun, loving the feel of it caressing my body...like a lover.

Mmm...yes, that was just the way a lover's hands should touch a woman's body....

I AWOKE TO the sound of knocking at the door. My first groggy thought was, *Blake will get it*. I turned over on my side to snuggle into the downy softness of the mattress, but the bed was hard as a rock.

Hard as—

The knocking made me sit upright and grab for my shirt.

I'd fallen asleep.

Out there like this.

Naked.

I pulled on the shirt, buttoned it as fast as I could and stepped into my jeans, nearly falling over myself.

My heart pounded in a furious, deep-sleep-interrupted panic. As if I'd been caught doing something wrong.

I ignored the shame as I blinked away the haze and opened the door. Étienne was standing there holding a travel-size bottle of shampoo.

"Bonjour, madame."

"Bonjour, Étienne. Don't call me *madame.* My name is Anna."

He glanced down at the shampoo, then lifted his gaze to mine. *"Bonjour,* Anna. Are you unwell? Your face is flushed."

I pressed my hand to my cheek and felt the warmth.

"Oh, no, I'm fine. I fell asleep out on the patio."

How much sun *had* I gotten? I glanced at my watch. Ten minutes after twelve. I'd slept for nearly three hours. No sunscreen. Great. From fish-belly white to lobster red in the span of a morning.

He held out the small bottle. "You left this in Monsieur Bernard's shower. I thought you might need it."

I reached out and took it. The motion caused the cotton shirt to rub across my bare breast and I was suddenly aware that I wasn't wearing a bra. I crossed my arms over my chest.

"Thank you for bringing it, Étienne. It must be Rita's, but I'll be able to use it."

An awkward silence ensued. I couldn't invite him in, the bed painting was sitting right in the middle of the floor—and I thought my underwear might be, too. I couldn't remember where I'd let it fall. I was just about to say goodbye when he said, "There is a festival happening today, La Fête du Pain. Would you care to accompany me?"

"Wait here just a minute."

I shut the door and carried the new painting to the patio. Silly to hide it, but I didn't want anyone looking at my work yet. I might even paint over the image. Although, at first glance, I liked what I saw. The partial image of the sculptor wasn't bad. It was coming along. I just needed to figure out what to do about the woman.

On the patio, I glanced up to make sure no rain clouds loomed. Not a cloud in the sky. The warm sun beat down through my shirt. The sting hinted at the severity of my sunburn, but I didn't have time to worry about it.

I shut the French doors, stashed my underwear in the bedroom and put on my bra. My sunburned breasts screamed at the invasion of elastic and wire, so I took it off.

I walked into the bathroom to inspect my bralessness in the mirror. The cotton shirt rubbed against my nipples and my nipples questioned the shirt's right to be there—over the bareness—since I was going out.

Thank goodness I wasn't overly endowed. Deciding I didn't look too obscene, I tied the shirt at the waist. Checked the mirror—yes, I could get away with this.

On my way to the front door to invite Étienne inside, I spied the empty easel. I don't know why I felt compelled, but I picked up a blank canvas and slid it onto the easel before opening the door.

It made it look as if I'd been doing *something,* or at least it looked like I was ready to do something. Étienne stood outside with one lanky arm braced against the doorjamb.

"Sorry about that. Come in."

He stepped inside. "So this is your studio? It is very nice."

"It's comfortable."

He walked around to look at the canvas on my easel. Then he looked at the blank canvases lining the walls, primed but empty.

That made me feel silly for putting the blank one up there.

"You have been here three weeks. Where is the work you have produced? You have already sold it?"

"No, I'm going through my white, minimalist phase right now. If you'll look closely at the canvas on the easel, you'll see a tiny black dot right in the center. That's the painting."

Étienne squinted and leaned in for a closer look. Then glanced at me, looking confused.

"I'm kidding," I said. "Don't believe everything I say."

"Such as when you rejected my marriage proposal? I should believe you really meant yes?"

"Well, no. I was serious about that. I can't marry you. I'm married to someone else."

He knit his brows. "You told me you were single."

Why did I open that can of worms? "It's complicated, Étienne. I'm getting a divorce."

Frowning, he said, "Your husband is an idiot to let you go."

The look of conviction on his face tugged at my heart. "French Boy, I like you." I winked at him to lighten the mood.

"Then you will go with me to *La Fête du Pain?* Please, it is much fun."

"*La Fête du Pain?* That means bread celebration?"

He nodded.

How in the world could I resist an opportunity to pay homage to bread?

"At *La Fête du Pain* you will sample a multitude of fresh-baked bread. *Boulangers* will have ovens outside and will bake the bread before your eyes. A good friend of mine will give a special presentation at three o'clock. I told him I would stop by. And you could come and help me practice my English so that when I meet my American woman who will marriage me, I will be ready, *non?*"

He smiled his Flirty French Boy smile. I had to admit he was adorable. Still, babies and puppies were adorable, but I didn't want or need either. Nor did I want or need a Flirty French Boy in my bed.

He reached out and touched my hair again.

I could hardly convince him that I was in the middle of something important. The blank canvases spoke for themselves. And I'd admitted I was sleeping when he arrived. Yesterday, it did me a world of good to get out—

For the first time in weeks, I'd painted something worth keeping. Perhaps a quick walk through *La Fête du Pain* would continue that trend. To tell the truth, as luxurious as being a lady of leisure sounded in theory—spending the day doing nothing but reading a book; lying naked in the sun all morning; accomplishing nothing tangible—I needed to do something constructive with my time. Perhaps going out again, *Paris* would refill my well.

"It sounds like fun, but I can't stay long."

Étienne dropped my curl and smiled. "*Oui,* I must work at three o'clock. But in this short time together I will be pleased to show you around. More of the real Paris, as you say."

Ah, the real Paris. Yes, there was that, too, and the bread. Wasn't bread the heart and soul of the real Paris?

"Have a seat while I change clothes."

I turned to go, but he grabbed my hand.

"*Non,* you look fine. I like your hair down that way."

I pulled my hand from his and touched my hair again, which I knew had to look wild after I'd slept on it all afternoon.

"Okay. Fine. Let's go."

As it turned out, *La Fête du Pain* was not just a huge Parisian bread festival, it was an annual event where bakers from all over Europe came to show off their baking prowess.

The plaza in front of the Hôtel de Ville (city hall) was covered with tents and wall-to-wall people. Large ovens had been set up for culinary artisans to display their expertise in rolling, dusting and baking breads of all types to crispy perfection.

The deliciously seductive aroma permeated the air and made me want to breathe deep. Étienne pulled me from tent to tent, elbowing his way to the samples, feeding me small morsels at each one. This one dipped in rosemary-garlic oil, that one spread with a particularly smelly cheese; yet another with a thin piece of pâté resting atop.

After we'd spent an hour stuffing ourselves with baguette, brown bread, challah and dozens more I couldn't begin to name, we watched his friend, Alain, who worked at the *crêperie,* present a demonstration on the fine art of crêpe making.

After Alain finished, Étienne introduced us. A stout man who looked to be in his mid-fifties, Alain kissed me on both cheeks and eyed me up and down in a manner that made me wish I'd taken the time to shower, apply makeup and dress properly for the occasion, rather than letting my wild hair fly free and tying up my big white man's shirt over my jeans. My flat sandals didn't help the ensemble, either. It didn't even cross my mind to put on my strappy ones.

Vive la différence between a Frenchwoman and me. Étienne

and Alain talked in French. Rather than stand there dumbly not understanding what they were saying, I walked over to the baguette stand next door and took the sample an older woman offered. Less than a minute later, Étienne appeared at my side with a bottle of red wine and two glasses.

"One of the benefits of the business," he said, gesturing to the bottle. "Why don't we sit on the fountain and enjoy it."

We managed to squeeze into a tight spot that seemed better suited for one person than two. I was beginning to understand that Étienne's invasion of my personal space was not so…well, *personal*, as much as it was a cultural thing.

French people, Frenchmen in particular, were just more intimate human beings, more prone to touch and stand close to a woman than Americans.

Sitting on the edge of the fountain, with our hips and shoulders pressed together, we toasted *La Fête du Pain* and friendship, American painters and French crêpe chefs.

"This is so much fun." The wine numbed my nose, and when I smiled, my entire face tingled. "I am so glad you talked me into this."

Étienne moved his arm behind me so that his palm rested on the edge of the fountain. It opened a bit more room, but also angled him so that my shoulder pressed into his chest.

He smelled musky and earthy, a bit more pungent than I was used to. Some women thought a man's natural scent was sexy, but I'd always preferred the clean smell of soap and aftershave. Today, in the spirit of the festival, I vowed not to let it bother me.

"You are not used to having fun?" he asked.

"What?"

"Your American husband did not take you fun places like *La Fête du Pain?* No wonder you are divorcing him. He did not properly care for you."

Oh. Whoa. I realized I hadn't thought of Blake in at least two hours and the realization crashed in like a chandelier falling from the sky. I didn't want Blake to ruin this otherwise perfect day.

"I have been meaning to ask you," I said, changing the subject. "Have you ever heard of a nineteenth-century French artist named Camille Deveau?"

He pursed his lips as if he was racking his brain, then shook his head.

"I hadn't either until that first day Rita and I arrived. We went to the Musée Picasso and there was an exhibit of her work. I went again yesterday to see it, but they had already taken it down. She was a really amazing person from the little I've read about her and I'd like to learn more. I was thinking about going to the library—um, to the *bibliothèque* to research her, but my French isn't strong enough to make much headway. Would you help me by translating for me?"

"Sure, you want to go now?"

I glanced at my watch. "It's quarter till three. Don't you have to work?"

He held up a finger. "Wait here. I'll be right back. One of the pleasures of being the boss is the—how you say—flexibility. I was to relieve Alain at the tent, but I will talk to him. I am sure he will not mind staying another hour. The *bibliothèque* is only open until four o'clock. We will go and do some quick research and then I will go to work and you will go home and paint."

THE LIBRARY WAS almost empty. After finding a couple of French reference books that mentioned Camille Deveau, we found a quiet corner table behind tall shelves. I set the books on the table, and Étienne glanced around and then pressed his finger to his lips. "Shh, don't tell anyone." He pulled out another bottle of wine from the inside of his jacket.

"We can't—" What I meant was *I* couldn't. I was already half-drunk from the first bottle.

Another difference between the French and me—they could hold their wine. But Étienne had pulled out a chair for me on the same side of the table where he sat, opened the bottle and poured two glasses before my numb brain could send a message to my even number lips to say "We are going to get kicked out of here, if we don't get arrested first."

Étienne made a *psssssh* sound and handed me a wineglass, clinking his to mine. "This is not America. The librarian would probably join us if we invited her. As long as we don't spill on the books."

Leaning back casually in his chair, he propped his left ankle on his knee and his left knee pressed against my thigh. He sipped his wine and read to me from one of the books we found on the shelves. I sipped and listened, enjoying the melodic sound of his accented English, the warm glow of wine and sunburn and the way his lips moved.

He didn't seem so boyish sitting there next to me.

"The author speculates that even though there was no documentation—no journals or letters to prove it—Camille Deveau was the lover of Georges Fonteneau, the famous nineteenth-century painter. She draws this conclusion based on a series of portraits Fonteneau painted of Camille Deveau."

I drained the last of the wine from my glass. "I knew they were close friends, but I didn't know they were lovers. I mean, Fonteneau was married and Camille Deveau was a proper lady."

Étienne shifted forward to pour more of the ruby-colored liquid into our glasses and his knee pressed more firmly into me.

"So what do you think of your little artist now? Taking a married lover?" He touched his glass to mine and held my gaze. I was so caught up in the exotic color of his eyes—I'd never noticed the flecks of green mixed in with brown and amber.

I didn't even notice him leaning in, until his lips were on mine, softly at first, tasting of the wine—of black currants, spice, coffee and tobacco.

"I think she has the right idea," he murmured.

I was so taken aback that I didn't object. He deepened the kiss a few layers. My whirling mind registered my pounding heart and the velvet feel of his lips on mine—skilled lips, capable lips. Why did I think he was too young? Because, my God, he was just so darn good at this. So good at invading my personal space.

Vaguely, somewhere in the fuzzy background, I heard a female voice say, *"Monsieur, Madame, la bibliothèque ferme dans cinq minutes."* I think she said the library would close in five minutes.

The kiss tapered off with slow, hungry, smaller kisses. My vision was blurry when he finally sat back in the chair. I blinked him into focus.

"So you see, the librarian, she is *obiblious* to our drinking wine in here." He trailed his thumb over my cheek, down my neck to the first button of my shirt. A hot surge of lusty longing coursed through me.

And I thought I wasn't attracted to him. Give a starving woman bread and water and it tastes like a feast.

"You have to go to work and I better go home—or at least somewhere far away from you before I get into trouble."

He arched a brow. "You told me on that first day I met you that you have a fondness for trouble."

He stood and pulled me to my feet. I swayed, unsteady, and he wrapped his hands around the small of my back, placing biting kisses on my neck, pulling me to him and pressing his erection into me.

Heat stirred and pooled in my belly and my body responded in a way that begged me to lay him flat on the table and show him just how much I loved trouble.

Oh my God, what was wrong with me?

My head lolled to the side, reveling in the skill of his lips and hands and—I wobbled again, sidestepping into a shelf, knocking over the books on the end.

Oh my God, I was *drunk. That's* what was wrong with me.

I was drunk and I was making out in a public library with a boy who kept mixing up his words. I was like a schoolgirl. And I liked it.

It was a damn good thing we were in a public place that was closing in the next minute or so because my body begged me to keep going.

"Let me come to you tonight after I quit work." Étienne's breath was hot in my ear.

If I let him we would probably... "No, we can't..."

His tongue was in my ear and he cupped my bottom so that my body was flush against him.

"Is this one of your noes I should not believe?" His hands traveled north and he unbuttoned my shirt, exposing my sunburned breasts, kneading them up and together like a skilled *boulanger.*

"Ouch, I'm sunburned." I tried to wriggle free, but he backed me against the shelf.

"I like it. It's very sexy, American Woman. You are not so much the uptight person as I first thought."

Just as his mouth ravaged one of my tender nipples, the librarian appeared at the entrance to our little alcove.

"Oh!" My gaze locked with hers. Pain mingled with ecstasy, which was nearly (but not quite) eclipsed by the horror of being discovered. All I could think was, *Oh my God, I should have worn a bra. I never go out without a bra.*

She pursed her lips, and as she walked away, I prayed she wasn't going to get security to throw us out.

The thought sobered me enough to realize library or no library, closing time or not, Étienne was going to keep going until he'd scored a home run. He slid his hand into my waistband, but I wriggled out of his grasp.

"Okay, French Boy, come on. It's time to go."

He stood there, breathing air in great gasps, his lips all wet and shiny, his hair mussed and his green shirt partially untucked.

As we walked to the metro on the crowded sidewalk, the traffic and harsh afternoon light curbed the lusty cravings that blossomed inside me in the library, leaving me feeling anxious and unsettled.

"I have to ask you something," I said.

"*Oui?*"

"How old are you?"

He knitted his brows and looked at me as if I'd asked him how many inches his penis measured.

"Why? Is that important to you?"

"Yes. It is. I usually like to know the age of the men I kiss."

He slanted me a perplexed sideways glance. "It seems irreverent to me. Because what is age but a chronological record of how long we have been on this earth?"

Irreverent?

"You mean *irrelevant?*"

He lifted one shoulder and let it fall.

"Okay, don't get all philosophical on me about age. Just answer my question."

"I am twenty-nine years last January."

It took my muzzy mind a few minutes to do the math, but I finally calculated the twelve-year age difference. So he was a few years older than I first thought, but he was still closer to Ben's age than mine. It made me want to ask what he was doing with *me* when any number of beautiful, young Frenchwomen—women much closer to his age—would line up for a man who could kiss like that.

Come to think of it, beautiful young *American* women would, too, and then he could have sex *and* get his green card.

We stopped at the entrance to my metro station. "Is this about the green card, Étienne? Because if it is, even when I get divorced, I'm not sure I ever want to get married again. Marriage is hard even when you do it for the right reasons. Don't marry someone just to get into the U.S."

He pulled me to him and ran his hands down the length of my back as he kissed me—right there in broad daylight at the entrance to the metro station.

I waited for the slow burn to ignite, but my body didn't respond the way it had before.

He pressed his lips to my ear and said, "*Non,* this is not about the green card. You do not need a green card for what I want to do with you."

His words made me blink and when he tried to kiss me, I turned my head to the side. He stepped back, looking a little insulted.

"Anna, I find you most attractive and I would like to be your lover. Does this trouble you?"

Did this trouble me? What a loaded question. Should I start with the age difference? Confess that despite my liking the *idea* of taking a younger lover, the reality was daunting; or did I tell him it had been eighteen years since I'd taken a lover and the man I chose ended up being gay?

Oh, no. No. I would *not* let the bad situation with Blake scare me away from healthy relationships.

It all came down to an issue of chemistry.

"Étienne, I'm just not…"

He looked down at me expectantly.

I sighed. "I'm still married and I guess until I sign the final divorce papers I just don't feel right about becoming someone's lover."

He looked at me as if I'd said something totally incomprehensible. I supposed since the two favorite sports of the French are eating and adultery, my reasoning for not being his lover sounded a little thin.

It *was* a thin excuse. But even though I responded to him when he kissed me—it had been ages since I'd had a man's hands on my body, so I think I would have responded if Quasimodo had ravished me. Not that Étienne was in any way Quasimodoish.

There was just no explaining chemistry.

"I will not force myself on you, but it is a shame that you let this man you are divorcing keep you from being truly free. Come to me at midnight, Anna, and I promise you won't regret it. I will work at the festival until six o'clock, then I will be at the restaurant waiting for you."

I opened my mouth to speak, though I don't know what I was going to say, but he dusted my lips with a feather-soft kiss.

As I watched his tall, thin frame walk away, I felt woozy and flattered and uncertain…and petrified all at once.

A GOOD FRIEND once said France would be lovely if not for the Frenchmen. Obviously, she hadn't been kissed senseless in the middle of the afternoon by a virile young Frenchman.

I never agreed with her. I'd had a love affair with France for as long as I could remember. Now, more than ever, I wholeheartedly disagreed with her. Sure, to the untrained eye most of the French seem to have two different moods: bored and downright disgusted.

Stereotypical.

After spending time in the library with Étienne, I'd learned one shouldn't judge a book by its cover. That's what I was thinking as I arrived at the center about half an hour later, a little more clearheaded than when I left Étienne, and beginning to feel the emotional fallout of our shameless library floor show.

Oh, God. I remembered the annoyed expression on the librarian's face. Was it really *me* standing there with my shirt unbuttoned while a man caressed my breasts in public? Well, that was the beauty of being a stranger in a strange land. If that had happened in Orlando, I would've—well, never mind. It wouldn't have happened in Orlando. Blake *never* kissed me that passionately, even in the beginning of our relationship, even in the privacy of our dark bedroom. He was much too staid, much too dull.

Another cue that clueless me should have picked up on. My God, I was starting to form a list:

Five Clues My Husband Was Gay

1. He had better decorating sense than I did. Of course, I attributed it to the fact that he was an architect and worked with designers....
2. We could walk on the beach and his hair looked better at the end of the walk than when we started. Of course, Blake hated the beach—too messy, all that sand tracking up the car—so we didn't go much. The hair thing could have been a fluke....
3. He counted calories more stringently than my physically fit girlfriends. Okay, I never could justify that one....
4. His blatant lack of interest in sex—with me, anyway. Which leads me full circle—
5. Never in the eighteen-year span of our relationship did he kiss me as passionately as Étienne did today,

not even in the beginning of our relationship. Blake was much too polite to fondle my breasts in public. Much too…gay.

Was it any wonder my body hummed at Étienne's touch? Yes, it *hummed*. Maybe I wasn't just drunk on the wine, I was drunk from being touched the way a woman should be touched.

Okay, actually, I *was* drunk from the wine, but my body *had* hummed.

My God, he wanted to be my lover. What was wrong with me? I guess the humming-body should negate the no-chemistry excuse. Shouldn't it?

I'd nearly failed chemistry in high school. So what did I know about it?

Maybe I was being hasty in writing him off. I mean, before I started analyzing the possibility of being his lover, my body responded. Maybe it wasn't a chemistry issue as much as I was just unprimed.

Maybe a younger lover was just what I needed to prime the old pump?

"Oh my God."

I sighed as I followed the path around a sharp, tree-lined bend and ran smack into Jacques Jauvert.

"Oh! *Bonjour,*" I said. Oh, yuck. It was the first time I'd seen the curmudgeon since the opening reception and—

He wasn't alone. Oooh…he was with one of the other residents—the guy from Argentina, I think—and they looked a little startled to see me.

"*Bonjour.*" Jauvert did not smile. The Argentinean stood stoically with his arms crossed. I got the distinct impression

I'd *interrupted* something because they stood a little too close, even for the French. I'd bet money Jauvert wasn't dissing Mr. Argentina's artwork.

Ha, ha, ha, *ookay,* I got it. Ya didn't have to tell me twice. My gaydar was fixed and fully operational. Hey, I'd just completed my Blake list, hadn't I?

Not a problem. Despite what happened with my husband, I didn't care what Jauvert's or Mr. Argentina's preferences were. Live and let live, that had always been my motto—just as long as Jauvert extended the same courtesy to my flowers.

The three yards I had to walk to pass them were the most awkward three yards I'd ever walked, but I rounded the next bend without another word and walked to my bungalow feeling a little woozy and a lot more uncertain about whether to make a midnight rendezvous with Étienne.

Come to me at midnight and I promise you won't regret it. The promise made my breath hitch.

The sculptor's studio door was open. I tuned in to read the emotional barometer. Were he and his lady fighting or making love? Though I'd never actually heard them doing the latter.

All was quiet and it hit me that it was a sad state when life came down to listening to see if I could hear other people making love.

Then I remembered Étienne.

I could make love if I wanted to.

The wind seemed to confirm as much. A strong gust blew through the courtyard, sounding the wind chimes above the sculptor's door.

The fat tomcat lay in a diminishing puddle of late-afternoon sunshine. His food dish was empty. He looked at me and *yowled,* a plaintive sound, as though he expected me to inform him when dinner would be served.

"What?" I said, unlocking my door.

He sauntered over and wound around my legs in that languid, sensual manner of a cat. I bent down and scratched him behind the ears.

"I'm sorry, I don't have anything for you."

He purred and nudged my hand into another stroke, walking away so my hand trailed the length of his back and tail. I noticed a tag on his collar read Guerrier. If I remembered correctly, *Guerrier* was French for *warrior.* He started to turn around for more, but a bird landed on the ground by the stucco studio wall and the cat lunged for it.

"I can't say I blame you, buddy. Don't wait for someone to serve you dinner. If you don't go get it yourself you just might miss out altogether."

The bird flew away and Guerrier plopped down as if the exertion had exhausted him.

As I stood to let myself inside I saw the sculptor at the window of his studio. He didn't wave or acknowledge me before he disappeared from view. I wondered if he even saw me.

AT ELEVEN FORTY-FIVE that night, I exited the Odéon metro station and walked down the boulevard Saint Germain to the rue de l'Ancienne Comédie. The street was flooded with people and the city was just starting to come alive.

It only took me five minutes to make it to Étienne's *crêperie.* As I approached, I noticed a group of four beautiful young women, early twenties, standing at the counter talking to him.

I hung back and watched. Perhaps they were ordering. But there was something in the way Étienne stood leaning with his elbows on the counter talking to them, something in the way they flipped their hair and laughed at what he said to them. Although I couldn't hear what he said.

Whether it was their microminiskirts or the way they carried their firm young bodies, I, now perfectly sober after our drunken afternoon gropefest, suddenly found the chasm that spanned the twelve years between us insurmountable.

I shoved my purse—and the five condoms tucked in the inside pocket—up under my arm and went home.

It wasn't because I was jealous of the younger women— well, maybe I envied their youth. It was a strange feeling for me because I'd never had a problem with age. But I would have felt like his mother walking up to greet him in my sandals that I thought were strappy and sexy, but now seemed like sensible shoes next to the young Parisian women.

I must have been crazy—or drunk—coming out at this hour to meet him.

Up on the boulevard Saint Germain, I hailed a cab rather than braving the metro at midnight, and rode back to the center.

The lights were still on in the sculptor's studio. No music or sounds of conversation, only the smell of his cigarette mixing with the jasmine—his calling card.

I went inside feeling foolish about how I had spent the day. I knew I should just let it go, there was no harm in getting drunk and making out in a public place with a man who was so much younger—then I cringed and flung my purse onto the couch.

What was I doing here? Why had I even come?

I wanted to be home in my studio by the lake; I wanted to be in a place where people bought my flowers; I wanted to talk to Rita. I glanced at my watch. With the time difference, it wasn't even six-thirty in the morning. She'd kill me if I called her this early, especially if it was to tell her that I had the chance to have sex but turned it down.

I went into the kitchen to see if there was anything to eat and all I found was a wedge of cheese starting to grow mold, a few shriveled-looking strawberries, a hunk of stale baguette, some coffee and—*ugh*—more red wine.

As I dumped the wasted food in the garbage can, a sad feeling washed over me. It wasn't the young women or Étienne or the age difference that made me run away tonight.

It was me.

Pure and simple, it was *me*.

Would I ever be able to love or make love again without the dark shadow of doubt hanging in the back of my mind? That there was something fundamentally wrong with me looming in the back of my mind?

I started shaking as the feeling seeped into my bone marrow. I pressed my hands to my face and my mind whirled from Étienne to Blake to Jauvert.

"No! I am not going to stand here and implode."

I got the bed painting from the patio and put it on the easel. I splashed bold strokes of color onto the white sheets, intensified the angles and shadows on the sculptor's face, and for want of being able to capture the blonde's features, I painted him in bed with a woman who ended up looking remarkably like Camille Deveau. She was lying on her back with her head hanging slightly over the edge of the wildly colored bed. The sculptor, with his wide, naked shoulders, lush mouth and seductive eyes was on top of her in the full throes of coital ecstasy.

I painted until the sun rose, throwing onto the canvas all the pent-up frustration I harbored over not being able to go to Étienne; all the hurt over Blake's lies; and all the anger for all those wasted years I stayed with a man who didn't love me the way I deserved to be loved.

TEN

I AWOKE THE next day to the sound of loud voices. Before I could force open my eyes, it sounded as if they were fighting right over me.

Oh, for God's sake. This was getting old.

I sat up and rubbed my eyes with my paint-splotched hands. I picked at the color that was caked under my fingernails.

The noise had faded and I wondered for a moment if I'd dreamt it. So I got up and kneaded my stiff neck as I looked at my watch.

It was one o'clock in the afternoon. A rush of guilt flooded through me. Staying up all night and sleeping away the day was becoming a habit.

I hadn't partied the night away or whiled away the hours making love....

I'd spent a drunken afternoon that almost led me to such exploits. I cringed as I thought about last night's close call with Étienne, and amazingly enough, rather than beating myself up over it, I was relieved nothing happened. My feelings confirmed that while I liked Étienne, I was right in not taking him as my lover.

I studied the canvas I'd worked on so hard all night. See, I'd gotten something done last night. No need to beat myself up over the turned-around days and nights.

I stared at the image, at the bright, wild colors and the way I'd defined the sculptor's face. Wow, it really did look like him. And I wasn't even a portrait painter. Not bad, if I did say so myself.

Now, the image of him making love to Camille Deveau... Hmm, I'd have to think about that. Perhaps I needed to paint over it and start again?

I decided to deliberate in the shower.

After I'd dressed in jeans and a short-sleeved mock turtleneck, leaving my hair down to air dry, I realized I was so hungry I considered eating the canvas rather than painting over Madame Deveau. So I grabbed my purse, not bothering to take the condoms out of the inner pocket, and stepped out of the studio to go to the market.

I had just shut and locked my door when the blonde came flying out of the sculptor's studio, shrieking at the top of her lungs, tears making her mascara run down her face in grotesque black streaks.

The sculptor was not far behind her.

"Matilde!"

He yelled something else after her. She stopped at the head of the path that led away from our courtyard and he caught up with her. He placed his hands on her shoulders and shook her gently, but she just cried and allowed herself to be shaken, like a rag doll in the hands of a child. Until she fell against him and sobbed, muttering something that sounded like a plea for—forgiveness? For love?

What? I wished I understood what they were saying.

Especially when he shook his head and repeated, *"Non."* Over and over, to everything she said, which just made her cry harder.

Was he breaking up with her?

It seemed so when she threw her arms around his neck and tried to kiss him, but he pushed her away.

"Non!" More unintelligible French. More hysterical sobs from the blonde.

Oh my God, is he gay, too?

Was the entire male population gay and I just didn't realize it?

Well, no, Étienne wasn't, but ugh, that was another problem unto itself.

Why else would the sculptor reject such a stunning woman who was so obviously in love with him?

He held her and let her sob into his chest for a few minutes and then he put a protective arm around her and they walked off together. He murmured soft French to her as they disappeared around the bend.

Well, now I knew what it felt like to be invisible, which was probably a good thing because it would have been very embarrassing if they'd realized I'd been watching them.

When I got to the gate, I saw that they'd turned to the left and were walking on the sidewalk. To avoid being seen, I kept a fair distance behind them. But I was so curious to know where they were going. Were they breaking up or was this just another chapter in their volatile relationship?

If I followed them I'd be able to observe the blonde and

I might be able to paint her likeness over Camille's face in *The Bed*. I'd have to paint in the mascara streaks. Even though it seemed a little extreme, it went well with the dramatic feel of the painting.

I followed them for miles, across the River Seine, from the left bank to the right, until they turned onto rue Pigalle. Not the nicest part of Paris. Even the air smelled different here—vaguely of garbage and cigar smoke melded with the cloying perfume and the sweat of broken dreams.

During World War II, American servicemen called this district "Pig Alley," because of all the hookers, sordid strip joints and sleazy sex clubs.

Although, I'd heard that it was starting to become a mecca for the famous creative types, at face value, it looked as if not much had changed.

I strolled past Joy's Sex Emporium and a place called Le Star Dust—Sexy Follies. The front of Le Star Dust was painted purple and a graffiti-covered metal security door was pulled halfway down over the entrance.

Right next door was what looked like a pawnshop. The sign hanging out over the sidewalk read Change, but the *g* was broken on the sign over the doorway and it read, Chance.

Which was it? Change or chance?

Perhaps one facilitated the other?

The sculptor and the blonde stopped in the middle of the sidewalk. She broke down in another fit, hitting him, banging on his chest with her fists, slapping him in the face before she ran away—in my direction.

To avoid being seen, I doubled back a few storefronts to a café, where I waited for them to pass.

When I emerged, I didn't see them in either direction. Either they'd ducked into a shop—a sex shop?—or they'd been swallowed up by the curious Pigalle crowds.

I walked up to rue Fontaine, wondering if perchance they'd somehow gotten back by me when I turned into the café. They weren't there.

Just as well. What was I supposed to do if I found them? Tell them I'd followed them to study the blonde's face for my painting? Or that I was dying to know what on earth they'd been fighting about over the three weeks I'd been here? Or perhaps I could explain that since coming to Paris, I'd been prone to flights of fancy that more often than not turned out to be wild-goose chases?

I sighed, seeing the most truth in the last claim.

But I could always keep this from becoming a flight of fancy if I had a look around.

That's what I did, for a long time. As the hours gave way one into the other, I wandered the streets, absorbing the strange and exotic sights of Paris's red-light district.

The lurid neon signs of the Sexodrome and the Musée de l'Érotisme were muted by the golden glow of the late-afternoon sun. Scantily clad prostitutes sprawled in brightly painted doorways lining the rue Fontaine. Most of them called out to me. Obviously, anyone who was willing to pay for services was welcome.

Women, some of whom I guessed were transvestites, hailed taxis on the rue Pigalle. Were they on their way to work the Bois de Boulogne on the west side?

Jauvert's introductory letter advised us to avoid the Bois at night. No matter how beautiful and serene the park seemed by day, he said, it transformed into the sleazy underbelly of the city after sunset. Perhaps, here before me in living color, were its inhabitants.

I wandered, mesmerized and sickened by the darker side of the City of Light; drawn in by this quarter where scandalous luxury mated with utter wretchedness in a streetside freak show that lured one closer, closer to the flame, until, I imagined, it consumed body and soul. Why had the sculptor and the blonde come here? Did one of them live here? Did they come here to indulge some kinky fetish? Maybe that's what had the blonde so riled up.

I strolled in awe through the curious blend of exquisite landmarks, such as the Moulin Rouge, and old burlesque theaters. I marveled at how the sex shops and prostitutes mixed with the occasional bourgeois building and the hordes of tourists.

It was all there: hope and despair, opportunity seeker and opportunist, wide-eyed innocent and jaded exhibitionist— stewing and melding, the stench lingering in the fetid air.

Did dreams beckon these people to Paris? Or had they, too, run away from the past? Selling their souls for a few months' reprieve or a way to anesthetize themselves against the future?

As the initial voyeuristic curiosity subsided, I decided Pigalle, simultaneously cruel and cunning, was no different from any other place in the world. The lost souls I'd seen wandering the street were not so dissimilar from me.

At least my running away from life in Orlando had plucked me from a soul-snuffing existence and deposited me into a situation ripe with opportunity for growth.

I guess it really was all up to me whether I grew or spent three months spinning my wheels.

As the sun set over Paris's eighteenth arrondissement, I decided it *was* up to me whether my Paris would be cruel or kind. But before I could decide, first I had to find my way back home.

I DECIDED TO take the metro since I was hungry and tired after walking around all day. I dug through my purse to get my train pass out of my wallet and discovered my wallet was missing.

Oh, for God's sake, did someone lift it out of my purse as I wandered the streets like a wide-eyed tourist? I turned in a quick circle as if I'd see someone standing close by looking through it.

People rushed past me in a hurry to get on the metro, but no one had my wallet. I checked the bottom of my purse to see if any coins had fallen out, but no luck. I even contemplated trying to push my way through on the tail of paying riders, but this was a station with large sliding doors that opened and shut fast and hard, allowing just one person to make it through.

If worst came to worst, perhaps I could find another metro station with turnstile entrances. And risk the chance of being caught?

I thought about the signs: Chance. Change. My legs ached as I mounted the steps to take me back up to the street.

I went to the closest café to ask for directions to the next closest metro station. The place wasn't as crowded as I thought it would be based on the steady flow of traffic outside.

I walked up to the bar.

"Excusez-moi, s'il vous plaît." The bartender cocked a brow at me and I said, *"Parlez-vous anglais?"*

Please speak English.

"Non." His voice was gruff, but he held up a finger, which I guessed meant he wanted me to wait. So I did, and that's when I noticed the sculptor seated across the bar in all his dark, rough-hewn glory. The blonde was not with him.

He must have sensed someone watching because he glanced up, but I ducked my head so he wouldn't catch me staring.

The bartender came back and said something in French to no one in particular.

"I speak English," said my neighbor.

The bartender gestured to me. I felt completely transparent, as if the sculptor knew I'd followed him up here. But then I decided it was a ridiculous thought. How could he know?

"May I help you?" he said from across the bar.

"I'm looking for the closest metro station. Um, beyond the one out there."

He nodded, downed his espresso, shoved his Gitane cigarettes in his pocket and tossed a few bills on the bar.

"I will show you."

"Oh, thank you, but that's not necessary. If you'll just point me in the right direction I can manage."

He ran a hand over the whiskered shadow on his cheeks and said, "A pretty foreigner should not wander the streets of Pigalle alone at night—unless she is seeking *that* sort of thing."

That sort of thing?

Pretty foreigner?— Ha, there's that word again—*pretty.* Just like…*pretty,* decorative little florals.

"I am on my way home." He walked around the bar and

stood in front of me. I hadn't realized just how tall and broad-shouldered he was. "You might as well come with me." My heart nearly leaped out of my chest. Oh my God, he *did* know. Or…wait…perhaps he thought I was after *that sort of thing.*

"I don't know you, *monsieur.* Why would I go with you?"

He laughed, and if I hadn't been so nervous, I might have liked the way his eyes crinkled at the corners in George Clooney fashion.

"Don't play coy. I am Jean Luc Le Garric. We are neighbors. You followed me up here this afternoon, *non?*"

ELEVEN

MAYBE IT WAS the fallout of seeing so many transvestites and prostitutes in one place, and all those hungry eyes and greedy hands eager to devour half-naked bodies and strip souls bare, but I was glad to get out of Pigalle.

I was glad to have someone accompany me home.

Even though I was embarrassed that Jean Luc Le Garric knew I'd followed him and even though I had to swallow my pride and borrow metro fare from him, my feet hurt so badly and I was so hungry that it was worth it.

Outside the café, he paused. "I don't understand why you want a different metro station. This is the one that will best take you home."

I couldn't bring myself to tell him I needed a station with turnstiles rather than doors so I could scoot through without paying. He'd think I was a complete and utter freak. If he didn't already.

So, I did the only thing I could do: I played dumb.

"Oh, I didn't realize that. Well, I guess you saved me a lot of needless walking."

Once we were on the train, he sat next to me. His long legs in their dark jeans bumped the seat in front of us. "Let me see your metro map. I will show you how to read it. To save you needless walking."

My cheeks flushed hot and I couldn't look at him. "I don't have it with me."

"You do not know Paris and yet you go out without a map and without your wallet? Is this how you do things in America?"

"My wallet may have been stolen."

"Did you report it to the police?"

"No. It might be in my studio. Last night, after I got home, I tossed my purse on the couch and it might have fallen out. At least that's what I'm hoping."

"Well if you insist on being a *flâneuse* at least make sure you have your map with you."

I blinked. "A what?"

"A *flâneuse*." I liked the way his accent caused the last syllables of the word to do an upturn, even though I had no idea what he was talking about.

He must have gathered as much because he said, "A *flâneur* is one who wanders the streets. Many great artists were notorious *flâneurs*. A *flâneuse* is a female wanderer."

A wanderer. I liked that.

The train stopped. A man in our car got out and a mother and her two children boarded.

"Does your girlfriend live in Pigalle?"

"My girlfriend? I do not have a girlfriend."

Oh. Perhaps they did break up.

"The woman who comes to your studio every day. I hear you arguing. Lucky for you my French is so poor. I don't mean to be nosy, but she's very beautiful and she seems to be crazy about you. Are you sure there's no way to work it out?"

He squinted at me, dark brown eyes that slanted down at the corners, framed by long, black lashes. "Do you speak of Matilde?"

"Is that her name?"

"Matilde is not my lover. Though she would like to be. That is why we fight. She is only my model, or she used to be. Her work with me is finished."

He was a bit arrogant.

"Matilde, hmm?" How could a heterosexual man refuse to be her lover? "She is so beautiful."

He made a disgusted noise designed to end the conversation and stared straight ahead as the train hummed along. I think it was the first time I'd ever ridden the metro when a busker wasn't in my face with his music. What I wouldn't give for the strains of an accordion or an off-key singer belting out, "I love Paris in the springtime..." That way I wouldn't feel such a competing need to fill the silence.

"So, I gather you are not part of the exchange program?"

"*Non.* I am a native Parisian."

"Really? I was under the impression that the Delacroix Centre was strictly an exchange center. Are you the only permanent artist?"

"*Oui.*"

"I would love to see your work sometime."

He nodded.

He didn't say anything else such as, *Sure, come on over,* or

How about when we get home? I took the hint from his short answers that I should quit asking questions. I mean, after all, he was nice enough to help me out of a bind. If not for him, I would still be walking.

We traveled in silence, changing trains twice, until we finally arrived at the École Militaire stop. It was beginning to feel familiar.

"This is us." He stood back and let me exit the train ahead of him. When we popped up onto the street again, night had fallen on the city and the air had taken on a chill. I ran my hands over my arms trying to warm up. As a native Floridian, I still wasn't in the habit of grabbing a jacket when I went out.

"You are cold?" Jean Luc asked.

I nodded.

"Please, take my jacket."

He placed it on my shoulders, the bulk of it hanging large on my frame. It smelled of cigarettes, cologne and man. The gesture touched me. It made me think of how gently he'd placed his arm around Matilde and how she'd leaned into him. Who could blame her for feeling the way she did?

I wished I could talk to her and tell her I knew how it felt to love a man who was emotionally unavailable. And that she would be... She would be okay. Eventually.

"How do you like Paris?" Jean Luc's voice startled me out of my thoughts.

"I like it. It has so much to offer. I really feel as if I'm just getting my bearings. And one third of the residency is over."

We turned down the pedestrian market street, rue Cler. All the shops were closed up for the night and it reminded me I had no food in the kitchen. Delicious aromas wafted from the café at the corner of rue Bosquet—people dined on sumptuous-looking meals that made my stomach growl. I put my hand over my belly and glanced up at Jean Luc.

He smiled. "Are you hungry?"

I nodded. "I set out to the market this afternoon, but somehow I ended up in Pigalle instead."

Shaking his head, he stopped in front of the café.

"Why don't we get something to eat."

"Oh, I would love to, but I don't have my wallet. Remember?"

"I am inviting you to be my guest."

A woman passed by with a tray loaded with bread, a carafe of white wine, some sort of chicken dish and a salad niçoise, the green beans, boiled eggs, potatoes and olives artfully arranged on the plate.

My mouth watered just looking at it.

"I should be taking you out to dinner for rescuing me."

He walked on ahead and I followed him. "We shall go see my friend Michel at the Bistro du Mars. It is just around the corner. Have you been there?"

I'd passed by this restaurant many times on my way home from shopping on the rue Cler but had never stopped and eaten there. In Paris there were so many restaurants it was almost overwhelming.

We stepped inside the intimate space that was no larger than my living room at home and had seating for about ten parties. Two of the tables were occupied, one with a couple and the other with a family of three.

Delectable smells greeted us and the white lace curtains and starched tablecloths stood out brilliantly against the red velvet banquettes, red carpet and textured red wallpaper.

"Jean Luc!" A tall, thin woman who looked to be in her mid-fifties, with a straight black chin-length bob moved gracefully from behind the bar toward us. She removed her rimless, rectangular glasses, which she wore low on her nose, before kissing him on each cheek and bubbling over in exuberant French. From the few words I understood, I gathered it had been a while since he'd been in.

"Marie-Grace, please allow me to introduce my friend and neighbor—" Jean Luc looked at me blankly and I realized I'd never told him my name.

"*Enchantée, madame. Je m'appelle* Annabelle."

"She is an American in Paris for the exchange program at the Delacroix Centre."

"Ahh, *enchantée, madame.*" Marie-Grace shoved her glasses back on, gave me the once-over, then leaned in and air-kissed both of my cheeks.

In the very back of the restaurant, a man in a white chef's coat opened a little window, set out two plates of salad and called a hearty greeting.

"Please, be seated." Marie-Grace gestured to a table in the corner. Then she and Jean Luc walked to the window. Marie-Grace retrieved the food and Jean Luc and the man, whom I presumed to be Michel, talked for a few minutes.

When I sat down, I realized how thoroughly exhausted I was. Starved and bone tired, but not too tired to watch Jean Luc at the back of the restaurant.

I decided his longish, curly dark hair made him look kind of like the actor Olivier Martinez. Olivier Martinez with amazing full lips, mile-wide shoulders and George Clooney eyes.

Lord, the combination worked.

Marie-Grace set a basket of fresh French bread and a carafe of water on the table, humming as she worked. It was a nice content sound and I relaxed into the red velvet banquette and watched Jean Luc walk toward me.

He ordered a bottle of white burgundy and we both took Marie-Grace's recommendation for the Dover sole.

When she walked away to place our order, Jean Luc said, "So, Annabelle, I may call you Annabelle, *non?*"

I nodded.

"Will you please explain why you were following me today?"

THANK GOD FOR good service.

Marie-Grace brought the wine just as I started to panic.

I managed to stammer out, "Well, it's complicated."

Voilà, she appeared with the bottle.

"Won't you have a drink with us?" I had no idea whether inviting the restaurateur to join you for a drink violated some esoteric French custom. All I knew was that it bought me more time.

"How lovely of you to ask, but I must decline so I may tend to my patrons." She nodded and resumed her humming as she walked away.

"That was a nice try," said Jean Luc. "But even if she would have joined us, I would not have forgotten the question, which was, will you please explain why you were following me today?"

I sipped my wine and tried to avoid looking at his eyes, but I could feel his penetrating gaze watching me, waiting expectantly.

I set down my glass and took a deep breath. "I don't know

why I followed you. Are you in some kind of trouble where you'd have to worry about being tailed?"

He laughed, and I was glad because it lightened the mood.

"No, I'm not in any sort of trouble. That's why I get alarmed when I discover someone is watching my every move."

"If someone did not know the circumstance, that could sound very paranoid."

"I suppose it might." He lifted the cloth on the breadbasket and offered me some. I took a piece and put it on my bread plate, ignoring my rumbling tummy, waiting to see where this conversation was leading before I tore into the food.

I folded my hands in my lap and leaned in. "Okay, here's the truth." Or at least part of the truth. "I've listened to you and your…Matilde fighting almost daily since I arrived. You're very loud, did you know that?"

He shook his head. "I was not aware. I beg your pardon." He picked up some bread, tore off a piece and spread it with butter. "And you were saying?"

I watched his sexy full lips as he bit into the bread.

"I was just curious about you. That's all." I sipped my wine. Over the top of my glass, I watched as his throat worked in a swallow.

"So what you are confessing is that you are nosy."

I almost choked. "I'm not nosy. I'm just…"

He smiled. His eyes crinkled and I lost my train of thought. My mind jumped back to the night I saw him standing in the window wearing the red bandanna, and my stomach fluttered. This time it wasn't because of hunger.

"You are poking fun at me," I said.

The image of him in the red bandanna made me remember Matilde standing naked in his studio and how he swore they were never lovers. He *had to be* gay to not want her.

I was such an idiot. After what I'd been through with Blake was I *really* developing a crush on a gay man? There was probably some sad psychological disorder that made women go after unattainable men.

His brows knit. "Poking fun? I do not understand."

Damn language barrier. I twisted the napkin in my lap. "Making fun of me?"

He stared at me blankly.

"Come on, your English is very good, surely you understand what I'm saying."

He arched a brow. "I am having fun at your expense."

I blinked once. Twice.

"Okay, you're a joker, aren't you? You knew exactly what I was saying." I buttered my bread and bit into it.

"Well, then, since I have a good sense of humor, I suppose I shall forgive you for following me today."

There was something in his gaze, the way it lingered bold and assessing, slowly and seductively searching my face, lingering on my lips, before returning to my eyes.

My head swam and my heart turned over.

Okay, maybe I'd been hasty. Gay men did not look at women the way he was looking at me.

We spent the rest of the evening talking about wine, the best nontouristy places to go in Paris, art—I learned that he taught sculpting at the École des Beaux-Arts, Paris's prestigious art school, a job he relished because he could divide his time between the school and his studio—and my new-found theories about Camille Deveau and Georges Fonteneau's

secret relationship. Yes, he'd heard of her, but not their pur-
ported love affair.

"It's such a sad story. Loving a man she can't have. I can
relate to this woman on so many levels."

"Did you come to Paris to escape a love you could not
have?"

I stared at the candle through the golden pool of wine
in my glass.

"I'll make a deal with you—tell me why you don't want
to be Matilde's lover, how you could refuse such a beautiful
woman who is obviously crazy about you, and I'll explain
exactly how I relate to Camille Deveau and why I came to
Paris. See, you'll get a two-for-one."

He dipped his head in acceptance. "Touché." He touched
his glass to mine. "The situation with Matilde is complicated. But just in case you wondered, I did not reject her
because I do not like women. *Au contraire*. I like women very
much."

Oh.

Something flared inside me so intense it made my breath
catch in my chest. I'd never felt so comfortable so fast with
a man. He was funny and interesting, not to mention what
he did to me when he smiled.

On the way home, walking on the uneven sidewalk under
an indigo sky so starry it could have been a Van Gogh painting, I said, "So you knew I was your neighbor? I always
thought you weren't aware of me."

"Unaware? Of you? *Non*. I saw you peering through your
windows at me."

I swatted him on the arm, noting that even earlier today,
I would have been mortified to know he saw me watching

him. But now I was completely at ease. "How come you didn't wave or say hello?"

"Are you kidding? Every time I would look out at you, you would turn your head or rush away from the window. I thought you were very unfriendly."

I laughed. If you only knew.

He waited with me as I unlocked the door. I realized, as I slid the key in the lock, I didn't want the evening to end.

On a wild hair, I said, "Would you like to come in? I have a bottle of red I've been needing a good excuse to open. Perhaps you'll accept a glass of wine in lieu of me reimbursing you for the metro ticket?"

"I think that sounds like an equitable exchange." He followed me inside.

"Make yourself at home." I went into the kitchen, opened the wine and got two glasses.

When I came back into the living room, he was standing in front of my easel…looking at *The Bed* painting.

TWELVE

JEAN LUC ARCHED a brow seductively. He tilted his head to the left and stared at the canvas.

"I recognize the man. It's an excellent likeness of me. But I must know, who is the beautiful woman I'm…*with*?" I set the wineglasses on the coffee table, trying to figure out how to explain why I'd painted such an intimate portrait of him. When I straightened, his gorgeous eyes were watching me, looking smug and amazed, as if he'd caught me naked. But the French didn't have nudity hang-ups. Americans had cornered that market, and in true form, I felt naked and exposed standing there unable to explain it away.

For a few breathless seconds, it felt as if my heart had stopped, until it kicked in and pounded double time and all the blood in my body rushed to my face.

"She's nobody," I said.

A reflex made me step forward and try to yank the painting off the easel. I just wanted to stash it out of sight, but Jean Luc stopped me with a firm, steady hand on top of mine. If I could've crawled under the couch I would have, but I couldn't even move my hand out from under his.

"*Personne?* Er, nobody?" His brows knit and he moved in closer to study the image of the woman. "She looks like your painter Deveau, the one with whom you identify. No?" A sly, knowing smile spread across his face.

"No." I jerked my hand away, and followed his gaze to the Camille Deveau biography lying on the table next to my easel.

Oh, God.

He picked it up, studying the photograph of her on the cover and looked back at the canvas. "You really are an accomplished portrait artist. I am impressed. And flattered."

I opened my mouth to say something, anything, racking my brain for a way out of this mortifying mess, but all that came out in one breathless rush was the truth.

"I intended to paint you with Matilde, but I never could capture her features." I turned around and walked back to the coffee table. With my back to him, I picked up my glass and gulped the wine. "Somehow Camille Deveau crept into your bed."

"And you see yourself in this tragic French painter? Is that why you painted her in my bed?"

I shrugged, still turned away from him.

"Does that mean you fancy yourself in my bed?"

My mind whirled and I heard his footsteps on the wooden floor. He stopped behind me.

Placing his hands on my shoulders, he gently turned me around and lifted my chin until I looked at him.

His question hung in the air between us as palpable as a lover's kiss, and he traced my bottom lip with his knuckle.

My body ached for his touch, and I caught his finger gently between my teeth, closing my eyes as I closed my lips around it.

"Come here," he murmured.

I don't know who moved first, but the next thing I knew we were in each other's arms.

His kiss sent new spirals of ecstasy unfurling in my body. I couldn't remember when I'd wanted a man as much as I wanted him.

I didn't care about Matilde or Blake or that Jean Luc had seen the painting. All I knew was, yes, I was the woman who should be in his bed.

I DIDN'T END UP in his bed.

He ended up in mine.

Thank God for Rita's going-away gift. Three down. Ninety-seven to go. It was a beautiful night.

He left at four-thirty because he had an early class to teach. I offered to get up and fix him some coffee, but he just kissed me and said, "Stay in bed. I'll see you later this afternoon."

I couldn't sleep after he left. I tossed and turned, the scent of our love still in the air. The day's turn of events swam in my head, merging with the Pigalle freak show.

I turned over and lay on my back, stretching my naked body. This time yesterday I never dreamt Jean Luc Le Garric would be in my bed.

This time yesterday I didn't even know his name was Jean Luc. He was simply the sculptor across the way. My, my, how fast things changed.

I got up, pulled on my big white shirt and padded into the kitchen on bare feet to fix myself a pot of coffee. As it brewed, I saw the corner of my wallet sticking out from beneath a pillow on the old couch. It must have fallen out of my purse when I tossed the bag on the sofa after my wildgoose chase to see Étienne. Finding it was a good omen. Yes, a very good sign.

With a hot cup in my hand, I put a blank canvas on my easel and drew with paint the image of one of the prostitutes I'd seen draped over a cobalt-painted chair in the bright red doorway of a sex shop.

A painted lady on a painted chair in a painted doorway.

It worked. I would call it simply *The Painted Lady*. The scene came from a new place in me just recently awakened. Albeit the image wasn't pretty, but there would be no more "...*pretty*, decorative little florals...."

At least not while I was in Paris.

Strange though, until now, I'd never aspired to the kind of painting that archived life. Life happened all around me. I always thought it was the egotistical souls who fancied their lives so interesting they were compelled to immortalize it on canvas.

That's why I painted flowers.

Maybe I painted flowers because nothing else around me was interesting enough to paint? Until now.

Obviously.

I sighed and drew brown streaks through the prostitute's blond hair. The thought of abandoning my flowers didn't settle well. I felt like a traitor, as if I was abandoning who I really was rather than growing into something bigger.

I stepped back and considered my work, then painted a crown of daisies on the hooker's head and a basket of roses at her feet.

I worked fast, using quick, shorthand strokes to rough in the images in my mind before the vivid details faded: the way a transvestite's miniskirt hiked up in back as he got into a cab, the tattooed woman in the sequined thong and itty-bitty bikini top that exposed half moons of dark nipples as she danced under the Folies Pigalle sign, the lingerie-clad "hostess" asleep in the window of the cabaret...

At about ten o'clock, when my stomach demanded I go to the market to pick up some breakfast, I was just wiping my paint-stained hands on a rag when someone knocked on the door. Contemplating not answering since I wasn't dressed, I peeked out a louver in the shutters to see who it was.

My breath caught. Jean Luc.

I was a mess. I wasn't expecting him for hours. Even so, I wasn't about to leave him standing out there.

I opened the door and he smiled that smile that made me dizzy, holding a loaf of bread, some cheese, salami and the most beautiful bouquet of mixed spring flowers.

"You weren't supposed to be here until this afternoon." I leaned in and kissed him long and deep. "I haven't even showered or dressed."

He didn't say a word, but dropped the groceries and flowers and pulled me into his arms, sliding his hands under my shirt to cup my bare bottom and pull me into him.

In the foggy recesses of my memory I vaguely remembered a time when I would have been mortified at the thought of having a man touch me in such intimate places when I wasn't shower fresh... But that was another life.

Letting everything lie where it fell, Jean Luc scooped me up and carried me into the bedroom and we picked up where we left off early that morning.

AFTERWARD, WE LAY in bed, my head on his shoulder, tucked into the crook of his neck. He held me possessively against him, gently stroking my arm.

"Ah, I forgot. The reason I came over here was to bring you a map. It would be a tragedy if my little *flâneuse* set out to wander and I was not there to help her find her way home."

I smiled up at him. "There's that word again. *Flâneuse.*"

"You act as if it is something distasteful. But it is not. The French writer Baudelaire— You have heard of him, *non?*"

I nodded.

"He once wrote, 'For the perfect *flâneur,* it is an immense joy to set up house in the heart of the multitude, amid the ebb and flow. To be away from home, yet to feel oneself everywhere at home, to see the world, to be at the center of the world, yet to remain hidden from the world—such are a few of the slightest pleasures of those independent, passionate, impartial natures which the tongue can but clumsily define.'"

"That's incredible. Do you always go around quoting literature?"

He tucked his hands behind his head, looking smug and pleased with himself.

I breathed in his scent, a mix of green, tobacco, spice and sex. It smelled like heaven. I closed my eyes and buried my nose in his neck, certain that any minute I would awaken to learn the past twenty-four hours had been one sexy dream.

Please, just five more minutes…

I propped myself up on my elbow and looked at him. "You know, we've made love four times, and I haven't even seen your studio. When do I get the grand tour?"

"Whenever you'd like."

"I'm going to shower, since that's where I was heading when you appeared. Make no mistake—I am not complaining, but I do need to freshen up."

I WRAPPED A TOWEL around myself and walked into the living room, blotting the excess water from my hair. "Jean Luc, what book was that Baudelaire piece you quoted—" Jean Luc stood at the door wearing nothing but his boxer shorts talking to Étienne.

Oh, shit.

WHILE JEAN LUC went out to get us something to eat, I called Rita.

"Oh my God. You had sex," said Rita. "I guess you're not homesick anymore?"

"Nope. All cured. He is incredible."

I fell back into the bed pillows and turned over on my side so I could sniff the pillowcase to see if it still smelled like him.

"Wait," said Rita. "Let me pour myself a glass of wine. Then I want details."

"Okay, hurry, he's going to be back soon and this is costing both of us a fortune." The line crackled as she set down the phone, but really I didn't care if it cost ten dollars a minute.

"I'm ready. Remember, details. Sexy details." I told her about Étienne and the library; about how I went to the restaurant at midnight but I couldn't go through with it and how he showed up at the door after Jean Luc and I had just had wild, passionate sex; and how Étienne was furious with me because I'd told him I didn't feel right about having sex because I was still married.

"Oh, you are such a liar."

"Well it was better than saying, 'Sorry, I'm just not that into you.'"

"Poor Étienne. It sounds like you broke his tender little heart."

"Something tells me Étienne's poor, tender little heart will be just fine. He'll find his middle-aged American woman to marry, he'll get his green card. He'll be happy, the woman will be *ecstatic* and they'll live happily ever after."

"Then get to the good stuff. So this other guy, Jean Luc? Is that his name?" She said it with a pinched, put-on French accent so it sounded more like Jaaahhn-Loook.

"Yes, that would be him." I flung my arm over my eyes and lay there smiling at the mental picture of him in my bed. "God, Ri, he's incredible."

"The sex is that good?"

"Mmm-hmm."

"Let me live vicariously through you. Details…"

"Which time?"

"Okay, nobody likes a braggart. But I'll forgive you and let you tell me about the steamiest, hottest, sexiest parts."

"All I'll say is that I haven't had this much fun since— I don't think I've ever had this much fun."

"So tell me…is he huge?"

"Ri! I can't believe you asked me that."

"Condom count? You are using them, aren't you?"

"Of course I am."

"How many?"

"Four."

"Four times? In twenty-four hours. I am so jealous. That's a good month for me. What about the blonde?"

I laughed to cover my annoyance.

"What about her? He said they're not involved."

"Yeah, right. Don't be naive."

"She was his model but not his lover. Did I tell you Ben's coming for a visit next month after his exams?"

"Anna! Don't change the subject and don't tell me you believe that line of crap about their being just friends. I saw them together. You don't fight like that unless you're doing it."

"Gee, thanks, Ri. Let's see if I have any other hot news you can pour ice water on."

I stared at the ceiling and willed myself not to succumb to the doubt.

"Rita, something's happened to me. It's like I'm finally free of all the shit that Blake put me through, and I'm talking eighteen years' worth. I look back now and I realize I never really lived. Until now."

Rita didn't respond.

"Everything's changed. My art's changed. I've changed. My God, I'm having red-hot, no-strings-attached sex—and might I add, it's the best sex I've ever had in my life. I'm happy, Rita, so don't spoil it."

I heard the front door open, the sound of Jean Luc rustling about in the kitchen. For a split second I wondered if going to the market was the only errand he ran. But I blinked away the thought as soon as it skittered into my head.

My sister sighed into the receiver. "I'm sorry. I am happy you're happy. And I'm jealous as hell you're having red-hot sex. Even if you won't tell me about it."

"Is everything all right with you and Fred?"

"Oh, yeah. We're just…married." She chuckled and the sound was kind of thin.

"Give him a hug for me, okay?"

I walked into the kitchen and mouthed the words *my sister*. Jean Luc smiled at me. He walked over, picked up my hair and started planting little kisses on the back of my neck.

"I will," she said. "And, Anna, I really am happy for you. That's why I left you the condoms, I wanted you to have a good time while you were there. A *lot* of good times. Just don't think you have to fall in love with the first guy you sleep with. I don't want you to get hurt again."

THIRTEEN

ONE MONTH LATER, lingering over cappuccinos with Jean Luc after a long walk through Luxembourg Gardens, it hit me. I had officially succumbed to the spell of springtime Paris. As we sat in companionable silence drinking in the city's charm, I couldn't remember the last time the chiding voices in my head were this quiet.

Here, in the heart of Paris, the voices quietly hummed a melodious tune, something vaguely familiar, but I couldn't quite put my finger on it.

Notes of promise?

I tilted my cup so that the dark coffee splashed up over the stiff white foam. It had been so long since I'd heard that tune, I couldn't remember. All I knew was it felt right.

Jean Luc lit a cigarette and turned his head to blow the smoke away from me.

"Will you to come to dinner with me at my parents' home on Sunday?"

Parents?

Over the month we'd been together he'd revealed a lot about himself—that he was forty-three years old, divorced for eight years and the father of a twenty-one-year-old daughter who went to college in Spain, which is where her mother lived.

When he wasn't at work or in his studio (where I now spent almost as much time as I did in my own), he was at his third-floor walk-up in a nineteenth-century building on the rue Guichard in the ritzy sixteenth arrondissement (teaching art in Paris must pay); his bedroom had an incredible, downy-soft featherbed, in which I could spend days (and we did when time permitted); his favorite kind of music was Portuguese fado; his favorite singer, Amália Rodriguez, owner of the sad, haunting voice I'd heard wailing from his studio before I met him; May was his favorite month of the year because the weather warmed up and he could enjoy the outdoors.

"En mai, fais ce qu'il te plaît." He said it meant, "In May, do what pleases you."

I loved the sound of that.

He told me he preferred to work all night and sleep all day, just like I did, but he said it was tough to pull it off when he had to teach an early class, and that he'd fallen into the upside-down cycle because he did not have anyone to share his bed at night.

I thought of all the times I'd heard Matilde and him laughing and fighting in the wee hours. And even worse, all the times when I saw the light on in his studio but I didn't hear them. But I hadn't seen hide nor hair of Matilde since that day I followed them to Pigalle. The day everything began.

I refused to let my mind create monsters because things were good. Too good. Not too-good-to-be-true. Just too good to mar with doubt over the shadow of a young, beautiful woman who was once a part of his life but seemed to have all but vanished.

I tried to ask about her, but he still refused to talk about her. Even after I spilled my guts over the reason my eighteen-year marriage ended.

I was starved for information about him, for clues to what composed the heart and soul of this complex, sexy man who was slowly but surely sweeping me off my feet.

One day when I went to an Internet café to do more research on Camille Deveau, I ended up typing in *Jean Luc Le Garric* instead. Here, I learned about his critically acclaimed Munich exhibit last March; it happened around the time I found out about Blake. How strange to put events that happened in his life before we met into context with mine.

Via the Internet, I also discovered he'd served on the faculty of the École des Beaux-Arts for fifteen years and was among the elite who'd graduated from said prestigious art school with unanimous accolades from his final-examination jury. A feat rarely accomplished by the few who gain admission to the school.

I knew all this, yet I hadn't heard a single word about his parents. I didn't even realize they lived locally.

Until now.

Family. That was so normal.

I was a woman who loved the calm comfort of family. The excitement of romance was fun for a while, but what I really craved was the simple security of family, the safety of it, the simplicity of it, the way you could come home and kick off your shoes, change into your jammies early on a Friday night and curl up on the couch.

In the days preceding the dinner, I felt alternately giddy and paralyzed at the prospect of dining with his family.

Because it was *his* family. Not mine.

For some reason the thought made me very sad. Maybe because it reminded me that other than Rita, Fred and Ben, I didn't have family. One of the hard things about losing Blake was that it was like losing my family all over again. It brought back shades of losing my parents. How even though Rita and I knew we'd always be a family, when they died it was as if our circle had been broken, flattened out into a straight line that we couldn't put back together again.

At one point I almost contemplated telling Jean Luc I couldn't go.

There would be too many questions.

My parents were dead. Yes, I had one sister and a son.

The son's father?

We're not divorced yet, but yes, I'm sleeping with your son.

Jean Luc told me in the French culture people did not ask such vulgar questions because they only served to embarrass the one being interrogated.

Speaking of questions, I had some for him.

Why did he want me to meet the folks?

What did this mean?

I couldn't ask, of course, for fear of being *vulgar*. Or maybe it was for fear of hearing what he'd say.

If he was introducing me for the reason most middle-aged men introduced women to their parents—I just wasn't ready for that yet, but I didn't know how to tell him that without making things weird between us.

So, that Sunday, I took out the cream cashmere sweater and navy trousers I'd worn on the airplane; donned my pearls, which I hadn't worn since arriving at the Delacroix Centre, and after smoothing my hair into a nice, neat chignon, I plucked out the errant gray. I was way overdue for a color and cut, but I hadn't noticed because of the camouflaging effect of wild curls *au naturel.*

My old uniform. It felt strange and looked stranger, as if I were staring in the mirror at someone I didn't recognize. But this was the only way I knew how to cope with meeting the parents.

When Jean Luc arrived at my door, dressed head to toe in his trademark black, he did a double take before hugging me.

"This is a different look for you."

I picked up the bouquet of hydrangeas I'd purchased for his mother and held them to my nose.

"You've never seen me dressed up," I said.

"I prefer you undressed." He buried his nose in the base of my neck. "Mmm, you smell nice."

He pulled away and looked at me. "It's just—it is not you. Your hair is pulled back so tightly it looks as if it hurts."

He reached around and his big hands fumbled with the band that held my hair, but I pulled out of his reach before he could free it.

"What are you doing?"

"I am returning you to the woman I know. To the woman with the curls. This one looks too uptight."

I was stunned. I couldn't help thinking of how Blake always preferred me to pull my hair back. Jean Luc caught my face in his hands and tilted it up to his.

"I love…"

His words trailed off, and the look on his face was soft as a caress. My stomach swirled in a slow spiral.

"I love your curls," he finally said.

As I let him reach back and free my hair, I realized I was glad he'd said *curls*.

I COULDN'T WAIT to call Rita the next day while Jean Luc was out. I guess I wanted to gloat since she'd been so sure he was going to sleep with me and go straight back to Matilde.

"I'm just glad I wore my pearls." I paced while I talked to her.

"That fancy, huh?"

"His parents' *house* was an eighteenth-century mansion near the Trocadéro. Rita, it was the most gorgeous place I'd ever seen. The dining room had these huge casement windows that framed this incredible view of the Eiffel Tower. It was unreal. I didn't think people really lived like that."

"So what were the folks like?"

The canvas on my easel caught my eye and I stopped in front of it, picked up my brush and dabbed some paint on the portrait of a Pigalle hooker. Despite the amount of time I'd been spending with Jean Luc, I'd managed to keep working and had finished fifteen paintings in the Pigalle series.

"*Maman* was very proper," I said. "Small and *très élégante*. Meticulously dressed. She wore her pearls, too. *Papa* was tall and handsome. That's where Jean Luc gets his looks. Strong resemblance."

"So does this mean things are serious?"

"No." I set down my brush and resumed pacing. "Absolutely not."

"Does Jean Luc know this?"

I COULDN'T WORK, I was distracted by a certain restlessness that had me throwing big gobs of paint on the canvas.

No rhyme.

No reason.

I was just too restless to stay inside and paint.

The Parisian wind told stories as it gusted in through the open eastern window and raced out in a cross-breeze through the French doors on the western side, only to circle around and flirt with me again.

It caressed my cheek, kissed my throat, whispered in my ear that there was so much out there that I needed to see. I closed my eyes against its lusty invitation and tried to resist, but I couldn't sit still for long.

Jean Luc must have picked up on my restlessness because he turned up at my door just as I was getting ready to go out.

I hated to admit it, but I really wished I hadn't taken the time to fuss with my hair because if I'd left five minutes earlier, I would have missed him and I could have taken my walk.

But he walked into my studio that beautiful morning and said, "Get your purse and lock your studio. I have something I want to show you."

"I was just getting ready to go out," I said.

"Where were you going?"

Why do you need to know?

"Nowhere, really. Just out for a walk."

God, I was a terrible person for feeling this way. He was so wonderful to me.

He led me to a gorgeous, silver Mercedes parked outside the center and opened the passenger-side door for me.

"Where are we going?"

"It is a surprise."

I played along, telling myself to relax when my body responded with prickles of irritation as he slid his hand underneath my skirt and up my thigh, teasing his fingers along the elastic of my underwear.

I closed my legs and angled them away from him. "Okay, Casanova, keep both hands on the wheel."

PMS?

Oversaturation?

I glanced over at him, his profile like a European god, and I decided it had to be PMS. Usually, one look at those eyes, those lips, those shoulders cured anything that ailed me.

It had to be PMS. Just relax.

"Jean Luc, we've been on the highway for an hour. Where are we going?"

He slanted a glance at me and smiled. My heart did a little two-step. That was more like it.

"Cannes."

"Cannes? What? That's at the other end of the country."

"I know. I have some business to tend to and I thought you might like to accompany me."

Annoyance stomped out the awareness that had bloomed in my belly. "Why didn't you tell me so that I could at least pack a toothbrush?"

"I have extra toothbrushes."

"I'll need a change of clothes."

He shot me a devilish grin and put his hand on my thigh again. "As far as I am concerned, my love, you won't need clothing."

I stared out the window, at war with myself, irritated because he didn't even give me the courtesy of asking whether I wanted to go. He must have sensed my irritation because we rode for miles in silence, past farm country and lavender fields. Finally, after I'd fumed enough, I convinced myself the impromptu trip was an adventure and forced myself into a better mood.

IT WAS ALMOST eight-thirty by the time we arrived at his family's Villa Angeline. A house with a name—actually it was a mansion from *who knows what century,* perched high on a Côte d'Azur cliff overlooking the Mediterranean Sea.

We stood on a balcony over the pool, looking down at the sea. The waxing moon shone like quicksilver on the water far below. Any residual irritation I felt earlier evaporated.

It really was mind-boggling to get in a car and end up on the other side of the country with only my purse and the clothes on my back. I thought of the green monster and the other baggage I'd dragged all the way to Paris and wanted to laugh.

If Rita could only see me now.

Jean Luc and I sat at a table on the terrace sipping champagne by candlelight and feasting on petits fours with caviar, crudités, fresh figs, foie gras, bread and an assortment of meats and cheeses Jean Luc had packed in a cooler and brought with us. He'd put so much thought into this trip. This surprise for me.

"When we go into town, I'd like to buy a bathing suit."

"You don't need one. It's very private up here."

"I'll need something if we go to the beach."

"Oh, did you want to do that?"

"Of course. I can't come all this way and not stick my feet in the Mediterranean Sea."

"Then I shall see that it happens." He reached out and took my hand. I couldn't decide if he was the most romantic man I'd ever met or controlling and chauvinistic for bringing me here this way.

Oh! What was wrong with me?

I stared at our fingers entwined. Things were going so well. Why was I spoiling it for myself by feeling like this? I'd always thought of happiness as a beautiful flower. So incredibly fragile and fine, and so short-lived. I guess from the moment Blake and I got married I was waiting for the bloom to fall off. Whether I realized it or not, I always felt as if he was just out of my grasp.

Now that I have a man who is treating me the way I *should* be treated, I feel like I can't get away fast enough. I hated the melancholy that was choking me.

It was just one of those days. All relationships had them. Never mind that this mood, these feelings of riding a careening cart rushing along out of control, started shortly after he invited me to dinner with his parents.

It had been a long tiring day of travel and I was exhausted. *Snap out of it, Annabelle.*

"How long are we staying?" I asked. "My son, Ben, arrives in three days."

"Not to worry. We can spend two days here and I will deliver you in time to receive him. We can pick him up together."

Hmm…I hadn't thought about that and I wasn't sure how I felt about it, either. What would Ben think of his mother getting involved before the divorce was final?

"While we're here we can get you some supplies if you would like to work," he said. "And did you realize your artist, Camille Deveau, spent the last years of her life in Cannes?"

Oh! That's right. "I read about that. It was just a brief passage in the biography, but I guess I was so swept away by the surprise of this spontaneous trip, I completely forgot about it."

Don't be bitchy.

"I thought you might like to have a look around her old neighborhood. How about if we do that tomorrow?"

I smiled and looked at the kind, beautiful man sitting across from me. Wanting to say, *You're divorced. How can you be so sure about life and love after losing yourself to someone and having it end badly?*

Instead, I sank into my chair and gazed up at the star-dotted indigo sky, breathing in the heady, salty air.

"I must go out and take care of something tonight. How about if you run yourself a bath upstairs and relax while I'm gone?"

It was almost ten o'clock.

"You have to go out tonight?"

He nodded. "It really can't wait. I will be gone about an hour, but when I get back, I promise to bring dessert."

He smiled that smile that could persuade me to dive off the hillside into the sea below. Then he led me upstairs and showed me the master bedroom.

It was decorated in traditional French white and gold,

with expensive-looking antiques. The floor was herring-bone parquet, topped with what I was sure were priceless Oriental rugs. The crowning glory was an immense four-poster bed, with a little wooden step so that you could climb in without having to hoist yourself up.

The bathroom was all marble, chrome and mirrors. Considerably more modern than the bedroom, and bigger than the first apartment I shared with a roommate when I was in college. The marble tub could have comfortably seated six.

But it was all for me.

Before he left, he ran my bath, dumping in gardenia-scented bath salts and attaching an air-filled pillow for me to rest my head on before he undressed me.

"Are you sure there's nothing I can do to persuade you to get in here with me?" If we could just get to that place where we connected so well I was sure everything would be fine.

He bit his bottom lip and closed his eyes. "You have no idea how you tempt me. But I must go. The sooner I go the sooner I will be back."

He left me to soak alone in that big, beautiful tub with air jets that kept the water warm. I felt like a princess for the first five minutes, but then the gardenia scent of the bath salts transported me back to my studio in Orlando, which made me think of the day Rita brought me the slides and the application for the residency trip.

Family.

Rita, Fred and Ben.

The quantity didn't matter, really, it was the quality of the relationship that counted. We shared a closer bond than some enormous families.

A pang of sadness morphed into homesickness, and I realized this was one of those times when I would have called my sister. But I didn't even have my cell phone with me. It was in Paris charging on the little café table by the kitchen.

The melancholy blue seeped into my pores, but I took a deep breath and blew it away, sinking deeper in the hot water, thinking about what I would have said if I could have talked to Rita.

I must have dozed as I steeped because I awoke with a start. For a moment I was disoriented and didn't remember where I was.

My skin was so waterlogged it was pruny.

I sat up, hit the button to stop the water jets and looked around. I had the eeriest feeling someone had been watching me. The bathroom door was cracked a bit, and I couldn't remember if Jean Luc had closed it all the way when he left.

Shuddering at the thought of being alone in this big, old unfamiliar house I climbed out of the tub and pulled on the white terry robe hanging on the back of the door.

I crept out of the bathroom hesitantly, with my ears trained to see if I could hear anything.

A door slammed somewhere downstairs, causing a little exclamation to jump to life in my throat.

I walked to the top of the staircase and listened for Jean Luc's footsteps, but all was quiet.

"Jean Luc?"

The only answer was the sound of my pounding heart.

FOURTEEN

I LOCKED MYSELF in the bedroom for a terrifying half hour. There was a telephone on the nightstand, but I had no idea how to dial French emergency.

Even if I'd known how, I had no idea how to ask for the police in French. I didn't have my lexicon with me. It, too, was back in Paris along with my passport.

All sorts of morbid thoughts flooded my mind.

The old house was just creepy. If I believed in ghosts my imagination would have really gotten carried away with me.

But I didn't believe in ghosts. Actually, ghosts were nothing compared to the monsters men could be.

I thought about the old cliché *If something's too good to be true it usually is.* Of course, it was happening again. Jean Luc *was* too good to be true. Men never did turn out to be who they claimed to be.

That was the banana peel that sent my exhausted, overactive mind slipping and sliding on a panicky collision course.

I sat down on the bed.

I'd known him for a few weeks, but did I really know him? Oh my God, what if he was some kind of deranged psychopath who used his charm and good looks to lure unsuspecting women into traps so he could kill them? Maybe that's what happened to Matilde.

Oh my God, I hadn't seen her since that day in Pigalle. It was as if she'd vanished.

Oh my God, I could see the headline—Mediocre Middle-aged Artist Disappears In Paris. Jacques Jauvert would insist on the word mediocre, that way he'd be able to inform the world just how bad my art was.

Okay, calm down. That's ridiculous. You've met his parents. He teaches at the Beaux-Arts. But I *knew* I heard a door slam. Someone was in here or had been in here.

Jean Luc said this place sat vacant most of the time, except for the caretakers. It was full of beautiful antiques and artwork. A burglar's dream.

I picked up a heavy silver candlestick off the bureau and sat next to the phone. If someone tried to break down the door, I'd dial O and take my chance that they'd *parlez-vous Anglais*. Never mind that I had no idea where the hell I was other than in Cannes.

How could I be so stupid letting him bring me here like this? I should have made him turn the car around.

I tried dialing Rita, just to tell her I loved her and in case I turned up dead she should tell Ben I loved him, too. But I couldn't remember the country code—was it zero, one, one or one, zero, one—all those damn numbers.

I was just about to take my chances and ask the operator to place the call for me when I heard a car pull into the driveway. I ran to the window and saw Jean Luc getting out of his silver Mercedes.

Relief flooded through me.

Feeling vaguely foolish about my earlier thoughts of him as a psycho-killer, I wanted to meet him at the door and throw myself into his arms, but what if I walked in on the intruder? They'd hear Jean Luc coming in and would have enough time to get away. I stood on the far side of the room clutching the candlestick, waiting for him to come up to me.

He tried to open the door, but it was locked. "Annabelle? It's me. The bedroom door's locked. Will you let me in, please?"

I did and he took one look and said, "What's the matter?"

I was shaking so hard the candlestick waved back and forth.

"Someone was here, in the house." My voice shook, too, and I was afraid I would buckle under all the emotion.

In the split second before he gathered me in his arms I saw a flash of panic in his eyes. If I hadn't been looking at him at that precise moment I would have missed it, and even though I had started to feel a little better about the situation, that little spark reignited the fear that something just wasn't right.

"What do you mean someone was here? Are you all right?"

With my cheek pressed against his chest, I told him how I'd dozed off in the tub, and though I didn't see anyone, I felt a presence and heard a door slam. "I know it wasn't just my imagination."

I waited for him to laugh and explain it away. To say it

was probably the caretaker or that the old house was drafty and made all kinds of creaks and groans, sounds like doors slamming. He didn't say any of those things, and when I pulled out of his arms, his mouth was set in a grim line.

Panic erupted in me all over again. So *maybe* he wasn't a psychopath, but I had no idea what kind of *business* he was conducting in Cannes in the middle of the night. What if his business was not on the up-and-up—drugs, money laundering, illegal weapons, white slavery—

Oh my God, this was how women were sold into slavery, never to be heard of again.

"I want to go back to Paris," I said.

He nodded. "We'll leave in the morning. We're both exhausted. Let's get some sleep."

After driving all this way, why was he so quick to agree? Why wasn't he trying to explain away the situation?

"No, I want to go now. I don't care if you have to put me on a train. I am not staying the night in this house."

WE DROVE STRAIGHT through and got back to Paris at six o'clock in the morning.

Jean Luc was not happy about my insisting we leave, but when I threatened to call a cab to take me to the train station (thank God he didn't call my bluff), he said, "I don't know that there is a train at this hour. You are being ridiculous."

I insisted, saying he had a lot of nerve just whisking me down here like this without asking me if I had engagements or if I even wanted to go. How dare he just assume I had nothing better to do. Everything I'd been feeling since I'd awakened to find myself in this lousy frame of mind came pouring out.

The grave hurt and insult of my words were apparent in his sigh.

He complied.

It was the longest eight hours of my life.

When we pulled up in front of the studio, I was surprised and relieved when he accepted my offer to make him coffee. I hoped that meant he'd stay and we'd crawl into my bed and hold each other while we slept so we could wake up and laugh about the whole fiasco.

He'd get a kick out of how I momentarily thought he'd kidnapped me and taken me down there for—God, I couldn't even remember. It all seemed so ridiculous now.

We were both silent as I measured water into the French press, transferred it to the kettle and set the water to boil. I arranged croissants (now two days old), grapes and melon slices on a plate.

I took out the new yellow linen place mats I'd purchased from the little rue Cler linen shop and put them on the café table by the kitchen window. I finished setting the table with my new blue cloth napkins and the flatware.

Blake always thought cloth table linens were impractical, so I never used them. Since arriving in France I'd made it a personal code never to use paper napkins on my table. I poured cream into a tiny porcelain pitcher, set out plates, juice glasses, coffee mugs the size of cereal bowls and all the while was aware of Jean Luc silently watching me, his arms folded across his chest and a grim, tired look on his face.

The kettle whistled. I poured the water over the coffee in the press pot, stirred it and gestured toward the table.

"Sit down."

He eyed the table, then looked back at me. "I think we need to spend some time apart, Anna."

His words hit like a slap, and my hand jerked. A tidal wave of water and grounds sloshed over the side onto the countertop. I grabbed a towel to wipe up the mess, thinking maybe if I acted like I didn't hear him he'd pretend he didn't say what he just said.

No such luck.

"You need to prepare for your son's visit, and I should be busy organizing the final jury examination of my students. I need to be fresh so I can give them the attention they deserve."

I wanted to tell him I only needed a day to prepare for Ben and ask him how he would've managed to organize the examination if we'd stayed in Cannes for another two days.

The questions rolled around in my mind like a tumbleweed getting tangled with absurd phrases like *Oh my God, he's a psycho-killer; this is how women are sold into slavery;* and *I want to go back to Paris now.* I couldn't unknot the words, "Please don't go." I just stood dumbly staring into the black abyss of my French press, stirring the coffee.

"I will talk to you soon," he said as he walked up behind me and brushed a featherlight kiss on the top of my head.

This time I knew without a doubt the door I heard shutting was not a figment of my imagination.

THE FIRST DAY'S separation reminded me that I was a strong, self-sufficient, independent woman. In fact, I was enjoying the time to myself. I'd missed this alone time. I painted a little and lay in the sun, totally nude, thank you very much. I even went and got my hair colored and trimmed (just a smidgen because I liked how long it was getting).

I felt like a million bucks.

He was probably missing me already.

THE SECOND DAY, I painted with the front door and all my windows open so I had a clear view of his studio—or should I say so that when he arrived at his studio *he* could see that I was doing perfectly fine, that I was a *talented,* strong, self-sufficient, independent woman.

WHEN HE HADN'T shown up by four o'clock on the second day, I took the metro over to his apartment and put a note on his door.

> I hope everything is going well as you organize your students' final exams. Please let me know if you're still planning on going with me to the airport to pick up Ben.
> Anna

Maybe I should have signed it *Love, Anna.* Nah, I was the one who had made the first move. *Anna,* plain and simple, was good enough.

I STILL HADN'T heard from Jean Luc on day number three, the day Ben would arrive. I awoke thinking the stand-off had gone on long enough.

Okay, fine. I was willing to throw in the towel and admit that I'd acted a little crazy. He could blame it on my being an "uptight American," if it made him feel better.

I'd tell him I was scared. Of us. Of where this relationship was heading, and I thought I had just broken through the other side of those fears.

I missed him. Plain and simple. I didn't want to spend any more time apart.

My son was arriving today and I wanted the two men I loved to—

Oh my God, there it was.

The *L* word.

I sat up in bed and covered my mouth with my hand as if I could shove the word back in before it made itself comfortable in my vocabulary, but it was already out. It had been out there for a long time, and that's what was wrong.

I loved him.

But it was okay.

It was more than okay.

It was time he knew it.

I had no idea what his student jury examinations entailed. Or if he'd even begun them. He could be finished for all I knew. It was worth a shot to go over to his apartment to see if I could catch him.

I didn't waste time showering for fear it would mean the difference between my finding him at home and missing him. I just pulled on my clothes, grabbed my purse and went.

I punched in the code to his building and walked up to his place on the third floor.

The message I'd left him yesterday still stuck out of the crevice between the door and the jamb.

Oh. He hadn't even been home.

Hmm. This was interesting. I wondered where he'd been if he wasn't sleeping here or at the studio.

I stood there a moment battling with a mental monster that pointed to all kinds of possibilities I didn't like, that twisted my stomach and made my heart ache.

I took down the note because it was irrelevant at that point. Obviously, Jean Luc wouldn't be taking me to meet Ben. But that was okay, because going by myself I could focus on Ben.

Really, it was better this way. In the meantime, I'd give Jean Luc the benefit of the doubt until I could ask him just where he'd been. Perhaps he still had business in Cannes.

Then why didn't he tell me? Why did he say the bit about the student exams?

I'd just turned to leave when I heard voices on the landing below; a deep, sexy French accent that started a passionate fluttering in my belly.

He was home.

But he wasn't alone.

A lilting French female voice floated up the stairs ahead of their footsteps. I thought I recognized the voice.

But I wasn't sure.

Until she laughed.

And then I knew.

Matilde.

I bit my lip until I could feel it throb in time with my pulse. So *that's* where he'd been for the past two days. Final student jury examinations, my ass.

He'd been with *her.*

Each footstep brought them closer to the third floor and made my heart pound harder. I looked around, trying to decide what to do. The only way out was to walk down the stairs past them.

I'd be damned if I'd let Jean Luc know I'd come over here ready to make up. That I— They'd both probably laugh in my face. *Stupid American.*

I took the only other possible option. I climbed up to the next floor to wait and watch.

FIFTEEN

I STRAIGHTENED THE studio and set out fresh linens to make up the couch for Ben's bed later that night. He only had four days in Paris because he was taking summer school to get ahead on his credits and only had a week between terms. Factor in two days spent flying and a day for jet lag recovery before jumping into class and that left a net total of four days to see Paris.

It was definitely better that Jean Luc was not in the picture vying for my attention. My stomach twisted at the memory of him unlocking his apartment door and holding it open for Matilde to enter. That's all I saw. The door shut and I beelined out of the building.

Bile rose in the back of my throat. I took a deep breath and willed my stomach to settle. I had too much to do today.

First order of business: Clear the studio of every trace of Jean Luc.

Second order of business: No moping over Jean Luc.

Third order of business: No mention of Jean Luc to Ben.

Fourth order of business: Quit thinking of Jean Luc!

I hadn't uttered a single word about him to Ben (and made Rita promise to be quiet, too) for precisely this reason.

Maybe somewhere in the recesses of my heart, I knew the relationship would end this way.

With Matilde.

Just like Rita predicted. I'd been so cocksure it wouldn't.

I trusted him.

He lied.

I was beginning to see a relationship pattern.

I trusted men.

They lied.

I spied the blue package of his Gitane cigarettes on the kitchen counter, and images of him in the stairwell with *the blonde* skittered through my mind. I closed my eyes against the ensuing ache.

This *would* happen right before Ben's visit.

Bad timing.

Bad judgment.

If it was destined to end, better he excused himself before meeting Ben.

I took a cigarette out of the pack, rolled it across my palm, then lifted it to my nose to inhale the tobacco that reminded me so much of him. I'd always been turned off by smokers, but there was something earthily sensual about his lips when he inhaled. Like foreign poetry.

Fifth order of business: Quit being pathetic.

I lifted the unlit cylinder to my lips, touched it to the tip of my tongue. The unfiltered end tasted of his raw, smoky essence.

Amazing how our tastes adapted to the whims of our hearts.

I snapped the cigarette in half, dumped the rest of the pack on the counter and finished off the job, sweeping the carnage into the trash.

Flopping down on the couch with a *pfff,* I forced all the air from my lungs and buried my face in my hands.

If I was going to cry, I'd better get on with it. Just get it over with now. Because I had exactly two hours to wallow and subsequently stash my feelings before my son arrived.

I sat staring into the blackness of my palms, waiting for the tears to burn my eyes and swim to the surface, but my hands smelled like broken cigarettes.

Like broken dreams?

No. I looked up. My dreams still belonged to me. That was one thing I did right this time.

I glanced around the modest studio, which looked different through my sad eyes. My gaze locked with Jean Luc's intense stare peering at me from *The Bed* painting hanging on the wall in front of me. My heart twisted.

He'd hung the canvas the afternoon after we first made love. He said such a special painting deserved a place of honor.

It was the only painting hanging on the wall; the rest of my work was lined up around the room on the paint-spattered wooden floor, propped up against the white stucco walls. The bizarre images looked like portals into some strange alternate universe.

As a whole, the body of work was about as different from the chaste flowers I used to paint as a hooker was from a debutante.

I raked my hair out of my eyes. God, what would Ben think of his mother now?

His dad was gay and his mom had gone off the deep end glorifying the seamy side of Paris. To hell with *La Tour Eiffel,* give me the whores and cross-dressers of Par-ee.

I swallowed hard. How come my work didn't seem so odious until I tried to see it through my son's eyes?

My assessment of the studio came full circle back to *The Bed*.

If Ben was sleeping on the couch, I couldn't have him staring at my former lover in the throes of passionate sex with a woman who was—a thinly veiled version of me.

Not that Ben would know, but still.

I took the canvas off the wall and carried the huge painting into the bedroom, my eyes searching for a place to stash it. The closet was too small, the bureau was flush against the wall and too heavy to pull out by myself. I could have stashed the canvas under the bed, but the mattress was on one of those solid platforms that didn't offer any storage space underneath.

I thought about hiding it at the back of a stack of canvases, but it was by far the largest painting in the studio; besides, the first thing people did when they walked into an artist's studio was to start looking at the work.

It annoyed me. People didn't walk into a writer's office and start reading their work in progress. For some reason painting lacked the privacy afforded to other creative work. For want of anything else to do with it, I turned it backward and propped it against the bedroom wall.

I went back to the living room to see if there was anything I missed, anything on which I should exercise parental discretion and remove.

The place really was small; fine for one person, but housing two was going to be a challenge.

As tight as Rita and I were, we'd have been at each other's

throats in such close quarters. Especially with one of us sleeping on the couch.

Habit made me glance out the window to see if Jean Luc's studio was open. It wasn't, of course. He was probably still with *her*.

Matilde is not my lover.

Her work with me is finished.

Liar.

I should take *The Bed* and nail it to his studio door. Let him have it and all the memories associated with it. Let him explain to Matilde about the woman he was making love to in the painting. But I didn't know when he'd be back and I didn't want to take the chance of it sitting there when Ben arrived.

What's that, Mom?

Oh, just a painting, Ben. In Paris, you find artwork in the most unlikely places.

The woman looks familiar.

Nobody you know, believe me.

I turned my back to the window and picked the wilting blooms out of the bouquet of freesias in the vase on the table. Too bad Ben and I weren't staying in Benoît Bernard's place like Rita and I did.

I lifted a dying blossom to my nose. It smelled of decay and perfume. A once-beautiful flower just past its prime.

Why not? Why couldn't we stay there?

He'd want to see my studio, of course, but maybe if I keep him busy enough…

Oh, gee, where did the time go, Ben? Too bad we didn't have a chance to see the studio. But you've seen one studio, you've seen them all.

Yeah, right. We'd cross that bridge when we came to it.

There was always the chance that the apartment wouldn't be available. What then?

How much to stay at the Ritz?

Okay, on my budget we'd have to settle for the Parisian equivalent of a Motel 6.

As long as we were anyplace but here.

I CALLED RITA and got Benoît Bernard's phone number. I left a message on his answering service, and he returned my call within the hour.

Good timing, he said. While he couldn't vacate the apartment in time for us to stay there that night, he said he welcomed the excuse to go to his place in Provence for a long weekend. We could have it for three nights starting tomorrow.

Perfect. Ben and I could take a quick overnight trip somewhere—Versailles? Giverny? I'd have to see what I could arrange in short order.

Monsieur Bernard said he would leave the key with Étienne at the crêpe restaurant.

Oh. God. That's right. Étienne.

I hadn't seen him since *that day.*

I had a flash of total clarity when I realized I'd made the right decision not sleeping with him. At least that was one thing I'd done right.

Étienne was a grown man. I'd give him the benefit of the doubt he'd conduct himself accordingly. In fact, he was probably already engaged to another middle-aged American woman who could give him his green card.

I hoped so.

I'd be cordial, but not *overly* friendly. Nothing to betray to

Ben what almost happened. After all, I was his mother. I wasn't even divorced from his father yet.

Since Ben and I weren't staying at the studio, I decided I'd wasted enough time cleaning and quickly changed gears. I packed an overnight bag, and took the early train to the airport, arriving about an hour before Ben's flight. It gave me time to check train schedules and map out a plan.

By the time his plane arrived we probably wouldn't be able to make the last train for Versailles, but Giverny would work.

Yes, that was it. I'd always wanted to see Monet's home and gardens. Too bad I didn't pack my easel.

I'd always been emotional—I cried when I was happy, I cried when I was sad. I cried when Ben emerged through the security gates. Seeing him felt like someone had sent a *rescuer* to save me, and I hugged him as if he were my life support.

My son.

"You're here," I said, holding him by the shoulders. "I have missed you so much."

"I missed you, too, Mom. Please don't cry."

I swiped at my eyes and nose, embarrassed at losing control. "I'm sorry. I've just missed you."

I hugged him again.

At Charles de Gaulle, international passengers get their baggage before they enter the airport's common areas. With that taken care of, we had just enough time to grab a bite to eat and make it to the Gare Saint-Lazare where we bought our tickets and boarded the train for Giverny.

"I know you're tired, but I thought we'd do this first so you could ease into your whirlwind tour of Paris."

It made sense.

He had dark circles under his eyes, and I wanted to gather him in my arms and let him sleep on my shoulder the way he did when he was a little boy.

"Why don't we just stay at your studio?"

I waved a hand nonchalantly. "Oh, it's too small for the two of us. Plus, this is your first time in Paris. I want everything to be perfect."

Little did he know.

The trip took about an hour, and I encouraged Ben to sleep after his long flight.

As I sat there looking at this man-child who was my son, my heart was so full, frankly I didn't care where we stayed, just as long as we were together. I was so glad to see my baby.

"You look so grown-up," I said.

He rolled his eyes. "Me? What about you? I mean, you don't look grown-up, you look…you look great. Younger, I think." He smiled at me. "Your hair's so long. I don't think I've ever seen you wear it this way. What did you do to it?"

I shrugged. "Not much. That's the beauty of it."

After about an hour, the train chugged into the station at Vernon. We took a ten-minute cab ride to the little Norman village of Giverny.

I'd secured us a room at a bed-and-breakfast called *Le Coin des Artistes,* which translated to the Artists' Corner. Located right on the rue Claude Monet, it was just down from the famous painter's home and gardens.

The B and B used to be an old café and general store, but the proprietor, Madame Laurence, had transformed it into a quaint four-guest room bed-and-breakfast.

She showed us to a double room. Ben swore he was too

keyed up to take a nap, so we strolled down to the Hôtel Baudy, a place I'd heard almost as much about as Monet's house.

In the late nineteenth century, the Hôtel Baudy was dubbed "the hotel of the American painters."

How appropriate, I thought as we chose a table with a yellow umbrella under the lime trees, by a low hedge that cordoned off the outer bounds of the terrace from a lush green field. It was approaching five o'clock and most of the tables were available. The rush of day tourists who came in to see Monet's house was starting to thin.

A small woman with dark hair handed us menus and said something in French I thought was, *I'll be right back.*

I studied the menu. "The drinking age in France is sixteen," I said. "Do you want to share a bottle of wine?"

Ben's gaze snapped to mine. "Really?"

"Well, we don't have to. I just thought—"

"Sure." He squared his shoulders and sat back, looking way too much like a man.

He was equal parts Blake and me. He had Blake's fair hair, but definitely my eyes and nose. The set of his jaw—that was all Blake, especially when I asked him if he'd spoken to his father.

"No."

Yes, just like his father. The word was delivered to end the conversation before it began. I didn't want to spoil the night so I didn't push.

After the server took our order—the salad with cold smoked salmon for me, the beef bourguignon for Ben, a bottle of Beaujolais for us to share—a hush fell between us.

As I gazed at the Hôtel Baudy, now only a restaurant, they

no longer let rooms to guests, I could feel Ben's distress emanating in waves.

I was sorry I'd mentioned Blake. I was just hoping they'd made some progress while I was gone. I hadn't talked to Blake since I'd been in Paris and chose not to waste my short weekly calls with Ben on the subject, so I didn't know.

It seemed as if with each passing moment, Ben sank deeper into silent despair.

No. This wouldn't do.

"I read that when Monet came to Giverny, the Hôtel Baudy was only a small place for travelers to eat and freshen up," I said, hoping to reclaim the light, relaxed mood we'd enjoyed a few minutes ago.

Ben nodded and stared somewhere over my shoulder.

"They built the hotel after all the American Impressionists started coming here." I gestured to the pink stucco building across the narrow rue Claude Monet from the terrace where we sat. There were sidewalks in some American cities wider than the street and I wondered what happened if two cars traveling in opposite directions met each other.

"The hotel has a rich history," I continued, keeping my voice light. "There's supposed to be a magical garden and artists' studio around back. If you're not too tired maybe we can take a look at it after we eat."

"Sure, Mom." Unenthused.

"It's been preserved to look as it did when the Baudys built it back in the late 1800s for all the Americans who came here to paint. You know how they discovered this place?"

My zeal must have sounded as canned as it felt, because Ben simply raised his eyebrows at my question.

God, I didn't blame him. I sounded like a travel guide, but

it was better than contemplating the ghost of the Blake we both thought we knew and once loved.

"It was because of the painter William Metcalf. He fell in love with this place and went back to Paris and told all his American friends. In fact, when he first stopped in for a meal at Baudys', Madame Baudy was afraid of him. She said he was a burly hirsute beast with no manners who spoke gibberish."

The server delivered the wine. I lifted my glass.

"A toast to you and Paris." We clinked glasses.

"I don't know if I'll ever be able to forgive him," Ben finally said. He rested his chin on his fist and looked so forlorn I almost couldn't bear it.

I touched his arm, wishing I could do something to fix this. "It doesn't change his love for you, honey."

Ben snorted as if the very thought was disgusting. "Yeah, but what does it mean about his love for you? Did he ever love you, Mom? Why did he even marry you?"

Those were the million-dollar questions. The questions that had sent me "Faraway" searching for answers.

I stroked his arm, surprised that for the first time contemplating the answers didn't leave me seething with anger or on the verge of tears. "I've asked myself those questions so many times, Ben, and the conclusion I've finally reached is that everything happens for a reason. Sometimes we don't know what that reason is, but we just have to go forward in blind faith. If I hadn't met your dad, I wouldn't have you. Being your mother is worth any price. If I can forgive him, I hope you can, too."

Ben contemplated his wine for a moment, then lifted his glass to mine.

"Nice thought, Mom, but easier said than done."

Just give it time, Ben.

After dinner we wandered back to the Hôtel Baudy garden. The replica of the nineteenth-century artists' studio sat so still and perfect with its ochre-washed walls and paint-spattered floor it looked as if a working artist had just stepped away for a bite to eat and would return to resume his work.

Several easels held canvases in various stages of progress; a swag of ivy had infiltrated the roof's far left corner, embedding itself in the plaster; pieces of pottery and sculpture lay scattered in random groupings around the space; under a magnificent window that stretched nearly the length of the right wall, a low, red-painted workbench held jewel-toned jars of pigment, paint palettes, jars of crusty old brushes and an open wooden painter's box.

It was as if we'd stepped back in time to a simpler era. I looked out the dusty, weathered window and squinted my eyes. I could almost see the haunting images the American painters came here to capture more than a century ago: the lush flora and fauna, the children playing in the garden, the well-dressed ladies with delicate parasols basking in the splendor of the blossoms.

Ben and I strolled side by side, in companionable silence, and I thought about what I'd said to him.

If I can forgive him, I hope you can, too.

Forgiveness.

Had I forgiven Blake? I hadn't even considered it until now. Really, it was the first step in the long journey toward healing.

The garden was laden with perfumed roses growing in enchanting abandon. Rustic perennials installed themselves under the canopy of trees, and vines snaked their way up the trunks. Daisies and hypericum guarded a winding path that led up to the summit of a hill.

It was so quiet it almost felt as if we were the only two people in the village. Just us and the souls of all those long-ago painters. People just like me and Camille Deveau who had lived and loved, celebrated great joys and endured unbearable heartbreak.

They'd all lived and loved and dealt with their share of betrayal and sadness, and the world went on after they were gone. Despite it all, they left behind their art and their flowers and their buildings that once rang with their laughter and tears.

The day I'd learned of Blake's betrayal, I was on my way to see the traveling collection of Monet's water-lily paintings. I never got to see them. Because of that, here I stood in the very place they originated. What a long, roundabout journey getting here.

I was starting to believe some things really did happen for a reason. So who was I to fancy that the pain I'd suffered was any worse than the anguish of those brave souls who came before me? They made it, didn't they? Perhaps some were better because of it.

As we walked back to *Le Coin des Artistes,* I stopped to inhale the sweet scent of an ancient rosebush bent under the weight of its blooms.

In a note that drifted in on the breeze, I closed my eyes and imagined Camille Deveau whispering, *The next step of your long, roundabout journey is learning to forgive yourself.*

SIXTEEN

WHEN BEN AND I returned to Paris, I was nervous about getting the key to the apartment from Étienne. I sent Ben across the street into the Nicholas shop to buy us a bottle of wine. Since he wasn't of age at home, I knew he'd get a kick out of being able to make the purchase legally here.

It also meant I could approach Étienne alone since I had no idea what he'd say or do. I mustered all my confidence and approached the crêpe restaurant.

He wasn't at the counter. I had to ask some guy I didn't recognize, if he knew where Étienne was. I wondered if he was one of the guys I saw out front the day I first arrived.

Less than a minute later, Étienne walked out from the back dangling the key between his right index finger and thumb. He stared at me for a moment, unsmiling, before he said, "Ah, *bonjour*, American Woman."

He leaned on the counter and made exaggerated glances up and down the street. "Where is your manfriend?"

My breath escaped in a rush that sounded more irritated than I'd intended. "Étienne, I'm here with my son. The key. Please?"

I held out my hand, but he held it just out of my reach. Was he going to drag this out until Ben came? For God's sake I hoped not.

"Where is he?" Étienne asked.

I wondered if he meant Ben or Jean Luc, so I took my chances. "My son is over at Nicholas across the street. If you're nice I'll introduce you to him. But only if you're nice."

"Is he by himself or is *You-Know-What* with him?"

I laughed. "You mean *You-Know-Who?*"

"I mean your *manfriend*. It is same thing, no?"

"Not exactly." *You-Know-What. Another priceless Étienne-ism. I'd have to remember it.* "No, my *manfriend* is not with us." For a second I considered telling Étienne that Jean Luc and I were finished, but then decided against it when the numbness I'd resurrected for the duration of Ben's visit started to fade.

What was the use of opening that vein of conversation?

Étienne pursed his lips and stroked his clean-shaven chin as if considering his options. Then he leaned in and dropped the key in my palm.

I kissed him on the cheek. "Thank you, French Boy."

He smiled. "If you ever leave *You-Know-What,* I will be right here."

I shook my head in mock disgust. "Until you find yourself another American woman and go off to the U.S. with her to open your restaurant."

He sighed dramatically and patted his heart. "*Non,* you are the only American woman for me."

"And the day I believe that, you can sell me the Eiffel Tower, okay?"

He shrugged and pursed his lips again. "I'll give you a good price."

ON BEN'S LAST morning in Paris, just as I feared, I could no longer dissuade him from seeing my studio.

"Do you think I came all this way not to see where you've been living for the past three months?"

"It hasn't been three months yet."

"Close enough. Come on, let's go."

Oh Lord. Here we go.

Étienne was at the counter when Ben and I stepped out onto the sidewalk. He waved, and when Ben turned his back, Étienne blew me a kiss. I blew him one back.

"Quit flirting and let's get a move on," Ben said, rolling his eyes.

Oops. "You weren't supposed to see that."

"I wish I hadn't." But he laughed when he said it, as if he was egging me on. It made me feel a little less nervous about showing him my new work.

Until the metro pulled to a screeching stop at the École Militaire stop.

Emerging from the darkness into the neighborhood I'd grown so accustomed to was like entering my own personal twilight zone. Everything looked the same—the market stalls on the rue Cler were in full swing; people crowded the streets buying bread, cheese and fresh produce; the vendors hollered their specials to passersby—but it all moved in a strange, warped slow-motion set to the sound track of my thudding heart, growing more intense as we turned onto the street that housed the Delacroix Centre.

Ben studied the map in his guidebook as we walked. "Wait a minute, this is near the Eiffel Tower, right?"

"Right."

"Why didn't we stop by yesterday when we were over here? I asked you when we were up at the top and you said— well, you handed me some lame excuse. What gives, Mom? Why don't you want me to see your place?"

I stopped, at a loss for words. God, when did the kid get to be so smart? What was I thinking? He'd always been smart.

"Oh, Ben, come here." We sat on a low stone wall about forty yards down from the center. He was an adult now. Maybe if I leveled with him—

"The work I've done here is a lot different from what I've done in the past. I don't know. I guess I'm just a little nervous about what you're going to think of it."

Of me?

He scrunched up his nose in a manner that was completely his own. "Get over it."

What?

He stood up.

"What did you say?"

"Get over it. You're an artist. Show me your work."

I blinked once. Twice. My God, he was right.

"Okay." I stood up, too. "That's what I thought you said."

Jean Luc's studio was shut up tight, but I noticed Guerrier's cat dish had food in it.

My body tensed.

He'd been there. Not long ago, judging by the amount of food in the bowl.

My hand shook a little as I inserted the key and I wasn't sure if it was because of narrowly missing Jean Luc or because on the walk it dawned on me that I hadn't tried to explain just *how different* my work was from what Ben was used to seeing. I took a steadying breath and reminded myself that he'd been away at school since I started painting again and hadn't seen the flowers. He really had no basis of comparison.

Still, some of the work was pretty bawdy.

I pushed open the door and stepped inside, first giving the place a once-over to make sure I hadn't forgotten to put away anything crucial—like an errant condom packet.

My God, it felt as if we'd switched roles. He was the adult and I was the kid trying to fool him into believing I'd behaved impeccably while I was on my own.

He was already inside looking at the canvases. I held my breath waiting for his critique.

He was silent for about five minutes, looking, slowly walking around the room from canvas to canvas.

While he looked, I busied myself at the table deadheading the freesias and sweeping up the blossoms that had fallen in my absence.

I should have stopped at the flower market on the rue Cler and bought new flowers—

"This is *your* work?" Ben stared at me wide-eyed.

Oh, no, here it came. I steeled myself, but that didn't extinguish the slow burn that rose from my belly upward.

"God, Mom. Why are you all red? These are cool."

I shrugged and crushed a dead freesia blossom between my fingers.

"You really painted these?"

I nodded and felt myself start to breathe again.

He liked them. My son liked the hookers and cross-dressers and transsexuals of Pigalle. God, after what happened with his father I would *never* tell him most of the *women* I'd painted were actually men. When I went back up there with Jean Luc—he insisted I shouldn't go alone—I was amazed at how some of the most beautiful of the bunch were actually men or beings caught in limbo between the sexes, thanks to hormones and plastic surgery. It was amazing. Some of the *men* actually make me feel unfeminine.

"Wow." Shaking his head, Ben started another circle around the room "You're really talented. No wonder they brought you to Paris."

"Choose the one you like and you can take it with you."

It was a test to see if he actually wanted one. I mean, I couldn't imagine him explaining to his dorm mates his mother was the artist.

"Really?"

But when he started picking up canvases and comparing them, eliminating some and narrowing down others, I realized he was serious. I also realized if I was ever going to move ahead on this solo journey, I did need, in the famous words of my son, to get over it.

I needed to hold my head up proud.

This is my work.

I experienced one last pang of weirdness when I wondered if I should tell Ben exactly what he was looking at...

But what was he looking at? What did *he* see?

A sensual woman or a man in drag?

It wasn't as if he were going to take the person home and unwrap him later and get the surprise of his life.

The interpretation of art should be left to the beholder.

The melodic sound of Matilde's laughter snapped me out of philosophizing. My attention snapped to the door and I saw her and Jean Luc outside of his studio.

For a moment, he stood transfixed, looking at me. I couldn't tell if it was a guilty look or one meant to say, *This is what you get.*

My gaze slid to Matilde; she looked at me as if seeing a ghost and all of a sudden I felt as if she'd slid her milky-white hands around my neck and started squeezing the life out of me.

I couldn't breathe as I glanced back at the bizarre Pigalle freak show lining my wall, and back at her.

Suddenly it was crystal clear why Jean Luc had been so evasive when it came to Matilde. Oh God, it all added up: Pigalle, the beautiful elusive Matilde, Jean Luc's tight-lipped silence… Oh, God.

Was Matilde a transsexual?

Was Jean Luc… I couldn't even say it.

The night I saw her modeling for him in his studio, she wore a G-string. On one of our trips to Pigalle, when I asked how transsexuals could parade in skimpy-next-to-nothings without ruining the "illusion of femininity," Jean Luc told me they "hid their candy."

They "tucked it away" so seamlessly that they could get away with short-shorts and G-strings.

I grabbed the back of the chair to steady myself. Why didn't it dawn on me sooner? How else would he have known all the sordid details?

"*Who* is the blonde?" Ben asked. "She's hot."

I almost fell over myself on my way to the door.

"She's nobody." Jean Luc had called her *nobody,* too, that very first day.

With a quick flick of my wrist, I slammed the door.

THERE WAS A note on my door when I got back from taking Ben to the airport.

Annabelle,
I must see you. It is most urgent. Please.
JLLG

He wanted to see me. Well, I didn't want to see him. Noooo. Fool me once, shame on me. Fool me twice—

No! He knew what I'd gone through with Blake, yet he'd intentionally led me on a chase. He knew it was my most vulnerable, raw, exposed nerve. My supposedly heterosexual husband left me for a man. Here Jean Luc was a switch-hitter who played on my vulnerability. I didn't care if he liked women *some of the time*.

Some of the time didn't get it. No. I was a full-time, one-man–one-woman show. How dare he do this to me.

I threw open the door and strode across the courtyard ready to tell him the *most urgent* things that were on my mind.

I didn't even knock. I threw open the door.

"How in the hell could you—"

Matilde stood in the middle of the floor.

Sans thong.

Totally nude. Most definitely, one-hundred-percent female. Unless she'd had some sort of miracle surgery that transformed her—

Jean Luc looked up from the big block of marble he'd been chipping away at with a hammer and chisel.

All I could manage was, "Oh!"

Matilde didn't even bother to cover herself. She looked

startlingly thin and I noticed tiny bruises marring the ivory skin of her arms.

Another act for my Pigalle freak show?

Nah, I'd had my fill.

Jean Luc stood, looking surprised to see me, but not angry. "Annabelle?"

I turned and walked out, trying to sort out if Matilde being a woman was a good thing or not. It was definitely better than *her* being a *him*. But then there was the small matter of her being there at all since the extent of what Jean Luc would tell me about her was that her work for him was finished.

I guess the hiring freeze had melted.

I'd just closed the door when it opened again. Jean Luc rushed in, his eyes looking wild.

"Please talk to me," he implored. "Where have you been? I have been worried sick about you."

Excuse me? Where have I been?

"I have nothing to say to you."

I went into the bedroom and shut the door.

Jean Luc pounded on it. "I am not leaving until we talk about this."

Realizing he probably meant what he said, I opened the door. "Okay, start talking." I glanced at my watch. "You have exactly two minutes."

He tried to take my hand. "Let's sit down or go get some coffee or a glass of wine—"

"You now have one minute and forty-five seconds."

He dropped my hand and turned his back to me, throwing his hands in the air and balling them into fists as if it helped him contain his frustration.

"How could you lie to me?" I said, unable to hold it in any

longer. The tears I'd held back since the morning he walked out of my studio more than a week ago flowed in torrents.

"I didn't—I mean, I know how it must look."

That was the *worst* thing he could have said.

"Stop it!" I screamed. "You told me she was gone and she's in your studio. You disappear for days, handing me a lame excuse about final exams and all the while you were with her—"

"Anna, listen to me. That's not the case—"

"I don't want your excuses."

I put my hands over my ears. He started to say something about reasons and explanations, but I cut him off.

"The only thing I'm willing to listen to is if you tell me who this woman is and what she means to you. And I want her in here so she can hear what you tell me."

He shrugged. "She doesn't speak English and you're not fluent in French so I don't know what that will solve. Anna, if you will sit down, I will tell you everything."

He looked so earnest that I sat and stared at his sad, handsome face as he told me Matilde was a prostitute and heroin addict.

"Didn't you see the track marks on her arms? How thin she'd gotten?"

He looked at me but I didn't say anything.

So he started from the beginning. He met her when she modeled for his class at Beaux-Arts.

"I admit that she is incredibly beautiful and in the beginning I was interested in her. Until I learned of her way of life. I promise you…" He touched my arm, but I pulled away. "I swear upon my father's good name that I have never made love with her."

He paused and looked at me, his eyes beseeching me to

believe him. They may not have made love—was that what we did?—but I wanted to ask him if they'd had *sex*. Down-and-dirty-what's-love-got-to-do-with-it sex. It's amazing how men can justify that there's a difference.

"It's a good thing we did not." He paused for a minute, swallowing against the emotion mounting in his voice. "Anna, she has AIDS."

Oh, God.

"All I wanted to do was help her get off the street and get clean. That's why I gave her all the work I could afford, but it wasn't enough to support her *habits*. She would not quit."

I stared at him, stunned speechless. He buried his face in his hands for a moment, then raked his hands through his hair.

"That night you and I met in the Pigalle café, that night you followed me when I walked Matilde home. I knew she had been shooting up again. She missed a couple of our sessions and I finally leveled the ultimatum. Either she quit the drugs or she was no longer welcome in my studio. That night she did not know she had been infected."

His angry words and the sadness in his eyes crushed me. He looked down, studied his hands. "The day we drove down to Cannes—"

My blood ran cold. I knew what he was going to say before he said it. "She was the business you had to take care of?"

He nodded but still wouldn't look at me. I hated myself for it, but pangs of jealousy coursed through me. I knew I should feel bad for this woman who'd been handed a death sentence, but just looking at him I knew he had feelings for Matilde. He and Matilde *would* have been lovers had she chosen him over sex for drugs and money.

Even if he didn't make love to Matilde, it was evident he loved her.

Of course he did.

She was beautiful. And young. I was just a substitute to pass the time with. I bristled at the irony. Just as I could not compete with a man for Blake's affections, I couldn't—*wouldn't* compete with the young, gorgeous, tragic Matilde for Jean Luc. The playing field was not level, and my heart was still too bruised and tender to have it ripped out and torn apart again.

"You love her."

He shook his head, still not looking me in the eyes.

Despite how he denied it, the woman had a hold on him.

"Jean Luc, it doesn't matter. I am going back to Florida in two weeks. You can love her and take care of her. You can do all the things you feel you need to do. Just do it."

"No, Anna, I do not want you to go."

I opened my mouth to speak, but all that came out was a perplexed grunt. A most unladylike, undignified sound, but I was so flummoxed by the whole turn of events I couldn't muster anything else.

"Please tell me you will consider staying in Paris after your residency."

"Doing what? Modeling for you? I can be your lover while Matilde is your love?"

I choked on the words as the tears started flowing again.

"You could stay and paint and write a book about this Camille Deveau who interests you so. You could live with me."

I shook my head, hating him for even mentioning it. Staying in Paris was not an option for me. With the stipend set to end with the residency, what would I do to support my-self? I wouldn't live with Jean Luc. Even the thought made me feel too vulnerable.

Once upon a time, I put my life in Blake's hands. What did that get me? Nothing but eighteen years of lies with a chaser of heartache. From now on, I was a one-woman show.

I got up and walked to the door, opened it. "You'll have to go now."

He sat there for a moment, his elbows braced on his knees, contemplating his hands. Then he stood and walked toward me.

"Jean Luc?"

"Yes?"

"Why did you go all the way to Cannes for her?"

He looked me in the eyes. "Earlier that week, Matilde took an overdose. She had learned of her condition and she wanted to...to end it.

"The hospital would not release her unless she was released into the care of someone. She called me because she had no one else."

Of course you went running right down there, didn't you?

I felt myself begin to back away emotionally. If I got caught in the middle of that messed-up relationship, I had no one else but myself to blame. But I still had to know—

"So what happened? You went out that night in Cannes and left me at the house in the tub. What did you do with Matilde?"

He rubbed his hand over his eyes before he looked at me. "I got her from the hospital. She seemed well enough. She wanted to come back to the villa with me—"

"Had you taken her there before?"

"No."

"Then how did she know about it?"

"She grew up in Antibes, which is twenty minutes from Cannes. When I first met her and learned of her association with the area, I told her my family spent time in Cannes. She knew of the Villa Angeline right away. She'd always wanted me to take her there."

"You didn't invite her to join us?" I knew it was a mean thing to say, but I couldn't help it.

He arched a brow and gave me a what-do-you-think shrug. "I told her she could not come to the villa because you were there. She ran away from me. I spent most of the time I was gone driving around looking for her—"

A chill passed over me. "She was there, wasn't she? She was the one inside the house." My hand flew to my mouth.

He bowed his head. "Yes, it was she. She told me as much." He searched my eyes. "She would never hurt you. She's not like that."

He touched my arm but I pulled away. I'd heard as much as I wanted to know. Just knowing she was there, looking at me as I lay in the tub, made every nerve in my body stand at red alert. I gestured at the door, hoping he would just go, because I was slowly coming undone.

"You must know she is only back for a short while. Just until she finishes this job for me."

"Until next time. Because there's always going to be a next time. You realize that, don't you?"

He squinted at me as if he didn't understand what I meant. But I didn't feel like explaining.

"May I see you tonight?" he said.

I shook my head, realizing he really didn't get it.

"No, Jean Luc, I can't see you anymore. I have to get ready

for the end-of-residency exhibit. You might say, I have to prepare for my own final exam."

AFTER FIVE DAYS without as much as a glimpse of Jean Luc, I realized he was honoring my request for him to leave me alone.

It was the best for all parties involved. Matilde needed him, he was devoted to her, and I had grown too fond of him for my own good.

I should have known I was not the kind of woman who could casually sleep with someone and write it off as a European fling. I envied women who could detach themselves that way. I wasn't cut from that cloth. I would have been lying if I said I didn't wonder where they'd gone. His studio was locked up tight. I didn't know if they'd gone elsewhere and started work on another project or—

It didn't matter.

I had the end-of-residency show to worry about. The way it worked was each resident chose five pieces to display in his or her studio. One week before the residency officially ended was the "studio walk." Jauvert, a center board member, an official from the City of Paris and one from the French Ministry of Foreign Affairs would walk into each studio and choose the one piece they deemed the best of the work displayed. That piece would be on exhibit in the gallery for the last week of the residency term.

The night before we bid each other *adieu* they would announce the winner of the one-hundred-thousand-dollar purchase prize.

I was proud of the work I'd produced.

Viewing it as a whole, I felt like I was ready to show what

I'd accomplished. *Let's see if I lived up to Jauvert's expectation that I would be the most improved.*

Frankly, I didn't care what he thought. I'd taken Ben's advice and *gotten over it*.

I chose four works from the Pigalle series, and just to throw Jauvert a curveball, I included *The Bed*.

As I set up for the studio walk, I almost chickened out of including it among the five. Out of respect to Jean Luc—it was his image captured in a most intimate moment.

If he'd been around, I would have asked his permission, but he wasn't. I could only go on gut instinct. Embarrassment didn't keep him from hanging the painting front and center on the living-room wall.

I sensed he would probably consider it an honor if I included it in the show.

I certainly hoped so, because the jury ended up choosing it as my entry in the end-of-residency show.

SEVENTEEN

JEAN LUC RETURNED the day before they announced the winner of the purchase prize. Since he'd been gone, I felt I owed it to him to tell him *The Bed* was selected for the show.

I stopped to pet Guerrier as I walked across the courtyard to talk to Jean Luc.

"I am going to miss you when I go back to the States," I said as I stroked the cat.

Jean Luc must have heard me talking to Guerrier because he came to the door holding his hammer and chisel, his jeans and gray shirt covered in a fine dust, before I even had a chance to knock.

"Is Matilde inside?" I didn't know why I asked. I didn't care if she was. Well, not much, anyway.

He shook his head. His hair looked glossy and almost black in the shadow of the doorway. "She is gone."

"Where did she go?" Guerrier rolled over on his side so I could scratch his belly.

"She has gone to London to a residential treatment center that specializes in treating people with AIDS."

I wondered how long it would take her to come bounding back into his life. I stood up and brushed the cat hair from my hands. "Jean Luc, she obviously loves you very much."

He shrugged. "I care for her very deeply, too. Just not in the way you assume. That is why I sent her to London. I hoped it would make you see that you are the person I care about."

That old familiar longing tugged at the pit of my stomach and I remembered with startling clarity the last time we made love. I tried to blink away the image.

"I'm not sure how you'll feel about me after you hear what I have to say."

He crossed his arms. "Why don't you come inside."

The sun beat down and it was turning out to be one of the warmest days we'd had since I'd arrived. Cooler than in Florida, but still warm enough to entice me to step inside his studio.

He went to the refrigerator and pulled out a bottle of Perrier and a lime.

He didn't ask me if I wanted some, just poured two glasses.

"So what is it you fear will change my opinion of you?"

He set a glass in front of me. "*The Bed,* er, my painting, *The Bed*, it's in the end-of-residency show. Jauvert and his band of merry men chose it as my entry."

He nodded. "Very good. Congratulations. What was your concern?"

I picked up the glass and sipped. "That you might not want it in the show."

He smiled. "Not to worry. I am honored."

He put the water and lime back in the refrigerator, then

picked up a box off his work bench. It was about the size of a shirt box and was tied with a red ribbon.

"This is for you."

A wave of apprehension swept through me. "Jean Luc, no. I can't."

"After Matilde left, I went back to Cannes. You see, there was another reason I brought you down there with me that day. There is an old woman in Cannes—a distant cousin of Camille Deveau's. Her last living relative. She holds some of her possessions. I asked some of my contacts at the École des Beaux-Arts and learned of her. I had to—how you say—jump through hoops, but I met her and obtained permission to copy Camille Deveau's remaining letters and her diaries. *Voilà*, for you, *madame*. What's more, she said she might be interested in working with someone to publish them. She has long thought that Camille would like the truth about her relationship with Georges Fonteneau to be known, that somehow it would validate their relationship. She said she did not know how to go about it, but would assist someone interested in researching and writing the book. You wouldn't know of anyone, would you?"

He held out the box and this time I accepted it, bewildered and bemused that he would go to so much trouble to do this for me. All I managed to stammer was, "Thank you."

"Anna, perhaps Camille has chosen you to tell her story and win her the recognition she is due?" Jean Luc said. "Can you really walk away from that?"

THE CORRESPONDENCE FILLED in the missing pieces of Camille Deveau's story. She and Georges Fonteneau were lovers deeply, passionately in love. They never married because he was not able to obtain a divorce from his wife.

When it all became too painful, she moved to Cannes to free herself from the one love she could never have.

Was she right in running away?

What would have happened if she'd stayed?

Even she pondered these questions, admittedly after it was too late.

The last page in the collection didn't have anything to do with Camille Deveau. It was from Jean Luc.

May I please have the honor of escorting you to the farewell reception?

JLLG

IN A PERFECT world, this is how I envisioned the end-of-residency award ceremony unfolding:

I would don a brand-new outfit purchased just for the occasion, a sexy red number that hugged me in all the right places, and new strappy sandals that looked very French, of course. I'd leave my hair down and let it curl exactly how it wanted to, and at precisely five minutes until eight o'clock, Jean Luc would knock on my door. He would take my hand and we would start toward the Delacroix Gallery.

At this point in my growth I would no longer care about being the first to arrive. I'd have transcended the stigma of caring what the others thought of me.

Jean Luc would open the heavy wooden gallery door for me and the first thing I would see when I entered was *The Bed* hanging front and center on the gallery wall. Then I'd vaguely register the Parisian Barbies who'd be talking to Jacques Jauvert. All three heads would swivel in our direction.

Jacques Jauvert would say, "*Bonsoir,* Madame Essex and Monsieur Le Garric."

We would return the greeting.

The Parisian Barbies would *bonsoir* in unison, and stand there perfectly coiffed and made up, holding their wineglasses by the stem, dainty pinkies extended, the same as they had that first night. I would wonder if Jauvert simply took them out of their boxes and set them on the floor for such occasions.

Jauvert would probably make some crack about my punctuality, but I would be secure enough to realize it wasn't personal, just his attempt to make conversation.

I would seize this opportunity to introduce myself to the attending members of the press and dignitaries from the City of Paris and the French Ministry of Foreign Affairs. After three months, I would be confident enough in the French I'd learned that I could carry on a basic conversation. Of course, they would be quite impressed at my willingness to communicate with them in their own language, but since they all spoke English fluently they'd help me out when I'd backed myself into a language corner.

Jean Luc and I would barely have enough time to wander around the gallery and look at the twelve pieces of artwork, each one accomplished in its own right, before the others would arrive; some looking even more anxious than they did that first evening three months ago.

But I would be calm and cool, not from overconfidence but because I was happy with my experience in Paris and the resulting work I'd produced. After all, wasn't that the real prize?

Mr. Argentina would nod to me, but rather than indulge the petty part of myself and wonder if he had an unfair edge for the hundred thousand since he and Jauvert were obviously involved, instead, I would nod back. I would probably even smile.

I might purposely make eye contact with Lesya Sokolov, the mixed-media artist from Romania. The faintest hint of a smile would tip the corners of her mouth, a sincere smile of solidarity. Even though we hadn't carried on a single conversation while at the center, I'd realize it was okay. I'd intuitively understand that we'd both found what we'd been seeking in Paris.

Although I'd still be the oldest person in the bunch, with the exception of the effeminate European painter, and the men who'd stood in a group on that first night would still huddle in an impenetrable clique, I would understand that was okay; that to the untrained eye, even though we all appeared very much the same as we did that first day, we were all leaving different people; that sometimes you have to look deeper to discover what's really there.

Even though I wouldn't have given much thought to the evening's announcement of the winner, my stomach would probably tighten in anticipation when Jacques Jauvert tapped his Montblanc pen on his wineglass and everyone gathered around the podium.

I would listen politely as he said, "Much of what this program encourages is the artist's personal self-discovery and growth. The jury was not only looking to purchase a great piece of artwork for the collection at the Museum of American Exchange, but also for evidence of how the artist had incorporated him- or herself into the body of work produced at the Delacroix Centre. For we believe self-discovery cannot be taught. It is up to the artist to seek what stimulates and appropriately apply it to his or her work."

Then he would commend each and every one of us for our

talent and dedication, and say, "There was one artist whose work unanimously captured the fancy of the selection committee...."

Even though I would be perfectly fine no matter who was named the winner, my mouth might go dry in the split seconds before Jauvert announced, "The winner of the Delacroix purchase prize award is, *The Bed* by Annabelle Essex."

My name would sound as if it had been called through an echo chamber. Every gaze in the room would turn to me and the gallery would reverberate with applause. Jauvert would motion for me to join him up front and the edges of my peripheral vision would turn white and wavy, enhanced by the strobe of camera flash exploding around me.

I would feel Jean Luc's steady hand touch my elbow. Then in slow motion, he would bend down and kiss me and we would share a private smile that would seem to last a lifetime, but all this would happen in the span of a few seconds. Jean Luc would take my wineglass, and somehow my feet would propel me forward toward Jacques Jauvert and the podium where he would quickly air kiss both of my cheeks; so would the group of dignitaries from the City of Paris and the French Ministry of Foreign Affairs.

All the while I would look at Jean Luc, who would smile his George Clooney smile, with one brow arched in a way that lit a flame deep inside me.

When quiet returned, Jauvert would continue, "In the fifteen years I've headed the exchange program, we've never granted a residency based on one piece of work."

I might start to worry, *Oh, no. Not that again,* but I would catch myself before I did. The old me would have done that. Now, it wouldn't bother me the way it did that first night.

Jacques Jauvert would say something about anticipating much growth from me and how I didn't disappoint him and the other members of the jury.

Then, just when I thought the evening couldn't get any better, Jauvert would present me with an oversize check for one hundred thousand dollars.

I would graciously accept it and think, *I knew I liked him from the beginning, I just had to grow into it.*

Then after all the excitement faded and Jean Luc and I found ourselves alone, I wouldn't waste time worrying about all the what-ifs and should'ves and could'ves that can make a person crazy.

He would pull me into his arms and say, "Anna, I love you. Please stay and walk beside me in this world."

I would say, "Of course I will, because I love you, too."

We would know that all that mattered was what was happening at that moment, that even though I had gone "Faraway" to find myself I'd come full circle in my journey.

Yes, in a perfect world, what was supposed to be my last evening in Paris would become the first day of the rest of my life with a lover I trusted and a career I loved.

Sometimes, when you want things badly enough all the stars line up, and for one perfect night you get that perfect world....

★ ★ ★ ★ ★

**For her fiftieth birthday party,
Ellie Frost will pretend that everything is fine.**

That she's celebrating, not mourning. That she and Curt are
still in love, not mentally signing divorce papers. For one
night, thrown closer together than they've been for months,
Ellie and Curt confront the betrayals and guilt that have
eaten away at their life together. But with love as the
foundation, their "home on Hope Street" still stands—they
just need the courage to cross the threshold again.

HOPE STREET

From acclaimed author
Judith Arnold

Don't miss this wonderful novel, available in stores now.

Free bonus book in this volume!

The Marriage Bed, where there is no room for
secrets between the sheets.

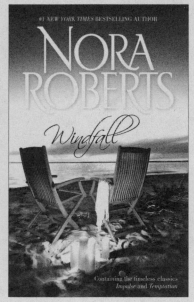